DIEGO KILLER

A Jake Smith Mystery

by
H. David Whalen

h david Whalen

For my wife, Patricia. Thank you for your love, patience, and support.

CHAPTER ONE
Murder Night

"KILL HIM!"

"Who?" the assassin queries. He did not have to ask. It is clear they both know.

"I want that bastard gone tonight! Understood?"

The two men raised their tequila shots and down them.

The joy swells inside the assassin. He had been looking forward to this for a long time. "What about his partner?" Hoping for a twosome.

"I still need him. His time will come soon enough."

"Consider it done!" The Enforcer spins and walks confidently out of the office.

It started when his boss called him to his office in early summer in nineteen seventy-three.

Back at his current hotel room, he phones San Diego and sets up a late night meeting. He gathers his tools of the trade, fills a black-leather satchel, and throws it on the unmade bed. The Enforcer walks to the closet and searches for the appropriate outfit for the evening's activities.

The killer chooses black dress shoes, a black turtleneck pullover, and black dress slacks. He takes his ensemble to the washroom, where he showers and shaves. After dressing, he grabs a dark-blue, almost black sports coat from the closet and heads downstairs to his De Ville.

A ragtag teenager guards his vehicle. He hands him an American fin. The car never needs looking after. The underbelly of Tijuana is well aware of the mid-night black Cadillac and gives it a wide berth.

The hitman drives to the border and crosses into the States. He checks the time. It is still early. He heads to a bar, which he is familiar with, in Chula Vista.

At Artio's Baja Sur Cantina, the man in black sits at the counter and orders a double neat whiskey and a cheeseburger. Mexican burgers do not hold a candle to the American version and he stops here every chance he gets. He sits alone for two hours before driving the waterfront route to downtown San Diego.

Pulling into an empty spot in front of the Star of India tall ship, the killer stays in the Cadillac. Slowly he draws on a Cuban Habanos cigar. After finishing his smoke, the Mexican man passes time strolling the waterfront park for more than an hour.

Well after ten o'clock, he returns to his vehicle. He stands beside the trunk for many minutes watching a few late night tourists mull the area. Eventually, he retrieves his gun, knife and other possibly needed items from the satchel. Tape, cable ties, flashlight, lock picking kit and a handful of extra shells all stuffed into familiar pockets. After double-checking that the small caliber pistol is fully loaded, it goes into the left-hand coat enclosure.

The fifteen-block march down Broadway takes him a mere nineteen minutes.

In the alley, at the back entrance, the killer checks for gawking eyes. None seen, he flicks his flashlight on, quickly picks the lock, and steps inside.

Before letting the door self-close, he examines the mechanism; it is Schlage's self-locking hardware, which requires key opening from either side. He keeps the door slightly propped open with his foot and pulls the small roll of duct tape from his pants. Tearing a strip, he covers the backset hole to prevent the tubular passage-latch from engaging.

The assassin climbs the stairs to office 604. All is dark. He assumes his target is a no-show. He tries the knob and surprised it turns. He enters and shines a beam around the room, stopping on the man sleeping in his chair. *This is too easy* he thinks as he stealthy approaches.

2

In one smooth action, he pulls a stiletto from his pants, clicks it open and stabs deep into the man's heart. No movement. No reflex. Nothing.

The assassin takes a Polaroid of the knife protruding from the man's chest for proof of death to give his boss. The flash momentarily lights the room.

After his eyes readjust, he spends an inordinate amount of time completely wiping down the office for any old fingerprints that he might have left previously. If nothing else, the man is thorough.

One last body inspection. Approaching, the intruder's foot slips on a sticky pool of liquid. He shines a beam down. The amount of blood is confusing. Anyway, he smears a wide oval through the patch before he wipes off his patent-leather sole with his soft wiping cloth. He carefully folds it with the wet patch in the middle surrounded by the dry parts and shoves it into a pocket. He will dispose of it once he is back at the wharf. He had planned to throw the gun into the bay but now decides to keep the unused weapon. There is no reason not to.

It is time to leave. Back downstairs, the assassin removes the tape and lets the door lock behind him.

Satisfied, the would-be murderer walks through the chilly coastal air to his car and drives south to Mexico.

CHAPTER TWO
Body Found

Sirens scream down the wide four-lane avenue. The call went out over the radio four minutes earlier, "10-46 male. 500 Broadway, corner of Columbia! Room Six-o-four! Repeat, 500 Broadway, room six-hundred-four!" The closest patrol unit responds to the dead-body code.

It is just after six o'clock Monday morning August 6 when two San Diego police officers sprint up the stairs. The top floor hallway of the six-story office building is tenebrous, except for the beacon of fluorescent light coming through the open door halfway down.

They bust into the room to encounter a late teen, early twenties, disheveled man huddling in a corner as white as vanilla ice cream and shaking uncontrollably.

A suited pop-eyed man stares blankly at the ceiling. A large pearl-handled stiletto sticks out of the corpse, which reclines in a high-back leather chair behind an oversized Mahogany desk.

Dried blood-infused foam residue surrounds the bloated body's mouth and nose. Additament lines of blood soused into the man's suit coat. Before drying, they had dripped onto the floor around the chair. Streaked through it appears to be a smeared shoe print.

The room reeks worse than a rented porta-potty. Other than the grotesque body, the room is neat, nothing tossed, nothing out of place.

One officer calls their findings into headquarters while the other escorts the young man into the hall, hoping for an easy confession.

Soon the room crams with firefighters and official personnel. It is busier than tuna evading hungry sharks. Scene investigators

4

place yellow numbered placards around the room, while flashbulbs go off like a dry summer lightning storm.

Three hours later, the building, normally filled with employees, is still empty. Officers corral them, along with hordes of spectators along the sidewalk, behind yellow crime scene tape. A tall, slender woman pushes to the front of the crowd. She flashes credentials to a sentinel and ducks under the tape. Behind her, another woman tries to follow, but the reporter does not get past the first guard. Her credentials not as important as the Senior District Attorneys are. Last, to arrive is the coroner who completes the manic party.

Detective Donald Terrance ruffles through a stack of papers on the desk in front of the victim. At the same time, his partner, Lead-Detective Stephen Lyle interviews their suspect in the bustling hallway.

"What's your name, Son?" Lyle questions.

"Gary Baird."

"What have you done here?"

"Nothing. I… I'm the janitor and when I got to this office, I found the guy." Baird mumbles, "I… I didn't know what to do so I called nine-one-one."

Lyle writes down his pertinent information. Gary is a student at Point Loma Nazarene University, a local Christian liberal arts college and he works early mornings as a janitor to pay for his schooling. Detective Lyle is suspicious of the seemingly unmentionable young man and tells him to stick around so they can talk later. He calls an officer over to keep an eye on Baird.

Lyle goes back inside the office to ascertain what his partner discovered. Detective Terrance has not found much on the desk, but he needs to call a locksmith to crack the sizable safe resting on the floor against the south wall. They split up to question the first responders and crime scene investigators.

The lead detective steps over to Edward Martin, the county coroner. "Hey Doc, find anything other than the obvious?" Lyle's meager attempt at humor.

"Good morning, Stephen. Nope, only the knife, which appears Mexican made and a slight smell of alcohol coming from the mouth. No other glaring wounds or abrasions at this time. I'll know more after the autopsy."

"As soon as possible, please?" He pats the man on the shoulder.

His partner approaches and reads aloud a business card. "Diego A. Ortiz, Esquire, Specializing in Immigration."

"Every lawyer in San Diego seems to be doing immigration these days," comments Lyle.

"Immigration or murder," replies a smiling Terrance.

"And ambulance chasers."

"And… "

Lyle walks away before Don can finish his thought. This nonsensical conversation could last the rest of the day.

Detective Terrance moves on to the lead CSI investigator. "Any fingerprints, Marv?"

"Not one, the place was wiped clean."

"Not even Ortiz's?"

"Not even his!"

"What about the footprints in the blood?" Donald points towards the body.

"Nothing usable. Only smears. Probably smooth-soled dress shoes," Marvin answers.

Lyle approaches. "Don, let's get Baird downtown."

CHAPTER THREE
Night Visitor

Diego Ortiz sat at his desk working late the previous Friday night after returning to his office. He was finishing up just after ten PM and put on his suit coat before locking up some paperwork in his safe. When he turned to leave, the door opened.

"We need to talk, Diego." Addressing the attorney by his first name, which was out of character and acting like old friends.

"We have nothing to discuss! I'm tired and going home to bed!"

"Not before we work this out!"

He gave in for the sake of a final compromise. "Would you like a nightcap?"

"Sure, what do you have?"

"We're drinking bourbon!" As Ortiz pulled out a bottle of Pappy Van Winkle's Family Reserve.

The twenty-year-old bourbon carried a five hundred dollar a bottle price tag and the only place in town to buy it was the Orange Street Liquor and Deli on Coronado Island. Coronado connected to the community of Imperial Beach via a tombolo named the Silver Strand or over the newly constructed Coronado Bridge from San Diego.

Routinely Ortiz picked up a couple of bottles when he was in Tijuana, where a friend's store kept it in stock just for him. If he were not going south of the border, which he did frequently, he would drive over the bridge and pick up a holdover bottle. He hated paying the bridge toll and even though owning Orange Street Liquor and purchasing at wholesale, it was still cheaper in Mexico.

"Bourbon's good." The visitor commented between sips.

7

The two sat drinking straight bourbon from two ordinary clear glass tumblers, and chit chatted for a while.

The visitor decided it was time to get down to business. "So Diego, you know why I'm here!"

"Can't say as I do," Ortiz answered. "I thought we were through with this."

"I know you don't want to go there, Sir, but I must insist this gets resolved tonight."

"Don't threaten me! I don't bend over for anyone!"

The caller rubbed eyes and forehead like massaging lotion onto an arm and looked back up. "Diego, how long have we been friends?"

"I wouldn't say we were ever friends, just a convenient relationship!"

Diego reached over and poured two more glasses of the smooth amber liquid. Neither one said a word for the longest time.

After each took another swig, Diego came to a resolution. "How about if you work for me full time? I will pay you more than you're making now."

"Work for you! That's not a solution!"

"Let me put a plan together for you to think about." The immigration attorney tried to convince the visitor.

"I can't make enough money working for you." The insulted guest responded.

"You'll make more than you imagine. I will take care of you. You won't want for anything." Diego's lies grew with every word. "And I'll supply you with benefits."

"Yeah? I'd rather work for myself…" The guest utilized an animated rolling-hand gesture. "as we keep talking about!"

"You know that's not possible, it is my business!" The attorney not conceding one iota.

They perpetuated discussing the problem and an amicable compromise. When the bottle of Pappy's was gone, Diego Ortiz stood and authoritatively mandated that the person sleeps on his proposal and they would talk the following week.

"Sit down!" A small semiautomatic twenty-two caliber pistol unexpectedly appeared.

The attorney surmised this was only a scare tactic. He motioned up his hands in front of him. "Just relax. You know we've worked out things before and this is no different. As I said, sleep on it and we'll meet in the morning." He upped the time frame just to get out of the room.

"I've given you every opportunity to work things out. Now it is too late. You leave me no choice!"

Perplexed, and after a short pause, the lawyer realized. "You came here to kill me. All this, work things out crap, is just that… CRAP!"

"No, you're wrong, Diego. I came here to talk some sense into you. You brought this on yourself!"

Ortiz collapsed into his chair. He rapidly scoured his desk for anything that would work as a weapon. He grasped a gold-plated Cross Pen and lunged, stabbing deep into the caller's left forearm. The killer did not flinch as blood commenced gushing from the wound onto the floor. A retaliatory twenty-two slug perforated Ortiz's heart. The slain attorney crumpled back into his chair, his eyes and mouth wide open in shock. The assassin watched the wounded man's chest slowly rise and fall to final heartbeats before death shrouded his body.

The gold pen pulled from the wounded arm and wiped clean of blood with a handkerchief. It replaced in the penholder on the wooden desk set from whence it came.

The handkerchief then twirled into a loose wound strand before wrapping it around the percolating wound and tying as a makeshift Band-Aid swathe.

The unwanted visitor threw the two drained glasses and empty bourbon bottle into the waste can, before glancing around the room to see if anything missed. Satisfied the visitor bent and grasped opposing corners of the plastic liner and tied them together. The killer slipped in the pooling blood beneath the body while pulling out the half-full bag. Catching the corner of the desk, the intruder did not go down but left a palm print.

9

Then the dark clothed person ran quickly from the death chamber and out the building. Entering the well-lit street, the killer nervously walked off into the warm August night.

Two blocks over, the bag of trash is thrown into a large outside construction dumpster.

CHAPTER FOUR
Murder Scene

Detectives Lyle and Terrance escort the young janitor out of the building, head to the station for an in-depth interview. As soon as they step through the front door, cameras whir and reporters inundate the detectives, firing nonstop questions. In attendance are the three local network television stations. Withal, endeavoring to stop the trio, are newspaper reporters for the San Diego Union and Tribune couple with the Daily Californian and more diminutive local community papers.

Jake Smith shoves his way to the front of the crowd, yelling, "Lyle, what's going on here?" above the reporter's monotone roar. Not one camera leaves its victim, but a few reporters glance in Smith's direction.

Lyle walks to the edge of the tape barrier. "Well, well, if it's not old Jack-off Smith! What are you doing here?" Lyle surprised to see Smith. It has been three years since Chief Baker fired Jake and he moved to Arkansas.

Ignoring Lyle's uncouth remark, Smith questions, "What's happening here?"

"What's your interest in this?"

"Simple human curiosity. Who died?"

"Nothing you'd be interested in, just some lawyer, with enemies." Grinning a cat-ate-the-mouse expression.

Smith ducks under the yellow tape. An officer grabs his arm. "You're not going anywhere!"

Smith looks back at the detective. "If it's Diego Ortiz, I work for him." He tries dangling a carrot. "I can let you know if anything is missing."

Terrance approaches dragging Baird. "You work for him? What are you a PI?" he pipes up.

"Exactly!"

"In town?"

"Exactly!"

His partner's intrusion gives Lyle a moment to think. "Let him pass!" he commands, "Smith, when you're finished, come by the station. We need to talk."

Smith overlooks thanking the detective but promises to see him later, with no intention of doing so.

The Chanel 8 reporter runs after Smith as soon as the detectives free him. As he strides past the officers. "Jake, wait up," Virginia Small shouts.

Before hitting the front door, he turns to see his old semifriend. "Virginia, how are you doing?"

"Fine, Jake. I thought you were in Oklahoma or some God forsaken state?"

"You got that right!" Referring to the description, not the location. "What did you do to your arm?" Smith notices gauze sticking out from under an Ace bandage wrapped tightly around Small's forearm.

"Oh, this? I slipped on the wet floor getting out of the shower this morning. Too big a hurry to get over here." She questions, "So you know the murdered guy?"

Jake fails to answer and continues through the door.

During the same time, Terrance questions his partner. "Why would you let him up there?"

"To see what he's after. I don't believe in coincidences and Smith being here and knowing the deceased is more than curiosity."

Detective Lyle is on his walkie-talkie to his boss upstairs. "Jake Smith is on his way up. Can you watch him and call me as soon as he leaves. I need to know what interests him."

Smith takes the stairs two at a time hoping to lose his tailing annoyance. On the sixth floor, he spies ADA Jillian Ross in the hallway talking with an officer.

Jake has not seen Jellybean since she cheated on him, New Year's Eve three years prior. *Crap,* he thinks to himself, *I'm outed now.*

Since returning to San Diego, he has kept a low profile and hasn't talked with any former acquaintances. Now, in the last five minutes, he has run into three people he had been specifically avoiding.

Jake approaches unnoticed. "Good morning, Ms. Ross."

Spinning at the familiar voice. "Jake! It's good to see you! When did you get back?" Shock and gladness encompass her at the same time.

"A while back," he answers nonchalantly. "How are you doing, Jill?"

She gives him a hug of familiarity and whispers in his ear, "A hell of a lot better now. I missed you, Jake." And, quickly separates.

"I can't say the same." He is still not over her misconduct.

Small makes it to the floor, completely out of breath, but in time to witness the hug. She walks rapidly to the old acquaintances. "Hello, Jill."

Ross snubs her. It does not surprise the reporter, they never got along and the ADA never had a comment for her newscast.

"Did you confirm the deceased?" Small tries to engage Smith.

"Haven't had a chance, dear," Acting overly friendly just to get under his ex's skin.

"It's Diego Ortiz." Directed at Smith, Ross tries to one-up the reporter.

San Diego Police Lieutenant, Stephen Holden steps out the open office door. "I'll be, Jake Smith, you're back?" Already alerted to Smith's arrival, but acting astonished at his presence.

"It kind of appears that way." Thinking *that's five out of seven.*

"What are you doing here?" Holden, referring to the crime scene.

"I'm doing some work for James." Smith uses the English translation of Diego. "I'm hoping to get into the room?"

"Who's James?"

"The dead guy."

"How long?" the lieutenant asks. His interest piques at Smith referring to Diego Ortiz as James.

"A few months, now."

"How long do you need in the room?" Holden clarifies.

"Five minutes."

"What are you looking for?" Holden bluntly rephrases his first question.

"Just here to help. I'll let you know if anything is missing. Was the room tossed?"

"What kind of work? I mean what you are doing now." Holden isn't going to give Smith anything on the room and wait to observe his impressions.

"A little investigative work." Smith underplays his answer.

"Good for you!" he patronizes, and continues the charade, "Did you run into Lyle and Terrance?"

"Unfortunately!"

Holden cannot contain a small chuckle. "After you're finished here, you'll need to come in and have a chat about your deceased client." Holden sticks out his hand. "It's good to see you, Jake."

Smith's reflects silently *it's not good to see anyone this morning,* however, he shakes the man's hand. "Thanks, Steve, I'll stop by in a few." He knows Stephen hates his name shortened and does it anyway. *Why do all Stephens have fixations over their name?*

The door guard steps aside for the entourage. Holden stays on Jake's heels like a fly on potato salad.

Small pulls a tiny camera from her bag and follows Jill following Holden into the room.

"Jeez, that's not good!" Smith comments, seeing the body with the large knife, untouched and protruding from the chest.

At the sound of the familiar voice, Ed Martin looks up. "Jake, it is nice to see you. Just get back?" The coroner truly happy to see his friend.

"Hey, Doc, likewise, though I wish it was better circumstances."

"This is a messy one!" Ed's unneeded comment. "Stop by the office sometime and we'll catch up."

"Will do, thanks, Doc."

Smith walks slowly around the room, looking carefully, but not touching.

Holden's suspicions of his former employee growing. "What exactly are you looking for, Jake?"

Smith is not mentioning that he got what he wanted as soon as he walked in and saw the Mexican stiletto. He turns to Holden and states, "Everything looks normal here… well, everything but Jim. I guess I better get out of your hair." He starts for the door.

"Jake, we'll see you at the station!" Holden reminds him to come in.

Unnoticed, Small snaps a quick photograph of the body. It will be the lead story on the five o'clock news broadcast.

CHAPTER FIVE
Jake Smith

Friday, February 2, nineteen-seventy-three, six months before the Ortiz murder, Detective Jake Smith walked into the Fayetteville Police headquarters after lunch. He opened the unusually closed detective's squad room door.

"SURPRISE!" everyone yells in unison.

Jake turned in his resignation two weeks prior and this is his last day on the job.

Someone handed him a scotch and water. His girlfriend, Alexis Dench, the Northwest Times reporter, ran up to him and hugged him hard while she whispered in his ear, "I'm so proud of you. I love you, Jake." The room burst into applause. Alex believed she might have been too loud and everyone overheard her. She turned three shades of scarlet and backed up giving Jake plenty of room.

"Speech! Speech!" The call goes out from various attendees.

Smith normally not one to be abashed, slowly raised his glass. "I don't know what to say."

The room laughs and someone yells, "Just lie, we'll try to believe it!" The room erupted.

"Well, all I can say is thank you for accepting me as one of you." He looked over the crowd, adding, "I don't know if that's a good thing." The group jeered and laughed more. They had probably been drinking the hour he was at lunch.

He continued more seriously. "I'll truly miss all of you. If anyone visits San Diego, you'll always have a place to stay."

"Get settled fast, Buddy, our bus is leaving next weekend!" his soon to be ex-partner, shouted.

Smith raised his glass and thanked the group again.

Diego Killer

The exuberant fun continued the rest of the afternoon and into the evening at a local bar.

The following morning Jake and Alexis left Arkansas in his Ferrari-red convertible Corvette. The soft-top up and packed compartment left barely enough room for them. Smith was leaving for good, but Alex had a return flight home two weeks later. She took vacation time off from work to help him move and settle in.

They loved each other and Jake had asked Alexis to marry him and move to San Diego. She did not say *yes* or *no* but tried to convince him to stay in Fayetteville, where they could build a life together.

Jake explained that he could not stay there; he just does not like the place. Moreover, Alex explained that she lived there her whole life and did not think she could ever leave. To solve the quandary, Alexis agreed to try San Diego for two weeks before making a final decision.

Six days later the pair pulled into the Southern California city, after sightseeing along the way at Carlsbad Caverns, the Grand Canyon, and other tourist attractions. They checked into a hotel on the La Jolla—Pacific Beach border, overlooking the Pacific Ocean, for the remaining week.

Smith showed his girlfriend a grand time, with two days in Los Angeles, one at Disneyland, and the other in Hollywood. Back in San Diego, they visited SeaWorld, the San Diego Zoo, and Balboa Park. Every evening featured a different restaurant and romantic moonlit walks on various beaches.

Dench, never having traveled outside of Arkansas, thought Southern California had to be the vacation spot of the world; the weather mild and the sun shone every day.

On the flip side, traffic was a nightmare. She was scared to death every time Jake hit freeway speeds over seventy miles per hour, weaving in and out of slower vehicles. Crowds of people clogged up every artery in the city, and they had to wait in line everywhere they went. Alex told Jake she will visit often, but refused to partake permanently in the nightmare.

The week ended too quickly for both and Jake dropped her off at Lindbergh Field, San Diego's International Airport for her trip home.

He returned to their hotel and checked out. Smith re-registered at the Padre Inn in Old Town and started looking for permanent accommodations.

The following Thursday, he found a second-floor loft on the corner of Fifth and Island a block south of Market Street downtown and signed a year lease beginning the first of the following month.

All through March, Jake remodeled his space. He partitioned off two front offices, leaving the immense single backroom and bathroom as living quarters. He bought cheap used furniture for both areas and worked on setting up his business.

Having previously been a police detective, obtaining his private investigator license was more a matter of filling out forms and paying the fee.

Jake did not want to use his name to avoid old friends for as long as possible. He called his small enterprise Hamilton-Adams Investigations, HAI for short. He figured two dead president's names sound traditional and a two-name masthead projected a larger firm perception. Image is critical. Smith does not realize his self-designed tyronic logo featuring a magnifying glass enlarging HAI projected the antithesis effect and had a small wooden plaque made. He nailed it to the front of the building.

By April, Hamilton-Adams Investigations had opened for business. It was a rough neighborhood and he did not expect walk-in traffic. Daily, Smith walked different sections of the downtown area introducing his incipient company to business owners and handing out cards. Unsurprisingly, nobody was in the market for his services and did not know anyone who was.

A week later, he got his first job. A man descried Smith's business card lying on a client's desk, phoned and wanted to meet with him.

The man told Jake that his wife, a shy and mostly a stay at home person, had ostensibly needed to give herself some sense of personal value. She took up selling Tupperware. The suspected problem arose the previous month with her business' suppositious boom and she now presented three to four home shows a week, but not bringing home any money.

HAI hired for five days to tail the woman. Smith got a photograph and the address of their residence.

The first evening on the job, Smith sat in his 'Vette down the block from the home. The man arrived from work just before six and she left shortly after that carrying a briefcase and a minuscule cardboard box. The PI followed her to a home in La Mesa. He watched as she knocked on the door. An older woman answered and the two talked for a few minutes. Smith snapped a couple of photographs of the pair. Eventually, the suspect handed over the small box and they said their goodbyes.

Jake again followed her to another home, in Clairemont. This time the woman made numerous trips into the house carrying many large boxes. Minutes after she unpacked, four more women showed up and went inside. Jake sat in his car and guzzled coffee from his thermos for three hours. Finally, the last women that arrived, left. Another half hour later, the Tupperware Lady walked out and drove home and so did Smith.

The following evening Smith again sat outside his client's home. Both adults and their three children never left the house.

The next evening while he sat in position, the woman of the house drove off with a preteen boy. Smith followed the dyad to a local Methodist church. She dropped the boy off and went back home.

Just before nine o'clock, the woman returned to the church and picked up her son.

Two more evenings of bloodhound work and the woman conducted two more, home shows.

Smith decided to see what she does during the day and sat outside the suspect's home Friday morning. Just before ten o'clock, she left. Jake followed her to a local Bank of America branch. When she went inside, Smith followed.

The woman walked to the self-service desk and filled out a deposit slip as Smith did the same. He struck up a little small talk. She asked if he was married. When he told her no, she asked about a girlfriend or neighbor that might be interested in a Tupperware demonstration. Smith did not know anyone. They part ways. She made a deposit and Smith left the bank. He sat in his car and made a note that the woman's deposit went into a savings account in her name only.

When the week of observation finished, Jake headed to the husband's office and showed the man the few pictures he had and told him that his wife did nothing but conduct Tupperware business. He also explained to him that she had a personal savings account at B of A.

They discussed whether to keep up the surveillance for an additional week. The man decided not to and terminated Smith. It will be up to the husband to ascertain if his wife was secretly stashing money to benefit their family or needed it to leave him.

The PI sat at his desk, worried over his next move. He had enough savings to keep HAI going for another three months, but if he cannot engender an income he will be broke and on the street.

CHAPTER SIX
Lynette Shaheen

Desperate by the commencement of the third month, Jake Smith sat at the counter, in Emily's Café, sipping his morning mug of coffee and endeavoring to deduce what to do. The first couple of struggling months, with only the one case, Smith had virtually depleted his savings account. He was on the verge of bankruptcy. Jake charged considerably less than his completion, though raising his hourly rate would not help when he had no clients. His week of surveillance work only extended the ineluctable foreordained by a few days.

While he waited for his runny eggs, the owner approached him. Jake, went there often, had become casual friends with her. They conducted a little small talk, and he mentioned that he was having trouble securing new clients. Emily responded that she was friends with an attorney. She would call him to see if he had anything available. When his breakfast arrived, she moved along to converse with other customers.

This statement made him think to cogitate lawyers. He returned to his office and called his attorney son in San Francisco for help.

Jake only had the one child. Cheryl got pregnant and gave birth to their son when she was twenty years old. She and Jake did not get married until two years later when he was a patrol officer for SDPD.

Adam advised his father to contact insurance companies. He relayed that a lot of indemnification businesses use outside investigators for suspected fraud cases.

Jake refused an offered loan, thanked his son, and signed off the long distance call.

21

Smith immediately started phoning insurance companies for appointments. His endeavor was unsuccessful and he did not secure a single interview.

Later that same evening, his phone rang. "Hello, HAI."

"When did *you* get back?"

"Happy to hear from you too! Who told you?" Jake asked his ex-wife Cheryl, who remarried a year after he moved to Arkansas. *Six of seven.*

"Adam called and told me."

"Now you know. What do you want?"

"Calm down Jake. I am only trying to help you. He said you needed some advice on your business and that he suggested insurance companies." Cheryl tried a little congeniality.

"I'm doing OK on my own. I only phoned Adam to see how *he* was doing," his indignant response.

"Well anyway, I talked to Roy over dinner. You know he's a successful businessman?" After a pause of smugness. "He has a job for you."

"What kind of job?"

"I'm not sure, but you can stop by his business in the morning." Cheryl gave Jake the address.

Smith eschewed writing it down; he refused to take charity from his ex.

"Did you get that, Jake?"

"Yeah, but I'm pretty busy on a case. I don't think I can help him right now."

The line went quiet for a long time. "Jake, I will have Roy call his insurance man and see if he can learn who you can talk to."

Moments later, Jake concedes minor defeat. "That's nice. I appreciate your help."

Two days after Cheryl's call, Jake's phone rang while he sat at his office desk lost in woe.

"Good morning, HAI Investigations."

"Jake, Roy here."

"Roy who?" Not relating this Roy to his ex-wife's new husband, whom he had never met.

"Roy Pickert, Roy, *and* Cheryl!"

"Oh, that Roy!" Smith realizes.

"Yes, *that* Roy." When Jake did not respond, he continued on, "Jake, I have a name for you at John Hancock Insurance who might be able to get you some work."

Roy related the name and phone number. Jake wrote this one down.

After thanking the man and promising to go over for a barbeque, Jake gets off the line.

He spent another fruitless day canvassing independent insurance underwriters trying to gather any names of people for the companies they represent. Specifically names of who was in charge of running investigations.

The first thing the following morning, Jake called Roy's given number and spoke to Lynette Shaheen. They made a lunch appointment for Tuesday, May 15.

When the lunch date arrived, Smith walked into the Grant Grill inside the historic US Grant Hotel on Broadway in the heart of downtown. He arrived a fashionable ten minutes late and asked the host if Ms. Shaheen was present. Jake directed to a white-clothed table in the center of the room.

"Ms. Shaheen?" Jake approached the table.

She glanced at her watch. "You're late!"

"Sorry, I had a little trouble parking."

"Then you should have left earlier. I don't waste my time waiting for anyone wanting a favor!' the woman bluntly responded.

Looking at the shameless corpulent woman, Smith thinks, *no doubt, this woman would wait eight hours for a meal.* Nevertheless, politely, as he took a seat, "I'll make sure it never happens again, Ms. Shaheen."

He erroneously expected her to respond with, please call me Lyn or Lynette. Instead, she states, "If there is a next time!"

"Let's order so you can get back to work. I'll fill you in on my background," Jake offered.

"I'm the office manager and don't have to account for my time. You're a little too presumptuous to be a detective, Smith."

Not sure if he should genuflect or kiss her ring, he overlooked her observation. "Would you like a drink?" He was sure she could use one.

At that instant, the waiter approached and sat a Baileys on ice in front of her. Then he asked Jake what he wanted to drink. Before Smith could answer, Shaheen, piped up, "I'll have the crab salad and bring some extra rolls and another Baileys."

"I'll have a tuna on rye and a glass of water, please." He realized if he did not get his order in expeditiously, he would not be eating.

"Alright Smith, so you think you're a detective?"

"Yes, I am! I worked as a detective for the San Diego PD for seven years. Then I transferred to Arkansas and was a detective in the Fayetteville Police Department before returning to San Diego to start my own firm, Hamilton-Adams Investigations." He goes on, "I was only in Arkansas for three years and maintain all my contacts here."

The waiter interrupted, delivering their food. "Enjoy! If I can get you anything else?"

"Another Baileys!" snapped the woman.

Shaheen did not waste a second shoveling in crab and spinach. "What contacts?" She asked through her overstuffed mouth.

Smith let his food sit. "I'm in tight with all the detectives and Chief Baker, which gives me access to their resources," Jake lied.

"Who else?" While stuffing in a mouthful of lettuce followed by half a French Roll.

He sarcastically asked the hippo, "Would you like me to get you a few more rolls?" Before the woman could spit more food particles across the table, he continued, "I'm also tight with the district attorney's office and all the local reporters, TV and newspaper."

"That's it?" Lynette's lack of diplomacy unbelievable.

24

"Of course not. I know many politicians and business owners! And regular folks, like yourself!" Smith more than fed up and ready to walk. He was craving a bite and Emily's Café fit the bill nicely.

"Well, you know I'll have to check your references!"

"Would you like me to do the investigation for you?" with abhorrence. He refused to concede to the uncouth woman.

"Not necessary. I use Newman Investigations. Ralph is ex-FBI and is *really* good," Shaheen jabbed back. "Are you going to eat your sandwich?"

"Help yourself." Smith pushed his plate across the table. "I really need to get going. I am working on another case at the moment. Should I stop by your office, say, in a day or two to pick up any paperwork… you know, release forms or insurance rider forms or whatever your organization uses?"

"You're ending our meeting!" In disbelieve.

Maybe you have never encountered a real man he abstains from voicing, but stands, and grins. "Unfortunately, I do have another commitment and I don't want to be *tardy*."

Lynette waved the waiter over and demanded he gave the lunch bill to Smith.

"Don't worry about paperwork at this point. After I check you out, I'll bring the necessary forms to our next meeting."

"Sounds good, Ms. Shaheen. When do you think that'll be?"

"We'll meet here next Tuesday, *at noon!*"

Smith immediately realized this was going to be a weekly commitment. He thinks *she better give me more business than she eats.*

CHAPTER SEVEN
Hancock Job

Jake Smith arrived at the Grant Grill by eleven-thirty, a half-hour early for his second meeting with Mrs. Lynette Shaheen, the Hancock Insurance manager. He sat at a table supping a mug of coffee when she walked in ten minutes late for their meeting. Smith thinks to himself that the arrogant woman is late just to spite him. He figured she had never been late for a free meal and now they are even. He stood and pulled a chair out for Shaheen. "Good afternoon, Lynette."

She sat. "I see you made it on time, this week!" Immediately the waiter set down a Baily's over ice in front of the woman, which Smith prearranged.

Lynette responded, "Take that back! I'll have a strawberry daiquiri," while glowering at Smith. Jake was never going to get ahead of this woman.

"So, Mrs. Shaheen, how did your background check go with Ralph?" he inquired.

"You squeaked by," she responded, though she never had Smith checked.

"Good. Did you bring the paperwork so I can get started?"

Shaheen ignored him and snapped her fingers at the waiter, who was already returning with her daiquiri. "I'll take the steak sandwich, with extra fries."

The young man turned to Jake. "For you Sir?"

"I'm good with coffee, thanks, John."

For the next ten minutes, while they waited for her lunch, Smith tried to converse with the obnoxious woman. For every

26

question or comment, she retorted with an inappropriate remark. She refrained from engaging conversation.

Smith watched her devourer her food. Steak sauce or ketchup continually ran down her chin. The scene disgusted him. When she finished every scrap of food on the table along with two more daiquiris, she asked, "Well, Smith, did you get a room?"

He never thought or would ever have considered it. "No, I didn't." Stunned at the insidious insinuation.

"What are you saying, Smith?"

"Uh… I thought you were married?" he stammered.

"What's that got to do with a little fun between friends?"

"Friends? I'm a business associate."

"Not yet, Smith!"

"It's clear this isn't going to work out!" Smith stood to leave.

"We'll see where we are next week then," Lynette bluntly stated.

"Sure, see you then." He walked toward the door, considering. *This woman is just too much. I have to figure out if the monetary value will, ever exceed the lunch bill.*

Their next meeting was a little different from the first two. Jake entered the grill, neither early nor late. Shaheen was already there.

If he were not so dire for a case, he would not have come back. Smith greeted the woman and sat. The first thing he noticed was a paper sitting face down in the center of the table.

"Good afternoon, Jake. I'm glad you came," she greeted him, shockingly pleasant. "I have a job for you," and she flipped the paper over. "This guy, Emery Fett, was in a car accident two months ago. He refused all offers of settlement and retained an attorney and doctor claiming back problems. He states he had to quit his job and his doctor says he will never work again. It was a small fender bender in a parking lot and I do not believe a word he's claiming. I need you to follow him and get pictures of him off his crutches or doing anything he claims he can't do."

"Right up my alley. I'll get this bum!"

"Good. This should be simple. It carries a flat five-hundred-dollar fee. All the information is here." Lynette handed Jake the paper.

"I'll need a retainer."

"You'll be paid when the job is complete!"

They ate lunch and carried on the congenial conversation. No mention of extra benefits surfaced. Jake realized he had passed her little test.

After lunch, Smith headed over to check out Fett's address. All was quiet around the abode and no one visible anywhere in the suburban neighborhood. He drove to his office and constructed a game plan.

Over the next few days, he visited the block at various times of day and night and never witnessed much activity, though there was an ever-present rear-dented old Rambler station wagon in the driveway.

On the fourth day, Jake sat in his car imbibing coffee from a foam go cup he purchased at a 7-Eleven, a couple of blocks over when Emery Fett emerged from the home on crutches with his neck in an obtrusive medical collar. Fett noticed the man in the car observing and awkwardly made his way to the street side mailbox. He fumbled around resting a crutch against the post and reached in snagging his mail. He secured the envelopes and fliers under his armpit and turned to smile at Smith, before struggling back inside.

Jake downed his last swallow of coffee and drove off. Half a block away, he noticed a puerile boy dragging a metal trashcan to the curb. He figured the following day was trash day. A plan formulated in his mind. On the way back to his loft, he stopped at an office supply store and purchased a hundred-pound bench scale with a twelve by twelve-inch platform.

That evening, Jake was back in Fett's neighborhood by nine-thirty. The past couple of nights Fett had turned his house lights off around ten o'clock and apparently retired for the night. Smith stopped a block away and walked to the man's location. He found a peacock blue over white VW Microbus with surfboard racks on its roof, parked across the street and casually leaned against it, hidden on the sidewalk side. His single-lens reflex Nikon F camera with mounted Nikkor 80-200mm telephoto lens dangled by a strap around his neck below his light summer jacket.

Not waiting long, Fett's porch and side-lane lights came out. The man appeared on his front porch with a crutch under each arm. The support collar was absent. He looked up and down the street. Smith clicked off a couple of pictures through the van windows.

Satisfied, he was alone Fett leaned the crutches against the wall and walked around the home and down the lane. A minute later, Smith observed the man as he carried a steel trashcan to the curb. It was stuffed and trash spilling over the top. After he dropped it, Fett returned and easily bent over and picked up the scattered mess and returned it to the container. Two more cans later, Fett retrieved his crutches and went into his home. Many minutes after that, all the house lights went out. Smith had a dozen photos of the activity.

Jake sauntered to his car. He remained there for an hour drinking coffee from his thermos. Not even a cat moved through the area.

Jake snatched his new scale from the trunk and headed back to the scene.

Another fifteen minutes concealed behind the van and he was satisfied. He walked across the street to the three cans. Smith took a final glance around; all was as still as a schoolyard on Christmas morning. He set his scale on the cement sidewalk and placed the first can on top. It registered forty-one pounds. Jack snapped a photo of the can and scale readout. The second can, thirty-four pounds, and another picture. He struggled with the third; it was heavy, full of yard trash, with trimmed branches and sawed-off pieces of wood sticking out. The photo documented sixty-nine pounds of weight. However, the report Shaheen gave Jake stated the man could not lift more than thirty pounds.

The PI grinned from ear to ear, as he drove back to his loft. Along the way, he picked up another coffee. It was going to be a long night.

As he entered his outer office, he decided to check his newfangled Phone-mate answering machine. He set down his camera and scale. Jake rewound the reel tape and pushed the start button. He listened to the message from his long-distance girlfriend, Alexis Dench in Arkansas. Her message told of how much she missed him and wanted him to call back. He hurriedly dialed the number. Even though it was already after one AM in Fayetteville, they talked for over an hour, telling each other how much they missed their time together and that she wanted to visit him in San Diego in two weeks.

After signing off, Smith hurried to his bathroom. He had purchased the consummate darkroom setup from a photographer who was going out of business, for an unheard of price of one grand. Besides the Beseler 23CII XL enlarger and everything needed to produce high-quality black and whites, the price also included the Nikon, with four bayonet-mount interchangeable lenses and a Rolleiflex T twin lens camera. Right after his purchase, Jake sealed the bathroom, turning it into a light-safe darkroom.

Smith carried in the enlarger and rested in on top of the closed toilet lid. He retrieved a piece of plywood; he had previously trimmed to size and set it over the sink, and laid out three developing trays. Finally, he unscrewed the white light bulb and replaced it with a red one. After filling the trays from the correct bottles of chemicals, he was ready to get to work.

Smith flicked on the red safelight and closed the door. He grabbed a film-developing canister and turned off the light to achieve total darkness. Jake opened the three-film can, and fumbled around in the dark, rolling one film at a time onto stainless steel spools. He dropped them into the container. With all three loaded, Jake screwed on the canister's lid and flicked the red light back on. In addition, Jake opened the door for increased visibility. He poured in film developer and used his automatic timer for the appropriate period. He repeated with a rinse, the fixer, and final rinse before he opened and hung the developed negatives the length of the shower curtain rod with clothespins, for drying.

Jake took a leak and made coffee while the negatives dried.

Retrieving the negs, he studied them over a small light table; he had placed on the kitchen-area counter and picked out a half a dozen to make 8 x 10 prints of.

Back in his makeshift darkroom, with the red light on, Jake placed the first negative into the enlarger and turned on the exposer bulb. Utilizing his Magnasight 8X Grain Focusing aid, he adjusted the lens. Next, he pulled a sheet of photo paper from his paper safe and inserted it into the adjustable print easel. He covered three-quarters of the photo paper with the stiffener sheet that came in the photo paper envelope and turned on the enlarger for five seconds. Taking care nothing jiggled, he moved the cardboard over to uncover another quarter of the sheet and flicked on the enlarger for another five seconds. Jake made two more exposures, the same way on the print paper and developed the sheet, going from tray to tray.

He returned to the kitchen area. After using his Premier Photo Dryer, he studied each of the four exposures and decided on the best one to use for the final prints.

Jake made two prints each of the six negatives he chose.

Before he cleaned up and shut down, Smith rolled half a dozen more film cassettes with Kodak Tri-X, using his bulk film roller. When all done, he looked at his watch, it was going on four AM.

Not having a permanent darkroom made photography work a tedious job. He stood at the bathroom door and studied his large living space. Jake decided to construct a permanent darkroom as soon as he could afford it. Looking back into the bathroom, he decided to clean up later and turned in for the rest of the night.

By nine o'clock the same morning, Smith waited for Lynette Shaheen to call him into her office. A half-hour went by before he got in.

"Good morning, Jake. What do you need?"

"I just am dropping off my report on Emery Fett." He laid a thick legal size manila envelope, printed with his logo, on her desk.

She glanced at her wall calendar. "That was quick. Are you sure you got enough?"

Without a response from Smith, she opened the envelope and carefully examined each photo, before she read his report. Jake sat quietly anticipating derogatory remarks.

The Hancock, manager leaned back in her chair. The chair made a loud crack! Smith was on alert, waiting for it to collapse under her weight. "Well, Jake, this looks great. How did you come up with the idea of weighting the cans?"

"I'm a professional with a large bag of tricks." He sported a toothy grin.

"I'll have a check cut for you. Can you stop by later this afternoon? It'll be at the front desk."

Smith stood. "That would be great. I'll see you at lunch, Lynette."

As he walked towards the door, she piped up, "I'm sure I'll have another investigation for you by then."

CHAPTER EIGHT
Alexis Dench

June 1, Alexis Dench returned to San Diego. Jake and Alex had been in constant contact over the telephone. Both excited to see each other. She arranged to fly back for an extended one-month visit. Jake hoped it turns permanent and she decided to marry him.

Smith parked in the San Diego airport lot early evening and walked into Terminal 1 to wait. He was walking-on-air and arrived an hour before her flight was scheduled to land. Jake sat on the end of a row of hard plastic chairs under the monstrous windows. The terminal was full of uniformed sailors and soldiers flying out on leave or flying in to report to local bases. Lovers entwined in happy hellos or sad goodbyes. He anxiously waited for his turn for a doting embrace.

His seat was next to a loquacious elderly woman waiting for her daughter. After a few minutes, she excused herself to go to the restroom. Instantly her vacant seat filled with a tall, well-dressed Mexican man, with a deplorable complexion and a rugged facial scar running down his left cheek. Smith nodded hello. The man ignored the intrusion.

Moments later, Jake stood and asked the man to save his seat. He desperately needed a cup of coffee, in addition, offered to get the stranger one for the favor. The man agreed to both requests. Smith returned with two paper cups and handed one to the man, thanking him. After retaking his seat, he introduced himself, "I'm Jake." He held out his hand.

"Nice to meet you, Jake. My name is Frank." Accepting the shake.

During their conversation, Frank told Jake that he lived in TJ but was flying to Guadalajara on business. When asked what he did, the man answered that he was a salesman for a Mexican furniture company. Smith thought it peculiar the man was flying out of San Diego rather than the Tijuana Airport but did not question the man's decision.

Jake handed the fellow his business card and said that if he was ever in need of a private investigator to give him a call. Smith also added, "Or if you're in San Diego, we could have a beer." Frank told Jake he was more of a bourbon-man, but promised to call him if he needed anything. Jake asked for his business card but told that he had run out of them.

Smith bade farewell and went upstairs to Alex's arriving gate.

Alexis' flight came in forty excruciating minutes late. She was close to the last person off and upon seeing her boyfriend, ran into his arms. While they waited to retrieve her luggage from the baggage carousel, Jake questioned about getting a bite to eat. Alex explained that it was a long fight and she was exhausted. She booked the least expensive she could find and had a two-hour layover in Dallas, and another longer one in Denver. Alex could not wait to take a shower and put on fresh clothes. She stated they could go out for a late meal after.

In Jake's loft, they made love and snuggled together for an hour before the pair drove to the Harbor House for fresh fish and a couple of cocktails. When dinner ended, Jake took her over the bridge to the famed Hotel Del Coronado and a leisurely romantic stroll along the beach. After which, the pair headed into the lounge for a nightcap.

Smith barely took his eyes off the woman and was startled when two men approached. "Jake, what a pleasant surprise?"

Jake spun in his chair and stood up. "Jim, it's good to see you." He was shocked that his new *friend,* Frank, was standing beside him. Smith introduced the men to his companion. He looked at Frank, and asked, "Did you miss your flight?"

"You know, Frank?" Ortiz shocked response.

"We just met at the airport."

"My boss called with a last minute change of plans. As I was leaving the airport, I ran into Diego. We're old friends." The Mexican man made a quick excuse and overlooked mentioning that he was actually at the terminal to pick up Ortiz.

"Well, we won't interrupt you two." Diego placed a hand on Jake's shoulder. "Give me a call next week." Looking at Alexis, he added, "Whenever you have time, it's not critical."

The pair of men strolled off and sat at a back table. Smith walked to the restroom and upon returning sat next to Alex, rather than taking his previous seat across from her, just so he could observe the men at the rear of the establishment.

"Honey, did you hear a word I said," Alex asked.

"Of course, dear."

"What did I say?"

"Uh… sorry I might not have got everything."

"Jake, who are those men you staring at?"

"Ortiz is an attorney I've done some work for. The other guy I sat next to at the airport. He was friendly yet standoffish if you know what I mean. Told me he was a salesman for a Mexican furniture company and flying south on business, but didn't even have a business card. Who goes on a sales trip and forgets to take cards? Also, he lives in Tijuana, so why did he come to San Diego to fly? Now he shows up here with some lame excuse!"

"Jake, is this trip going to be all business?"

"Of course not, dear. It's just doesn't make sense, that's all." Jake cannot help himself, something is erroneous with the picture he's observing.

"Look at that!" The PI whispers, "This Frank guy dominates the conversation and looks pissed. I can't see Jim's face, but he keeps squirming in his seat."

After staring for a couple more minutes, Jake suggests, "Alex, let's get out of here. I'll go see Jim on Monday."

CHAPTER NINE
Marriage Proposal

Saturday morning Alexis was up by four o'clock local time. It was already six in Arkansas and her regular rising time. She spent a quiet couple of hours at the only table in the room, drinking coffee and watching Jake sleep in the corner bed. Alex had missed her boyfriend's quick wit and unorthodox humor more than she realized.

Eventually, Alex washed the frying pan that had been sitting dirty in the sink, probably for more than a week. In the apartment-sized refrigerator, she found a couple eggs and half a loaf of wheat bread and commenced making breakfast.

The pleasant whiff of hot buttered toast, sizzling eggs, and freshly brewed coffee woke the slumbering man. Groggy and through half-opened eyes, he wished Alex, "Good morning, dear. You're up early?"

"Hi, honey. Just making us a little breakfast." Alex responded without taking her eyes off the stove top."

"Do I have time for a shower?"

"No. It'll be ready in a minute or two."

After a sitting for an hour eating and sharing wonderful Arkansas memories, they returned to bed for a little extra morning activity. After making love, still entwined, both expressed how good it was to be together again.

They both took showers and sat for another cup of coffee.

The rest of the day the pair relaxed and dined out at Anthony's on the Wharf after walking the Embarcadero and taking the ferry to Coronado and back.

Diego Killer

The following day they drove up the coast highway before Jake turned inland and they toured Palomar Mountain and the famed observatory featuring a two hundred inch ground-glass reflective telescope. Alex and Jake had a home-cooked chicken cordon bleu supper at the Ramona Cafe before returning to the loft.

Monday morning Alex slept late. Jake kissed her softly on the forehead and left a note telling her that he will be back before noon. He headed up the block to Emily's Cafe. He sat at the counter and consumed a buttered English muffin sans jelly, and coffee before heading to Ortiz's office.

It was an enjoyable late spring morning. The coastal eddy blanketed the city in low cooling clouds and Smith decided to walk the fourteen blocks. He strolled Fifth Avenue north past the Pussy Cat Theater and strip-clubs in the pornography district before arriving at his destination just after ten o'clock.

Smith entered Ortiz's office and greeted by the receptionist, Donna. She tells him that he can go right in.

Jim, as he knows the attorney, looked up and addressed him, "Good morning, Jake. It was nice running into you and Alexis the other night. She seems like a wonderful lady. You're a lucky man."

"You're right there. I've been trying to get her to marry me, but she's resisting." He quickly added, "Not me per say, but living in a big city."

They both shared a small laugh.

"So what brings you in?"

"Well, Jim, I'm a little concerned about your friend, Frank," bluntly stated, Smith jumped to the point of his visit.

"Frank's alright. I've known him for a number of years."

"From your school days?"

"No. Long after that. Why does he bother you?"

Smith related meeting Frank at the airport and his furniture salesman story, and how he was flying to Guadalajara on business. He goes on telling of his observations later in the lounge. Moreover, Jake ended with, "Nothing is as he told me and that shady character is lying."

Ortiz's does not indulge deep into his and the man's history, or what they discussed, but emphasized that Smith needs to stay away from him… for his own safety. "Frank Trujillo is not a nice man."

Smith, left, telling Diego that if help needed he was available.

On the trek back, the overcast sky was breaking up and the sun started to beat down on the San Diego streets. Another hour and it will turn into a seasonal hot day. Jake wondered what James had gotten involved with and whom Frank really worked for. He decided to look into the man's history now that he knows Frank's last name is Trujillo. If that truly was his name.

Smith was getting frequent jobs from Lynette, at Hartford and had started courting other large insurance companies. His business on the cusp of exploding. Far more than he could handle alone. Jake makes the decision to again, ask Alex, to marry him. He thought they could be a great team, with her people skills and research background as a reporter. She could handle the inside operation and he the outside investigations.

Now it was just a matter of timing. Everything must be perfect for Jake to expose his plan to Alexis.

Jake entered his office; Alex was sitting at his desk on the telephone. While he sits in a chair to wait, Alexis was laughing and listening. She responded, "He just came in. We'll finish this later," with a small giggle.

She listened and laughed again. "All right, we'll do lunch later in the week. I'll give you a call."

Listening again.

"Great, I'll see you there, Lyn." Alex hung up.

"Please tell me that wasn't Lynette Shaheen."

"What A nice person. We're going to be great friends."

"If you're meeting that woman for lunch, make it a buffet!" Smith cannot help himself.

"Jake, don't be mean! She adores you."

"The only thing she adores is pork chops and my checkbook."

Alex gave him a disgusted look. "You better treat her right; she just gave us another case."

Us? Smith reflected. *This is going to be easier than I thought* and smiled. "What kind of case?"

"There was a five-car pileup on Interstate 5 a week ago. The woman that caused it is claiming Hartford's client was at fault and started the chain reaction. The kid in the fourth car back is siding with her. All we have to do is re-interview everyone and proof the woman is lying. She wants me to stop by this afternoon and pick up the file."

"I'll drive you." Smith knew she did not like all the one-way streets and gets confused over directions.

"No Jake, I'll go alone. I need to get comfortable driving in the city." She continued, "And on the interstates."

"What are you saying, Alexis?"

"Nothing. Tell me about your morning?"

"I left you a note."

Alex gave him an eye roll. "I saw it. What did James tell you about that man?"

"Oh, not so much." Smith went on and told her that Diego made it clear to stay away from Franco Trujillo. "He's a killer!"

"He told you that man kills people?" Eyes wide open and mouth the same.

"Not in so many words, but what else would I have to be afraid of?"

"Jake, you need to reassess your relationship with Ortiz! Lynette has plenty of work for us."

"But Lynette eats more than she pays!"

Another eye-roll.

Alex's first two weeks were a blur. Jake was working on two cases for Hartford, following a man for Ortiz, and picked up a trial job from Farmers Insurance. This left Alexis alone most evenings and a good part of the day. Smith rented her a car so she could circumvent the city and have as good a vacation as possible under the circumstances.

Unknown to Jake, Alex called people back in Fayetteville and had a malefactor and personal check run on Franco Trujillo.

However, nothing came back, but she did not give up. More than a week later, she received a call from Detective Overstreet, Smiths ex-partner in Arkansas. He expounded that he spoke with a man at the Tijuana Police Station and told Trujillo was a known enforcer for the Melendez Drug Cartel.

That evening Alexis explained to Jake what she found out. He was mystified why Ortiz would have any dealings with that group.

The last week of her vacation arrived. Smith was running out of time to convince his girlfriend to become his wife and business partner.

Sunday evening he took Alex to dinner. Jake mandated that she dress up. This was what she had been waiting for and had packed the perfect dress.

After his shower, he put on his Navy-blue suit, accented with a soft sky-blue tie. He even shined his black penny loafer dress shoes, which he had not done in years. The stitching frayed and he vowed to go shopping.

Two hours after he was ready, she came out of the washroom. Alexis was stunning.

After the Kats' massacre, on New Year's Eve, in Fayetteville, two years prior, Jake's blood had ruined the new designer dress she had bought just for him. Unknown to Jake, Alexis re-bought the exact dress immediately, but left it hanging in her closet and never worn it.

Smith commented on how gorgeous she was, though he did not recognize the dress. She was disappointed and her look fortified it.

"What's wrong, honey?" he questioned.

With a half-smile. "Nothing, dear. I'm excited about spending time with you."

Staring at her for the longest time, he asked, "That dress looks familiar?"

Alexis did not let him off the hook by responding.

He slapped his forehead, "I knew I recognized it! I thought it was ruined?"

Her eyes sparkled and a broad smile pushed her cheeks high. "I knew you liked it so I bought *us* another one."

Us again not verbalizing. Jake states, "Let's get moving," more like police jargon.

Always on the job Alex thinks.

They arrived at the Marine Room on Spindrift Drive in La Jolla, after driving up the beach route. As they made their way along Rivera Drive, around Sail Bay, Smith pulled over to watch the last sailboats heading for the marina in the dim orange twilight. They stood on the cement walk holding hands, with Alexis' head on his shoulder.

Finally, at the restaurant, the maitre d' sat them under the vast wall of windows watching the surf pound La Jolla Shores beach. A bottle of Dom Perignon Brut Champaign already at tableside in a high polished chilled stainless steel ice-filled bucket nestled in a tri-leg matching stand.

The restaurant's sommelier marched, behind the waiter. A silver tastevin cellarman's cup hanging on a silver chain from his neck and a white towel draped over his left arm. The server wearing a dark coat and tie. The sommelier in a black tuxedo.

The wine steward nodded and greeted the couple without a word, before lifting the bottle from its cradle. He wrapped the towel around it, careful not to impede the label. The man held the bottle towards Jake for his inspection. Jake read every word, or at least acted as if he had, and made a short head-bow in acceptance.

The man pulled a wine key from his pocket and opened the bottle. POP! The cork came free. Not a drop hit Jake's lap. Not a bubble lost. The sommelier poured a scintilla of the liquid into his tastevin. He inspected tiny breaking globules on the Champaign's surface, afore tasting. Once in his mouth, he swirled the small sample around while looking up and concentrating. Finally, he turned to the server, who handed him a crystal glass. He put the goblet to his mouth, and let the used wine trickled in.

Satisfied he turned back to his patrons and poured a small taste into Smith's glass. Jake does not have a clue about wines but put

41

on an impressive show for his date. He followed the sommelier's lead and visually inspected the liquid as he swirled the glass before taking a sip. Jake unsure what to do next, swallowed the mouthful. He looked at the steward and quietly nodded.

"Very good, Sir." Two half glasses are poured for the guests before both employees left the table.

"Wow! I didn't know you were a wine connoisseur?" Alex stated.

Blushed and lying, "I know a little."

Jake and Alexis sat for an hour drinking the champagne and basking in each other's company before ordering.

After an extra-long, leisurely meal, sharing a medium prepared Chateaubriand and steamed broccoli, with each having a glass of Château Tour des Gendres Sauvignon, they left the establishment and walked, carrying their shoes, barefoot along the sandy beach to Scripts' Pier.

The tide was out and Jake and Alexis stood under the powder horn moon watching the small breakers crash into the cement pillars lining the sides of the wharf. The spot was perfect. The time was perfect. The evening was perfect. Jake slipped his hand into his pocket and slid his pinky into the ring. He dropped to one knee and asked Alexis to be his wife.

With no hesitation this go-around, she immediately said, "Yes."

Jake rose and slid the ring on her finger. They kissed and held each other for the longest time.

Finally, parting, Alex looked in surprise at the ring. It was considerably larger than the solitaire from Jake's first proposal in Arkansas. The platinum band supported a raised voluminous round diamond flanked by three marque cut stones set in silver leaves on each side. It was gorgeous!

Alex was curious as to what happened to the other ring, but in good taste, refrained from asking.

The following morning Alex canceled her return flight.

CHAPTER TEN
Alphabet Agencies

The day after Diego Ortiz's body found Lieutenant Holden comes through the detective squad room door. "Where's Lyle and Terrance?" he questions loudly, to no one in particular.

"Not here yet!" someone responds, equipollently loud.

"Marsh, get on the horn, and get them in here! As soon as they arrive send them to the third-floor conference room," Holden orders.

The lieutenant heads upstairs to see what is bothering the chief.

He enters the conference room. Chief Baker is sitting at the head of the twenty-seat high polished blonde maple-veneered table slightly reclining in a large armrest chair. Along the far side sits five dark-suited men and a woman dressed in business attire. All have a mug of coffee or a large glass water in front of them. Holden acknowledges his boss and nods to the others, before walking to the back of the room and getting his own coffee. He selects a seat on the opposite side of the table from the congregated unknowns, juxtaposition to his boss.

The woman and man continue their whispering conversation while the other four shuffle papers or sit quietly with folded hands. The Chief asks about his two detectives and Holden replies that they will be along shortly. The lieutenant asks what is going on, but his boss only states they will get into it as soon as the others arrive.

Twenty minutes of small talk, later, Lyle and Terrance enter the room.

Lyle looks around the group. "Hope we didn't miss any of the fun?"

43

"Take a seat, gentlemen," Holden demands overlooking his detective's smart-ass remark.

Terrance thinks better of getting a coffee; Lyle does not and heads to the back of the room, ignoring the direct command.

Lyle fiddles with his coffee for as long as he thinks he can get away with it, before taking the seat next to his partner.

"All right, let's go around the table and introduce yourselves and state exactly why you're here." Baker starts.

The first man, not standing, sets the protocol and replies, "Special Agent Davis, San Diego FBI Unit. I've been investigating Diego Alphonse Ortiz for the past eleven months on a number of Federal Offenses. First and foremost, Racketeering, plus Criminal Enterprise, Human Trafficking, and others."

Next to him. "Nathan Morris, Special Agent, FBI Dallas Division. I've been in San Diego for five months assisting Agent Davis."

Continuing along. "Beverly Good, CBI. I came down from Sacramento four months ago investigating Ortiz on falsifying documents. Specifically DMV records and related items."

Next. "Scott Radclif, DEA, San Diego. I'm on the drug side of Ortiz's investigation and head up a local team. I'm…"

"Hold on a second," Baker interrupts. "Agent Radcliff, how long has your investigation been ongoing?"

"It's close to two years now, Chief. I believe we've been investigating him longer than anyone."

The chief shows a look of dismay, which turns to anger, and he snaps. "Why wasn't I informed of *that*, two years ago?"

"It's Federal. Of course, when we conclude, you and your men will be brought in to assist in the arrests," Radclif lies.

"Please continue."

"Stationed right here in San Diego for fourteen years."

The next man. "The INS is looking at Ortiz's smuggling of illegal aliens across the border. Here and Calexico. And, we're working with agents in Arizona, New Mexico, and Texas. Oh, I'm Agent Adams."

"Crap, how big is… err, was his operation?" Terrance questions.

"Large! We are trying to find out just how extensive before making arrests. And now that Ortiz is dead, who's taking charge," Adam answers. "Oh, and we've been on to him for two and a half years!" Not to be outdone by the Drug Enforcement Agency, and grinning at Radclif.

The next fellow's turn. "Wallace Bruce, Postal Inspector. Everyone calls me Wally. The FBI recently brought us in to look at mail and wire fraud. We think he used the Post Office to send cash and documents back and forth across the Mexican and state borders."

"That does it, then?" Baker asks.

"There are a couple more, Pitts with AFT and Gentry with the IRS that I know about," Special Agent Davis speaks up.

"Ok, Lieutenant Holden, you've met, Lyle, you're up," the chief continues.

"*Special* Detective Stephen Lyle, San Diego Police Department." He smiles at each of the FBI Special Agents. Neither Baker nor Holden thinks it is funny. "We're investigating Ortiz's murder. So, I imagine, with him dead, all your cases wrapped and you guys… " He looks at Beverly and adds, "And gal, can take the bus home."

"Not so fast, Detective," DEA Agent Radclif chirps up, "Ortiz might be gone, but his assets are alive and well. And I'm going to get every one of them!"

That starts twenty minutes of bickering between all the Feds on who has rights of seizure and which agency has priority and who is getting there first.

Chief Baker tries desperately to quiet everyone down. He finally does by standing and loudly proclaiming, "Let me make this crystal clear! San Diego Police is investigating a murder! It's our turf and we have priority over everyone. What I suggest, for the benefit of all concerned, is that we work together and share information. Otherwise, no one is getting onto any scene that I determine crucial to *my* investigation. That does not mean just the murder scene, but all his properties. Am I clear?"

"It's our case in total now, including the murder, Chief. The FBI is in charge of everything. I'll need to be briefed on whatever you guys found so far… as soon as this morning's circus is over!" Davis bluntly states.

"No, the murder is SDPD's jurisdiction and we'll be handling it on our own!" Holden asserts.

"Afraid not, Lieutenant. Ortiz's murder is definitely mob orientated. Federal law trumps you!" Davis surmises.

"Calm down gentleman! We are on the same side here!" Baker, still standing, states, "We *will* work together, understand!"

The left side of the table all stand at once. FBI Special Agent Morris speaks for the first time, "Detectives," addressing Lyle and Terrance, "let's go to your office!"

"Holden, my office!" Baker tells his subordinate.

Lyle and Terrance stomp out of the conference room and head downstairs. The parade of agents follows. No one is going to chance to be out of the loop.

In the Chief's office, Baker and Holden discuss their orchestration for SDPD's murder investigation. They decide every agency is on their own and they are not going to be the FED's 411 Information Service. Holden dismissed rushes downstairs.

Detectives Lyle and Terrance are at their desks surrounded by the standing carnival troop. The ringmaster, Davis is cracking his superfluous whip, while his partner is loading the cannon. Clowns Radclif and Adams are trying to put on their act in ring two. Lyle slowly and as loudly as he possibly can, slurps his coffee, while Terrance pretends to be looking through a stack of files.

"Lyle, hand over everything you have!" Davis Demands.

"Don't have anything yet. The scene is still being processed." Lyle grins.

"We aren't playing chess here! And it's not your move!" The agent goes on, "Give me your prelims, now!"

"No prelims! At least not until I have my coffee," retorts Lyle, and he takes another loud slurp.

Holden steps through the door. "Lyle, Terrance, my office!"

The three of them go over what they are willing to share and what will be their little secrets.

Returning to their desks Lyle tells Terrance to make copies of the initial findings from the murder scene.

Terrance is gone for thirty-six minutes and returns with six mimeographed sheets. Each copy only has Ortiz's office address, phone number, and occupation, which is already common knowledge. The only other reference on the page is to Private Investigator Jake Smith; Name, number, and address.

While his partner was out of the room, Lyle shoved everything from their desks into a bottom drawer and leaned smugly back in his chair with his hands folded behind his head.

Terrance returns and hands out the sheets.

"What the hell is this?" snaps Davis.

"That's what we have so far." Terrance smiles.

"This is bull-crap!" Morris pipes up.

"Sorry, we can't be more helpful at this time. If you guys can come back tomorrow, I'm sure we'll have another sheet, maybe two," Lyle mordaciously states.

"Who's Jake Smith?" asks Beverly Good, of the California Bureau of Investigation.

"He's a PI who worked for Ortiz, and a person of interest."

As soon as all the alphabet agencies file out, Lyle turns to Terrance. "Sic'm on Smith, that was brilliant, buddy."

CHAPTER ELEVEN
SDPD Headquarters

Earlier that morning, San Diego's Police Chief gets to work. He phones Jake Smith. Baker has no forehand knowledge the Feds will be in his office by nine.

It is just after eight o'clock and Jake's still in the living section of his loft reading the morning edition of the San Diego Union and drinking coffee. The vexing telephone ring breaks his concentration.

Jake saunters to the wall phone. "Good morning, Hamilton-Adams Investigations."

"Good morning, Jake, Chief Baker here."

"Hey Chief, long time no talk," Smith's casual, but on alert. *That makes seven of seven!*

"You were going to stop by the station yesterday? Lyle really needs to speak to you regarding your client."

"Oh yeah, I forgot. I'll try and swing by this morning."

"Come on Jake, there is no way you forget your one client was murdered! You're acting like a suspect again!"

"A suspect? Why would I murder my only paying client? I have a penchant for eating."

"Jake, if you're not here in a half hour, we'll be sending a car around for you!"

"Now you're talking, I always wanted a chauffeur." Smith has never given Baker a break.

Click! The man on the other end terminates the call.

Jake dumps his cold coffee and pours a fresh one. He sits back at his table and rereads Clyford Rampton's article. It is a fluff piece with a lot of supposition and not many facts. Typical breaking news rhetoric.

He pulls a couple of slices of wheat bread from the bag and plops them into his toaster. As Jake stands to wonder who wanted his client dead, there is a knock on the door. Glancing at his watch, it is not even eight-thirty yet and his office does not open until nine. He finishes buttering his toast and reaches for the jar of grape jelly when the knock turns into pounding and yelling. "Police! Open up!"

Crap! Don't these guys have anything better to do? Jake reflects and lets them beat his door while he sits back down to eat.

"Honey, who is pounding on the door," asks blurry-eyed Alex as she sits up in bed.

"Nobody important. Try to go back to sleep."

Many minutes of silence later, it starts in again. Bam! Bam! Bam! "SMITH! OPEN UP! Or we're breaking it down!"

Repulsed, Alex gets up and toddles to the restroom.

Jake saunters to the front door. He listens to them trying to shoulder it open. Then the kicking starts. It gratifies him that he installed a steel security bar on the inside. There is no physical way they are getting in. Two full minutes later Smith leans against the doorframe and yells, "I'm getting dressed! I'll be ready in a few minutes!" He goes back to finish the toast and coffee.

Ten more minutes later, Jake opens the door. "Good morning, Officers. What can I do for you today?"

"Smith, you're coming with us!" Officer Carndy demands.

"What's the problem, Dan?" Smith knows the man from his previous tenure with the department.

"You know damn well what the problem is! Baker sent us down to bring you in."

"Well, isn't that gentlemanly of him?"

"Let's go!" The officer jostles Smith's arm.

Jake jerks free. "I'll grab my coat and be right with you."

"You don't need a coat; it's going to be ninety-seven degrees today!"

"Dan, if you want to make detective, appearance is important" He pats the officer's bicep, before turning back into his apartment.

"Is this guy always such an ass?" questions the officer unknown to Smith.

"Yeah. You gotta like him," Dan retorts.

Alex is emerging from the bathroom, and Jake mentions, "I'm going down to headquarters. I'll be back in an hour or so."

"What's going on Jake?"

"A little Q & A session. No big thing. I'll see you soon, dear."

At the station, the desk sergeant stops Smith and the officers. "You'll have to wait here a while. Something came up. Take a seat!"

Almost an hour later. The desk phone rings. "Ok guys, take him up."

Holden, waiting for the three to pass his office, intercepts them, "Come on in here for a minute, Jake. Lyle and Terrance are tied up. They shouldn't be too long, now."

Smith looks out Holden's window over the squad room and spies the activity around the detectives. "Who's all those guys?" he asks.

"Just some Feds trying to interfere with our investigation," the lieutenant answers.

"What do they have to do with a local murder?" Jake unprepared to let it go.

"I don't know! Lyle will straighten them out. Tell me how you're doing, Jake?"

The old, boss and subordinate talk until the detectives are alone.

"They're free now. You can go on in, Jake," Holden states. "Stop by anytime."

Detectives Lyle and Terrance sitting and whispering, at their desks, as Jake closes the office door a little too hard.

Everyone in the room looks up. "Glad you decided to stop by, Smith!" Terrance's sarcasm is no match for Jake's wit.

"Stevie, could you pull a chair over for me? I am going to get a cup of Joe. Be right back." Smith jets into the hall before he receives a response. Jake knows nobody ever gets away with calling the aloof Stephen Lyle, Stevie or even Steve, without a blatant correction and apocalyptic threat. Smith smiles to himself.

Ten minutes or so later, after chatting with everyone he runs into, Smith returns without his coffee.

"Where's your coffee, Smith?" Lyle barks.

"Oh, I got busy and forgot it." He spins around and back down the hallway.

"That idiot isn't ever going to change," Terrance comments to his partner.

Eventually, Smith wanders back in and takes his assigned seat. "So have you guys solved this thing yet?"

"Where were you Friday night?" Lyle gets straight into inculpations.

"Friday night? Is that when Doc told you it happened?"

The detectives received the autopsy report late Monday afternoon after Coroner Martin rushed it. Diego Ortiz was a prominent attorney, who deserved priority status.

"We're asking the questions! Where were you?" Lyle demands a response.

"Let's see… Friday… " Smith scratches his head and displays a look of dismay. "Friday… Friday… I believe I was busy."

"Busy where?" Terrance is almost yelling in frustration.

"Where… where… " Again the same gestures. "I believe I was tailing a guy in National City. I'll check my calendar and get back to you on that one." Jake stands and asks, "Is that it?"

"Sit down, Smith!" Again, Detective Lyle.

Lieutenant Holden comes through his office door after listening to the Mutt and Jeff routine; he determined he would have to mediate. "Jake, if you can just answer the questions, you'll be out of here post haste." Condescending, "We all miss your jokes, though."

"Yeah, I should be on stage… the one-twenty to Yuma." Jake is not ready to give in and not in any hurry to leave.

Holden fakes a diminutive laugh, recollecting the last time they investigated Smith he fled to Yuma. "We are going to need your assistance solving this case. How long have you been doing work for Ortiz?"

"I did a couple of background checks for Diego last month."

"Who did you look into for him?"

"I don't want to misspeak off the top of my head. I'll check my records and get back to you on that item too." Jake turns to Terrance. "Are you making a to-do list for me? My memory isn't what it used to be."

More pissed off than he has ever been with Smith, Terrance grabs a notepad and scribbles, *Alibi* and *Clients*.

"What type of clients did he represent?" Back to Holden.

"Criminals, I imagine. What other types of clients do lawyers represent?"

"That's what we're trying to find out. There weren't any files, other than immigration cases."

"There you have it!" Smith stands.

"Not quite yet, please sit down, Jake." The lieutenant has never been so cordial.

"What did you find at his house?" Smith questions.

"It's clean. He didn't have any papers, to speak of, there. Where else did Ortiz keep files?"

"Don't have a clue, Stephen. Like, I said, I did a couple of investigations, Ortiz and I weren't drinking buddies." He utilizes Holden's given name to piss off Lyle.

"So you don't know who his friends are?" Lyle roughly asks.

"He had friends?' Smith acts shocked. He's not about to reveal Franco Trujillo's visit.

"What did you discuss at your meeting Friday?" Holden gets tougher.

"No meeting. He called and canceled."

"Phone records are easy to check, Jake. You'd better be leveling with me!"

"Why aren't you guys out looking for the real killer?"

52

"Because we're looking at him! How did you know to show up at the scene?" Holden still unconvinced.

"You're getting as senile as these two!" Smith is angry.

"Answer my question, Smith!"

"You're not the only guys with radios! I heard the call!" Jake lies. The murder had gone through Ortiz's organization faster than a mudslide, and Emily phoned him.

"And you thought it was in your best interest to return to the scene?"

"I wasn't returning anywhere! I thought I could help."

"What were you looking for in his office?"

"Clues."

"Clues you might have left?"

"That's ridiculous!" Smith retaliates.

"Is it? Why were you so interested in the waste bin?"

"I noticed the bag was missing and wondering what was in it?"

"What *was* in it?"

"Trash, I assume. Do you have it?"

"Of course, along with your fingerprints." Holden tries to bait him.

"Charge me or I'm out of here!" Smith jumps to his feet.

"Stay in town, Smith. We'll come for you as soon as the warrant's ready!"

"I'll mark my calendar!" He knows Holden is lying. They would not let him walk out otherwise.

CHAPTER TWELVE
Evidence Boxes

"Crap! Ortiz was shot to death!" Terrance visually examines the death certificate and hands it to his partner.

San Diego Police Detectives Stephen Lyle and Donald Terrance are sitting at their desks. Doc Martin had sent it over the autopsy report late in the afternoon the day before, but disrupted by the Feds surprise morning visit and Smith's interview, they had not the time to read it.

"I see that." Lyle reading the report. "It says here that the knife had been inserted postmortem."

"Why would someone shoot him, and then stab him?" thinking aloud. "For good measure?" Terrence questions.

"Make a statement. Personal… or maybe a signature? Do you recall any other murders where a stiletto was left?"

"Sure don't. I'm positive I would have remembered that. I'll check nationally," assures Terrance.

Finishing the report, Lyle sets it down and states, "The knife went into the same hole the bullet made."

"Not too bright if they thought they were covering up the cause of death."

"Nobody's that stupid."

Lyle calls the scene investigator to check on evidence processing.

Off the phone, Lyle tells his partner, "Marvin," referring to SDPD's Chief Crime Scene Investigator, Marvin Kenny, "is bringing over what he's processed so far and his report"

"What does he have?" asks Terrance.

"They got into the safe. It had Ortiz's bank records and some cash. He also has the plastic trash bag. It recovered from a construction dumpster a few blocks away. He'll go over everything when he gets here."

The pair spends the next hour or so drinking coffee and making lists of what they know. They plan on stopping by Point Loma Nazarene University after lunch and checking Gary Baird's references and talking to his acquaintances to get an idea of what kind of person he is. Baird had told them at the scene that he never met Ortiz and hired by the building manager.

Kenny walks into the squad room and approaches the detectives. "Hey, Guys. Here's what we got so far." He set the three boxes he is juggling on the floor beside the detective's desks.

The first evidence he reveals, "Diego Ortiz was shot to death with a twenty-two long rifle bullet. The stiletto was shoved in to make the murder look like a stabbing!" Investigator Kenny lays the slug on the desk along with the stiletto.

"We got that from the autopsy," Lyle responds.

Terrance hustles a chair over for Marvin to sit in.

"I picked up the slug, yesterday, for ballistics," Marvin mentions. "The lab matched it to a Browning semi-automatic, which hasn't been located."

The investigator opens the top box and pulls out his list and report. He hands Lyle the report and lays the list in front of himself. Marvin puts a check mark next to *Weapon*.

The boxes arranged in list order and he grabs the next item. Banded packages of bills and a few loose ones. Marvin stacks them on Lyle's desk.

"Here's the cash, fourteen thousand and three hundred eighty dollars."

"Doesn't he believe in banks?" Terrance ruminates.

"We'll get to his bank accounts next," as he checks, *Cash*, the second notation on his list. Marvin pulls a file out and reads it. Ortiz has records of two accounts, a checking account with three thousand and change and savings that carry's a balance of a little over ten grand."

"That's it! I thought he was successful?" Lyle comments, not really a question.

"That's it for the safe's records. There could be and I suspect more accounts. You'll need to find them. Probably at his house," the CSI suggests.

"Weren't there." Terrance comments. They had searched the house the day before and had not found much. It was virtually as if nobody lived there, other than sleeping, dressing and utilizing the restroom.

Marvin checks off *Accounts*.

Lyle picks up the bullet to examine and questions if there were any fingerprints in the room.

"Only Ortiz's," comes the answer. "And only in obscure places. The room was wiped!"

He checks *Fingerprints*, further down the list.

The next item is a jewelry box sized steel-container. The lid badly damaged around the lock, as they had to pry it open. "He also accumulated a little gold. Ten South African Kuggerans, and fifteen Canadian Maple Leafs." Referring to his list. "A 1927 D St Gaudens Double Eagle, also gold. A silver 1794 Flowing Hair dollar and an 1838 O Capped Bust half-dollar. The gold coins worth a little over six thousand dollars, but the other three rare coins, together, value at around a half million. There are other common silver coins, which only amount to a few hundred." Another check mark.

"We found a 9mm Luger from WW II and a newer 357 Smith & Wesson, setting the pistols on the desk. The Luger hasn't been fired recently, and the 357 has never been shot."

Guns checked as Lyle asks, "Were they loaded."

"Hollow points in the 357. Nothing in the Luger. No shell boxes present."

The next item from the first box is a photo album. "There are a few old pictures of a Mexican woman, which could be his mother. None showing a father figure. In addition, more recent pictures of an attractive, younger Mexican woman who could be a wife or sister. A couple of photos show children, which we don't have any idea who they are. Could be his, nieces, nephews or someone else's."

"Any of Ortiz?" Lyle asks.

"None!" Marvin adds two full bottles of Pappy's bourbon to the desk without commenting. "That's all for the safe. I would have thought there would have been more, but it was mostly empty."

Kenny sets the top empty box on the floor and opens the next one. "In here we have his desk files. The top half is current clients, and the rest of the box seems to be a hodgepodge of people over the last few years, as far back as '68. Nothing anywhere within the office from before that time." He set a stack of legal-size file folders on top of a pile of paper since; the desk did not have any more unused space.

"So there's a few clients and not much money in the bank." Terrance more to himself, while writing a note.

"Surprising, huh? He must have outside file storage somewhere," Kenny reiterates, then checks off the last two items he missed *Album* and *Liquor*, then *Current Files*. He stacks the second empty box on top of the first.

Opening the final box, "This contains items we found in the dumpster." Marvin pulls out a white plastic trash bag, and closes the box-top flaps and places the bag on top of the desk mess. "This is the garbage bag from his office waste container. Presumably removed and dump after the murder."

The detective's eyes widen.

"First, we have an empty bottle of Pappy Van Winkle's bourbon and two empty used glasses. Ortiz has expensive tastes. He must have generated far more income than his records show. The glasses have bourbon residue. Apparently, Ortiz and an unknown person had a drink… maybe even the whole bottle. Doc does not have the tox-report yet. The seal appears to have been broken recently and he sets the cap on the desk. I doubt it was a client at that time of night and the price of the liquor. More likely a close friend or business acquaintance he wanted to impress."

"What time do you think the murder occurred?" Lyle asks.

"Martin," referring to the coroner, "told me the victim had steak, lobster, and wine in his stomach that was well digested. A meal like that probably isn't lunch. So he was killed well after dinner."

The rest of the bag is regular office trash; discarded notes, a fast food lunch bag and cup, and tissues, etc. Nothing of consequence!"

"Any receipts?"

"A couple. They're here." He points at three crinkled up small papers.

"Fingerprints?" Terrance asks, hoping Smith's was on something.

"All Ortiz's. According to his schedule, he met with three clients and Jake Smith that day. As I stated, none of their prints were anywhere in the room."

"Are you working on anything else?" Lyle questions Kenny.

"Not until you guys give me more."

"Ok, Marv, thanks for your help, we'll be in touch." Lyle adds, "Don't let out the cause of death was a bullet. The news already reported it as a stabbing. Only the three of us and Doc will know."

"My lips are sealed." Kenny stands. "We'll talk," he tells the detectives and leaves the room.

Detective Lyle turns to his partner for the same acknowledgment. In addition, thinks *we'll nail that bastard this time.*

CHAPTER THIRTEEN
Smith Verses FBI

Banging starts on HAI's steel freight-size office door. Smith is at his backroom table drinking his morning coffee and reading a *True Detective* magazine. He ignores the interruption.

Egan Davis keeps banging.

"Where could this guy be, it's not even eight-thirty yet?" FBI Special Agent Morris asks his partner.

"No idea!" Agent Davis answers, as his hand tires from pounding.

Suddenly there is a faint voice from within, "I open at nine," spoken with wanton disregard.

"FBI, OPEN UP!" screams Davis.

No response.

The agent starts pounding and yelling again. Five minutes later Morris grabs his partner's sleeve. He takes a quick look at his watch. "Let's grab a cup of coffee. We'll be back by nine."

Looking through disgusted eyes. "I'll wait here so he doesn't try and sneak out! Black and strong."

Many minutes later Morris returns with two coffees and two glazed donuts. They wait, one after the other continuously glancing at his wristwatch. At straight-up nine o'clock, its Morris's turn to pound and scream.

Nine minutes later the steel door squeaks and grinds along its top rollers. Jake Smith stands in front of the agents grinning, "You guys are up early. What can I do for you?"

"Jake Smith?" asks one of them.

"In the flesh," not budging or inviting them inside.

"We need to talk! Can we come in?" Davis is not asking.

Jake takes a long look at his watch. "Sorry guys, I have a nine o'clock. I'll check my calendar, maybe we can meet tomorrow or later in the week?"

"Your appointment is late!" Morris bluntly responds.

"You guys know criminals have a hard time sticking to schedules."

"Cut the crap, Smith! There's no appointment, and we're not leaving!"

"Did you bring a whole box?" Smith notices a mostly munched donut in Morris' hand.

Morris tries the nice-cop routine. "Jake, can we have five minutes. When your appointment shows, we're gone." All three obviously aware there is not going to be any five-minute discussion.

"Well, if you put it that way, I can spare five." Smith pivots and sits behind Alex's desk. Both agents pull their own chairs over and sit opposite him.

"Jake Smith, we are Special Agents Davis and Morr… "

"I've got to take a leak," interrupting the introduction, Smith is gone from the room faster than flicking a light switch.

"That SOB… " Morris starts.

Davis looks at his partner, putting an index finger to his lips, before pointing around the room. Morris nods acknowledgment and they sit quietly until Jake returns.

"Sorry about that… a little too much coffee." Not sitting, Smith glances at the large white-dialed wall clock. "I'm afraid our five minutes is up, gentlemen."

Glaring through squinted eyes, neither agent twitches a muscle. "We're investigating Ortiz and told you are the man to talk to," Davis states.

"Cortiz? Who's that?" Jake deliberately mispronounces the name.

Morris stands. "Jake, you know the drill… we either talk here and now or we're taking the ride downtown!"

"We are downtown," Smith, reminds him.

Davis joins his partner, standing. "Let's go!"

"Who's driving?" The grinning Jake joins them standing. He does not have anything better to do today than play with these guys.

The three men arrive at SDPD headquarters in the FBI's company car and approach the front desk. "Special Agents Davis and Morris we need a room to question this man. Can you alert Lyle and his partner to sit in?"

"Morn'n, Jake," the desk Sergeant nods at Smith.

"Good morning, Cal," Smith dips his head back.

"I'll check with Lieutenant Holden and see what's available. You guys can take a seat," Cal responds as he picks up the interoffice phone.

Five minutes later, Lyle and Terrance appear. "Follow us!" Lyle tells the agents.

On their way to the second floor, "I'm surprised you brought him here?" Lyle asks Davis.

"I understood we're working in cooperation, and just being accommodating. But, we're asking all the questions! Understood?" explains the agent. They are there because the FBI does not know the history between Smith and Lyle, and Davis mistakenly thought Jake might be more open in familiar surroundings.

"Completely," Lyle lies, knowing his partner and he are not overlooking any opportunity.

The five sit in Interrogation Room A. Lieutenant Holden is behind the glass, observing.

Davis takes the lead. "I'm recording this!"

Smith chuckles. "If you must. I haven't had enough coffee this morning and my mind is still a little foggy. I only hope this isn't going to be a waste of your time."

"Can you state your name for the record?"

Smith feigns trying to remember and turns to Lyle. "Stevie, maybe a fresh cup will help. I'm sure you remember how to fix it... I like it black!" His eyebrows rise for acknowledgment.

Behind the glass, Holden thinks to himself *it's been a little dull around here without him.*

After a long glare, Lyle barks, "Don, get him a coffee!"

The other three officials sit in quiet contempt eyeing Smith, who is acting fuzzy and swaying a little from side to side. His eyes closed, but the smile never leaves his face.

Terrance comes back and sets a piping hot mug of the brown liquid in front of Jake. He microwaved it for three minutes in hope Smith burns his tongue.

"I'm sorry Don, but I need a napkin."

"You're not getting a F****** napkin!" Lyle snaps almost screaming.

"Let's everyone calm down and we'll get through this as quickly as possible." Morris tries.

"Great, I have important things to do today," Smith chirps up.

Davis resets the recorder. "Name?"

"Jake Smith."

"Occupation?"

"PI."

Davis reiterates for the recording, "Private Investigator."

The formalities continue without incident. Then they get to the meaty questions.

"Did work for Diego Ortiz?"

"Her again? Who is that?" Smith acts as if he does not know the name.

"You were at *his* murder scene and knew *him* then!" Lyle interjects.

"Detective, you know the rules!" Glares Davis. He turns back to Jake and asks, "What about that, Smith?"

Acting demented and taking small sips of the burning coffee. "Oh, you mean James?" Smith finally mutters.

"James?"

"That's how I knew him. He likes to be called James." Smith throws them a tidbit, "I worked two background investigations for him, but didn't really *know* him, if you know what I mean?"

"So he paid you and signed the checks, *Diego Ortiz* and you're telling me you don't know his name?"

"You guys, you're trying to fool me." As sweet as he can, though he has them right where he wants them.

"I need you to quit trying to mess with us and just answer the questions!" Davis, now as pissed as Lyle.

"Sure, Egore, is it? No checks, cash! So I never really knew his name," Smith fibs.

"Cash? Didn't you find that strange?" Egan overlooks the label.

"Business 101… Egore."

"EEE-GAN!"

"Ok. EEE-GAN. As I was saying, Business 101, never refuse cash!" Smith schools the agent.

Davis goes on asking about the jobs. Moreover, what they entailed. Jake cannot seem to remember specifics, just that they were background checks or something on a couple different people. Of course, he states that he will look for his records and get back to them, though he has no intention of either.

"So, why were you at the scene?" Morris quickly asks.

"I was walking down the street and saw the commotion and wandered over," states Smith.

"That's not what you told us yesterday!" Lyle lets go.

"Morning exercise, you know," Smith answers Davis, overlooking Lyle.

"How often do you exercise?" Lyle asks, staying in the conversation, and knowing Smith is anything but a fitness freak.

"Oh Stevie, you know how important it is to stay in shape." Jake glances at the man's paunch, "Or maybe you don't."

Lyle cannot contain himself and springs to his feet at Jake's personal jab.

"Sit down, Stephen!" Terrance grabs his partner's arm before a fistfight breaks out.

Smith riposte, "A little touchy over your weight problem there, Stevie." Trying to push him over the edge.

"THAT'S ENOUGH!" Davis, almost yelling. He turns to Smith and gets to his feet. "You and I are going back to your office and get the names of the people you investigated for Ortiz,"

"Great, EEE-GAN. I'm not the best record keeper. Why don't you bring your lunch along, it might take a few hours," giddy Smith replies.

"*You* go get your records in order! We'll be along in a couple of hours!" Davis, way past the slow burn stage.

"Sit down Smith. We're not finished!" Terrance now involved and wanting a crack.

Smith complies, "Steve, I'm starting to fade, can you grab me another coffee?"

"Would you like a spike of Pappy in it?" Terrance asks, trying to set him up.

"I'm not that way!" Jake turns the liquor reference into an off-color joke. He had shared Pappy's Bourbon with James before, and aware of what Terrance is really up to.

"It's high-end bourbon, moron!" Terrance joins his partner, out of control.

"Oh! I've been known to take a little nip… now and again, you know. Maybe today is a good day to take up serious drinking."

"We know you and Ortiz shared a bottle Friday night!"

"Friday? Which Friday would that be, Don?"

"The Friday you murdered your employer!"

"Don, Don, Don." Shaking his head, "I wasn't anywhere near him that night."

"I'm sure you have an airtight alibi?" Davis, back on lead.

"Let me think about it. I know I can come up with one!" Smith cannot wipe the smile off his face. He now knows Ortiz was drinking with someone he knew when he was murdered. If they were drinking Pappy's, it was a friend. Everyone else gets Harpers. Another tick for Frank Trujillo.

After two minutes of boring Smith's eyeballs, Lyle slowly stands and walks out in disgust. And, not to play coffee girl.

Holden emerges from the observation room and confronts him in the hall. "When the FBI cuts Smith loose, put a tail on him. Find out where he goes and who he talks to. I just joined your team!"

CHAPTER FOURTEEN
The Landrys

Thursday morning, Lyle and Terrance decide to run over to Ortiz's office and interview all the other tenants to see who knew him, and what they can find out.

Arriving they find the building's small parking lot full, and park down the street, in a lot owned by an independent company and pay the five-dollar fee.

Walking around the corner of the building, Terrance notices a small plaque bolted onto the brick front, reading, "RLD, Inc., 930 Prospect Avenue, La Jolla, California". It lacks a personal name or phone number. He makes a note.

It is an old brick six-story walk-up. There is an open main stairway at one end of the floors and the other end features an additional fire escape stairway behind a door. Each level contains eight suites, four on each side of the corridor.

The detectives enter the first office they encounter. The door sign reads, South Coast Remodeling. Terrance admires the framed and hung large photograph depicting a tangerine glowing moon reflecting off the ocean. He recognizes the location as somewhere along Sunset Cliffs.

Lyle approaches the young man sitting behind the only desk in the reception area. He shows his badge and asks the man if he knew Diego Ortiz. "Only by name and seeing him in the halls." The detective questions whether Ortiz used their services and if his boss knew the attorney. No to these questions too.

The detectives continue calling on every office in the building. They cannot find anyone who had more than a passing conversation with the lawyer. Not one business worked with him.

"Who is this apparition? Terrance questions his partner.

"That, my friend, is precisely what we're going to find out. We are going to visit every haunt he visited. Talk to every spirit he talked to. Look in every web he spun!"

Besides the deceased's top floor office, resides Filson Accounting. The door is locked and nobody's at work. The other six offices on the top floor, sans signs, appear to be vacant.

Tearing off the yellow crime scene tape, and letting it drop to the floor, they slip into Ortiz's rooms. The investigators re-examine each area. In the big office, they go straight to the open safe. CSI cleaned out everything of importance and nothing new found.

Terrance pulls out his notebook, walks to the desk and phones information for RLD's number. He dials the given number and questions the receptionist under the guise of wanting to lease an empty commercial suite in the building. The woman does not think there are any empty units in that particular building but suggests he come in, and talk with Reena Landry, who has numerous available places downtown. Terrance leaves his name and tells her that he will be there in an hour, roughly the time told Reena would be back in her office.

As Terrance is on the phone, Lyle walks around the room looking at the hanging art. He stops in front of the smallest one and fixates on it.

Off the phone, Terrance holds his palm-up hands like a St. Francis garden statue. "What are you looking at? All these nice pictures in here, you're admiring the one that looks like my kid could have painted!"

"What's this supposed to be… is that blue thing in the middle a turtle?" Lyle takes a closer look. "Henri Matisse. Hmm… nobody, I know." He turns, "Let go rent an office!"

"Hold up a minute." Terrance walks around, fingering each picture. "All these are painted, but your favorite is a cheap print in an expensive frame." He stands puzzled and glances around at each one again.

"Maybe he just liked the colors. Let's go!" Lyle commands.

The pair walks to their plain wrap and drives to the La Jolla office of RLD, Incorporated.

Terrance asks the receptionist if Reena is available stating he is the man who called about downtown office space. The detectives asked to take a seat and told that the owner will be off the phone shortly.

Almost thirty minutes later, the receptionist lets them into Reena Landry's office.

"Good morning Mrs. Landry, I'm Don and this is my partner Stephen."

"Good morning, gentlemen, I understand you're looking for office space downtown?"

"Yes, we're interested in a place at 500 Broadway. It's an ideal spot for us."

"What type of business do you have?" Reena asks.

"We're architects," Lyle responds.

"I have the perfect place for you in the one-thousand block of Front Street. It's only a few blocks from there."

"We're really interested in the Broadway address," Terrance again.

"I'm sorry; there is nothing available in that building."

"We've visited the place and it appears the sixth floor only has two tenants."

"Sorry, one client leases the entire floor."

"Is that so?" Lyle ends the charade and pulls his badge.

Perplexed, she asks, "Why didn't you just say who you are!"

"We're investigating Diego Ortiz's murder. So he leases the whole floor?"

"I can't divulge information about my clients."

"Why would he need that many suites for a small law firm?"

"I lease space. I don't question what they need it for."

"The first question you asked us was what we did!" Terrance notes.

"Of course I knew he was a lawyer, but not privy to the ins and outs of his business."

"Can you give us a key to all the rooms on the sixth floor?" Lyle questions.

"Not without a search warrant. I must protect my client's privacy."

"Ex-client, Mrs. Landry! What are you hiding?"

"Hiding! I have nothing to hide! Now if you'll excuse me, I have work to do!" Insulted by the insinuation.

The detectives leave the room and close the door behind them as asked. Lyle immediately notices a light start blinking on the receptionist's phone and sticks his head back into Reena's office. He overhears the woman say, "Hayden, the police were just here..." upon hearing the door open, she spins her chair around. "Get out of here!" screaming at the detective.

"Sorry, I just had one more question."

"Not without my attorney present! Now get the hell out!"

Outside, on their way to the car, Lyle tells his partner that they need to find out who Hayden is and what she is concealing.

Back at the station, Lyle gets on the horn to Jillian Ross. He explains the situation and asks the ADA if she can get a search warrant for the entire sixth floor.

Jill states she will see what she can do, but it is a long shot. She asks him if Ortiz's lease was in any of the confiscated files.

"Didn't see it."

She continues, "If you can't get her to voluntarily hand over the keys, we would need a court order for the warrant. From what you told me, it sounds like she never specifically said his name. Therefore, to get a court to support us, we would have to prove that Ortiz is the leaseholder. If she will not give up the keys, she certainly won't turn over the lease. Without her, we need collaboration, probably from another tenant that actually witnessed him going into the rooms. It could take weeks."

"We don't have weeks!"

"Find his lease! He's got a copy somewhere."

In the meantime, Terrance researches Hayden. He discovers the man is Reena's husband and owns a financial business in the same building as RLD.

The detectives drive back to La Jolla. They do not have to scour the directory board; Hayden Landry Financial, Inc. is the second name, right under his wife's business. They discover the office front door locked and nobody home.

Lyle shoves a business card in the door crack and they return to the station empty-handed.

Again, sitting at their desks, Lyle notices a large clasp-envelope from the DMV had arrived. He tears it open. It contains Ortiz's records. They already have the lawyer's Cadillac impounded, and the DMV records are not helpful.

The telephone rings. Stephen picks up.

"Good afternoon, Special Agent, Davis here."

"Egan, what can I do for you?"

"Just checking in to see if you have anything new on Ortiz?"

Lyle quickly decides to let Davis in. He figures if he gives something up the agent will do likewise. "We talked with a woman named Reena Landry. Her husband and she are hiding something. In addition, Ortiz leased the whole floor of offices at the Broadway address, including Filson Accounting's suite next to his. We're trying to get search warrants now."

Davis responds, "I been in the other rooms. They're mostly empty. My guess, he just didn't want neighbors. The last one on the left has been turned into an apartment. My guess is Ortiz lived there most of the time."

"What do you know about the Landrys?"

"Mrs. Landry and Ortiz had a couple businesses together."

Lyle sees the light, "Holy crap! That's what she's hiding!"

"Not anymore. The IRS is looking at them. You've met Fraser Gentry, right."

"Not yet. I assume he'll stop by?"

"Don't know. Anyway, Reena could have a motive to off Ortiz." Davis' offhanded comment.

"That she could!" Detective Lyle, one-step ahead of Davis.

After hanging up, Stephen tells his partner that they have another suspect.

CHAPTER FIFTEEN
Siena Herrera

After the FBI release Private Investigator Jake Smith, he leaves the police station. No one would give him a ride.

Outside, Jake decides to walk over to Ortiz's office and have a quick look around.

The crime scene tape already pulled off the door and lays on the hallway floor. Jake enters.

The cops tore every inch of the office apart and left it a mess. The only things in place are the painting around the perimeter, and there isn't a straight one in the lot. The investigators obviously looked behind each one.

Smith stands in the center of the room realizing this was a waste of time.

Out of respect for the pictures, he walks slowly around straightening each one. The last one he gets to is the Matisse print. He stands, lost in thought, staring at the colorful modern art, trying to figure out what the picture depicts. It dawns on him it is the only one still hanging straight.

Jake unhangs the picture, curious as for why it appears untouched. He had no knowledge that Detective Lyle had straightened when he was studying it. He turns it over. Nothing is unusual. He takes it to the desk and lays it face down. Jake pulls a penknife from his pocket and removes the backboard.

There, hidden behind the print, he discovers an out of focus black and white eight by ten, of a man and woman making love on a floor. He does not know either party.

Jake finds a rubber band and rolls up the photo and sticks it in his inside coat pocket.

A final glance around the room and he walks out, leaving the torn apart frame on the desk.

He sits in his office telling Alexis about the experience. Moreover, that something fishy is going on, "They are investigating *ME* as a murder suspect!"

By this time its mid-afternoon on the tenth. Their conversation interrupted by an attractive early thirties Mexican woman coming through the door.

Alex rapidly walks into her office and asks, "Hello, can I help you?"

Finally, alone for a second, Jake removes the stolen photo and slips it into his bottom desk drawer.

"I'm not sure I'm in the right place, I'm Siena Herrera and would like you to investigate Juan's death. I believe you did work for him."

Alex asks her to hold on a minute and calls Jake to her office.

The woman repeats her request.

"Sorry Mrs. Herrera, I'm not familiar with him," Jake answers.

"You might know my husband as Diego Ortiz."

"Jim?" Shocked, both, by his true name, and that he is married.

"Yes, James. Juan goes by that name," she retorts.

"Why would he use a different name?" inquires bewildered Smith.

"He thought that name was more conducive to his business. He actually had it legally changed many years ago."

"We are sorry for your loss, Mrs. Herrera," Alexis interrupts.

"Thank you. It is a terrible situation. Our children are having a difficult time. They're so young."

"James has children?" Smith cannot believe what he hears.

"A boy seven and Estefania is four," she offers.

"I'm sorry, Mrs. Herrera," Jake turn at apologizing.

"Please call me Siena," she interjects.

"Of course, Siena," Smith continues, "can you tell me where you and Jim... uh, Juan live?"

"He has a small house on this side of the border but comes home most weekends. We have a beach house south of Rosarito off the old highway to Ensenada."

"Where is his house here?" questions Smith.

"I don't know. I've never been there."

"You never visited him?" Alexis is amazed.

"Of course the children and I have been to the United States many times, but mostly to shop or visit attractions around California. We always met Juan at his office or wherever we were going for the day."

"What would you like me to do for you, Siena?" Smith asks.

"I want to hire you to find my husband's murderer and explain to me why this… this thing happened to Juan," Siena, starting to choke up.

"The police are investigating. I'll be happy to go with you to see them," Jake volunteers.

"My husband never trusted the police. I think it began when he was a young boy growing up on the streets of Tijuana."

Jake never knew James was a Mexican National and he does not respond. There obviously is a lot he never knew about his former client. "What can you tell me about his business and associates?"

"Not much. I was not allowed to know about his business. You could start by talking to Jose Contreras."

Mrs. Herrera continues to give Smith information on Diego's partner in Mexico. "Contreras is an attorney with an office just north of the Tijuana's Arch, on *Av Revolución*. Jose and Juan grew up together, hawking Chiclets gum, as young boys, along the bridge crossing over the Tijuana River just west of the El Chaparral border crossing. It is the main walking thoroughfare for tourists going downtown.

"By the time they turned ten or eleven; the pair was living on the streets and working for the bazaars along Revolution Avenue, enticing foreigners into souvenir shops. A year later, they graduated to handing out leaflets advertising topless dancing clubs, and dragging unsuspecting men into prostitution bars. It wasn't long until Juan and his partner was pipping prostitutes and selling marijuana cigarettes.

"When Juan turned nineteen years of age, he alone crossed the border into the States. On a dark moonless night, he climbed the border fence and snuck through the dry-grass and rocky canyons east of the Chula Vista."

"From what he told me," Siena goes on, "he worked odd jobs washing dishes, cleaning warehouses and such for three years. Apparently, he stole food and slept in alleys while saving every penny he could. Juan was smart. He found a man to help him. An elderly man. Like the father, Juan never had. I do not know all the details, but Mr. Brown somehow got him legalized and through school, getting him an education and becoming a lawyer."

"I'm not sure, but I think Juan paid for Jose to become a lawyer in Tijuana. That would be before they went into business together. That is about all I know. Can you help me?"

"What can you tell me about Mr. Brown?"

"Nothing, except he died before Juan graduated college. I don't believe he had any relatives and left everything to Juan."

"Do you know his full name?" Jake asks.

"Clarence Brown, he was a lawyer here in San Diego. I do not know more than that."

"Of course we can look into it. I can't promise anything but we'll do our best for you, Siena," Jake sympathetically states.

Siena pulls a bundle of hundreds, rubber banded together, from her purse. "Here is ten-thousand dollars to get started. Let me know when you need more."

Alexis writes out a receipt and gets the woman's contact information. Siena thanks them and goes on her way.

"This is going to be a tough case!" Jake mumbles to his partner. He removes five bills from the bundle and shoves them into his pocket. "Can you deposit the rest into our account? I'm going over to see Emily Vargas and will be back by dinner time."

"Any special requests?" Alex, referring to food.

She receives an *I don't care* response, and he tells her, "I'm leaving now and will see you later." Jake kisses her forehead.

Jake strolls into Emily's Cafe and sits at the counter ordering a coffee. He asks a waitress if Emily is around, and told that she is out and will be back in a few minutes.

Emily Vargas was instrumental in getting Smith and Ortiz together. Jake knows they were good friends and wants to see if she can enlighten him on a reason someone wanted him dead.

After an hour of drinking too much coffee, Smith asks for the check. At that instant, the owner makes it back to work. Emily and Jake chat for a while before he takes off and goes back to his loft.

Smith sits at his desk making a list and a plan of attack for the Ortiz case when Alexis enters. Her arms juggling cartons of Chinese takeout. "I brought dinner," gleefully she tells.

Jake slams the steel door shut, locking up the office while Alex sets out white cartons of spicy Szechuan beef, egg foo young and steamed white rice on their small inside table.

During dinner, Jake explains what he had learned from Vargas. "Emily was very candid. She wants to help any way she can." He tells Alex that Diego helped her and her family across the border and arranged immigration papers. Smith also states that Emily and Diego were partners in the café, and when Diego died, the business and the building became solely hers!" Jake takes a few seconds, thinking. "That's motive." Though quickly dismissing the notion. He continues, "The best part. She gave me Ortiz's home address in Chula Vista. As soon as it's dark, we'll pay a visit."

"Sounds good. Tomorrow I'm going to see what I can find out about Clarence Brown," Alex comments.

"And I'm going to TJ to see his partner."

CHAPTER SIXTEEN
Search Warrant

FBI Agents Davis and Morris secure a search warrant for both, Reena and Hayden Landry's offices. They recruit an additional twelve agents from the San Diego FBI headquarters and convoy to the La Jolla location by nine o'clock Friday morning.

Morris takes six agents and goes to Hayden Landry Financial, while the other seven agents swarm RLD. Neither Hayden nor his wife has been in their office yet today, but each called immediately by unknown employees.

The principles show up shorty and demand to know what they are looking for. Both teams spend hours tearing apart their respective assignments. In addition, they load several vehicles with full boxes of files, and every scrap of paper deemed important.

At the end of the fiasco, the agents drive away. Both Hayden and Reena close their businesses and send their employees home. They leave together in his recently purchased full-size GMC Sierra pickup.

Back at the local FBI headquarters, Davis and Morris oversee every available agent inspecting each, and every snippet of paper seized from the Landry's businesses. The FBI is specifically looking for anything pertaining to Diego Ortiz or other major accounts, large and frequent transactions, and they flag all cash dealings.

Just before two PM, a woman agent screams out, "Holy crap! They use a file storage facility in Sorrento Valley!"

Davis immediately sends Morris and two agents to the Sorrento Record Storage Corporation on Sorrento Valley Road. It is their assignment to secure the business until Davis meets them there with a search warrant.

Agent Davis telephones Senior ADA Jillian Ross and asks her to type up a search warrant and get it signed. Jill mentions that she will use the same judge who signed the Landry warrant and should have it within an hour. The FBI man tells her that he is on his way to her office and will wait for it.

Morris' team arrives at the business, which locked with a handwritten note taped to the door:

CLOSED UNTIL MONDAY
FOR INVENTORY.
SORRY FOR THE INCONVENIENCE.
IF THIS IS AN EMERGENCY, PLEASE CALL
619-555-5855.

Morris directs the two add-on agents to go to the alley and watch the back door. He sits in his white company Impala guarding the front.

A little more than two hours later Special Agent Davis pulls into the lot. Behind him is a cavalcade of vehicles full of agents. He jumps from his car, search warrant in hand. "What's happening?" Davis questions his partner.

"They're closed."

"Get the ram. We're going in!"

As the front door caves, the alarm starts blaring. "Someone find that siren and get it off!" Davis spits out.

He then divides the men and woman into four teams and assigns each a quadrant to search.

As everyone dissipates, two rent-a-cops spring through the broken open door, guns were drawn. "What's going on here?" screams one of them.

"FBI!" Davis shows his badge. "Put those guns away before you shoot someone! And, get out of here!"

Not long after the private security officers arrived, the president and vice president of Sorrento Storage screech into the parking lot. One car following the other. They burst into their business and demand to know what is happening. The company president tells the intruders to stop until their attorney arrives.

Agent Davis emphatically states, "Nobody's stopping. Stand over there," pointing at a corner of the office.

When the two newcomers refuse to comply and demand more answers. A couple of agents escorts the men outside, and point-blank tells them that if they interfere, they will be arrested and removed, from the area.

Their attorney arrives and talks with his clients for a couple of minutes.

It is his turn to make demands. He marches inside, followed by the company officers. After watching the commotion for a few seconds, the lawyer observes two agents conversing and approaches and stipulates to see the warrant. After handed the search warrant, he scans through it. Turning to his clients, he explains that the agents are searching for any records relating to the Landry's or their companies specifically related to Diego Ortiz.

The company men look at each other and laugh. Their attorney asks what is so funny.

"The Landrys picked up *all* their records three hours ago."

"What reason did they give you?"

"Something about getting everything together for a tax audit," the vice-president explains.

"Ortiz?" Isn't that the attorney who was murdered a few days ago?" the lawyer questions.

"I believe so. But again, it has nothing to do with us!"

The lawyer is not so sure. "The FBI doesn't investigate local murders. There is more to this!"

"We just store files and don't know what's in them. They cannot have anything on us! We didn't break any laws!"

The FBI search comes up empty.

CHAPTER SEVENTEEN
Ortiz Home

He steps into the backyard and shines his flashlight around. His partner continues to search inside. The yard well kept, though the police left the house a mess, and Smith thinks *Ortiz must own a landscaping company or at the very least has one of his immigrate clients do yard work.*

Smith stops the beam on the back wall of the garage. He stares at the structure for a long time. Something is amiss; he just cannot put a finger on what! The wall is not in plane with the house.

Going inside, he continues to look hard at the other side of the same wall. Jake walks along inspecting and tapping on various spots. At the far end, he slides away a shelving unit. The drywall pieced together in an odd pattern, the top third or so has three smaller pieces while the bottom part is a single half-sheet.

He pushes and bangs along the edges of the lower portion with nothing happening.

"I wondered where you got to." Alexis asks as she enters the garage through the kitchen door. "What are you doing?"

"I don't know! This wall appears thick to me. I'm probably just imaging." Jake shakes his head. "Did you find anything in the house?"

His partner smiles and holds up a weird steel shaft. It is three inches long, tapered with a small square flange protruding from the thinner end.

"What is that thing?"

"Actually, I was hoping you'd know?" Alexis, hands over the implement.

Looking absent-mindedly at the wall adjacent to where her man was tapping, "I found it on a hook, behind the facing board under the kitchen sink."

Without warning, "Step aside buddy!" She pulls Jake's arm until he is out of the space between the wall and the moved shelving unit.

Alex bends over, placing her middle finger of her left hand over a black spot near the floor and rubs the area. "It's a hole! Give me back my key!"

After a quiet click, the lower drywall section springs ajar. She steps back and lets Smith take a first look. Alexis is not about to join the rats, spiders and other creatures living within!

Jake shines his flashlight around. He spots a light switch on the wall and flicks it on. Feeling safer, Alex follows him into the long, narrow room.

Industrial shelving lines the back wall. They are full of cardboard file boxes, each labeled chronologically. They walk down the row reading assorted labels.

"Honey, can you check the boxes with the latest and earliest dates first?"

"Sure. What are you going to do?" questions Alex.

"I'm going to check the house again. For secret panels." Jake beams.

He starts in the master bedroom. Smith opens the closet and pushes all the hanging clothes to the far right to look at the end and back walls. Nothing. He shoves the clothes to the opposite end. He spots a panel just above the flooring and pushes around every edge. Finally, he shines a beam of light around the area and finds a small hole near the top corner of the chamber wall. Jake inserts the same funny key into the cavity and the panel swings open, revealing a two by two-foot floor safe.

Jake prays the unit not bolted to the floor and struggles to pull it from the enclosure. Slowly it gives way and moves an inch. Five minutes later the safe is sitting on the open floor. There is no way he can open or move it any further, and he returns to the garage to see how Alexis is making out.

"How's it coming?" Jake asks.

"It looks like he changed his marketing strategy in '68. That's when his business boomed."

"What did he do… start smuggling in clients?" sarcastically asks Jake.

"It certainly appears that way. I've put some of the questionable files in those three boxes to take with us." Alex points at the stack.

"You're kidding!" Jake's shocked comment.

Alexis asks, "You were gone a long time, find anything?"

"A safe. Can you bring the car around? Just back it into the driveway."

His partner leaves to retrieve their vehicle and Jake looks for a hand-truck.

Seven minutes later the 'Vette backs into position.

It is after three-thirty in the morning and the neighborhood is quiet and vacant. Jake asks Alex to follow him to the location of the safe. He needs help getting the hand-truck under it and rocking it back onto the platform to roll out of there.

"What are you going to do with it now?" she questions.

"We have to get it into the car."

"And how do you expect we are going to do that?" She shakes her head in disbelieve.

"I'll figure it out." Every man's standard answer.

At the car, Jake struggles, unable to lift the safe into the trunk. He looks over his vehicle. "I'm afraid we have to put this thing in the passenger seat."

"That's obvious. Anyone could see it wouldn't have fit in the trunk."

Jake gives her a frown. "It would've fit. Though, the lid probably wouldn't have closed. But I could have tied it."

He goes to the garage and finds three two by fours and returns to the car. Jake lays two of the eight-foot planks with one end resting on the car seat and the other stretched out onto the grass. They position the hand-truck between the ends of the boards and stand it upright with the unit resting on his makeshift ramp. Using the final board, Jake leverages the safe an inch or two, at a time, up the boards. At the top, they both roll the unit face down onto the car seat.

Jack takes the dolly into the garage and returns with the three cardboard file boxes. Two, fit into the trunk and the third goes onto the small back seat. Alexis shoehorns herself behind the driver's seat, next to the box, while Jake returns to the garage, secures the hidden room, and replaces the moved shelf. He quickly takes a final look through the house to make sure nothing left out of place.

As he fires up his Corvette, a paperboy pedals past, throwing the morning edition on the lawn with the six previous days unpicked up newspapers.

The teenager waves at Jake. Smith acknowledges back before shooting down the street.

Returning to their loft, Jake makes three trips carrying the boxes upstairs, while Alex makes a pot of coffee and a couple pieces of cinnamon and sugar toast.

"What are you going to do about the safe?"

"I have to leave it in the car for now." Jake cannot come up with a better solution.

He grabs a blanket and goes back downstairs. Smith drives up Fifth Avenue and parks in his rented underground space. After covering the safe with the blanket, he locks the car and returns to the loft.

The pair sits at the small kitchen table, drinking coffee, eating toast and discussing what to do about the safe.

"I'm taking it to San Diego Locksmith in the morning. Jesse will get it open." Jake glances at his watch. "We better get some shut eye."

CHAPTER EIGHTEEN
Ortiz's Safe

San Diego Locksmith opens at eight-thirty and Smith pulls into the parking lot early to wait. Jake's radio is blaring Neil Diamond's, *Cracklin' Rosie*. He leaves his car running to finish the song. Smith did not notice the car follow him in. Diego's safe is next to him, filling the passenger seat. A large paper cup of coffee sits in the plastic cup holder hanging off the window seal.

Jake grabs the coffee. As the cup hits his lip, "JAKE! JAKE!" screamed above the music, through the downed passenger window. Stunned, he jerks his head to the right, spilling coffee down the front of his shirt. He squirms around, holding the paper cup high and away from him, as he frantically wipes the burning liquid with his other hand.

"WHAT THE HELL ARE YOU DOING?" Looking and stilling wiping.

"TURN OFF THE RADIO!" Virginia Small yells.

Minutes later, radio off and everything under control, Jake asks, "What are you doing here?"

"We only had a second to talk at the scene and I saw you driving, so I followed. Just wanted to say hi and see how you're doing." Virginia next apologies. "Sorry about the coffee. I didn't mean to scare you. Are you ok?"

"No! I'm not! You could have honked or something!"

"I said I'm sorry. So tell me how was Oklahoma?"

"Arkansas! I really don't have time for this now."

"How about lunch at AP's deli? Say, noon? My treat."

"Not today. I'm working."

"On the Ortiz murder?"

"No… no… are you looking for a story?"

"Is that Ortiz's safe?"

A white van pulls in and parks next to the bright-red Corvette. The magnet attached to the door advertises San Diego Locksmith. A man jumps out, bends over to look through the driver's window. "Hey Jake, you're here early."

Turning back to the reporter, Jake states forcefully, "Virginia, leave us alone!"

"I can help," Virginia suggests.

Jake's angry scowl says everything.

"Ok, Jake, I'm leaving. Lunch tomorrow then. I'll call you."

Jake does not say a word until her car is out of the lot. "What a pain in the ass!"

Turning back to the locksmith. "Morning, Jesse. I have a job for you." He puts his hand on the safe.

"You're supposed to be watching homes, not burglarizing them," the man jests.

"Perks of the job," Smith jokes back.

"Let me open up and I'll get a dolly."

Jake had met Jesse when he first rented the loft and had the locks changed and some added features installed. They included a closed-circuit camera system, with one camera outside the front door, viewing the sidewalk, one in the hallway, one in the office and the fourth inside his loft. The pair became instant friends.

As Jesse comes around the corner from the back of his building. Jake throws down the only gulp of coffee left and gets out of his car.

Jesse looks at Jake's shirt and then around the sky. Back to Smith. "Looks like a flock of seagulls crapped on you."

"A real comedian! Can we get this thing inside?"

"It's going to be heavy," the locksmith visualizes and verbalizes.

"You're telling me?"

"How did you get it in there?"

"One-handed it. I expect you to do the same getting it out." They stare at each other and break into laughter.

84

After the pair struggle trying to lift it. "Why don't you pull around back? I have a come-along. I'll attach it to the roll-up door frame and we can hoist it out," Jesse suggests.

"I like easy. Meet you around back."

After they remove the safe from Smith's vehicle, Jesse lowers it onto a heavy-duty rolling cart. "Do you want to wait? I'll open it right now. Should take a half-hour or so," the locksmith tells Jake.

"That'll be great. What can I do?" Smith asks.

"It's extra if you help," grins Jesse.

The safecracker examines the unit. "I'll have to drill it. The safe will be inoperable after."

"Go for it!"

Jesse retrieves a large hammer-drill and diamond tipped drill bits. He punches a small dimple in the front of the dial and starts drilling. After a quite a few minutes and two ruined drill bits, he grabs a punch rod and a hammer. He pounds on the cam and pushes it away from the bolt. With no obstructions, he reaches in with a steel rod and opens the unit.

Looking inside the safe, Smith pulls out a wooden box, a locked steel box, and a stack of loose files. "Can we open the lockbox?" he asks his partner in crime.

"That one is easy. I have a master that'll open it."

While Jesse goes to look for his key, Smith looks in the wooden box, it filled with high-end, mostly woman's jewelry. He thinks to himself, *I wonder if this is his wife's or mistress'*. After picking up a man's watch *or he took it in lieu of payments for services rendered.*

The locksmith returns and tries a couple of keys before the steel box opens. It contains a ledger and various documents.

Jesse hands Jake a cardboard box to carry the bounty in. Smith asks him to dispose of the safe, pays him two hundred dollars for the job and drives back to HAI.

Alexis is waiting in Jake's adjoining office looking through some files from Ortiz's home. She notices her fiancé coming up the sidewalk on the black and white monitor and goes to the living quarters to get him a mug of coffee.

Smith's at his desk by the time Alex brings him the steaming mug. "What happened to your shirt?"

"Good morning to you too," his smiling response.

"Looks like you struck gold?" seeing jewelry spread out over the desk.

"Gold, silver, and gemstones. A pirate's booty," Jake kids.

He hands her a large diamond encrusted sparkly bracket. "Look at that!"

Alex fondles the piece. "You think it's real?"

"Absolutely! He wouldn't lock up costume jewelry!"

"What's all this stuff worth?"

"Have no idea, maybe tens of thousands?"

Jake grabs some documents from the steel box and starts reading. Alex picks up the ledger from the same box. Each is engrossed for more than an hour before Jake sets down his papers and stares at Alex.

"What's wrong, honey?" she asks.

"Both Ortiz parents *and* baby Diego died in a house fire in Phoenix back in nineteen-forty-one." He hands her a yellowed newspaper clipping.

"The poor baby. Less than a year old." Alexis reads the article. "What do you make of this?"

Smith surmises, "It appears that when Clarence Brown took Juan under his wing, he found the death records and set up him to assume the dead boy's identity. I'll bet Juan and Diego were born the same year." Jake hands her more documents.

"Why would he want Juan to have a false identity?"

"Don't know." After a few moments of thought. "Maybe to skirt Juan's criminal record in Mexico. You know give him a clean start. There are also school records."

"What schools?" Alex asks.

"San Diego High School and San Diego City Junior College. San Diego State and Western School of Law records too. Here's a picture of Diego, graduating Western."

Alex looks them over. "So?"

"So they're fake. We know Juan grew up in TJ, but this is a history of him growing up in San Diego. Look at the picture. It shows him in a graduation gown in front of Westerns monument sign shaking an old man's hand, who's probably Brown. But Siena told us, Brown was dead before he graduated college."

"What are you saying?" Alex does not understand.

"There's no one else anywhere in the picture, only the school facade and them. If it was taken at the ceremony, certainly, someone would have gotten in it, even if by accident. I'm thinking they just rented a robe and went to the school, maybe early on a Sunday morning, or something, you know when no one was around and took the picture. Then faked everything."

They are both deadly silent, trying to figure it out.

"Ortiz wasn't really a lawyer?" she questions, looking confused.

"Let's look at the timeline." Smith gets a grasp on the situation. "We're assuming he was born in forty-one. So, Juan is nineteen when he arrives, which would have been nineteen-sixty." Jake hands Alex the high school records.

"They say he attended from fifty-five to fifty-nine. He was still in Mexico!"

Alexis' light bulb bursts. "And then has years of college."

"Right. To get a law degree takes seven to eight years…" Jake shuffles through the papers and pulls out the Western Law Degree. "It's dated sixty-sixty."

"How do you know that?" Alex interrupts.

"It says so right here." Jake points to the date beside the signature.

"No. How long it takes to get a law degree?"

"Thought about going once." Jakes goes back to the problem at hand. "So, all these records are fake and Diego's life a shame!"

Alex thinks about it. "You're probably right. Diego, err Juan couldn't have gotten through law school anyway. Brown must have taught him everything he knew!"

"Agreed. That's why he took up immigration law and not criminal or civil law."

"What's the difference?"

"A narrower specific field. More paperwork and no court appearances? And, working with desperate immigrates, nobody is going to scrutinize his credentials. He just hangs fake certificates on the wall!"

After giving Alex time to let it sink in, Jake asks, "Anything interesting in the ledger?"

"I need more time to analyze, but it looks like Ortiz kept good records," Dench voices."

She starts scouring the client files while Smith takes a second run through Ortiz's identification papers and school records.

A while later. "Did you find anything definitive on Ortiz bringing in his own clients," Jake asks.

Alex absent-mindedly comments, "Not yet."

"What are you reading?" Jake inquires.

"Emily Vargas' file notes. He met her working at Agua Caliente. The next entry, two weeks later, shows she moved into an apartment in San Diego. That is just too quick anyway you look at it! Is Agua Caliente a restaurant?"

"Horse racing track," Jake states. Thinking about the time factor, he agrees. "You're right on."

CHAPTER NINETEEN
Marsh and Romero

The previous day, Lyle and Terrance called to their boss' office. Detectives Marsh and Romero already sitting when they walked in.

"Detectives, pull up a couple of chairs," Lieutenant Holden directed them.

They both glanced at the two-seated detectives. "What's up?" Terrance asked as they sat.

"I assigned Max and Maurio to assist you guys to wrap up the Ortiz investigation."

"Don't need help! Almost got to the bottom of this thing," Lyle objected.

"Good, but they *are* going to assist you guys!" persisted Holden. "This investigation is getting complicated with the insertion of the Feds. It certainly won't hurt to have a few more eyes on the ground. We're not going to be aced out by Davis and Morris!" He looked Lyle directly in the eye. "You are still running the case, use them where you can!"

"Yes, Sir!"

The four detectives returned to the squad room, "Ok, bring us up to speed and tells where you need us," Detective Max Marsh stated.

"We need you to hit the ground running. To start with, I want Smith followed twenty-four seven. He's up to his eyeballs in this and we need to know what he's doing!"

Every officer hates stakeouts. "What else?" Detective Maurio Romero is hoping for more interesting assignments.

"There will be plenty for you to do, but Smith is the priority!" Terrance added.

"We'll stick to him like Elmer's glue," Romero assured.

The two new-to-the-case detectives walked out, heading to their unmarked vehicle.

As they drove slowly pass Smith's loft, they observed an attractive Mexican woman leaving. "Stop!" screamed Romero. Marsh rapidly hit the brakes. Romero grabbed his camera and snapped photos of the woman.

Late that evening, after a boring afternoon, Junior Detective Romero is first up to sit in the hot car watching HAI, on the warmer than the usual summer night. Marsh leaves him and will be back to take over in the morning.

Just after sunset, Smith, and Dench appear. Both dressed in dark clothing. The detective wasn't prepared and misses the photo-op. Romero watches them walk briskly up the street. He starts his car and creeps along far behind.

Minutes later the PI and his girlfriend turn into a parking garage.

When Smith's 'Vette emerges, the detective follows them south to Chula Vista.

The PI ignores the yellow police tape and they disappear into a dark home. Romero notes the address and takes a picture.

After sitting in his car for hours, Dench eventually appears and walks away. Romero assumes she was going a block over to retrieve their Corvette and will be back to pick up Smith. He holds position.

After Alex returns and backs into the driveway, Romero cannot get enough photos of the two loading the car with the safe and boxes.

The last photo from this location is a newspaper kid, waving goodbye to the would-be burglars.

Back at the loft, the rest of the night is quiet. Romero catnaps. By five o'clock, Marsh slides into the seat next to his partner. He is juggling two large throw-a-way cups of black coffee and a bag of donuts. "Breakfast!"

"Glad to see you, partner," Romero comments.

"Long quiet night?"

"Hell no! Lyle's right, Smith and his girlfriend are up to their asses in this."

"Do tell!" gleefully, Max directs.

Romero tells his partner everything that transpired during the night, while frequently glancing at his notes and patting his camera.

Marsh suggests his partner go home and close his eyes for a few hours. Yawning, Romero agrees. He mentions that he will drop off the film at their lab on his way and heads out.

Three hours later, Detective Marsh follows Smith to San Diego Locksmith.

He parks across the street, a couple of doors away and watches. Marsh recognizes Small's car park beside Smith. He grabs the camera and sneaks into a neighboring business' yard next to the locksmith.

Moving in as close as he dares Marsh stands behind the neighbor's cement block wall. He takes quick chancy glances over the top. He cannot hear, but dying to know Smith and Small's conversation. He observes the owner pull up and open the store, and Smith driving around back.

In turn, Marsh runs to the backend of the wall and peeks over the corner. He watches them unload the safe and takes many photos.

As soon as Jake drives away, Marsh goes around to the front door and speaks to the proprietor.

Jesse keeps his mouth shut, even after threatened with arrest.

The only excitement remaining that day is the FBI visiting Smith. Moreover, the rest of the weekend is boring.

CHAPTER TWENTY
Timeline

Detective Donald Terrance joins his partner in the squad room Friday morning, August 10. Stephen Lyle is sitting at his desk making notes.

"Good morning," Don greets.

Lyle ignores him and keeps writing. Terrance grabs Lyle's almost empty coffee mug and returns with a coffee for himself and a refill for his partner.

Stopping his note taking, Lyle leans back in his chair. "Thanks."

"What are you working on?" asks Terrance.

"Making a list of people we need to re-interview, everyone Ortiz knew. We need to construct a timeline of his movements before the murder." On top of the list is Jake Smith and Alexis Dench.

Terrance takes a small notepad and writes Ortiz, Smith, Dench, and Baird on separate pages. Then he goes to the corkboard and pins them up. Ortiz top dead center and the rest in a second row below.

Lyle looks at the large ticking wall clock. "Smith first!"

"Let's stop for breakfast, along the way. I know a small cafe close to his office, we can go to," Terrance suggests.

Twenty minutes later the detectives sit at the counter of Emily's Cafe. "A black coffee and a toasted English muffin." Stephen turns to Don, "Know what you want?"

"I'll have the same."

A Mexican woman emerges from the back kitchen and delivers their orders. "Good morning, Detectives, haven't seen you guys around here?"

"It's that obvious?" Terrance comments.

"Yeah." The proprietor laughs. "I'm Emily, the owner."

"You won't happen to know a guy named Jake Smith, would you?" Lyle fishes.

"He comes in here. Why?"

"He's an old friend. Just heard he is back in town and would like to look him up," Lyle deceives.

"Jake and his fiancé live right around the corner on Island."

"Fiancé? That won't be Alexis would it?" Terrance continues the charade.

"You know her? Wonderful lady," remarks Emily.

"I heard Smith was doing work for Diego Ortiz?" Lyle wondering if she knew him too.

"That was so sad. He was my attorney when I first immigrated here."

"What a coincidence, we're investigating that case."

The owner looks shocked. After a few moments of thought. "Is that why you're looking for Jake?"

Not acknowledging her question, "When was the last time you saw Diego?"

"He came in at least once a week. I guess the last time was a week ago?"

"You mean last Friday?"

"That sounds right."

"How did he act? I mean, did he seem nervous or upset?"

"No. He was always in a great mood. Nothing seemed to bother him."

"What time was he here?" Lyle continues.

"Not sure, but he usually came by around eight-thirty or so. Listen, I must get back to work. It was nice talking with you." Emily starts to walk off.

"One more question, please?" Lyle speaks a little louder.

Emily turns back around, fearing she said too much already. "Yes?"

"When was the last time Smith came in?"

"Hard to tell, Jakes comes in often."

"Did he ever sit with Diego?"

"Of course, if they ran into each other." Scrunching up her face and looking up to the left. "I don't believe they ever met here on purpose."

"Were they together last Friday morning?"

"I think they were. If you'll excuse me." Emily walks quickly back into the kitchen.

"Crap, they were together twice, the day Ortiz was murdered. Here and at Ortiz's office," Terrance comments.

"Shove in your muffin. Let's find Smith." Lyle stands and includes, "We'll get back to Emily. I'm sure that woman knows more than she's telling."

They climb the stairs to Jake's place. The office door is already open and Alex is sitting at the desk reading a file.

"Good morning, Ms. Dench. Congratulations on your engagement." Lyle acts friendly.

Startled, Alex looks up. She quickly closes the file and shoves a stack of them into a desk drawer. "Detectives."

"Is Jake around?"

"No, he's already gone," Alex, tells them.

Looking at his watch, Terrance asks, "A little early for Smith isn't it?"

"No, we never get much sleep." Dench grins at her insinuation.

"We need to speak with him, where can we find him?"

"Don't know, he was gone when I got up." Still grinning.

Lyle lays his card on the desk. "Have him give me a call!"

"Looks like you guys have a case?" Terrance not letting the hidden files go unnoticed.

"Yeah, we're really busy at the moment."

"Ortiz?"

"Feigning a surprised look. Alex fabricates, "Ortiz? Oh no, just routine insurance cases.""

"Must be sensitive? You sure put them away quickly."

"All our clients deserve confidentiality." Another large grin blankets her face.

"We've heard that before," Terrance states to his partner.

"Have Jake call me," Lyle repeats as he turns to leave.

"Did you ever meet Diego Ortiz?" Terrance not ready to give up.

"Once."

"When was that?"

"Not sure… sometime around the first of June, I believe."

They thank Alexis and drive to Nazarene University to find Gary Baird.

The pair of detectives walks directly to the school administration building to find out if Baird is on campus, and where he can be located. The secretary directs them to the Social Sciences building and room 110.

They enter without knocking. "Excuse us, Professor. We need to speak to Gary Baird."

Somewhere in the middle of the lecture hall, Baird stands and follows the men to the outside hallway. He overlooks that every eye in the room follows him.

"I've told you guys that I don't know anything other than I found him dead."

"We know. We're putting together a timeline and need to know if you ran into him the week before you found the body," Lyle returns.

"No, I've never run into him. I work early mornings before he gets work."

"Ever see anyone else around the building?"

"No… wait a minute. There was a guy! A couple months back. When I arrived he came out and stood for a second looking my way, and then walked in the opposite direction."

"Which day of the week was that?" Terrance tries to pin him down.

"Not exactly sure, you know."

"What did look like?"

"Couldn't see. He could have been Mexican!"

"There's quite a bit of light in that area. Can you describe him? Scars, marks, what he was wearing?"

"I only have a key for the alley door and its dark back there. But, he was large. I hurried inside and made sure the door locked behind me."

"You saw him leave by the back door?" Lyle clarifies.

"Ya, the inside light was off. Couldn't see much. Like I said, he walked away from me."

"No communication?"

"Not a word," Baird comments.

"Ok Gary, if you remember anything else, give me a call," Lyle hands him another business card.

Walking back to the parking lot. "What do you think?" Terrance asks.

"Smith has kind of an olive complexion." Lyle draws a simile.

"You think someone was casing the place?"

"It could have been anyone. Probably just a tenant putting in a late night. Let's find Donna King!"

"Who's that?"

"Ortiz's secretary. Her name and phone number came up, on a paper I looked at this morning."

They find a pay phone and Lyle makes the call. "Ms. King?"

"Yes."

"This is Detective Stephen Lyle of the San Diego Police Department. Did you work for Diego Ortiz?"

"Oh yes. Since I retired my daughter, Donna, took over my position and has been his secretary ever since."

They talk for a few minutes and Lyle tells her they need to speak to Donna and asks for her address. Mrs. King tells him that they live together. He gets the address and states that they will be there shortly.

Donna, in anticipation of the visit, answers the doorbell and lets the detectives into her living room. She is an attractive young African-American woman.

After introductions and formalities, "How long have you worked for Ortiz?" one of the detectives asks.

"A little over two years. I started part-time while I was a senior at San Diego State and went full time two months after graduation," Donna tells the men.

"How did you find the job?" Lyle questions, though he already knows the answer.

"My mother worked for him since he started his practice. I took over when Dad got sick and she quit to take care of him."

"What type of clients did he have?"

"All foreigners trying to get naturalized or permanent alien status."

"No other types of clients?"

"No, just immigration. It was his specialty."

"Did you ever witness a disgruntled client or your boss having a disagreement?" Lyle questions.

"Not that I can recall. Everyone liked Mr. Ortiz and he was an excellent attorney. He always put his client's needs first."

"Do you know Jake Smith?"

"Sure. He's so funny. Jake did some work for my boss."

"How did Smith and Ortiz get along? Asks Terrance.

"Good, as far as I know." After a moment of thought, she questions, "You don't think Mr. Smith did it?"

"Oh no," Lyle quickly states. "We just have to talk to everyone Ortiz knew." He changes back to a previous question and rewords, "So, no one threatened or yelled at Mr. Ortiz, that you know of?"

"You already asked me that. Come to think of it. There was one guy. A large man. Big! He wasn't a client but would come in once in a while. From what I saw, they weren't really friends. Mr. Ortiz told me they were associates... whatever that means. The guy certainly didn't look like a businessman, more of a thug is you ask me."

"What did they talk about? Do you know the man's name?" Two rapid questions.

"Uh, I think it's Frank. Don't know what was discussed. They always had the door closed. But, one time, about a couple of weeks ago, maybe, my boss yelled, 'Get out of my office and don't come back. And, tell Pedro to quit bothering me! My answer is *no* and will always be *no*'." Donna recalls. "I think that was the last time I ever saw the guy."

"Who's Pedro?"

"No idea. Not even sure, that's the name. Could have been Pancho, Pablo, or something like that. I'm pretty sure it started with a *P* though."

"Did Ortiz tell to you what they argued about?"

"Just said he was sorry I had to hear it. It's the only time I ever heard him raise his voice."

"What about cases he was currently working on? Any problems?" Lyle changes the subject.

"None I know about. He was busy and I just did a little filing and typing, and made phone calls for him."

"And set appointments?" Terrance puts in.

"No, I never made any appointments. Mr. Ortiz always did that personally, I guess. I don't know where he got his clients. Hardly anyone ever came into the office."

"Who did you have to call?"

"Just check up on passport photos, documents and such. I called Mr. Tignor a lot," Donna, mentions.

"Who's Mr. Tignor?"

"He works at the immigration office. I think he's a supervisor."

"Do you know his first name?"

"Fenton."

"Did you keep any client files on your desk or do you happen to have any here?"

"No, my boss keeps all the files."

The detectives thank her and hit the street.

CHAPTER TWENTY-ONE
FBI Searches

While Jake and Alex are looking through Ortiz's safe contents in their office, Special Agents Davis and Morris lead four agents into Ortiz's Chula Vista home.

They had not bothered rushing right over after the murder, as they wiretapped the house a year earlier. There was almost nil movement on the property. Moreover, more than once, one of their own made illegal entries and peeked around.

Entering the upturned home, Morris comments, "Our boys in blue were here."

This day the team of six agents looks through the premises.

An hour later, the quiet neighborhood erupts with unmarked vehicles and officers. Windows fill with prying eyes. A few gawkers congregate on the sidewalks and front lawns.

Davis commands the newbies, "You two canvass the neighbors!" Pointing out a couple female agents. "The rest follows me."

In the living room, Agent Davis addresses the contingency. "I want this place torn to shreds! Not an inch of this house missed! To start with, it looks like someone might have removed a file cabinet or safe from the master bedroom closet. Also, there is a secret room in the garage filled with boxes. Blazer, take five agents and search that garage, top to bottom!"

Five hours later, not one drawer left intact. Not one closet or cupboard holds an item. Everything overturned onto the floor. The place looks as though a category five hurricane came through, reversed direction and torn through the second time. They even ripped up sections of carpet and sledgehammered holes in the walls.

The thorough men and women found everything worth finding sans what Jake and Alex had already absconded the night before.

By two-fifteen, Davis and Morris stand in the living room, Morris asks, "So there was obviously a safe removed from the master bedroom closet, who got it?"

"Those asshole detectives would be my guess!" Davis responds.

"Excuse me," Agent Gail Andover interrupts. "We've been going through the boxes in the garage room, and there appear to be quite a few missing dates."

"Earlier or later dates, Agent?"

"Random. Well, probably not random, but definitely from various specific years." Andover answers.

"Thanks, Gail." Davis turns back to his partner. "Get everyone loading the vans and taking the evidence to the office. As soon as we're done here, you and I are going to find those detectives!"

Twenty minutes later. "They can finish loading. Let's get out of here," Davis tells his partner.

Just as Morris is starting their vehicle the two canvassing agents approach with a longhaired teenager. Davis rolls down his passenger window. "Who's this?"

"The kid saw a red Corvette backed into the driveway around four o'clock this morning. Just as he passed, it took off south." Pointing down the street.

Davis steps from his vehicle. "What's your name son?"

"Philly, man."

"So Philly Man, what were you doing up so early?"

"Making money, man!" smart-ass Philly.

"Stealing cars?" Davis, not to be outdone.

"No way, man! Delivering the Union."

"So Phil, tell me about your morning."

"Not much to tell, man, just routing!" Grinning at his pun. When Davis sports a look of confusion, "Paper route – I was routing, get it?"

"You're a funny guy. Tell me about the car?"

"Oh, you mean the 'Vette? Sweet ride. I need to steal one of those," patronizing Davis back.

"Did you see the person driving?"

"Sure, man, I'm not blind! And, the woman in the back seat."

"A man driving and a woman in the back seat?" Thinking about it. "Who was in the passenger seat?"

"No one, man, empty."

"Do you think you could recognize the driver or the woman in the back seat?"

"It was dark. I couldn't really see faces and such. I was checking out the car, anyway."

"Did you check out the license plate number?"

"I ain't the FBI, man."

Laughing, Davis adds, "You could be!" The smart aleck kid growing on him.

Morris, listening to the interview, pulls Smith's picture from his briefcase and circles the car to his partner's location. "Is this the man?" He hands the photo to Phil.

"Can't tell... could be or couldn't be." Phil shrugs and hands back the picture.

"Anything unusual about the car?" Morris questions.

"Nah, it was a standard Mille Miglia Red Chevrolet Corvette Sting Ray convertible C3 automobile featuring the M22 4 speed *Rock Crusher* transmission!" The kid grins.

"Your favorite ride?" Davis smiles back.

"I like cars. Fast get-a-way cars!" Philly beams.

Davis writes down the newspaper boy's name, address and phone number before he hands over his card. "Keep in touch, Phil." He turns back to the agents, and asks, "Is that all?"

"We went to every house on both sides of this block and the three behind on the next block over. Everyone said, basically, the same thing, nobody knew the homeowner more than a passing nod. Ortiz usually came home late, if at all and left early. He was never outside and avoided conversation," one agent volunteers.

"How could he not be in his yard mowing the grass or washing his car?"

"Had a kid come every couple of weeks to cut the lawn. Probably him." Gesturing at Phil walking away.

"What about visitors or a girlfriend?"

"No one ever saw anyone come or go! When he was home, as I said, he stayed inside. He was also extremely quiet, no loud music, TV or any noise what-so-ever!"

"The perfect neighbor!" Morris smirks.

Davis thanks the agents, and tells them to assist with the box loading, after which to go back to the office with everyone else. "If we're not back, start helping catalog the information."

The Davis-Morris team drives off. On their way to the police station, they decide to stop by Smith's after.

At police headquarters, they're told that Detectives Lyle and Terrance have checked out for the day. Davis demands to speak with Lieutenant Holden.

After making a call and many moments later, the desk sergeant tells the agents they can go up.

Holden acts friendly, but does not know or is not willing to divulge where his detectives are. He knows nothing of any missing evidence from Ortiz's Chula Vista home.

They thank him and go back downstairs to leave.

"Hold up a second," Davis tells his subordinate. He strolls up to the front desk, and approaches the sergeant, "Holden said I could get Detective Lyle's where about from you."

"Just a minute."

After checking logs and radio communications. "Looks like they're on their way to Jake Smith's office."

As the agents start for the door, Morris turns back. "You know Jake Smith?" After an uncomplimentary affirmative. "What about his ride... any idea what he drives?"

"A red Corvette convertible. Don't know where that bum gets the money!"

CHAPTER TWENTY-TWO
Descent on HAI

Detectives Lyle and Terrance just entered Smith's outer office. Jake and Alexis are in the inner office still pondering over the files and ledgers they stole from Ortiz's home.

Jake did not see them on the sidewalk or in the hallway on his monitor, but as soon as they cross his office threshold, he hears the bell chime and glances at the screen. "Crap, the two-man dog and pony show just walked in!"

He jumps up and heads to the closed door. "Hide all the files and throw the ledger into the safe.

Jake had put in two doors in his office when he constructed it. One leads into the reception office and the second into the backroom. San Diego Locksmith installed a small wall safe in the living area at that time.

Dench grabs everything and scoots to the back. Smith opens the locked door and enters his reception room. He greets his nemesis, "Stevie, good to see you," sarcastically.

"Smith, what are you hiding!" Lyle growls.

"Me, hiding? What are you talking about?" His eyebrows arch, hands go up, acting as innocent as a newborn.

"What's behind locked doors?" Terrance, before his partner can respond.

"Oh, Don, you know… uh, Alex and me were busy." Jake projects a satisfied grin.

"Looks like the gang's all here!" FBI Davis comments as he and Morris stroll into the office.

"Glad you guys came to save me!" Jake beams.

"What are you doing here!" demands Lyle. The detectives had not the time to show Smith the pictures Marsh and Romero took. The plan had been to pressure him and find out who the woman seen leaving Hamilton-Adams Investigations, was and where everything taken from Ortiz's house is. Including what was in the safe at San Diego Locksmith.

"Probably the same reason you're here!" responds Davis. "We want the Ortiz's files that Smith stole from his Chula Vista house!" Accusingly, he looks Smith over.

"Stolen files?" Smith acts shocked. "So why come here? I don't have any files! I've had nothing to do with Ortiz since his murder."

"We have an eyewitness who saw you and Dench leaving Ortiz's early this morning!" Davis bluntly throws out the information.

"This morning? Oh yeah, we couldn't sleep and went out to get donuts and coffee. Ended up driving around for a while. I think I backed into a driveway in Chula Vista to turn around and waved at a newspaper boy. Was *that* Ortiz's house?" Smith acts stunned.

"You went into the house!" Lyle accuses and lays an array of the photos on the desk.

The FBI men are as surprised as Smith is, at the pictures.

"You want to tell me again that you didn't steal files and a safe?" Officer Lyle questions.

"Come on guys, lighten up!" Jake continues, "I lost a client, why would I need his files?" Smith wants to turn the tables by asking verses answering.

"That's exactly what you're going to tell us!" Terrance's turn.

Smith just sports a tooth-baring grin and says nothing, while stealing a glance at the pictures strewn across the table. It never dawned on him that he is a serious enough suspect to follow.

"All right, let's look around!" states Lyle.

"Not *without* a search warrant!" Jake acts pissed that they would suspect him.

"What are you hiding?" continues the detective.

"Hiding? Nothing! Protecting! My privacy as an American tax paying citizen!"

"You want to play hardball? Alright with me." Agent Davis takes control. "Morris stay here and don't let Smith out of your sight. I'm getting a search warrant!" He stomps out.

"You guys can all wait on the sidewalk. I got real work to do." Smith walks to the front sliding steel door and starts to pull it closed. "Gentleman, leave forthwith!"

"We aren't going anywhere, Smith!" Morris contends.

"You don't have a choice!" Smith fires back.

"You going to call your attorney?" Smirking. "I hear he is dead!" Terrance asserts, eyes glistening.

Smith walks to the desk, picks up the telephone, and dials. He calls the automatic *time* phone service and fakes talking to a receptionist and asking to speak to Dewey. While he feigns on-hold, Jake covers the mouthpiece and states, "I work for a lot of attorneys!"

Lyle moves to the desk and pushes the hang-up button, "Smith, we are waiting here or you're going downtown. Your choice! What's it going to be?"

"Let me grab my coat!"

"Get Dench. She coming too!" Terrance puts in.

"And what has she got to with anything. She never even met Ortiz."

"Most burglars don't meet their victims!" Morris chimes.

"I'll see if I can get a hold of her and have her meet us at the station."

"She's in the back! Remember, you and her were behind the locked door… uh, talking. Get her out here!"

Thinking fast on his feet. "That was just my little joke. Alex is not here! I think she's meeting with a client at the Grant Grill." Smith lies.

"Think? You don't know where your partner is?"

"I'm not her Mother! She comes and goes all day long."

"You fellas take him downtown. I'll wait in the hall for my partner. Don't worry, nobody's getting in or out of this place!"

Alex keeps listening from the back room over the intercom until the door slams shut. The office is quiet and she peeks around the door to be sure everyone has gone. *What now?* She thinks *I've got to get those files out of here.*

She looks at the security camera screen. Morris is on the sidewalk having a smoke. Terrance and his partner are walking off with Jake in tow. Alex runs to retrieve two of the boxes of files and Jake's lockpick tools. She carries them downstairs to the lower floor bathroom, which always kept locked. Setting the boxes down, she struggles to try to pick the lock.

"Can I help you?" A man interrupts.

Startled, Alex jumps up and whips around. "Oh Gene, you frightened me. I'm locked out of our unit and desperately need to use the restroom."

Gene rents a unit downstairs, and pulls his key from his pocket and lets Alex in. "There you go. If you want to wait for Jake in my place, you're welcome to."

"I'll be fine. Thank you, Gene." Alex picks up her boxes and goes inside. She rips a small piece of cardboard from a box flap. Alex checks that the hallway is clear. She steps outside the small room and holds the torn cardboard in place while she tugs the door closed.

Alexis returns with the last box and the ledgers and pushes the bathroom door open. She stacks the carton on top of the first two.

After her last trip bringing down Ortiz's steel and wooden boxes, she closes and relocks the door and returns upstairs to wait.

An hour and a half later Agents Davis and Morris enter the front office and hand Alex the warrant. They spend over two hours searching through all the desks, cabinets, and drawers in the loft.

"What's the combination?" Morris, looking at the safe, asks Alex.

"I don't know!"

"Have it your way!" Davis gets on the phone and calls his office. "We need a safe opened." Moreover, she listens to him explain the rest of the search.

"I think I might remember it now. I watched Jake open it once." Alex approaches the unit and opens it. "There you go!"

The agents do not find a trace of Diego Ortiz in HAI offices. "What are you and your boyfriend trying to pull here?"

"Us, pull something? We don't have anything to hide!"

"Then why did you make us jump through hoops to find nothing!" Davis snaps.

"Thought you guys liked to play games." Alexis puts on her sweetest smile.

"This isn't over! You two are hiding evidence and going to jail!" Morris threatens.

"How's the food in there?" Jake's a good mentor.

The agents stomp out. Another hour later, Jake walks back in. "Hi, honey. What happened?"

"You're back early! What happened with Lyle?"

"They're following us! Have pictures of us at Ortiz's house taking the safe and files. They also have a picture of Siena, and wanted to know who she is," Smith relates. "And they know I took the safe to Jesse."

"Why did they let you go!" shocked Alex responds.

"Don't exactly know. After the FBI called, things changed. I told them Diego's wife hired us to retrieve those items and that's all we did. We turned everything over to her and don't know what was in the safe or files!" Jake curiously asks, "I wonder what the FBI told them? They did the files, right?"

"I need to go downstairs to the washroom," Alex interrupts.

"Has ours clogged again?" A look of disgust blankets his face.

Alex is already in the hallway, and Jake hustles to catch up.

Downstairs at the bathroom door, Alex hands Jake his kit. He quickly opens the door, and spies the stack and starts laughing. "I love you, Alexis Dench."

CHAPTER TWENTY-THREE
Elon Mensah, Esquire

Early Saturday morning, August 11, Reena Landry sits in her office in the solemn thought of the events of the day before. RLD is usually open on Saturdays, though she normally takes weekends off unless she has a prearranged meeting with a client. This day a handwritten, 'Closed until Monday' sign posted on her glass front doors, and she is alone.

She hears the door's mail slot bang close. Reena looks out her front office window and observes the mail carrier leaving the courtyard and heads to the receptionist's office to check what arrived. After accumulating the scattered envelopes and advertising fliers off the floor, she takes the handful of mail back to her office.

Reena looks through the stack. Only one envelope piques her attention. The rest can wait until Monday. She studies the unopened IRS communique for the longest time before ripping it open. Mrs. Landry gradually reads every word. She is subject to an upcoming audit.

Mrs. Landry seizes her key ring and goes across the courtyard to her husbands, also closed, office. She finds his mail on the floor behind the door and drops to her knees scouring the mess. There it is. His audit notice. Expeditiously she scoops it up, stands and tears it open. The letter is word-for-word identical to hers.

She runs back to her business and phones Hayden, waking him up. After explaining the situation, her husband phones their tax attorney and arranges to meet him at RLD in an hour. He dresses and rushes to the office.

Reena and Hayden sit discussing their books and money laundering operation. They are convinced the second real-set of books well hidden.

Years earlier Hayden had set up a fictitious client file under the name Howard Griffin. Their actual books locked in a safe deposit box under that designation.

Elon Mensah, the Landry's Harvard Law graduate attorney, arrives and pounds on the locked front doors. After letting him in and given coffee, the three of them get comfortable in Reena's plush-casual client conference room.

The lawyer stares at his clients until Reena opens her mouth, "I think we might be in trouble."

"What's going on?" Elon, hoping to find their underlying cause of grieve.

"Nothing to get worked up about, we're both being audited by the IRS," Hayden admits.

"If there is nothing to worry about, why am I here?"

Back to Reena. "Hayden and I discussed our situation and thought we need some legal advice."

"Ok. You know I'm precluded from disclosing anything we discuss, so be veracious and tell me your concerns."

"We might have done a few things that are not above board. I'm sure the IRS can't discover anything, but..." looking at his wife, "but thought we should be prepared just to be on the safe side."

"You mean illicit endeavors?"

"I'm sure you heard of Diego Ortiz's murder?" Reena butts in.

"I read about it in the paper, but never met the man."

"We assisted in hiding some of his assets."

Thinking it over. "You laundered his money?"

Looking down. "Exactly," Reena confesses. She looks back up at the lawyer. "We're clean, Elon."

"Clean? You mean undetectable?"

"We think so," Hayden mumbles.

"You better tell me the whole story, guys. Start at the beginning!"

Hayden goes first. He tells about one of his first clients, Howard Griffin. "Griffin ran a semi-successful plumbing business and made decent money. When his father passed away and he inherited just under two million dollars. I invested half of the money in blue-chip stocks, a quarter of it went into offshore accounts and the remainder went into business assets and operating capital. As he grew and made real money, we invested in IRAs for him, and his wife, and mutual funds and some riskier high yield investments."

He perpetuates the story, "Griffin died young, at age forty-eight, from congested heart failure. He worked hard and played harder. His wife moved back to Ohio and left me in charge of managing their assets. Before he passed, I set them up in a living trust with me as their trustee."

After a long pause, considering how much he should divulge, Hayden goes on, "I made them a lot of money and... and probably took higher fees than I should have. Nevertheless, Mrs. Griffin could not have children and they did not think any other relatives deserved their financial prosperity. They had more money than they ever needed." He integrates, "No harm, no foul!"

"So how much did you take?" Mensah inquires.

"Not quite sure... anyway, my stake... I mean, what I earned from their money grew rather substantially. After Howard passed, I used his name and set up a separate account with me as the only signer at a small local bank in Santee. I used that account to funnel funds into Reena's and my investments. In my safe deposit box, at the bank, are all the records."

"So that's it?" The attorney softly mentions more to himself than his clients. "What about Ortiz? How's he involved?"

"I'll let Reena tell you, then finish what I did."

Elon sits quietly, looking at Reena, and waiting.

"Diego came to me to buy some property. He wanted apartments and commercial buildings to lease. He was a great client and bought a lot of property. We even set up a few of LLCs together and developed a couple of strip malls and other projects."

"That's not a problem!" the lawyer comments.

"Not at first," Reena tells the man that they became quite close and very profitable. She also mentions that one time, Diego told her that he wasn't 'a nice man anymore'."

"What does that mean?"

"He didn't come right out and say, but I got the impression he was a real criminal. I'm afraid if they find anything on him, I'll be branded by association because of our partnerships." After a little tear time, the strong woman wipes her eyes and blows her nose. "The bigger picture is Ortiz was laundering money through our projects and skimming off his own rentals and businesses."

The lawyer pushes. "He told you that?"

"Yes," looking embarrassed, "and taught me how to save… I mean hide money from the IRS through my properties."

"So where's all the cash?"

Hayden speaks up again, "That's where I came in. I set up offshore accounts for him and us. And, layers of shell accounts that we both used to hide assets. Almost everything Reena and I own is in one company or another."

After rubbing his forehead and eyes, the lawyer asks, "So your trepidation is the IRS will easily find that you're living well beyond your reported means and you don't have a paper trail for all your business and personal assets?"

"That's the problem! Everything and I *mean* everything, is off-books," Hayden admits, while his wife starts to puddle up again.

"When are your audits?"

"The letter states an introductory meeting with Agent Fraser Gentry will be Monday morning at nine o'clock." Reena checks her letter.

"Something is wrong! The IRS never gives you the name of the inspector or has an introductory meeting. They phone you to inform you that they'll be on the following day to start going over your books." The attorney ponders. "And, if they suspect illegal activity, they just show up unannounced!"

"Start? How long does this take?" Reena, overlooking the obvious problem.

"Sometimes months or even years with larger companies. You're still using Filson Accounting, aren't you?"

"Yes." Without elaborating.

Elon stands, "I'll call you this afternoon after I speak to a couple of IRS contacts I have and find out what's really going on here." After some thought, "Oy vey! It's the weekend. I'll see here Monday!"

CHAPTER TWENTY-FOUR
Smith in Tijuana

Monday morning Smith decides to go to TJ and meet Jose Contreras, Diego's Mexican partner. He asks Alex to look into Clarence Brown while he is gone.

After Marsh and Romero took Sunday night off, the detectives are together Monday morning, watching. It is not long before Smith leaves alone and the boys follow him to Mexico.

Jake parks in a large dirt lot on the U.S. side and pays for a day of parking. He enters Mexico through the walk-across corridor, passing Mexican border agents holding automatic weapons. One officer stops him and inquiries about his business in Mexico. Jake tells the guard he is a tourist and going souvenir shopping along Revolution Avenue. They allowed him to pass.

On the Mexican side of the border, men and boys deluge Jake, soliciting for dozens of cabs lining the lot and streets. Jake flips a kid a buck and says he is going downtown. The lad hustles him to an old large red Chevrolet Caprice with red and green intermixed dingle balls hanging across the inside windshield. In addition, there is a plastic statue of the Virgin Mary attached to the center-top of the cracked dashboard and a Mexican flag decal on the glove box. A string of rosary beads hangs from the statue halfway to the floor.

"Donde vas, Señor?"

Smith hands the drive a slip of paper with Contreras's address written on it.

"Si, Si, Señor." The man drops the column-mounted gearshift into drive and squeals the tires. They sped past the bullring weaving in and out of thick traffic. The honking and yelling are

worse than New York City during rush hour. Smith holds on for dear life, praying that it is a short drive.

"Relájate y disfruta del viaje." Smith does not understand the words mean *relax and enjoy the drive,* as the car veers down an unpaved alley.

They bounce through potholes spraying muddy sewage over buildings and pedestrians. *"Más rápido, Señor."* The driver smiles in the rear-view mirror. Smith would rather a safer trip versus a quicker one and wishes the man would keep his eyes on the road. Five minutes later the cab screeches to a halt in front of Contreras' office. *"Cinco dólares, Señor."*

Smith hands the cabby a ten and hurries from the death machine, yelling, *"Gracias! Gracias!"*

The PI enters the lobby and approaches a young receptionist sitting behind a desk. "Contreras?"

"Señor Jose Contreras, Abogado?"

Does anyone speak English Smith thinks and tries the foreign language, *"Si... uh, donda?"*

She responds to his incorrect verbiage, "Second floor, Room 202, Sir."

"Well, that wasn't so difficult!"

"Perdón?" Acting as if she did not understand Jake's sarcasm.

Upstairs, Jake finds 202 and enters. This older secretary speaks perfect English to the American. She asks him to take a seat and informs her boss that he has a visitor.

A couple of minutes later a short round man emerges and holds out his hand. "Good morning, Sir, Jose Contreras. What can I do for you today?"

"Jake Smith. I'm investigating Diego Ortiz's murder." Jake quickly flips open his old SDPD badge and closes it just as fast.

"Officer Smith, nice to meet you. Please come in."

Jake follows Jose into the inner sanctuary and sits at the front of the desk across from the Mexican lawyer.

"Would like a drink, soda, water, or something stronger?"

"I'm fine, Jose. May, I call you Jose?"

"That will be fine, Jake. I am sorry for Diego, but what can I help you with?"

"Mrs. Herrera hired me to find out what transpired," Jake frankly states and watches for a reaction.

"Siena is a nice woman. I'm worried about her and the children's wellbeing."

"Why? Is someone after the family?"

"Oh no. Not that I'm aware of anyway, but I wasn't worried about my partner either until it was too late. So we just don't know."

"Do we know why or who Ortiz had problems with?"

"It is a cruel world, Mr. Smith. When Juan and I grew up on the streets, we made enemies."

"That's was many years ago. Why would anyone hold a grudge that long?" Smith believes it must be a current enemy.

"Well, as we matured and grew prosperous, so did our rivals. Anyone of them could have had contact with Juan that I'm not aware of."

"What was your business dealings with Diego?"

"Mostly paperwork. When he had immigration clients, I supplied Mexican support documents and family histories for him. Nothing more."

Jose's lie does not convince Smith. "He could have hired anyone for research and filings. Why a partnership?" Smith is looking for deeper understanding.

"As I stated, we grew up together, closer than brothers, as he became wealthy, he wanted to help me do the same. *La Familia es lo más importante!*"

"I understand. Can you give me the names of the men you think Diego had trouble with?"

"*Señor*, you do not want to go there. These are very bad men… worst of the worst."

Smith tries a fishing expedition. "Diego's and your business grew exponentially in the last three years, I found evidence that he was smuggling in his own clientele! You had to know, and are involved. With Diego out of the way you have the whole enchilada!"

"You know not of what you're speaking, *Señor*. For your sake, I suggest you go home and mind your own business. Now if you'll excuse me, I have work to do." Contreras stands but does not extend his hand.

"Thank you for your time, Jose. I'm sure we'll talk again, maybe over tequila and more pleasant times." Jake turns to leave.

"One moment, *Señor*, it's not what you think! Diego was not involved in alien transportation. Other people do the smuggling and he just helped the poorer families to establish after the fact! He was a good, compassionate man, just trying to help his people."

"With the legal work…" Thinking about the logistics, Jake changes his question in mid-sentence, "Where did these families stay during the process and how did Diego assist them after legalization?"

"Juan is… was a resourceful man, *Señor*. He owned many properties and businesses. Whether he needed more help or not, he hired them anyway. Such a strong heart!"

With Smith's confirmation of alien smuggling, he is convinced Ortiz was more involved than Jose is admitting.

Back on the street, he makes notes to find property and businesses Diego owned and background checks on the employees.

He wanders south along the street planning his next move. Jake stops in front of an out of place large Woolworth's Department Store, in the next block.

During the time, Smith had crossed the border and grabbed a cab, Marsh, and Romero had done likewise. Watching and following. They are standing across the street and observe Smith leave Contreras' building. The detectives need to know what Smith was doing and what he found out.

They never speak to the lawyer, out find enough from his receptionist. She openly admits Ortiz and her boss were business partners and childhood friends.

Quickly returning to the street, Smith, nowhere found, and they assume he headed home. Their next stop is the Tijuana Police Station.

They find a young investigator that speaks fluent English and is eager to get involved. The Mexican detective had never heard of Diego Ortiz. However, divulges that Jose Contreras is the attorney of record for the Melendez drug cartel.

They jump in a cab and head for the border.

By now, a street vendor is yelling at Smith and a ragtag youth pulling at his sleeve. "Picture with Zebra, *Señor*. Your wife like!"

Smith laughs. "How did you know?" He steps over to the colorful patched wooden cart with a black and white paint-striped burro attached.

"Señor, por favor sientate." The photographer pats the cart bench seat and hands, Smith, a huge decorated sombrero.

Jake sits and adjusts his hat at an angle trying to look like a Bandido as the vendor steps behind a large old wooden box camera and ducks under a lightproof black cloth. A moment later, a hand rises from beneath the cloth. *"Estate quieto!"*

Jake does not understand but sits still. A large flashbulb explodes. When the man emerges, he waves the photo around the air for a while before putting the black and white in a paper souvenir frame and handing it to the sucker. Jake gives him five dollars and thanks him before entering Woolworth's.

After looking around the establishment, Jake buys Alex a bottle of Channel #5 from the perfume counter, to accompany the photo, and heads back to the street.

He spots a taxi though it is not hard as handfuls of kids are barking at him, "Taxi, *Señor*? Taxi, *Señor*! Take to border, *Señor!*"

However, inside a different cab, it looks very similar to his last ride. Jake hands the driver another slip of paper. This one has Siena Herrera's beach home address scrawled across it.

The driver studies the address. *"Si, Señor. Veinte dólares, Señor."*

Not understanding, he repeats, *"Veinte?"*

"Si Señor, veinte… uh, twenty *dólares."*

"Twenty dollars, right," confirms Jake.

They take the old road through the hills of South TJ, past rundown lower-class houses mixed with large opulent gated mansions. Smith wonders if Contreras or some old Diego's old friends live in them.

Just north of Rosarito, the taxi turns onto the newer toll road for the next five or six miles before getting off and finding the address.

Smith gets out of the car and hands the taxi driver a fifty-dollar bill. "Wait here. One hour." Holding up his index finger, he shows the man a second fifty in his other hand.

Catching on, the driver agrees, *"Una hora. Si, Si, Señor. Una hora."*

Herrera's estate home looms over the glistening blue Pacific, back an acre or more off the road. It enclosed behind a high cement block wall. Smith walks the drive to the locked ostentatious wrought-iron double gate. Two barking Doberman Pinschers appear galloping across the gigantic field. They attack the iron slats, snapping and growling, trying to get at the intruder.

"Calm down, boys. I'm friendly." Smith puts his hand close for a sniff. Snarling teeth lunge voraciously through the bars. Jake jumps back. "I guess you don't understand English!"

He looks around and finds a speaker box with a call button, attached to the gatepost. He pushes it and waits.

"Hola?"

"Hello, Mrs. Herrera?"

"Un momento, por favor."

Almost five minutes later. "Hello?"

"Mrs. Herrera it's Jake Smith."

"Just a minute, I'll send a car for you."

Another five minutes and a silver Cadillac pulls up, inside the gate. A man gets out and yells at the barking dogs in unknown Spanish. He picks up a stick and swings it. The dogs run off in the direction they came. He opens one gate and leads Smith to the car.

When they arrive under the covered car porch, an older woman is standing at the open front door. Smith diligently looks around for the Dobermans before getting out and greeting her.

She takes Jake through the mansion and out double-hung French doors onto a patio. Going through the house, Smith believes he must in the Mexican National Museum by mistake. It's filled with antiquities and art treasures.

Siena is standing beside the patio table, smiling. "Jake, it's nice to see you again. Good news, I hope?"

"I'm afraid not yet," he replies.

"Please have a seat. Would you like a glass of iced tea or a soft drink?"

"Tea will be nice, thank you." Smith sits, with a seat between them. "What a beautiful view!"

"Yes, it is nice and so peaceful here."

Siena calls the old woman over and speaks to her in Spanish. The woman scurries off.

Jake jumps into the reason for his visit. "I talked with Jose Contreras today. What can you tell me about him and Diego's... uh, Juan's business?"

"Nothing. I was not allowed to know their business."

Jake thanks the elderly woman as she reappears carrying a tray with a tall Crystal glass of translucent amber liquid. The silver serving platter also holds a generous bowl of sugar and another with ice.

"This is Juan's mother, Rosa."

Smith jumps to his feet. "It's a pleasure to meet you, Mrs. Herrera."

The woman smiles and nods before quickly turning and leaving.

"Sorry, Jake, she doesn't speak English."

"Oh." Back to business. "Did Juan keep any files or hopefully a ledger book here?"

"Not that I know about, though there is a safe in his office. Would you like me to show you the office?"

"Please." He takes a big gulp of tea and stands.

Entering the room, Smith is astounded. Jim's office, as large as his entire loft, finished all in solid oak panels and a marble floor. The Walnut desk is three times the size of his kitchen table. The remainder of the room immaculately furnished with the highest quality pieces of original oil paintings. Jake recognizes a couple of Picasso's and a Renoir. He is not familiar with marble statues or other works.

"Where is the safe?" Not seeing it.

Siena walks to a wall bookcase and presses an unseen button. One section slowly opens revealing the double door, floor to ceiling, safe. "Sorry, I do not know how to open it."

"Does he have a file cabinet somewhere in here?"

Siena walks to the other end of the bookcase and presses another button revealing two large desk-matching file units.

"May I?" Smith asks as he walks towards the Walnut veneer Steelcase drawers.

"Of course, Jake. Anything that will help."

He starts opening drawer after drawer. All contain hanging files. Scanning the header tabs, in the last bottom drawer, he finds a file marked *Personal*. Jake pulls it out and moves to the desk, He lays the folder down and starts browsing through it. Closest to the last paper, he stops. There is the Tech Guard Safe registration papers and information. He asks Siena if she can make a Xerox.

She moves to a matching bureau behind the desk and opens one of the two doors. It contains Juan's Xerox 813 desktop copier and she runs off a duplicate of the sheet for Jake.

Jake returns the file to its home and continues, now looking through the desk. In the top drawer on the other side of the desk, he finds a ledger. He does not touch it, but stands and asks Siena if it is possible to get a drink of water. She questions if he would rather have another ice tea and he states that water would be fine. As soon as she leaves Jake alone, he pulls the ledger out and shoves is in the back of his waistband and untucks his shirt covering the book.

Siena returns with his drink and he quickly downs it and looks at his watch, telling her he must be going but would like to come back with his assistant to go through the files more carefully.

Jake gets a ride with the same man across the yard and to his waiting taxi. "To the border, please," Jake instructs the driver.

"Frontera, Si Señor."

Marsh and Romero, already back at their office, escort Lyle and Terrance to a private conference room. They bring them up to speed on Smith's activities, including following him to Mexico and speaking to Jose Contreras and the Tijuana police.

Terrance stunned. He never really thought Smith was involved at that level. Lyle, on the other hand, is elated. "Great work guys. Stay on him like flies on a fresh turd!"

Lyle looks at his watch, and tells his partner, "We need to find out who this woman is," holding up the photo of Siena Herrera.

"That must be Ortiz's wife."

Lyle responds, "That's what I'm thinking. We're going to the FBI lab tomorrow."

CHAPTER TWENTY-FIVE
Agent Gentry

Internal Revenue Service Agent Fraser Gentry shows up at RLD offices Monday, August 13, at precisely nine Am, for their scheduled pre-audit meeting. Reena, Hayden and their tax attorney, Elon Mensah are waiting.

Introductions made and they all go into the conference room to talk.

Attorney Mensah immediately starts off, "Mr. Gentry, I'm a little confused. What is this meeting about?"

"Mr. Mensah, let me first state that I am not an audit agent, though I can mandate one if necessary. What I am here about is Diego Ortiz. I, rather we have been investigating him for a few months. If you cooperate with my investigation… well, that is really all I'm concerned about at this time."

Elon quickly answers, "Please call me Elon, Fraser. We will be nothing but cooperative. From what I understand, the deceased Ortiz was not an ethical person. My clients," he waves his hand in the direction of Reena and Hayden, "actually dropped him as a client some time ago. From what I have been advised, Mr. Ortiz approached my clients with a money laundering scheme and they immediately refused to be involved with any illegal activities," the attorney bold-faced lies.

"I'm pleased to hear that. Now if I can directly ask your clients a few questions?"

"Of course, as I stated, they have nothing to hide."

"Mrs. Landry, you run a Real Estate sales and property-development company?"

"That is correct, Mr. Gentry." Reena trying to act polite through her searing disposition.

"So, what kind of scheme did Ortiz purpose to you?"

"He started out as a good... a great client actually, buying numerous commercial and residential rental properties. One day, about a year ago I believe, he came to a meeting and purposed we undercharge market leasing rates, but enter overcharged figures in the books on some of our shared investment properties."

"So if I understand correctly, for simplicity's sake, you would charge a lesser amount, let's just say, a hundred dollars and enter a payment of a hundred-fifty dollars in the books, thus depositing the hundred coupled with fifty of other monies?"

"That was basically his idea, along with a high forty-eight percent non-vacancy rate, so he would deposit the full amount of... of *dirty* money on vacant units and enter the payment under fictitious names and lease agreements."

"Hmm." Thinking it over. "Where does this other money come from?"

"I don't know where Diego's came from, but he suggested I... and Hayden under-report income from our businesses to use."

"What about developments?"

"Same idea for storefronts or business units. He owned quite a few small businesses, which he ran money through. My understanding is he would overstate purchase orders while understating inventories, and bogus sales." Reena acts as if she is thinking it over. "That's all I know."

"You and your husband own a lot of rentals too, don't you?" Gentry is hunting.

"Of course, but our books are clean and all above board!"

"Everything is legal on our end!" reiterates Elon.

"Good." Turning to Hayden. "What was your connection to Ortiz?"

"Straight retirement investments... oh, he dabbled in some high-risk stock, but most of those lost money." Mr. Landry states.

"So his losses, also masked other income?"

"I don't know how he could have. Everything is stringently regulated!"

"But he could take a loss and state it as a gain and deposit money?"

"It might be possible, but honestly, I wouldn't know how." Hayden lies through his teeth.

"What about overstating trading commissions?"

"Are you accusing me?"

"No. I'm thinking it's all on his end and his books," Agent Gentry states, but thinks *this man knows too much, not to have been involved.*

"Neither Reena nor myself have anything to do with our clients' books!"

"Of course not. I wasn't suggesting that. I was just thinking out loud," he covers.

"Can I get a copy of all the properties and transactions the two of you had with him?"

Mensah speaks up, "Of course, Agent. It will take a week or two with the mass of purchases, and as my clients stated that was a while ago, and they will have to get the records out of storage."

"That would be Sorrento Valley Storage?"

Crap, this guy knows more than he's letting on. What else does he already know? Thinks the Landry's attorney.

"That's correct, Mr. Gentry," Hayden puts in.

Agent Fraser Gentry gets to his feet. "All right then, I'll wait for you to get back to me. If I can think of anything else I'll swing by." He hands each of them a business card. "I'm sure we'll meet again." After shaking their hands, he steps out.

Alone, Elon tells his clients. "Don't trust that man. This isn't even *close* to being over!"

"I didn't like him!" Reena adds.

"Get all Ortiz's documents and your books to me ASAP. I'll prepare a report and supporting papers for Gentry." The lawyer looks hard into each of their eyes. "You'll need to prepare for *your* audit immediately!"

"I thought he wasn't worried about auditing us?"

"Don't kid yourself!"

As soon as IRS Agent, Fraser Gentry returns to his office, he calls for an immediate audit of RLD, and Hayden Landry Financial. He figures they are up to no good and far more involved with Diego Ortiz than they care to admit.

Next, Fraser Gentry picks up the phone, and calls FBI Agent Davis and requests Xerox's of all financial documents impounded on the Landrys and Ortiz from Sorrento Valley Storage.

CHAPTER TWENTY-SIX
FBI Visit

Lyle and Terrance are pissed. They just informed that the FBI raided Ortiz's private residence in Chula Vista. Even though they had searched the home immediately after the murder, before knowledge of the Feds running investigations. Lyle thinks they are supposed to be working together and should have been included.

Lyle rises from his desk. "Let's go to FBI headquarters and confront Davis and Morris!"

"You think they're going to share?"

"No, but we have to find out who the woman in the picture is and where to find her."

The detectives head over to the FBI's downtown field offices.

When they enter the front reception room Lyle shows his badge and demands to see Agent Davis. Eventually, Davis appears in the room. "Good morning, Detectives."

"Agent Davis, we need a word!" Lyle takes charge.

"Of course, Stephen. Let's step in here," opening an adjoining door.

The three men enter and sit at a round table. "Where's your partner?" Lyle questions.

"He's involved at the moment and won't be joining us. What's on your mind?"

"Ortiz's Chula Vista home! I thought we were in this together?"

"We are Detective. As soon as all the evidence is processed, I'll be sending over our report."

"We need to see what you have now!" Terrance pipes up.

"Sorry, that isn't possible, Don. First, most of the files are in our lab, the only thing we have here is a couple of folders."

"Don't BS me! Your lab is in the basement. Let's take a walk down there?"

"As I stated, that isn't possible at this time. There are dozens of boxes and thousands of files. Presently we have a handful of agents reading and sorting through everything. It will take at least a week. And, we can't have you guys slowing down the process."

"Us guys! If you remember, we are lead on Ortiz's murder!" Lyle angrily states.

Terrance, on the other hand, didn't miss the *dozens of boxes and thousands of files*. "Where the hell did you find all that?"

Ignoring Terrance, Davis addressed Lyle's concern. "I remember. The key word here is *murder* and if we find anything pertaining to that, you will be the first to know. Our investigation is restricted to Rico violations and related Federal crimes."

"How do we know your information doesn't relate to our case?" Terrance tries, "We need to see what you have!"

"You don't, but as I stated, anything we discover pertaining to your investigation will be sent to you forthwith. Now if we're done here, I have to get back to work." Agent Davis stands to conclude the meeting.

Both detectives remain in their seats. "Look, Egan," Lyle, a little more pleasant by using his first name, "we only want to observe your procedure for a couple of minutes and then we'll be on our way."

Exacerbated Davis gives in. "Ok, five minutes. Follow me."

Before they enter the room. "No talking. Do not disturb their work!" Davis commands and he opens the door.

The large room consists of three rows of long tables pushed together. There is an agent sitting on each side of each table in a rolling office chair. Periodically a chair creaks over to a stack of new files and the man or woman grabs a few, before rolling back to an empty table spot and looking through them. On the last row, a woman picks up an empty box to remove from her station and retrieves a new full one from the stack at the end of the row.

"Take a look around. NO DISRUPTIONS!" Davis moves over to the woman who had just grab the new box. "How's it going, Cecelia?"

"Slow and tedious," comes the reply. "We have a long way to go."

"Crap! Did all this come from Ortiz's?" whispers Terrance.

Lyle and Terrance stick together walking slowly around the large tables, looking at laid out files over the shoulders of various agents to observe what being read. In the middle of the second table, Terrance stops and pulls a pen and pad from his top pocket. He writes Emily Vargas, Emily's Cafe, Fidel Caballero, Orange Street Liquor & Deli, Cristian Pabón, Southend Printing and Pasqual Agosto, Public Portrait.

Lyle keeps walking and at the last table, writes a note of his own.

"Alright, gentlemen, the tour's over," barks Davis. The three men leave the room.

Back in the hall. "Again, I'll get all the pertinent info to you as soon as everything is ready."

Terrance whips out his photograph. "Do you know this woman?"

After looking at the photo, Davis tells the men he does not know the woman and walks back into the room.

"Do you think he's lying?"

"He knows exactly who she is!"

At their vehicle, Lyle asks Terrance, "What did you find so interesting in there?"

"Four names and businesses. I assume Ortiz was involved with each. We need to check them out. What about you?"

"The mystery woman is Siena Herrera. Ortiz's wife in Mexico."

They decide to talk to Emily again on their way back to the station.

They enter the cafe and sit at the counter each ordering a coffee and a glass of water. Lyle without ice, Terrance with. They spot the woman, through the open kitchen order window and wave her over.

"Hi, Ms. Vargas," Terrance speaks first.

"Detectives, it's good to see you again," Emily responds.

"A couple of questions if you don't mind?" Lyle asks.

"Anything to help find Diego's killer."

"What was your relationship to Ortiz?"

"He was my attorney and helped me with my American Citizenship."

"And?"

Emily only gives a quizzical look, remaining silent.

"We know he is involved in your cafe?" Not waiting and hoping for more.

"Well, yes, we were partners. He funded the cafe, and I do the work."

"So who's your new partner, now?"

"I don't understand?"

"With him gone, who took over his obligations with you?" Lyle clarifies.

"No one. I received sole ownership." Emily has nothing to hide.

"You own the whole café now?" Terrance quickly realizes she has a motive.

"Lock, stock, and barrel!" Smiling proudly.

"His death is quite advantageous for you?" Terrance accusingly states.

"Hardly, Ortiz did all the accounting… well, he furnished his accountant to handle the business end," and adds, "he was involved in printing the menus, signage and helped with hiring. Plus, many other duties I don't have time for. I'm at a loss on how to run this place on my own." Emily wants the detectives to understand, Ortiz's death was not good for her.

"So, when he came in once a week, it wasn't a social call, but business?"

"No, it was social and to eat. We were more than partners, we were friends," Emily emphatically states.

"Did Ortiz tell you how to run this place? You know the day to day operations."

"Of course not. As long as I was making money, he was happy. Besides, he didn't have time to be involved at that level. I saw Mr. Filson far more frequently."

"Who's that?"

"The accountant."

"What's his first name and name of his business?"

"Derrik. His office is right next door to Diego's."

They both gulp their coffee and stand, "Thank you, Ms. Vargas. You've been very helpful."

Lyle and Terrance walk into the offices of Filson Accounting on the sixth floor of Ortiz's building on Broadway.

After getting by the receptionist, they meet with Derrik Filson. The accountant seems visually upset talking about Diego's passing. The three discuss Ortiz's involvement, how their businesses intertwine. The detectives told that Ortiz was a silent partner and how he recruited him right out of college and set up the business.

The accountant has no clients other than Diego Ortiz and his many business ventures. It seems Ortiz financed a dozen small local businesses and numerous properties.

One of the operations, the lawyer owned, is a property management company, Ortiz Development, which oversees various individual property managers and takes care of maintenance, landscaping, and leasing. In addition, the company researches new properties to buy and land to develop.

Filson tells the detectives of other business ventures Ortiz is involved with. He talks a lot and has nothing to hide. Derrik states that he is unsure of his future with his partner gone. He definitely does not prosper from Diego Ortiz's early demise.

The detectives leave going to the Ortiz Development across town.

This office is busy with many people on phone calls from their local managers. Everyone has problems and needs babysitting. It is almost an hour before they get into Erwin Rookey's office.

"Sorry to keep you waiting, a lot of fires to put out with Diego gone."

Erwin is extremely friendly, a true saleswoman, but offers little help. Almost every question asked, answered with a question.

The detectives talk for as long as they can before asked to leave.

The men go to the station to research Ortiz's other businesses. They now have a list, thanks to the FBI and Derrik Filson.

CHAPTER TWENTY-SEVEN
Mexico Again

Jake approaches the counter and rings the silver push-button counter bell. A minute later, Jesse emerges from the back room and greets Jake.

"I have another job for you, Jesse," Smith says.

"Great, I hope it's harder than the last one," the locksmith's sarcastic response.

"Your wish is coming true. There is a double-door safe south of TJ that I need opened."

"You know, if I drill it, the safe is ruined."

"I know, but it's imperative that I get in."

"What brand is it?"

Jake pulls the copied safe information sheet from his pocket and hands it to the locksmith. Jesse unfolds the sheet and reads it. "This is easy. You have the registration number and owner info. I can request the combination from the manufacturer."

"Wonderful. How long will that take?"

"It depends if I can convince them to give it to me over the phone, or have to mail in a written request and wait for them to get back to me."

"What're the chances they just tell you?"

"Fifty-fifty. I don't stock floor safes but I have sold a couple of theirs on drop shipments. I'll call Angela. She's the saleswoman and knows me. With luck, I can get a favor."

Jake hopes so too. He thanks, Jesse, and lets him know he will check in later that afternoon.

While Jake is looking into the Ortiz safe problem, Alex is going to the County Recorder for a background check on Clarence Brown, Diego's mentor, and pseudo-father.

Alexis walks into the downtown recorder's office. She stands and looks at all the department identification signs and heads the *Property Records* desk. After waiting in line, her turn arrives, and she approaches the clerk. Alex asks for the Deed of Record for all the properties owned by Clarence Brown and any listed for Diego Ortiz. She orders copies of the records. The clerk tells her to a seat in the waiting area.

After a while, a man sits next to Alex. They end up chatting as they wait. Clyford Rampton tells her he is a reporter for the San Diego Union newspaper. She reciprocates that she works for Hamilton-Adams Investigations.

"You work with Jake Smith?"

"That's correct."

"Are you an investigator too?"

Laughing, she answers, "Oh no, I do research. So you know Jake?"

"We crossed paths when he was an SDPD detective..."

"Number sixty-seven window four!" blares over the speaker system.

"That's me. It was nice meeting you...?"

"Alexis."

"Alexis. Say hi to Jake for me." They shake hands and Rampton scurries off.

An hour and eight minutes and almost one hundred dollars later she thanks the clerk and walks over to the *Birth/Death & Marriage License* counter.

There again, she has the clerk lookup, Brown, and Ortiz. There is not any history of either man married, but she obtains birth and death certificates for Clarence Brown. He was born at Balboa Naval Hospital and was a San Diego native. Brown died in early nineteen-sixty-seven. Nothing on record for a Diego Ortiz.

Alexis immediately realizes, Brown died in January sixty-seven, and Ortiz supposedly graduated law school, after the summer session, in August. Siena was right, Clarence Brown passed before graduation. That picture, with him and Diego, couldn't have been taken at the ceremony!

Alex is about to leave and takes a final look at the signs. She makes her way to the *Business License* counter, to look up the businesses listed in Ortiz's ledger, and adds businesses owned by Clarence Brown. Brown's records show only his law firm, but under Ortiz, there is a variety including Filson Accounting, Inc. and Emily's Cafe. She next has the clerk look up all the partnerships listed in his ledger. Again, copies of everything ordered. After almost four hours in the department, Alex takes the box of Xerox's and goes back to HAI offices.

Jake and his partner spend the rest of the afternoon categorizing and listing people they need to speak to, and in which order.

At four-fifty-six, the phone rings. Alex picks up. Jesse is on the line and he asks to speak with Jake. He got Diego's safe combination.

Jesse verbally walks Jake through the process of how to unlock the unit, which direction to spin the dial and how many turns between numbers.

After getting off the phone, "I'm going back to Siena's in the morning, would like you to come. Two sets of eyes will be helpful."

"I would love to go with you, Jake," Alex answers. She has never been out of the country and is looking forward to the adventure.

Smith and Dench show up at Diego's Mexican shore estate, late the next morning.

While Jake is opening the safe, Siena gives Alex a tour of the mansion. Alex possesses an easy outgoing, charismatic personality. She and Siena get along swimmingly. They end their tour on the patio sipping ice tea and sharing girl talk.

Siena confesses her disdain for her husband. Diego was aloof and conducted many out of marriage affairs. The philandering started before their union and continued thereafter. At one point, Siena hired a private eye and had her husband followed for more than a year. She knows of numerous trysts. Many one-nighters and a three-year affair.

In the meantime, Jake recovers four more ledgers, Diego's business investment ledger, his alien smuggling books, a drug record, and his money-laundering scheme.

After Jake and Alex leave the estate, they decide to spend the afternoon visiting shops along Revolution Avenue. Dench stashes the four books in her purse.

Late in the afternoon, they are in a tourist mall off the main street down a steep stairway. Jake is looking through a belt rack in a small leather shop and Alex decides to go to the pottery bazaar, a few stalls down. He plans to catch up with her as soon as he finds what he is looking for.

As soon as Smith steps onto the wide crowded walkway with his purchase, he hears, "Good afternoon, Jake."

Surprised at the man's voice, he whirls to see Franco Trujillo leaning against the wall. "Frank, what are you doing here?"

"Looking for you, Jake. My boss would like to have a word."

Smith quickly glances around the crowd. Nobody stands out. "Who's your boss and where is he?"

"I have a car. We'll go to him." Frank tries to come across as friendly.

"I don't think so," Jake states and starts to move off.

Frank throws Jakes into a plywood wall. The stall shakes like it's going to crumble and draws attention. The Mexican thug ignores the stares and throws a quick blow to Jake's right cheek. "I'm not asking. You are coming to see him!" Trujillo grabs Smith's left arm and spins him around while shoving an ATM AutoMag IV pistol into Smith's kidneys. "Let's go!"

The assailant, gripping Jake's bicep, strides off pushing Smith in front.

As soon as they pass the pottery shop, Dench sees her lover. "Jake, in here!" She yells and waves.

Frank whips his head to see whose shouting. Smith jerks free and starts darting between tourists and locals, through the crowd. Frank recovers quickly and is on Jake's heals.

Dench is running as fast as she can, trying to catch up, but the throng is thick and does not let her pass easily. A half a block away, Alex trips on the uneven walkway and skins her knee. With adrenaline rushing through her body, she does not feel the blood dripping as she jumps back to her feet and pushes on.

She rounds the corner and spots Frank pistol-whipping Jake against a cement-block wall. She screams for help just as a black Lincoln screeches up in front of the men.

Alex is still screaming at the top of her lungs as Frank pushes her partner into the back seat of the large sedan. He turns to Alex, twenty feet away and gives her a large smile and one-finger salute before jumping in beside Jake. The vehicle quickly lost in traffic.

Dench, still yelling and frantically looking for help, spies a policeman running towards her.

"What's the problem, Miss?" In English, but a heavy Spanish accent.

"They took my husband!" Her voice piercing the air above the noisy tourists.

"Please calm down! Who took your husband?" the officer asks.

"I don't know. A man was chasing him with a gun. His head is bleeding."

"You don't know the man?"

"I think his name is Frank Trujillo!"

"Frank Trujillo? Are you sure?"

"Yes! Yes! I met him once. I'm sure it was him!" Dench screams.

"You better come with me, *Señora*. What is your name?"

Dench looks over the police officer. He wears a brown uniform. Jake had warned her about the Tijuana police; green-uniformed men are *Federales* and employed by the government, but brown uniformed officers are city police. They make most of their money accepting bribes and working on the side.

"I need to go home!"

"No, you must come with me now," the man insists.

Alex takes off running back into the crowd. He chases after her, constantly blowing a loud whistle and yelling, *"Alto! Alto!"*

She runs back into the pottery shop and weaves around giant stacks of clay pots. Alex accidentally bumps into one and sending it crashing to the floor. Everyone stops and stares at her fleeing body and the littered broken pottery. In unison, they turn at the sound of the shrieking whistle as the officer runs into the bazaar yelling, *"Dónde Señora! Dónde Señora!* Where is the woman?" While Dench slips through the back rooms and the open door.

Not one patron or employee whispers a word and the officer quickly returns to the outside mall, back through the front of the shop, and continues searching.

Alex busts onto the sidewalk straight into a taco cart. She picks herself up, and jumps into a taxi sitting at the curb, "To the border!" and throws a twenty at the driver. He snatches the bill and takes off.

CHAPTER TWENTY-EIGHT
Drug Dealer

Stephen Lyle turns to Donald Terrance. "Well, look at this." He hands his partner the top sheet of Gary Baird's bank statement.

"When did you get that?"

"It came in this morning."

Looking at the sheet. "Holy cow! Baird deposited two thousand in cash on the second and five on the sixth, the day we discovered the body!"

Lyle responds, "That could be a payment for a hit. Seven thousand in cash is a lot of money for a struggling student."

"We're on the same page there, partner. Let's bring him in again!" Terrance shakes his head in disbelieve.

"I'm calling Ross first, to get a search warrant for his dorm and vehicle."

By noon, the detectives are on their way to the Nazarene University. First stop is Baird's residence hall.

The door is unlocked and they enter. The room is free of Baird and his roommate. The two men tear apart the dorm looking for evidence of the murder, specifically, the murder weapon and blood-splattered clothing, shoes or gloves. When they finish, the detectives are empty-handed.

Terrance stands in the middle of the room looking around to see what they missed. He stares at the high-wall heating vent. "Does that look crooked to you?"

"Could be, hard to tell," Lyle replies.

The detective drags a desk chair over. "Do you have your Swiss Army knife?"

"Never leave home without it," Lyle states, smiling.

Climbing on the chair seat, Terrance examines the vent, "Can you pull out your slot screwdriver and hand it to me?"

Lyle pulls the multi-tool Swiss Army knife from his pocket, flips out the driver, and hands it to his partner.

Terrance removes the grate and peers into the dark chamber. Reaching in, he pulls a small faded Levi knapsack from the cavity and hands it down to Lyle, who tears into it and puts baggies of marijuana on the closest unmade bed. "Looks like our upstanding Christian student is a drug dealer," he comments.

"The search warrant doesn't specifically cover drugs," Lyle mumbles.

"Let's take him downtown. We won't mention the drugs until after we hear about the cash deposits."

Back at the station, the three men sit in Interview Room D.

"Why are you guys harassing me?" Baird questions.

Lyle turns on the recorder. "Tells again how you pay for school, Gary?"

"I work... you know as a janitor."

"And?"

"And, I have a couple school loans."

"And?"

"And what? That's it!" Gary starts to get nervous.

"Gary," Terrance is the good guy half of the team, "does your job pay you in cash?"

"No, check." Wondering where this is leading.

"How about your loans? Cash or check?"

"Check. What are you getting at?"

"Since the first of the month, you made two cash deposits for seven thousand dollars." Both detectives sit quietly waiting for Baird's explanation.

Finally, he speaks, "My mother sent me some money." Quickly adding, "I ran a little short this month."

"We think you were paid in cash to kill Ortiz!" Lyle flat out accuses the shaking young man.

"No! No… no, I didn't kill anyone!" Tears start to flow as he realizes what is happening.

"Gary, I think maybe you were justified. Maybe Ortiz came on to you and you had to defend yourself," Terrance suggests.

"NO! I *did not* murder Diego!"

"Diego? I thought you never met the man." Lyle knows Baird just misspoke.

After sobbing uncontrollably for five minutes. "I… I… I knew him, OK, but not the way you think."

Terrance stands. "Gary, I'll get you a drink of water." While he is gone, Lyle just stares at the student. Baird does not realize it, as he never looks up.

Terrance returns with the drink and a box of tissues.

They give Baird a few minutes to compose himself before Lyle starts back in, "We're going to need a blood sample and your fingerprints."

"What for," he asks.

"To match the scene evidence. Do you know what blood type you are?"

"B negative," comes the answer from the rattled student.

"Gary, you must know that is the second rarest blood type there is. Only two percent of the population is B negative."

"Yeah, I know, hope I never need a transfusion."

"Funny thing though, Gary, the killer's blood was all over the floor at the Ortiz murder. Want to guess what type it is?"

"No! I wasn't there. Why don't you believe me?" Through sobs.

"What *way* did you know Diego?" Terrance goes back to the last question before the break.

"Uh, I asked him for some legal help once and he let me call him if I needed more."

"What kind of legal help?"

"Uh, some guys were harassing me at school and I didn't know what to do."

"So what did Ortiz tell you to do?"

"He told me to go to administration and tell them to fix the problem or I was getting a restraining order and my lawyer would sue the school. Diego told me to use his name and give them a business card."

"And what happened?"

The school stopped the problem. I don't know how, but it never happened again."

"Ok Gary, now tell us about your drug business." Terrance takes over.

"What drug business?"

Before he could add another word, Lyle reaches down beside his chair, grabs the backpack and sets it on the table.

Baird knows he is busted, and breaks down again, grabbing handfuls of tissues. After working on him for another hour, the detectives break Baird and he comes clean.

"I sold a little weed to help pay for school. Just to a couple of friends. My job didn't pay enough. I was desperate. I didn't have enough money for the next semester. I'm sorry," and quickly adds, "I'll never do it again."

"Who is your supplier?"

"I... I don't know. A guy at school set me up and I found the weed behind the trash can in the alley at work."

"You're going to have to do better than that if you want to stay out of jail!" Lyle threatens.

"Walk us through the exact procedure, Gary."

"I would leave money in a backpack and put it behind the trash bin when I went to work. Then when I left I would pick up the pack and it would have the weed in it."

"Gary, that doesn't fly! You better get real and fast if you want our help." Terrance's turn to lay down a threat.

Baird sits quietly for the longest time, before saying, "I guess it doesn't matter now anyway, he's dead." Another moment of thought, Baird tells all. "Diego recruited me when I went to him for help. He fronted me the first *buy* and after that, I would leave my backpack in his office and pick it up the next night."

"And the deposits?"

141

"I saved up the money for a couple of months. I… I was afraid to deposit it. I knew it was wrong. I'm so sorry. But I didn't kill him!"

"Gary, I believe you. We're not going to mention this to narcotics… this time, but it had better be over! Understand?"

"Yes, Sir! Thank you, Sir. It'll never happen again, Sir."

"Get out of here," Lyle commands.

Baird stands and vigorously shakes both detective's hands, before darting out of the room. "Thank you! Thank you, it'll never happen again. I promise. I learned my lesson!"

"Get out of here before I change my mind!" Lyle demands.

After Baird is gone. "Well, we scared the piss out him," Terrance laughs.

"Yeah," joining in the laughter. "Do you believe him?"

"I do. He was too scared to deposit the money, he would have had died of a heart attack if he did the murder." Laughing harder than ever.

"But that makes Ortiz a drug dealer and opens the suspect list to dealers and junkies." Lyle thinks out-loud.

"We better find out who Diego is supplying! Let's find Joe Olson and see what the word on the street is," referring to one of their informants.

CHAPTER TWENTY-NINE
Jake Meets Pablo

Jake Smith was thrown into the back seat of an ebony Lincoln Continental Towncar, featuring a larger than the normal driver and just as large a man in the passenger seat. Another colossal man pulls Jake into the center and Trujillo squeezes in beside him.

"Trujillo, what the hell are you doing?" Smith yells at him. His head has not quit bleeding from the gun-barrel whipping and his shirt absorbed all it could hold. It drips onto the leather seat and carpet.

"You idiot. Get that blood stopped! As soon as we get there, you better get that mess cleaned up or it'll be your blood next!" shouts Trujillo at the guy beside Smith.

The giant jerks Smith shirt inside out over his head, twists, and ties it off with a large cable tie. With his new hood, Smith cannot see. Then the man takes out a handkerchief and feebly tries to clean the immaculate carpet.

"Jake, I asked nicely. You have should come along, it didn't have to be like this," Trujillo addresses Smith.

"Where are you taking me?"

"Sorry Jake, I can't understand what you're saying."

The rest of the ride is in silence. The man in the passenger seat and the other in the back did not want to chance to upset Trujillo, and the driver concentrates on the road.

Smith listens for familiar noises, and counts the right and left turns.

The vehicle stops after a twenty-minute drive. Jake listens closely to a warehouse door squeak and clank as it rolls up. As soon as it bangs against the top stop, the car jerks hard as the driver floors the gas. It stops just as quickly. Nobody moves until the closing noise of the door finishes and the loud click of the floor locks kicked into place.

Jake, dragged from the car and pushed hard to the cement floor. The passenger pulls a Naugahyde chair over. The seat and back ripped and fibers stick out. The chrome armrests and legs are dented and rusting.

Smith's hands and feet bound together and around the chair with matte-silver duct tape. The Melendez soldiers use two more rolls making their prisoner and the steel-frame chair one. They tip the unit back on two legs and drag it across the large greasy floor. During the process of getting him through a door, they bang him into a doorframe cracking his elbow. Ignoring the loud yelp and cursing from Smith, they continue into the next room. With a hard thump, the chair tips upright. Smith sits quietly waiting for the hammer to fall.

He flinches at the sharp prick of a knifepoint on his neck before his shirt sliced and torn off.

Jake blinks rapidly trying to adjust his eyes in the dim light. All he sees is blurred shadows moving around the room. Suddenly a stand comes ablaze with four industrial flood lamps all pointed at Smith's face. He instantly closes his eyes and turns his head from the retina-burning light. Next, both his shoes ripped off his feet.

"Mr. Smith, tell me about your involvement with Diego Ortiz?"

The captive turns his head forward and squints through the high-intensity glare. He spots what appears to be the outline of a short, fat man sitting in a chair asking the question.

"I worked on a background case for him... that's all," Smith squeals out.

"That is not all! You can make this easier on yourself by being truthful. We'll start with what you were talking to Contreras about?" The same unknown man demands.

"Before Diego's untimely death, he suggested that Contreras might have a job for me. When I went to see about it, he told me that he did not have anything." Jake makes up a cover story as he goes.

"Mr. Contreras told me you are investigating Ortiz!"

So, these guys talked to Jose Smith thinks. "Only as far as settling his affairs for his wife."

"Mrs. Herrera hired you?"

"She wants her husband's assets determined to settle the matters." Smith lies.

"So you want to do this the hard way?" The boss addresses, Franco, "Work your magic!"

Smith sits quietly and wonders what is about to happen. He hears a click and quick buzz as sparks fly. Next to the cart, appears Trujillo, his face momentarily lights up, and he's holding the jumper cables. Jake's eyes try to adjust, but all he sees is the bright flash embossed across on his cornea.

Seconds later, he screams in pain as two excoriating clamps impale his chest. Blood immediately pours past his nipples and down his body.

"Now Mr. Smith, please tell me what you are investigating and what you found out?"

"Nothing… I… I already told you… I…" barely speaking above the pain.

Zap! Electricity surges through his body as it jumps uncontrollably. He screams in agony. "Stop! Stop!"

"It pains me to see you like this, Mr. Smith. It all stops when you tell me what I want to know," the leader states.

"I… I don't know what you want." Smith body could not stop shaking.

"I want to know what Contreras told you."

"Nothing!"

The volts surged through Smith's body again. He could not contain himself and his pants filled with warm flowing urine. Soon there is a pool on the floor beneath him.

"Piss around your socked feet. Docs not look good, Mr. Smith." Trujillo laughs.

Jake knows the next surge of electricity will be more painful than he can bear. "I'm… I'm telling the truth!" He is unprepared for the shock.

"Who do you think killed Ortiz?"

"I… I… I don't know, and don't care," Smith babbles. "Why are you asking?"

"I am not asking again."

Yeeeeow! Another lightening jolt and another uncontrollable spasm consume his body.

"Ok! Ok! He told me you did it, but I didn't ask," Smith fabricates.

"Did what?"

"Murder… Killed Ortiz!" Quickly thinking *killed sounds better than murdered.*

"That's better. What did he tell you about our business?" Trujillo questions.

"Nothi… " Jake stopped short of finishing. "He said you're not a good person, though nothing about your affairs."

"What did Siena tell you?"

"Who's Siena?" He knew that was the wrong answer even before his body jerks again, and more urine flows.

"Mr. Smith, I know you visited her twice in as many days."

"You don't appear to like the pain?" Trujillo adds. "Why don't you just tell us the truth and this all goes away."

"You're going to kill me. Why don't you just get it over?"

"Oh no, Mr. Smith, you are going to live for days." The room breaks into jubilee.

Smith decides not to say another word. The pain will never stop anyway, and death will come quicker. He says a silent prayer.

CHAPTER THIRTY
FBI Called

Alex Dench, riding in a Tijuana taxi, approaches the Mexican side of the border. She is on high alert, eyes dart for unusual activity. She spies half a dozen brown uniform officers scanning the crossers and tells the driver to take her back to the closest shops.

She pays the driver and finds a clothing shop. Inside, Alex buys a large-lens pair of sunglasses, a colorfully striped serape poncho, scarf and small straw sombrero with a colorful cloth edge band sewn around the brim. At the shop next door, she buys a multicolored donkey *piñata* and pink plaster piggy bank. In addition, Alex buys a mishmash of smaller souvenirs and gets a used plastic bag to carry them.

She puts on her disguise and juggles the *piñata* under one arm and the plaster pig, with the bag of souvenirs hanging below, in the other. She looks like the quintessential tourist.

She walks back to the border crossing and enters a duty-free liquor store. Alex browsers the bottles while watching the Americans, through the front window, heading back to the U.S. Finally, a family of four passes the store and she quickly follows them walking close enough to be one of the group.

At the last door before entering US Customs two Mexican police officers, review the group closely. Alex starts talking to the young girl about her day in Mexico. The officers, satisfied, turn their attention to the next set of returning people.

As the father opens the door to the inside corridor, a local officer yells, *"Alto! Stop!"*

Alex glances over her shoulder, he is yelling at her. She pushes past the family knocking over the girl. The father quickly attends to his fallen daughter while looking and shouting at the strangely dressed women, "What the hell, lady!"

Alex does not hear him, as she runs towards American officials, constantly screaming, "Help me!"

A U.S. Custom's guard grabs her arm. "What's going on?"

Before she can answer, the two Mexican uniforms grab her free arm. One yells, "You're coming with us!"

The American states back, "No! She's a US citizen and in our custody!"

"She's committed a Mexican crime and we're in charge!"

Soon, a multitude of officials, from both countries, surrounds Alex. Everyone is talking at once claiming jurisdiction and no one pays attention to Alex's jumbled explanation and pleas for help.

Finally, a commander for the U.S. side comes to her rescue. "Everyone, get your hands off this woman! We are taking her in! If she has committed a Mexican crime she will be turned over to you," addressing what appears to be a senior officer of the opposition. Looking back at his men, he commands, "Bring her to my office!"

Without passing the checkpoint, the gaggle of Americans officers escort Alex to a room off the main hallway and sit her down in front of the desk while the rest stand behind ensuring her entrapment. The lead man takes his seat. "What's going on?"

Before she can answer, a uniformed man pulls a chair over and immediately rifles through her souvenir bag and purse. He pulls out the ledgers. "What are these?" as he thumbs through them.

"Confidential client records!" Alex turns to the man in charge, and changes the subject, explaining the abduction of Jake Smith and orders them to start an immediate search. In addition, Alex demands to talk with FBI Agents Davis and Morris. When questioned on why she fibs that they are all working together on the Ortiz case.

The Customs man calls the San Diego FBI office.

An hour later, Davis and his partner push through the still waiting Mexican officers and into the room. After all the introductions, Alex explains that they visited Diego's wife and home in Rosarito and the events that followed. She omits telling them that Smith found ledgers, which put back in her purse when she minimized their importance. In addition, she overlooked mentioning that Siena Herrera has a motive to eliminate her husband.

Davis states that he has worked with Edwardo Prieto, a Captain of the Federal Judicial Police and will give him a call. He then asks the Border Patrol lieutenant if someone can give Alex a ride home.

While Alexis scours the newfound ledgers back in her loft, Davis and Morris meet with *Capitán* Prieto in the Tijuana Police Headquarters.

As soon as Davis tells Prieto the name of the man, Alex identified, is Frank Trujillo, the Mexican agent knows exactly what is going on. He explains Trujillo has been a suspect in numerous murders for the Melendez drug ring, for years, but they could never pin anything directly on him.

He goes on to say that, he believes they are probably holding Smith in a warehouse on the East Mesa. Prieto puts together a team of soldiers, each sporting machine guns and side arms and wearing bulletproof vests for the warehouse search.

Davis, Morris, and Prieto meet the teams down the street from the building and the Mexican captain hands out assignments and explains the plan to find and liberate Jake Smith.

Within minutes, they descend on the warehouse, breaking open doors and barging in. Gunfire erupts simultaneously from both factions. In the war zone, men are falling, wounded or dead. Morris takes a shot to the shoulder and goes down. The blasts are earsplitting and bullets whizzing throughout the building. People are running helter-skelter in every direction or diving for cover. Vehicles heard peeling out as fugitives exit the scene as fast as possible.

Twenty minutes later the gun battle is over. Prieto's men victorious. Many criminals are dead or in custody. Many more have fled to safety.

Soldiers are running through the building looking for their captive. One team bursts through a closed door into a large room. It is empty but for Private Investigator, Jake Smith. He sits strapped to a chair in the center. Next, to him, a cart holding a car battery. Connected are two jumper cables leading to Smith's chest.

He wrung out, head down, and unconscious with sweat pouring uncontrollably from his half-naked body, and blood trails running down. A large lake of urine mixed blood blankets the floor beneath him.

The lead officer yells, *"Obtener medico!"* Get medical, in Spanish.

Moments later two men are attending to Smith. He is weak and close to death. They quickly transport him to Hospital Guadalajara.

Morris also took to the same hospital. Davis rides in the ambulance with his partner.

After Morris undergoes surgery to remove the slug from his shoulder and is in recovery, Davis goes in search of Smith. He finds him lying in a room, receiving hydration through a tube, and numerous attached monitor wires leading to a digital display. The open wounds on his chest oozing, and smeared with a thick layer of greasy ointment. His breathing slow and sporadic. He is under sedation, appearing to be asleep. Davis looks over the distressed man for several minutes before approaching. "Jake, can you hear me?" he softly asks.

After a few moments, Smith slightly moves, and quietly responds, "Yes," followed by a slight opening of his black and blue swollen eyes.

"Special Agent Egan Davis."

"I can see that." though, Smith only sees a dark fuzzy shadow.

"I need to ask you what happened."

There is no response, and a full minute later, Davis asks, "Smith?"

"I'm not sure," Smith responds. "I was kind of hoping you could tell me." A small, painful smile crosses his face. Smith is conscious enough to know he isn't willing to share anything with the agent that suspects him of hiding and stealing evidence, even if Davis is right on both accounts.

"Try to think about it. I'm going to check on Morris. If he's alright, we'll be back."

"What happened?" Smith questions, barely above a whisper.

"He was shot in the shoulder while we were searching for you."

Jake did not hear the man, as he was already back asleep with drugs consuming his body.

Davis approaches the nurse's station to inquire about his partner. Before he can speak. "Agent Davis?"

Turning, he sees the white lab-coated doctor who worked on his partner. "Yes."

"I am pleased to inform you, Mr. Morris is doing fine. We remover the bullet from his shoulder and he should fully recover. He was extremely lucky. The slug, a hollow-point, did not shatter as designed. It was found lodged in the flesh right beneath the clavicle. He's anxious to get out of here, but I'm hesitant to discharge him. He really should be admitted for a couple of day's observation."

"Do you suspect complications?"

"Oh no, but infection is always a strong possibility. I would hate for him to survive the shot only to suffer permanent damage from bacterial complications, or even contracting pneumonia."

"Hey, Partner, we ready to blow this joint?" Morris emerges through the double swinging aluminum doors with two nurses on his tail.

"Agent Morris you really need to stay with us, at least overnight," the head nurse interrupts the reunion.

"Nonsense, you did your job, and a mighty fine job at that, I must say. But I have to get back to work."

"You wouldn't be going back to work for a few weeks, Mr. Morris," the doctor chimes in.

"Don't worry about me, Doc, I'm a fast healer." Turning to Davis. "Let's go."

Egan shrugs his shoulders at the medical staff, displaying a, *what can I do* look. Davis turns and starts walking down the hall. Morris is on his heels.

In the elevator, Davis pushed the up button.

"We want down!" Morris blurts out.

"Have to pay Smith a visit first."

Minutes later, Morris follows Davis into Smith's room. He is awake and a nurse attending to his wounds. The two men stand silently waiting.

"Hey, guys." Smith gurgles to them, as the nurse is leaving.

"Looks like you're feeling a little better, Jake," Davis comments.

"Yeah, the drugs are starting to wear off. Could you get me a drink of water, Morris?" He adds, "With your good arm?" Morris' cast consumes his upper chest and right arm sticks out horizontally in an *L* shape.

As the agent looks around for a plastic cup, Davis questions, "So now, do you remember what happened?"

Still fuzzy and gesturing at Morris. "What happened to him?"

"I was here a little while ago. Do you remember?"

Jake does not remember anyone visiting him and hopes he did not spill the beans. "I'm sure I'm alright and ready to get out of here. Can I hitch a ride with you guys?"

Davis asks, "Tells me what happened?"

Morris hands Smith a small cup of water. "Here you go, Jake."

What's up? These guys are acting as if I'm a long-lost cousin Smith thinks to himself, but voices. "I'm a little sore, but it's nothing I can take care of at home." It suddenly dawns on him and he bolts upright while the bandages pull from his chest and flop freely, "Crap!" he screams and reels in pain, "Where's Alexis? Is she alright?"

A nurse runs into the room. "Gentlemen, you need to leave, NOW!" As she runs to Smith and gently lays him, back down. "Mr. Smith, you must lay still!" She retrieves new bandages from the wall cabinet and starts working on his chest.

"I'm checking out and going with these guys. I'm a fast healer and will be more comfortable at home."

"Todos los estadounidenses son sanadores rápidos!" The nurse laughs at her; *all Americans are fast healers* joke.

After re-bandaging, the nurse moves on to her next patient, and Smith tenderly slides on his pants. His shirt nowhere found and he slips his arms into a light blue backward gown. "Let's go!"

The trio walks past the nurse's station, with a woman yelling, "You can't leave!" While frantically paging the doctor.

On the drive back to San Diego, Davis explains that Dench is fine, and relays her story, plus the story of the raid and rescue.

Smith, in and out of consciousness, does not comprehend a word said.

CHAPTER THIRTY-ONE
Melendez Organization

Pablo Melendez grew up in the Mexican border town of Juárez across from El Paso, Texas. He fled to Tijuana when he was twenty-eight years old, in nineteen fifty-six. It had not taken him long to get into the marijuana selling business.

Juan Herrera and Jose Contreras were both sixteen years of age hustling everything they could get their hands on when they met Pablo outside of a whorehouse on Revolution Avenue.

Contreras approached him and endeavored to get him a date inside the bordello. The young Contreras would not take no for an answer and persisted to pressure the older man. Melendez was impressed with the truculent youth and offered him a lucrative opportunity, by integrating weed dealing with his repertoire. Melendez knew he could not sell enough on his own and needed street dealers to expand. Jose called his partner over and they both got involved. Melendez fronted them the first two buys and hooked the kids into his enterprise.

For the next three years, the teenagers brought in more business than Pablo could have imagined. Their boss capitalized on the growth, adding every illegal drug he could get his hands on. Business boomed. Melendez grew to the largest drug distributor in Tijuana.

Juan and Jose decided Pablo was not sharing enough of the wealth and they needed to go on their own. They took what money they had saved and rented a small storage space on the outskirts of town and started bringing in their own drugs. The pair had not told their boss, and immediately sold less of his product and more of their own.

Diego Killer

A few months downline, Pablo called a meeting and confronted them on their dwindling sales. Juan made excuses for the lower volumes. Pablo told him that he understood, but they had no choice but to increase their output or face consequences.

Melendez had not believed a word Juan told him. His other dealers showed no sign of slowing. He started having the pair followed.

Not long after their meeting, Pablo discovered the traitors rented a unit and that they were selling their own drugs. One night, shortly before Juan turned nineteen, their storage unit and entire inventory burnt to the ground.

The word on the street was Melendez did it personally. He could not appear weak to the rest of his organization. He liked the boys as brothers, but if the situation ignored, two renegades could quickly turn into a full-blown coupe. Pablo Melendez had little choice but to put out a hit contract on Juan and Jose.

The young entrepreneurs, warned by another of Pablo's dealers, ran. Contreras hid out in the small village of Telchac Puerto, on the Yucatan Peninsula, in southern Mexico and Herrera snuck across the border to San Diego. With the two AWOL, Melendez proudly spread the word that the bodies would never be found. In addition, if anyone ever tried this again, not only would the Benedict Arnold be tortured beyond recognition, but also his mother, father and all relatives included.

Right after the boys went into hiding, Melendez met, and hired Franco Trujillo to head his enforcement division. After that, nobody ever left the organization, alive!

Over the next ten years, the Melendez Drug Cartel became the largest in Mexico. The bulk of their money made exporting weed, cocaine, meth, and heroin into the United States. He had his own methamphetamine labs cooking the substance throughout Baja California and mainland Mexico. Other drugs imported from Central and South America, while heroin came from Southeast Asia.

Any competition was subject to death by Trujillo's hand. Drug wars piled up and so did the bodies.

155

By the late sixties, Pablo expanded into kidnapping wealthy Mexican citizens and collected ransoms. Even after being paid off many victims never lived through Franco's wrath.

In nineteen-seventy Pablo, discovered Jose Contreras was back and had an office in downtown TJ. He was an attorney. Pablo paid his old employee a visit. Melendez easily convinced Contreras to become his lawyer. Of course, only as retribution for Jose's past indiscretion. No money ever exchanged hands.

Contreras knew he had no choice or it would be his and his family's slow tortuous demise.

Juan Herrera lived in San Diego under the name Diego Ortiz. He was no wiser to the fact that his partner was working for Pablo again and went to his grave unaware.

When Melendez found out about Herrera, he visited his other traitor in San Diego.

By this time, Ortiz was a force in his own right. He refused to understand that he owed Pablo for his youthful mistakes and declined to merge their enterprises.

They fought for over a year, with neither man conceding the position he had built.

CHAPTER THIRTY-TWO
Under Suspicion

Dench leaves her fiancé sleeping and quietly slips out for coffee.

Clyford Rampton, the San Diego Union reporter runs into Alexis at a local 7-Eleven convenience store. He recognizes her from the County Recorder's office where they previously met and had a brief conversation. During the talk, he asked what she was looking up, as by that time she had an armload of copies and still waiting for more. Dench mentioned she worked with Smith, and she was doing a little research.

"Good morning, Ms. Dench, it's nice to see you again," Clyford greets.

"Hi. It's Biff isn't it?" She remembers the face, but not his name.

"Cliff, with the Union."

"Oh, that's right, sorry."

"So how's it going working with Smith?"

"Jake had a little accident in Mexico and he's now home recuperating," Alex comments.

"I'm sorry to hear that. I wish him a speedy recovery."

"Thanks, I'll let him know," Alex responds.

"I'll stop by your office and wish him well in person. Any idea when he'll be working again?" Rampton, the consummate reporter thinks there might be a small filler story here; *"LOCAL PI HAS MISHAP IN MEXICO"*.

"You know Jake, a day or two at the longest," giggles Alex. "I better get back before he pushes it."

"Has Virginia Small stopped by yet?" Cliff questions.

157

"I don't know her. Jake just got back last evening I doubt anyone knows. Why would she come by?"

"Well," hesitantly, "they've been friends for a long time. I just thought... it doesn't matter. She's probably still mourning Ortiz's murder anyway."

"Small and Ortiz? How long has that gone on?" Alex asks.

"I shouldn't have said anything. I thought Jake would have told you since he is... err, was friends with both."

"He never said a word. I don't think he knows." She turns on *her* reporter side. "How do you know?"

"Ah, it's the best-kept secret in San Diego. You know Diego was such a philanderer. He was always on our social page with one woman or another. I shouldn't spread gossip, but I overheard them arguing at a restaurant in Pacific Beach the night Ortiz was murdered. Couldn't hear much until she stood and screamed, go f*** yourself." He adds, "She pulled off a ring and threw it at him before storming off. I guess that ended it. Well, that and Ortiz's death."

"That's interesting," Dench, voices while thinking *there's a scorned woman with a motive!*

"Please keep this to yourself. I just assumed, Jake, if anyone, would know."

"Mum's the word. I better get back." Alex whirls and leaves almost running. Her partner, working or not, needs to hear this.

Jake is sitting painfully slumped over at his desk as Alex enters their loft.

She sees him and sits. "How are you feeling, dear?"

"Good... well a little sore, but I'll be alright," he answers.

"Ran into Clyford Rampton while I was getting us some coffee. He told me an interesting story. Do you know Virginia Small?"

"Sure, she's a news reporter. I had a few dealings with her back when I was San Diego PD."

Dench overlooks questioning exactly what kind of dealings. "Virginia and Diego were an item! Apparently engaged. They had a public fight and Virginia ended it!"

"Ortiz and Small? I had no idea!" He states with a puzzled expression.

"No one else did either. Rampton observed them arguing at a restaurant on the same night Diego was murdered! Small got up and threw a ring at him and stomped out."

"What do you make of that?" Smith questions.

"Looks like she ended an engagement. A scorned woman sure has a motive for murder!" Alex bluntly lays it on the table.

"Yeah... but Virginia, I just don't see it." Jake falls into deep contemplation.

"We never really know another person. She could have more hidden rage than anyone knew," Alexis continues the conversation.

Still thinking quietly, Jake finally states, "I don't buy it! However, this could be good for us. I'm going to put Lyle on to her. It'll take the investigation off me and if she is guilty, they'll find out and if she's not it doesn't matter."

"I like it." Alex sees the logic. "Tell me about Mexico and Trujillo. Why would he hurt you?"

"From what I can remember... I didn't get the whole story before passing out." Jake goes on to tell his fiancé the intricate horrors of being shocked and their mutilating his body in graphic detail. Alex is stunned at the torture he endured.

Jake finishes the hurtful story and Alex asks what would constitute that kind of treatment.

"The best I can figure out is Trujillo works for this little Mexican dude and they are in cahoots with Contreras. I don't think Diego knew it. But, at the same time, this guy was after Ortiz for some reason. Contreras must have set his partner up."

"So they murdered Ortiz?"

"That's what I'm thinking. Also, they asked about Siena. I don't know what they think she's into."

They discuss what happened and why and what they should do. The pair is deep into the conversation, for over an hour, when Lyle and Terrance walk in.

"Hey, buddy, how you hanging?" asks Lyle.

"Good as new, *Buddy*," Smith retorts sarcastically.

"Glad to see you're alright, Jake, "Terrance sincerely voices.
"Thanks, Don."

"What's going on, Jake?" Lyle demands.

"Just another day at the office, Steve."

"What were you doing in Mexico?" Lyle cuts to the chase.

"Just a little outing," Smith says. "You know shopping and enjoying the day."

"And you are kidnapped?" unbelieving Terrance.

"Must have thought I was a rich American," grins Smith. "Lucky Alex got away and Davis saved me."

Turning to Alex. "How did you get away?" Lyle not having heard the whole story from Davis and surprised that Alex had been with Jake.

"I wasn't with Jake at the instant he was grabbed and was in another shop." Without elaborating.

"I solved another case for you guys," Smith pops up, smiling.

"Which one would that be?" Lyle asks before Jake can continue.

"Ortiz's murder. You should take a hard look at Virginia Small."

"Small? What has she got to do with it?"

"Ask her about their broken engagement."

"Small and Ortiz? I..."

The group interrupted. "Good morning, Gentlemen." Reporter Small sticks her head through the door.

"Ms. Small, what are you doing here?" Terrance questions, but cannot believe their good luck.

"Came to check on Jake." She looks at Smith with sympathetic eyes.

"I'm fine, Virginia, thanks," Smith acknowledges. "How did you hear?"

"It's all over town... you know there aren't any secrets."

"Virginia, we were coming to see you after checking on Jake here." Terrance slyly winks at the reporter.

"Great, do you have a story that needs reporting?"
Nevertheless, thinking *it's about time these Bozo's start co-operating with me.*

"Yes, a good one!" Lyle grins from ear to ear. "Let's give Jake a break and we can go to our office and have a little talk!" Commanding more than suggesting.

As the three get into the hall out HAI's office, FBI agents, Davis and Morris turn the corner, off the stairway.

"Popular spot," Davis quips. Turning to his partner. "We'll have to come here more often."

"Agents," acknowledges Lyle. "He's all yours. Good luck!"

Morris and Davis enter Smith's office. "Good morning Jake, Alex," together as if they were twins.

"I'm going to start charging admission." Smith looks disgusted. He was hoping to lay down for a while.

"How are you feeling, Jake?" asks Special Agent Davis.

"It would be better if I could get a little peace and quiet!"

"We'll be quick. Just need to know what you can tell us about yesterday?"

"I already told you everything I know on the ride back. I don't remember if I thanked you guys. I really, really appreciate you saving me. Surely would be dead otherwise."

"Just doing our job, Jake. And I'm sure you would have done the same for us," Morris comments.

"I'm not so sure," jests Jake.

"So tell us everything you remember. Who took you and why?"

"It's like I just told the traveling dog and pony team, don't know why I was chosen, maybe mistaken identity, for ransom or whatever."

"What did they ask you?"

"About family and friends. I think they wanted to know who has money... you know who would pay for my freedom. It's a short list." He smiles at Alex.

"Then why would they hurt you?" Davis does not trust a word, leaving Smith's parted lips.

161

"They didn't like my sunny disposition?" Eyebrows raise.

"Jake, we know it has to do with Ortiz smuggling drugs and the Melendez Cartel!"

Drugs think Smith. Now he knows how his client was involved. He needs to get these people out of here so Alex and he has a chance to go over the new ledgers. *I hope Alex still has them* still to himself. He looks questioningly at his partner.

Alex does not have a clue what he is on his mind and only smiles back.

"They didn't mention drugs, but come to think of it, they did ask about Ortiz's business. Maybe they thought I was more involved with Diego than just doing a couple simple background checks for him."

"Who did you investigate for Ortiz?"

Back to this crap! "Some Mexican National, trying to get legalized, Jesus Jimenez or something like that. All Spanish names sound alike to me." Winging it as he goes.

"Ortiz was an immigration attorney for years. He must have already had an investigator. Why would he always a sudden come to you?"

"Diego and Emily Vargas have been friends for years and she got me in."

"Your friends with the owner of Emily's Cafe?"

"I've been going there ever since I came back to San Diego. We got to know each other."

"Got back to San Diego?" Morris surprised. "You lived here before?"

"SDPD for years," Smith looks gleeful.

"And you quit and left and came back?"

"Got tired and moved to Arkansas for a little slower pace." Jake looks at his fiancé. "Best move I ever made."

"So why did you come back?"

"Wanted to start my own business and Arkansas didn't offer a big enough market. Besides, I know people here who could refer clients to me. It's was the logical choice."

"Give us specific questions they asked you!" demands Davis, back to the subject at hand.

"Sorry, Chief, I was so out of it, I don't remember much." He decides to give them a tidbit to get them to go out investigating and leave him alone. "They did ask about Diego's wife in Mexico." Jake tries to conclude the interview. "That's when I passed out and never heard another thing!"

"Alright, Jake, we'll let you get some rest. Call us if remember anything."

Back in the hall, Davis is pissed. "Smith isn't telling what he knows!"

CHAPTER THIRTY-THREE
Lyle Interviews Small

Detectives Stephen Lyle and Donald Terrance arrive at the station with Virginia Small in tow, to interview her about the Ortiz relationship.

Terrance pulls a chair to the edge of the desk in the squad room for her to sit in. They are going to talk to her in the more casual setting than in an interrogation room. Not to tip her off, before they pounce.

Terrance asks if she would like a coffee, and told yes with cream and two sugars. He heads off to accommodate the reporter and grab a cup for Lyle and himself. In the meantime, Lyle conducts small talk with the woman, asking about her job and if she has heard anything new about the Ortiz murder.

She responds, "No, I was hoping you had something to share. The streets are quiet and nobody is opening up. I don't think anybody really knew him."

Don returns with the three coffees and sits to join the conversation. He overhears her last comment and responds, "I think there are people who were close to him. You know at least a girlfriend or two."

"A girlfriend? I've seen the articles about his entertaining various woman, but I always thought he was gay, and that was just a put on."

"Gay!" Lyle exclaims, "I understand you were engaged to him!" Obviously, the time arrives to apply pressure on the woman.

Her turn to act surprised. "Engaged! Heavens NO! I barely knew the man and only from a reporter's standpoint!"

"Well… if he was gay, do you think he gave Clyford Rampton a ring too?" Lyle grins.

It is the first time the detectives ever saw Small turn a bright shade of red and at a loss for words. *So, that's why I'm here* she thinks as she tries to formulate a response to the question.

"Ms. Small, you were enraged to Ortiz weren't you?" Lyle bluntly asks.

"I… I was until he told me the wedding was off because he found a man," She fibs.

"What man was that?"

"I don't know, he wouldn't say."

"Virginia, we need you, to be honest with us!" Terrance demands. "We have a witness to your conversation and actions at the Pacific Beach Cafe on the night *you* broke off your engagement and there wasn't any talk of another man!" He flat out lies.

Back in quiet thought, it is several minutes before Virginia answers. "When he asked me out that night, I could tell there were problems and pushed him. That's when he told me… his sexual preference. The restaurant incident was only the final act. Returning the ring." Making it up as she goes along.

"Where were you Friday night, August third?" He adds, "After your dinner with Ortiz."

"I… I went for a drive up the coast. Stopped at the cove and watched night divers' lights shining on the ocean surface for hours, before going home to bed." The fibs keep coming.

"What time did you get home?"

"I don't remember. It was late, maybe two or three in the morning."

"Any you *stopped* by Diego's office on the way!"

"No, I never saw that man again! Do I need a lawyer?"

"That's up to you! Who saw you at the cove?" The questions keep coming.

"I don't know, tourists, I imagine. Nobody I personally knew."

"And did anyone see you at your house?"

"I want a lawyer now!"

Lyle slides the phone across the desk. "Call him. Then we all will continue!"

The detectives leave the room and go into Lieutenant Holden's office. Terrance stands at the blinds and keeps an eye on Small while Lyle explains the situation.

"Good work, detectives. How did you get onto Small?" Holden asks after Lyle finishes his story.

Sheepishly, "Jake Smith told us."

Breaking out in a hearty laugh. "Stephen, you're never going to be rid of Smith."

"Give me a break, Lieutenant, Smith has been friends with Small for years. He just happened to let it slip." Lyle is becoming a chronic liar.

"Or Smith is just trying to divert attention from himself!" It dawns on Terrance and he voices his thought.

A half-hour later, Cooper Madison strolls into the squad room and talks quietly with Virginia. The detectives re-enter their office and suggest they all go to an interview room.

"I need to be alone with my client first!" demands Madison.

"Fine, let me show you to a room." Terrance leads the pair down the hall to Interrogation Room C.

The detectives sit at their desks for a half hour, before Madison enters the squad room. "Detectives, my client has nothing to say at this time. If you're not charging her with any crime, we're leaving." He stands and waits to see if they really have something or not.

"Don't let her leave town, Madison!" Lyle commands. "We'll have everything together soon enough!"

Small and her attorney leave the station and Lyle gets on the horn to ADA Jillian Ross. He needs a search warrant for Small's home, car, and office.

After explaining to the ADA, what he has, Ross retorts, "You might have enough, showing they had a violent public argument on the same night as the murder. Let me see if… " After a moment of contemplation, "Judge Huater will sign one. I'll get back to you."

CLICK!

For the next hour, the detectives call Smith, Small's boss and peers, and Emily Vargas. Smith admits Rampton, the Union reporter, is the one that confided to Alexis, and Lyle speaks directly to her to get the exact conversation before phoning Rampton.

Terrance is on the phone to Chanel 8's News Room talking to Virginia's manager and co-workers. None of them admits to knowing of the Small-Ortiz relationship. Next, he calls Emily Vargas.

After putting Emily on the spot and mildly threatening her with police interference charges, she admits that she was aware of the engagement. The cafe owner freely badmouths Small and emphatically states that they were not a good match and Diego would have been better off without her. In addition, she had witnessed Small's hidden rage, and that she saw her actually hit Diego in the face on one occasion. Emily changes *hit* to *slap*. Terrance also discovers Diego has a wife and family in Mexico.

Off the phones, the detectives exchange information.

"Now, we know why Smith was in Mexico!" screams Lyle, as he is dialing Smith again.

Alex tells the detective that Jake had just stepped out. "What do you mean stepped out? I thought he could barely move?"

"You know Jake, can't keep a wounded dog down for long!" Giggles Alex as Lyle slams down the phone.

RING! RING!" Detective Terrance here." After a brief listen. "Thanks, Jill."

"We got the warrant! Let's go!"

CHAPTER THIRTY-FOUR
No Gun

ADA Jillian Ross gets off the phone with Detective Terrance and immediately calls Private Investigator Jake Smith, her former lover. "Hello Alex, may I speak to Jake?"

Minutes later. "Hello Ms. Ross, what's up?"

"Jake you don't have to be so formal, why don't you call me Jellybean?" Jill offers.

No response as he tries to figure out the implications of using his former pet name for his former lover.

"Jake, are you still there?"

"Oh yeah, I'm here. What can I do for you?" Deciding not to use any label for her at this time.

"I just heard about your condition and wanted to see how you're making out?" Jill asks.

"I *make out* really well, thank you!" Jake answers sarcastically with a pun.

A small giggle. "You don't have to remind me!" Receiving no response. "I thought you would like to know Lyle has a search warrant for Virginia Small."

Pseudo shock. "Virginia! What on earth for?"

"Jake, you don't have to play dumb with me. I know you sicced them on her!"

"I only mentioned that Diego and she had been engaged... at one point. Don't know how long their affair went on or when they broke up. You know Ortiz was a real player?"

"Well, they're searching her place as we speak. Oh, and she lawyered up. Do you know Cooper Madison?"

"Doesn't ring a bell."

Diego Killer

"He's fairly new in town. I guess you were in Arkansas when he breezed in. Young, good looking and unbelievably aggressive!"

"Young, good looking and aggressive, sounds like you definitely met him! How is Jerrod anyway?"

"Jake, you know as well as I, that was only a wakeup call for *you.* I'm so sorry it ever happened."

"Water under the bridge. I better get back to work." Thinking *how can she blame me when she was the one that cheated!*

"If you need anything, chicken soup or something else, or if you just want to talk, please call me."

"I don't have your number anymore!" Hoping she gets the message.

"It's the same as always, and you know where I live. Take care of yourself and I hope to see you soon, Jake." In her most sultry voice.

He hangs up without answering. Though Jake does not admit it, he misses Jellybean.

"What did that woman want?" Alex enters Jake's office. She knows the story of how Jillian Ross broke up with her man.

"Just wanted to let *us* know that Lyle and Terrance are searching Small's place. She hired an attorney." Considering the current state of affairs. "Maybe she did do it," mumbling almost to himself.

"Maybe? I don't know her, but a rejected woman in love can be capable of anything. So you better watch your step, Mister!" She kids her fiancé.

"Yeah." Not really listening. "I think I'm going to drive over and see how the search is going." Jake struggles to stand while gripping his chest and exhausting a slight moan.

"Honey, you not up to working yet. You need at least a week to recuperate! Besides, they wouldn't let you in. And I'm sure Lyle, won't tell you anything!"

"They won't even have Small if it weren't for me... err you. I'll explain in unequivocal terms that they own us!"

Jake is struggling to put on his coat and Alex jumps in to assist him. "I'm driving!"

169

"I thought you'd never ask." He smiles broadly.

"I'm *not* asking!" She grins back.

On the ride over, with Alex driving and Jake navigating, she looks hard at her man. "How do you know where she lives?"

Breaking out of deep thought. "Huh?"

"I asked how you know where we are going?" rephrasing.

"Oh, I went there once."

"When!" she demands.

"It was a long time ago. I think I was dropping off a deposition or something. Anyway, I wasn't supposed to collaborate with her, but thought something in the news might help our investigation."

"And you still remember where she lives?" Getting madder by the second.

Laughing hysterically between coughing and gasping for breath as his chest rips into uncontrollable convulsions.

Alexis slams the car to the curb. "Jake, Jake! You have to calm down!" After watching for less than a minute, she drops the shifter back into drive and takes off like a rocket heading to the nearest hospital.

After an EKG to check for heart complications, Jake injected with muscle relaxants, painkillers, and a sleeping aid.

He wakes hours later, still in an emergency room curtained cubicle. He peers groggily through hazed eyes around the dimly lit room trying to figure out where he is.

The curtain whips back and head jettisons in. "Sorry to disturb you, Sir. Housekeeping." The older woman scurries around picking up small wrappers and other insignificant trash from the floor and dumping the corner can into a large heavy-duty plastic bag suspended in a frame on her cart.

As she is about to close the curtain, a nurse catches the hem. "Thank you, Maria, I'm going in."

"Mr. Smith, glad you're back in our world."

Jake puts his hand on his chest. It feels different. He lifts the neckline of the ill-fitting loose gown and peers in. There are large lumps under a new Ace bandage wrapped tightly around his body. "Jeez, how many rolls of tape did you use?"

"I'm your nurse. My name is Judith. How are you feeling, Mr. Smith?" She grabs a blood pressure cuff and thermometer.

"I'm fine. Only the wraps are too tight. I can hardly breathe!"

"That's the idea, no breathing, no moving! When you leave here in a couple of days, you're going straight home to bed for two weeks minimum!"

"I'm ready to get out of here now! Where's Alex?" Jake tries to sit up.

Nurse Judith pushes him down. "You don't want me to restrain you!"

She takes his blood pressure and temperature. "Everything looks good." The nurse looks Jake over. "Do you need another blanket or pillow?"

"I need to leave!"

"You're not going anywhere until Dr. Ittingen releases you!"

"Great. Send him in."

"The Doctor is in surgery. *She* should be here again in the morning."

"In the morning! She'll have to visit me at home!" Jake commands.

"Can I get you something to eat or drink?" The nurse refuses to acknowledge his comment.

Rubbing his eyes in disbelief. "Coffee, black and strong… and throw in a little brandy… on second thought make it a lot of brandy!"

The nurse smiles at him and leaves. She has heard that stupid remark at least once a day since graduate school.

Late that afternoon, Alex is back. Jake has dozed off and she sits quietly watching the sheets rise and fall. The curtain pulls back. "Oh! You surprised me, I didn't notice you sneak in." The late shift nurse enters.

"I don't sneak!" Alexis almost offended.

"I didn't mean it literally!" Apologetically.

Jake's eyes pop open, noticing Alex. "Hi honey, are we ready to go?"

The nurse moves and catches Jake's eye. "I don't think you've been released yet." She picks up his chart. "Sorry, Mr. Smith, it looks like you're staying for a day or two anyway. I'm your nurse for the evening…"

Before she can introduce herself, Smith interjects, "We're not getting acquainted. I'm leaving NOW!"

The nurse pulls a syringe and a small bottle out of a locked cabinet.

"What do you think you're doing?"

"This will help you relax." She squeezes the liquid, through the needle into the IV tube.

"I don't need to relax and NO more drugs!" Smith screams too late.

"Mr. Smith, glad you're awake. I hear you were spunky last evening! I'm Dr. Ittingen." The visitor enters Smith's cubicle. We'll just have a quick peek and you how you're doing."

"I'm feeling great, Doc. Really great! Will be much better recuperating at home though!"

After Ittingen's half-hour quick peek, Jake's discharge takes almost two hours.

As Alex is driving Jake to their loft, "You need a few days of rest. Doctor's orders, dear! By the way, we got a new client yesterday. It'll take me a couple of days of research while you get on your feet."

She waits for a response.

Finally, Jake asks, "Do I have to guess?"

"I think that would be fun. Let's see, the first hint, the last name starts with M."

"M? I was thinking S!"

"You're no fun! How did you know it was Small?"

"I had a lucent moment early this morning and gave her a jingle to see how the search went. Who's M?"

Diego Killer

"Madison, her attorney!"

CHAPTER THIRTY-FIVE
Murder Arrest

Lyle and Terrance serve the search warrant on Small's home and office. Nothing found in the office. In her home, they find a shoebox filled with love letters and notes from Diego Ortiz, dating back three years. The box also contains a few letters to Ortiz that she never sent.

They put out a BOLO on Virginia Small's puke-green VW bug.

Within a few minutes, they get a hit on the vehicle; it parked a half a block from Smith's office. Lyle and Terrance saddle up and ride to Smith's place.

Walking into HAI, the detectives overhear Virginia Small talking to Jake and Alex in the inner office. They stand quietly eavesdropping from the other room.

"I just don't know what to do," Virginia comments.

"If you're innocent you have nothing to hide. If I were you, I would cooperate with SDPD. Alex and I will get started on your investigation today and see what they have!" Smith responds.

Since Small's attorney hired them the day before, the PI has already made a couple of phone calls trying to confirm her alibi. The only one who saw her that night was the restaurant manager and he confirmed the argument and Small furiously leaving in the middle of their meal.

"Virginia Small, you are under arrest for the murder of Diego Ortiz!" Lyle proclaims loudly while the detectives break in on the meeting. He continues, "Please stand and turn around!"

Virginia cannot hold back the tears as she complies, with Terrance locking on the cuffs behind her back.

"Jake, please hurry! I won't make it in jail!" she sobs.

"I'll call Madison and have him meet you at the station!" Smith directs, "Stay strong and don't say a word until your attorney is present!"

Lyle glares at Smith. "Now, you're giving legal advice!"

"Not *one* word, Virginia!" Smith repeats.

At the station, the detectives escort Small into an interview room and remove her cuffs. "Have a seat!" commands Lyle. As she sits, Lyle walks around the table and sits across from her. Terrance leans casually against the adjacent wall, arms crossed in a dominant position.

"While we're waiting for Madison, why don't you tell us how you hurt your arm, Virginia?" Lyle questions while looking at her left arm scab, which was a fully wrapped wound at the murder scene.

"I… I slipped into the edge of my car door on spilled gasoline while filling my car the other day." She makes up, not remembering the story she told Smith at the scene.

"Can you empty your purse on the table?" Lyle continues.

"No! I'll wait for my lawyer."

"It's not a question!" Terrance moves to the table and grabs her purse off her shoulder. He dumps the contents on the workstation. "Well, looky here!" Small's Beretta Model 70 pistol clangs as it hits the wooden tabletop.

Lyle grabs the gun and checks the chamber. The gun is not loaded. He removes the clip and pushes seven live twenty-two long rifle shells from the eight-shell clip. One bullet is missing. "When was the last time you fired this weapon?" he asks while smelling the barrel.

"A couple of weeks ago."

"Friday night, August third?" Lyle asks.

"Ye… Yes!" The tears flow uncontrollably.

"That's the night, Ortiz was murdered!" Lyle loudly notes, slamming his hand on the table, scaring the bejesus out of the already terrified woman.

"B… but he was stabbed," she cries.

"Virginia, do not say another word!" Madison stomps through the door. "Detectives, you know better than to question my client without my presence!"

"We're just having a voluntary chat."

"If Ms. Small hasn't been formally booked or Mirandized yet, we're leaving! Come on, Virginia!"

Lyle stands, "Virginia Small, you are charged with the murder of Diego Ortiz. You have the right to remain silent. Anything you say can and will be used against you in a court of law. You have the right to an attorney. If you cannot afford an attorney, one will be provided for you. Do you understand the rights I have just read to you? With these rights in mind, do you wish to speak to me?"

"No, she doesn't!" responds her lawyer.

"Ms. Small I need to hear it from you."

Virginia nods her head.

"You must verbalize your answer for the tape!" Lyle states.

"Yes, I understand!"

"Let's go to booking!"

The four of them retreat to fingerprint and mug shot the suspect. In the hallway, they run into ADA Ross and exchange greetings.

Lieutenant Holden sticks his head out of observation room where he is overseeing the interview. "Ms. Ross, you can step in here." Holden briefs Ross as what has happened so far, and Small's responses.

"They shouldn't have talked with her without Madison present," the ADA comments, and then adds, "What's so interesting about the gun, Ortiz was stabbed?"

Holden backs up his detectives, stating that Small had not been officially charged, or booked, before their discussion. Ross is defiant that the detectives knew she had lawyered up and they should have waited. She adds that the detectives probably did not overstep, but certainly it is a gray area, and contestable in court.

Their conversation halts as the four return to the interview room.

"Ms. Small, can you tell us where you were when you fired your gun?" Lyle jumps right in where he left off.

"Detectives, I'm going to need some time to talk with my client before any further questioning," Madison speaks up.

Lyle and Terrance leave the two alone and step into the adjacent room with Ross and Holden.

"Let's go to my office," Holden offers. They have to give the lawyer and client, privacy.

Ross immediately asks about the gun again. Holden admits, Ortiz shot with a twenty-two and stabbed in the same hole after death.

An hour or so later the guard officer knocks on Holden's door and tells the group, "They're ready!"

Back in the room, Lyle repeats, his *where were you when you fired your gun* question.

Madison pats Virginia's arm. "It's alright to tell them."

"I was on the far end of La Jolla Shores, north of Scripts pier. It was late and the beach deserted. I… I was upset and took out my gun and fired it out to sea."

"And, nobody heard the gun go off?"

"I don't think so. Nobody came out. The houses in that area are higher up the cliff."

"What's the interest in the gun, Detectives?" asks the attorney.

"Diego Ortiz was murdered with a twenty-two long rifle," bluntly states Detective Lyle, "and Ms. Small admits to shooting her gun on the same night the murder took place."

"I thought he was stabbed to death?" The attorney caught off-guard.

"That's what the news reported," smiling at Small, "but it's inaccurate, he was shot first as she well knows!"

The shocked suspect and her representative are at a loss for words.

"Is it true, Ms. Small, that you had a long-term love affair with Mr. Ortiz, and he publicly broke it off, humiliating you the same night he was murdered?"

"It wasn't…"

"Don't answer that!" Madison interrupts.

"I want to," she goes on, "that is all true and why I was upset and went for a walk on the beach, and fired my gun."

"We're not answering any more questions at this time!" Madison stands.

Terrance looks at his partner. Lyle nods and Terrance opens the door and asks the guard to escort Ms. Small to a cell.

CHAPTER THIRTY-SIX
Business Ledger

The sun is rising above the downtown skyscrapers. It is going to be another August scorcher in Southern California. Jake suffered a painfully long night. His throbbing wounds only afforded an hour or so of sleep. Ortiz's six ledgers lay on the Smith's kitchen area table. It is just after six AM and Jake is staring at the stack of books, waiting for coffee to brew. Alex is still asleep in the open loft corner bed.

He walks to the window and watches the light Saturday morning traffic, wondering how Virginia Small is after her first night in jail. Alex rolls over in bed breaking his concentration and he snaps back into reality. Jake grabs a cup of black coffee and sits down at the table.

Spreading out the ledgers, he looks over the titles. *Law Business, Property Investments, Business Endeavors, Immigration Cases, Import Records* and *Money Channels*. Jake and Alex have already gone through the first two. The last four Alex had smuggled back from Rosarito a couple of days earlier, but they had not had the time to examine.

He grabs the *Business Endeavors* book and opens to the handwritten index. It lists five group headings and he turns to the beginning section, *Restaurants*.

The first page lists Emily's Cafe, and underneath, 1970: 80/20: weekly. Next tells a brief history in five bulleted descriptions. The first bullet, *Ensenada, Mexico in 1969; 1*. Second, *Aemilia Vargas, Montes Vargas, Tajo Vargas, Rosalinde Vargas*. Below that, *US citizenship; 1970*. Fourth, *433 Market Street, Downtown, San Diego*. Last, *1001*. Jake confused, wonders what those designations refer to, specifically, the numbers 1 and 1001. The others entries seem self-explanatory; Ortiz met Emily in sixty-eight, she's married and has two children, they are American citizens thanks to Diego and the cafe's location.

He continues to the next page, which starts with columns of numbers and entries for buying the cafe, remodeling, initial inventory and all related expenses for opening the business. The far right column shows the running total reflecting a deficit of $52,412.22.

Jake runs his index finger down the columns. During the first six months, the losses continue to increase, after which the cafe starts to make small gains. Four pages and a year and a half later, they are showing a profit. The profits grew slowly and steadily until present. One column lists payments to Emily, presumably wages or draws on the net profit, and another, lists considerably larger payments to Ortiz. By the time of his murder, Emily Vargas still owes him over forty-nine thousand dollars.

Smith jots down some numbers, makes a couple of calculations and studies them. Diego is taking eighty percent of profits plus a payment for the investment. At this rate, Emily Vargas will be paying him off until she turns one-hundred-sixteen years old. Jake thinks the business arrangement amounts to Emily being barely above slave labor and slowing starving.

Further into the book, the next restaurant, Surf Deli, and underneath, *1970: 70/30: weekly* and like entries to Emily's page. Subsequent pages are again columns of numbers. There are two more eating establishments containing same type entries. The ending business, in this section, is the Orange Street Liquor & Deli on Coronado Island.

Jake turns to the next section, *Stores*. First listed is South Border Foods, followed by a boutique and two clothing stores.

Onto the *Services* section. Listed is Southend Printing and Public Portrait. Both show Diego owning one-hundred percent and run by managers.

The fourth and fifth sections are *Legal & Accounting* and *Moving & Storage*. *Legal & Accounting* have entries for Filson

Accounting, the law offices of Hanover & Jackson and First Insurance, which includes a notary public, while the last section has three entries, Best Automotive, selling and servicing used vehicles, North Moving & Storage and City Trash Collection. North Moving pages show ownership in two storage facilities and a moving company. City Trash appears to collect waste from business and residents restricted to Diego's properties.

"Good morning, honey." Alex props up on her elbow looking at Jake. "How long have you been up?"

"A couple of hours. After your coffee and breakfast, we have some things to go over!"

An hour later, Jake is explaining what he found in the ledger.

Alex concludes, after looking through a couple sections, "The numbers, 1, 2, 3, etc., must be the order he set up each business and the four digit numbers are probably file numbers correlating to personal records."

They decide to start visiting businesses right away and see if any are open on Saturday. Sunday they reserve to examine the last three ledgers.

Alex makes a list in the order of places to stop by according to location. She uses their Thomas Brother's map book to construe a route. It circumscribes the county in a large jagged circle starting and ending at their loft.

By ten o'clock, the pair walks up Fifth Avenue to Public Portrait. The trek slow and tedious with Jake in a lot of pain and stopping frequently. Alex keeps suggesting he go back to the loft and she will investigate alone. He keeps refusing and pushing on.

The business is open and the small space crammed with men, women, and children waiting for passport photos. There is a fellow taking the pictures from an old bellows-extended press camera at a makeshift sitting area against the south wall. The opposite wall is loaded with formal portraits from their backroom studio.

"Please take a number!" A woman yells, above the room buzz at the couple.

The new arrivals approach the counter. Smith reviews his notes before asking, "Is Pasqual Agosto here?"

"He's busy." Pointing at the man behind the camera. "Your turn will be in an hour. Name?" Pen in hand, ready to write.

Smith immediately flashes his outdated SDPD badge. "Better make it now!"

"I'm Mrs. Agosto. I help you?" answering in broken English.

"We're investigating the Ortiz murder!" Smith states and stands quiet, watching for a response.

"Diego wonderful man. He help us immigrate here."

"And your boss. He owns this place!" Smith pushes.

"*Si*, help us and work for him. He always be… " searching for a word, and ends in Spanish, "*muy generoso.*"

Both PI's know that is a lie. Alex tries a little sweetener, "Alda, we know he underpays you and works you to death. We're here to help you."

"How you know my name?"

"We know a lot about your family, and like I said, we are here to help you get treated fairly."

"What can police do? Diego dead. Mr. Filson new boss."

"Derrik Filson, the accountant?" Smith surprised.

"*Si*, take over *negocio*… ah, company."

Smith thanks her and leaves with Alex trailing behind. On the sidewalk, she asks, "What are you thinking, she was talking freely, we could have found out a lot more about Diego's methods of operation!"

As they struggle back to their car, parked close to HAI, Smith explains his theory. The only two businesses that Diego was involved with, as a minority owner, are the accounting and other attorney firms. The rest, he controls up to a one-hundred percent! These two; he only owned twenty percent of each even though he put up a hundred percent of the cash to open them." Jake goes on to surmise that Diego needed those people to be loyal beyond the realm. They must know everything Diego did, and help control the kingdom!

After listening to Jake's conjecture. "Filson controls the money and the law firm could specialize in immigration, too. So both firms are in as deep as Ortiz!" Walking quietly for a couple of blocks, "We suspect they were smuggling in their own clients. Maybe Diego worked behind the scenes with the other lawyers being the front men. You know an extra layer of protection for him." Alex goes on, "So, Melendez wants in on the action and snatches you, to see if you're involved. You know, since you suddenly start showing up in Mexico, talking with Contreras and Siena."

"Or, just maybe, Filson and Contreras teamed up with Melendez to get rid of Ortiz and take over the complete operation," Smith verbalizes his thoughts.

"That would mean Small really has nothing to do with the whole mess," Alex states, though she had been excited to get Small out of Jake's life.

By noon, they pull into the parking area of Southend Printing. The business is closed. Alex checks her map and they move on to the other destinations. The only ones open are the retail and eating-places. All speak highly of Diego and not admit to any problems.

They end at Emily's Café, for an early supper, and hope the proprietor will be working. They are in luck. While eating Emily Vargas approaches their table. *"Buenas tardes, Amigos."*

"Good afternoon, Emily. Do you have a minute?" Alexis asks as she slides over on the bench seat. "Sit with us."

The cafe is slow before the dinner rush. Emily looks over the almost empty room. "I do need a break." She sidles in beside Alex.

"Emily, we've been friends for a long time," Jake starts. "You introduced me to Diego and got me a job with him."

"Oh yes, I like to help people," she responds.

"And I appreciate your help and friendship. It's time I return the favor!" Jakes sets her up.

"You owe me nothing, Jake. I helped both, you and Diego."

"But you didn't help yourself." It is time to get to the point. "I have Diego's records of your dealings with him. He screwed you!"

"Oh no, *Señor*, he saved me… and my family!"

"Emily, we both know two things. One, he did save you from whatever your life was in Mexico, but two, he exploited you in the process!" Smith waits. When no response comes, he continues,

"You do all the work and Diego took eighty percent of the profits, plus loan payments He was charging you for the total setup of this." he waves his hands around the room. "You know you work like a dog for very little money and you'll never own the cafe?"

"Not true, Jake, I own it now… building and all, one hundred percent!" Smiling wide, showing every tooth.

"You own everything?" Quickly putting it together. "Free and clear with Diego's passing?"

"Yes, that was our deal, though I will really miss, Diego."

"Whose idea was it to bequeath this to you?"

"The accountant's, I think. Or maybe the bank's, I'm not sure." Emily acts confused.

"Why would a bank be involved?"

"Diego took out a loan to open the cafe. He was struggling in those days and didn't have the money. It is a government insured SBA loan with Union First. As a partner, I had to sign the papers too. The bank insisted we both take out a term life policy for the loan naming each other as Beneficiary. With the unfortunate death of Diego, I get everything."

"But, you still own the bank?" Smith not fully understanding.

"No, the insurance paid off the loan."

"Congratulations, Emily, we're so happy for you," Alex chimes in.

As the front doorbell keeps going off, Emily looks around. "I better get back to work now. I'll see you guys soon."

CHAPTER THIRTY-SEVEN
Business Visits

Even though Lyle and Terrance believe the murder case solved with Virginia Small in jail, they decide to start visiting Ortiz's businesses. The idea is to dig up enough dirt on Smith to put him away or the very least get his PI license revoked. Their first stop is Public Portrait.

Entering the downtown studio early Monday morning, they approach the man behind the counter, and show their credentials and ask to speak to the owner.

"I'm Pasqual Agosto, the manager. How can I help you? My wife told the other policemen everything."

"What other policemen?" pops up Detective Lyle.

"The man and woman who were here Saturday morning."

"That damn, Smith," Terrance mutters.

Lyle overlooks his partner's observation and asks, "Who is the owner?"

"The business is owned by Mr. Filson."

Shocked at Filson's name, "What about Diego Ortiz?"

Puzzled, Pasqual states, "Mr. Ortiz died. When I first came to this country. I was a photographer in Mexico when I met him and he told me he could help us move to San Diego and get me a job."

"So you were trying to emigrate and was referred to Ortiz?"

"I was not doing well and running a Zebra cart in Tijuana. Mr. Ortiz and a very attractive brown-haired woman sat for a souvenir picture. That's how we met."

"And you found out he was a lawyer and asked about coming to America?" Lyle puts words in the man's mouth.

"Oh no, Mr. Ortiz asked me if I would like to move to San Diego. He assured me he could get me American citizenship and a job at his photo business," the manager is forthcoming.

"So Ortiz approached you? Tell us about the process to enter this country!" demands Lyle.

"Process?"

"Yes, process! What did Ortiz do for you?"

"First, he got me a work visa. For almost a year I walked across the border and a car picked me up and dropped me off here."

"That must have been expensive! How did you pay for it?"

"Mr. Ortiz is truly a saint. He paid for everything and we pay him back with a small amount from our paychecks."

"Your attorney put all the money up front… as a loan, and then, got you a job to pay him back?" Lyle is confused

"Yes. When Mr. Ortiz had finished the paperwork, me and my wife moved here. Mr. Ortiz found us an apartment and got us a car. He is sent from God!"

The detectives thank the man and leave. Sitting in their department vehicle, they go over what the photo store manager told them.

Finally, Terrance asks, more to himself than his partner, "What kind of attorney goes around soliciting clients in TJ, supplies them with papers, transportation, an apartment and a car, all upfront, and then takes payments."

"One that's betting on the long game! And a bigger payoff somewhere downline!" Lyle spits out.

"And what about Smith and Dench. We need to pick them up for obstruction, interference and impersonating police officers!" Terrance changes the subject.

Lyle and Terrance spend the day going from one Ortiz business to another. They find about half the stories similar to the Agosto's tale and most others did not comment either way, with two not available for the interview. Many mentioned the previous police visit.

Back at their office late that afternoon, Lyle phones NIS Agent Silvester Adams, who had been at the alphabet agencies meeting, the day after the murder. Adams is investigating Ortiz as a *coyote*, a human smuggler. He had been on Ortiz's trail the longest of all investigators.

Detective Lyle explains what they have discovered about Ortiz funding the immigration of families and how the operation worked, or that least how it started.

Lyle's openness to cooperate with NIS prompted Agent Adams to follow suit, telling what he had discovered. "What I have found is he had multiple layers with each doing different jobs." He continues, "The first layer is located in Tijuana. I feel Ortiz had a manager who oversaw a team of recruiters in TJ and Mexicali across the California border from Calexico. And, separate managers for Nogales, below Arizona, in Sonora and Juarez, south of El Paso and Matamoros across from Brownsville in Texas. Each city manager has several people under them. The bottom layer pays well and receives incentive bonuses to keep their confidence. I never got to the city manager level, until a couple of months ago, with a newer street level hire. This woman had only been with the organization for a couple of weeks and had no loyalty when one of our agents got to her."

She ratted out her boss. Lucky for us he lived in Tucson and we picked him up."

"So you got a break. Did he lay out the organizational structure?" inquires Lyle.

"Well, sort of. No names, or locations, but he inadvertently made reference to four levels. That's how I figured out Ortiz's position, though there certainly could be more layers, and this guy just didn't know."

"Do you think Ortiz has other attorneys across the country doing the same thing he did personally in San Diego?"

"That's the million dollar question!" Agent Adams responds. "At this point, I think he must have people in the corresponding U.S. cities to facilitate the logistics of transportation and housing, and maybe temporary work situations, but... " he stops short.

"But?"

After a longer than normal pause, "But, I just don't know."

"How is he getting them across?" The detective, not ready to give up.

Another longer pause, "I don't see how any of that helps your investigation?"

Lyle's turn to think. Finally, "Silvester, your revelations are more helpful than you know. We now have many suspects to narrow down. All I need is a few local names of people Ortiz represented. If I can squeeze one of them into talking, it'll help both of us."

"Don't you have his client list?" surprised Adams.

"Not really. We're working on it, but there again… well, there's a lot of levels." Lyle not willing to admit the FBI is not sharing if they know and that bastard Smith is hiding everything.

"I have to get going, Stephen. We'll talk soon." Silvester hangs up on Lyle.

"That sounded interesting," comments Terrance.

"Yeah, really interesting. Let's pick up Smith. I'll tell you the rest on the road."

At Smith's office, Alex Dench tells the men that Jake went back to Mexico.

"Mexico! I thought he was in too much pain to work?" Terrance gushes out.

CHAPTER THIRTY-EIGHT
Small's Arraignment

Small, transported from jail to court for her arrangement hearing. Attorney Cooper Madison is waiting in a courthouse interview room. ADA Jillian Ross en route.

Two-court appointed sheriff's deputies drop-off Virginia to her waiting lawyer. Upon entering the room, one of them removes the handcuffs and orders her to take a seat. He tells Madison that they will be right outside and knock when he finishes. He locks the door behind him as he steps out.

After the *how are you* and small talk, they get down to business. Cooper explains the procedure for the arrangement and the probable outcome. "The Court will read the charges and ask for a plea. The State will try to insert some strong evidence while requesting no bail. I will tell that you're tied to the community and not a flight risk and ask for reduced bail. If we're lucky, really lucky, you could be out of here this afternoon."

"What exactly does that mean?" Virginia asks.

"If the judge grants bail, which I must tell you, in a capital murder case is unlikely, but if he does we can post bail and you can go home until the trial."

Tears well up in her eye sockets, "How long until a trial starts?" She knows from covering many murder cases for the news, that it could take a year or two or even longer.

"The Sixth Amendment gives you the right to a speedy trial. The problem there is it's a crapshoot. The State will try to request more time in continuances if their case is weak and they are looking for more evidence. Right now, all we know for sure is that they have circumstantial evidence, but that doesn't mean it's a weak case. On our side, the more time we have, the better the chance of preparing a winning case. I would not suggest a speedy trial!"

"I'm innocent! What could they have to prove otherwise?"

"Virginia, I'm sorry to say this, but it's not a case of innocence or guilt. It's what a jury believes and determines."

"I didn't do anything and want... *need* to get out of here! I can't live in jail for years!"

"Let's wait and hear what the judge says. We have sixty days from today's decision to request a speedy trial. But there again, they can request delays, and there is no time definition of what constitutes a speedy trial." Cooper adds, "We've got a little time, let's go through your story again."

They hear the door unlock and turn to look. A guard sticks his head in. "You're wanted in court!"

Small follows one guard down the hall with the second behind her and Madison trailing. The gaggle enters the side courtroom door. The room is almost empty, but every eye is on Small. ADA Jillian Ross sits confidently at the plaintiff table, wearing a fitted gray women's suit jacket over a solid pastel pink blouse and a small string of freshwater pearls, which Jake had given to her for the last birthday they spent together. The ensemble complete with a matching knee-length slightly darker charcoal skirt. She had been anticipating that Jake would show up for the hearing and wore the pearls to let him know she is still interested.

The black-robed judicature enters and the bailiff yells, "All rise! The Honorable Susanne Jenkins presiding."

She climbs into the box without looking at anyone and sits arranging a small stack of papers.

"Please be seated. The State of California versus Virginia Small." The bailiff finishes and moves to the sidewall. He stands defiantly, arms crossed, glaring at the defendant.

Judge Jenkins looks up. "Good morning, Miss Ross." Turning to the defendant's table. "And who do I have the pleasure of today?" Looking at the standing Madison. After returning acknowledgments, she looks at Small. "This is an arraignment hearing for the sole purpose of entering a plea and setting bail. Please stand for the reading of the charges."

ADA Ross jumps to her feet. "Your Honor, we waive the reading."

"Mr. Madison?" Jenkins looks at him.

"Your honor, we would like to hear the charges my client is accused of."

The judge gives a disgusted look at Madison. After, *the look* has time to sink in, "Are you sure, Mr. Madison?"

"Yes, Your Honor."

Succeeding the lengthy list of charges, Jenkins glares back at Small's attorney. "Are we good now?" However, it is a rhetorical question and she is not expecting an answer.

Madison leaps up. "Yes, Your Honor. Thank you, Your Honor," And he starts out of turn, "In the interest of saving time, the State has very little circumstantial evidence regarding my client's alleged involvement in the murder of Diego Ortiz. She…"

"Ross jumps faster than a mother stepping on a diaper pin, "Your Honor, this is not a trial and certainly not the time to turn it into one!"

Madison quickly throws out, "I just believe this travesty of justice should be terminated immediately, and if Miss Ross ever comes up with a definitive allegation it can be revisited at that time!"

"What are you talking about? My case is solid and ready to go now!" Ross, as mad as someone late for lunch, and getting pulled over for speeding.

The courtroom visitors are buzzing! The gavel is banging! "Everyone, sit down!" screams Judge Jenkins at the attorneys. "This is just an *arrangement* and continuing as scheduled! If there is another outburst, the room will be cleared, the suspect will be remanded to her cell and I will set bail as I see fit! Are we clear?" She glares at Small's lawyer.

Cooper Madison nods and sits. Ross still on her feet, as mad as hell.

H. David Whalen

"Miss Ross please take your seat!" The judge breaks Jill's raged hypnotic glare at Cooper. He casually smiles back.

"Ms. Ross, SIT DOWN!"

"Sorry, Your Honor," as she takes her seat, though not sorry in the slightest.

"Ms. Small, do you understand the charges brought against you?" the Judge asks.

"Yes," in a weak voice.

"Ms. Small you will have to speak up. How do you plea?"

"Not Guilty, Your Honor!" Madison breaks in, again jumping to his feet.

"I would like to hear it from your client, Mr. Madison!"

"Not guilty!" Virginia, loud enough to be heard from the sidewalk.

"Very well, now, let's get to bail. Ms. Ross?"

She stands. "Diego Ortiz was a very prominent attorney and outstanding citizen of our fair city. Ms. Small… " Pointing and looking at Virginia, she continues, "… has the means to flee this jurisdiction and the motive." Jill sneaks in, "As his jilted lover."

"Objection! There is no evidence that Ms. Small and Mr. Ortiz were lovers."

Judge Jenkins reprimands Small's attorney, "Mr. Madison, save your objections for the trial!"

Ross turns back to the bench. "Our overworked police force does not have the manpower to babysit Ms. Small until a trial can be set. I request no bail!"

"Mr. Cooper?"

"Your Honor, my esteem colleague appears to be overreacting. Virginia," using her first name to humanize her, "as a longtime public figure possesses unbreakable ties to this community. She only wants justice done and would never consider fleeing." He laughs and turns back to Jill, before continuing, "A flight risk is just ludicrous in this situation, I request release on her own recognizance." Cooper knows full well, that is a fallacy, but hopes for a reasonable bail.

"Bail set at one million dollars. Defendant remanded to custody. Bailiff, please restrain, Ms. Small." The gavel bangs!

CHAPTER THIRTY-NINE
Montes Vargas

Alex is up early. Jake is already dressed and at the table drinking coffee and reading the Union's article on Small's arraignment. She pours herself a mug and joins him.

"Anything interesting?" Alex inquires.

Jake lays the newspaper down. "Just Rampton's report on Small's hearing. She received a million dollar bail and is stuck in jail."

"That doesn't surprise me. "You need to let Small go through the court system. If she's innocent it'll come out." Alex tries to reassure Jake.

"I know she didn't do it. With all the illegal activity going on and so much money surrounding Ortiz, my bet is on Melendez. Besides, Virginia is a strong woman, and this isn't the first time a relationship didn't work out."

"And money is a stronger motive than jilted love?" Alex questions, "Sounds like you have firsthand knowledge of Virginia's love life?" Jealousy flows through her body.

Jake laughs heartily for many minutes. Finally, under control, "Honey, there was *never* anything between Virginia and me, other than a little professional courtesy, and I couldn't trust her in that area either." Remembering the times, she lied to him and screwed him over for the sake of a story.

"It doesn't matter now, Jake. How are you feeling?"

"Great! I'm a fast healer… and the Darvon doesn't hurt," he comments and smiles.

"Do you have plans for today?" Alex asks.

"I'm going to see Emily and then back to Mexico."

"Oh Jake, do you think that's a good idea?" Alex's face scrunched in concern.

"I need to press Siena on how much she really knows about Diego's affairs, business and personal. I better get going." After the last swallow of coffee, he mentions, "I think I'll stop and see Ed Martin too."

Jake walks down the block to Emily's Cafe.

"Hi, Maria, is Emily around?" He asks the only waitress he sees.

"Hey, Jake. No, she called in sick today."

He thanks her, and asks for Emily's home address saying he would like to send some get-well flowers. Maria knows Emily likes and trusts the PI and retrieves the Vargas' address for him.

After picking up his Corvette from the parking lot, Jake drives to the county morgue.

He peeks through the small glass window in the door. Inside the examination room, he observes coroner, Ed Martin is working on the first body in a full room of waiting cadavers.

Pushing the door open, "Morning, Doc."

Martin does not look up but keeps working. He pulls out a badly scared, dark brown three-pound liver and throws it into the stainless steel basket suspended from a hanging scale. Martin talks into the microphone hanging from his neck and describes the organ. He mentions the body's yellow jaundice appearance and concludes the woman was a chronic alcoholic. Finishing his entry, he glances up. "Hi, Jake, it's about time you came around." Ed briefly talked with his friend at the crime scene, for the first time in three years. He moves over to the visitor, removing the blue plastic gloves and shakes Jake's hand.

Smith and Martin have always got along well and actually like each other. "Sorry, I should have come in earlier, but was trying to keep a low profile for a while," Jake, making an excuse.

"Oh, I understand. I assume the Ortiz murder forced you out of the woodwork?"

Jakes breaks up and between laughter, "You know it did!"

"Let me get you a cup of coffee and you can tell me what's happening in your life."

The pair sits and talks for a while. Jake tells him about his new firm and engagement to Alex. The doctor is genuinely pleased for his friend. Then Smith gets to the real reason for the intrusion, Ortiz's murder. He explains his relationship with the victim and Small's arrest, and whom he thinks is the real killer.

"Of course I've been following Small's arrest. I never believed Virginia had murder in her blood." Doc inserts, "But, you might have something on your other suspect."

"Yeah, stabbing isn't the method of choice for a woman!" Smith states. "Poison, shooting or running over is a more believable modus operandi."

"Don't say shooting! Ortiz *was* shot. The knife, inserted after death and only as a misdirection!"

"Diego was shot to death!" The first time Smith hears the actual cause of death.

"I shouldn't have let that slip. It's kind of a secret, Jake. You can't tell a soul until the police publicize it!"

"My lips are sealed, Doc," Jake assures him and Martin trusts Smith. "But that certainly screws up my theory!"

"Don't let it! Keep on the associate angle. I certainly think that's more feasible."

"Thanks, Ed," Jake had never called him anything but Doc. "Let's get together. I'll have Alexis make a dinner."

"Sounds great. I would like to meet her. Just let me know where and when."

The men shake in unabridged friendship and Jake leaves ready to visit Emily.

He drives slowly down Logan Avenue until he spots the address.

At the door, Jake hears children crying and a dog barking. He reaches over and rings the bell. He has to ring it three more times before someone hears it and a man answers the door.

"Hola, Señor."

"Hi, uh *hola*. Is Emily here?" Smith asks.

"Un momento." He yells above the noise, "Amelia!"

"Shh, silencio!" the woman screams. *"Sacar al perro!"*

Jake assumes *perro* means dog and someone is going to remove the animal from the room.

Soon it is somewhat quiet and she comes to her husband's side. "Jake, what are you doing here?" Stunned at his presence.

"Hi, Emily. May I come in?"

"Of course." Directed to her husband, *"Déjalo entrar,"* as she steps inside and scurries around picking up toys and clutter.

Jake is shown to the couch and offered ice tea and cookies, which he refuses. Emily introduces Montes to him and tells Jake her husband speaks very little English.

"So what can I do for you, Jake?" she inquires.

"I'm sorry to come at such a bad time, with you sick and all."

She giggles. "Oh, I'm only sick of work and wanted a day off."

"I glad to hear that. You need a break from the cafe anytime you can get it," Jake responds with his own little laugh.

A small girl comes running to her Mother's side crying her eye's out. They speak back and forth in Spanish. Emily excuses herself and goes to another room to stop her children's bickering.

Jake addresses the man in the worn out recliner, "So Montes, what do you do?" He wants to be cordial and includes the man.

"Yo... I do... de mantenimieto." Not coming up the English work for maintenance.

"He's a handyman for Diego." Emily is back.

"You both work for Ortiz?" Surprised Jake.

"Diego buys a lot of houses and Montes fixes them up for families coming from Mexico."

"That's wonderful." Thinking about it, "I guess he's out of a job now?"

"Oh no, Montes is going to help me in the cafe," Emily shows her delight.

Smith realizes Diego's death is good for both of them.

H. David Whalen

"I just wanted to ask you if you know anyone who had a motive for killing Ortiz. I'm thinking Jose Contreras, in particular."

"I never meet him, though Diego mentioned him to me a couple of times. They were great friends… since childhood." Pondering for a couple of minutes. "I don't think Jose would ever have a reason to kill Diego." She adds, "I read in the paper they arrested that TV woman. She did it, huh?"

"The police think she did, but I'm not so sure," Jake responds.

They talk for a few more minutes. Emily does not admit to ever hearing of Pablo Melendez.

Jake excuses himself. He is going to Mexico.

CHAPTER FORTY
Mexican Federales

FBI Special Agent's Davis and Blazer sit in *Federales Capitán*, Edwardo Prieto's Tijuana office. Davis has worked with Prieto before, and the men do not particularly like each other. Nevertheless, they respect the other's position.

The men discuss Smith and Morris' health. Robert Blazer brought in, from Cincinnati, as Davis' new field partner, leaves Morris on desk-duty until his shoulder heals. During the time in Prieto's office, Bobby sits quietly and only listens.

"So, Agent Davis, what brings you to Mexico?" the *Federales* asks.

"Please call me Egan. I'm interested in a joint task force to bring down the Ortiz and Melendez organizations."

"We've been working on Melendez for quite some time. He is a real fox. I'm not familiar with Ortiz."

"Diego Ortiz is believed to be Melendez's U.S. conduit for drug imports." Davis goes on to bolster the perceived connection.

"I see," the captain, answers at the end of the agent's soliloquy.

"If you can turn up the heat down here and us, in the states maybe we can simultaneously break their criminal enterprises. Ortiz was murdered last week and with a battle for control, now the timing is right!"

Thoughtfully. "Do you know who is taking over this Ortiz business?"

"We think it is two-part, there is an accountant in San Diego and an attorney here."

Before Davis can go on, the *Capitán* asks, "Jose Contreras?"

"You're familiar with Contreras?"

"Yes, he is part of the Melendez gang. He represents them in court and spends too much time at Pablo's Ranchito."

"You have been following him?" Davis observes.

"We follow a lot of the Melendez's people." Especially Jose Contreras and Franco Trujillo."

"Who's Trujillo?"

"He's a bad man… a murderer. They call him Enforcer. This man travels constantly throughout Mexico and America. He has killed more than one of my men! We just haven't been able to catch him in the act or collect enough proof."

"Can you give me a copy of his and Contreras' files? I'll send them to Quantico and see what we have on them.

"Yes, we strike together! I'll get the files for you."

Prieto has a low-ranked man retrieve, and copy both files they have, including a recent photograph of each man.

The two officers put together a tentative plan contingent on the FBI's research on the Enforcer and the lawyer. The joint task force consummated. Prieto gives Davis a secure phone number to get in touch with him and Davis does likewise.

Outside on the street, Davis tells Blazer that they never had a connection between Ortiz and Melendez. He postulates that it is likely the two entities could have been fighting over the U.S. market and the Enforcer murdered Ortiz in an attempt for Pablo Melendez to take sole control.

They approach their vehicle and head home.

Once back at the San Diego FBI Headquarters, Blazer Xerox's the files Prieto gave them and arranges to have them overnighted to Virginia. Davis gets on their teleprinter machine, contacting Quantico, and notifies them of the coming files and request. He asks them to get together, anything they have on Franco Trujillo, Jose Contreras and Pablo Melendez. Davis already has an extensive file on Diego Ortiz.

Davis makes a matter-of-fact directive, "We need to take another crack at Smith. He must have Ortiz's missing files somewhere."

Without uttering a word, Blazer picks up the phone and calls Smith's office. While talking, his face turns white. He hangs up and cries, "That damn fool has gone back to Mexico!"

"When?"

"His secretary told me he headed there this morning, but had a couple of stops in town first."

Davis glances at the wall clock. It clicks eleven thirty-two. He gets on the horn to NIS officer Adams. "Sylvester, Smith is heading to Mexico!"

His partner overhears, "I don't know."… "It's possible he hasn't crossed the border."… "Put a BOLO on him."… "Have agents check all the parking lots for his Corvette!" Davis continues to relate all Smith's vehicle information, year, model, color and license number.

He hangs up and rotates to Agent Blazer. "Let's go to the border. If he's still in the country, they'll get him and hold him for us!"

Halfway to their destination, the radio comes alive. "Agent Davis, the Border Patrol has Jake Smith in custody. He is being held in room 214 on the second level. 10-4."

"At least we aren't picking up a body!" Davis breathes deep.

At the border campus, the FBI agents escorted upstairs. Blazer holds the door for his partner. Davis bursts into the room screaming, "Smith, what the hell do you think you're doing!"

"Agent Davis, it's nice to see you care!" Smith's sarcastic response.

"You *know* this isn't over! I need to know why they're after you!"

"The price you pay for fame and glory," grins Smith.

"It's time to cut the crap. This isn't a joke!" Blazer inserts.

"No *yoke*?" Jake cannot help himself.

"Can we have the room, gentlemen?" Agent Davis asks the three present Border Patrol officers.

When Smith, Davis, and Blazer are alone, "Jake, let me level with you, you are in the middle of a war between the Ortiz and Melendez organizations. We have set up a joint task force with the

Mexican *Federales* and are taking them both down." After a pause for effect, "Jake, I want to keep you alive and out of jail. To accomplish this fact, we need your cooperation." He waits for a response.

"We are on the same page, agent. I want to keep waking up on this side of the dirt, too. I don't know what I can help you with?"

"For starters, we need the files you stole from Ortiz's Chula Vista home."

"You searched my home and office, I don't have any files," Smith emphatically states.

"Jake, the paperboy saw you loading your car. It is time to work together." It kills Davis to be diplomatic with this unsavory man.

After a long silent pause. "Ok, Egan, I have some files and will turn them over to you," knowing the feds are never getting the six ledgers. Moreover, Alex has already made Xeroxes of the relative pages from the file boxes.

"Good Jake, you're making the right decision." Davis stands, Blazer and Smith follow suit. Egan shakes the PI's hand. "We'll follow you back to your office and pick them up."

"They're not there, as you well know. I'll get them and bring them to your office this afternoon."

"We'll all go to the location now, and you can hand them over." Blazer quickly suggests.

"I thought we are going to trust each other!" Smith stares at the new agent.

"We are, Jake, that'll be fine. This afternoon!"

"Of course, Egan."

The three walk out together. Outside, Smith leaves the agents at their vehicle, parked under the canopy and walks to the large dirt parking lot across the street to his car.

"We're going to trust that guy?" Blazer snaps at Davis.

"Hell no! Call the office and get everyone who is free in the south bay area positioned to trade off following him. We'll take it from, since he knows we're already heading in the same direction, and hand him off as soon as he tries to ditch us!"

Smith sits in his car with binoculars watching for the agents to leave. He cannot see their location under the carport and keeps his eyes fixed on the exits for twenty minutes. Not eyeing them, he assumes they got out before he arrived at his car. He leaves for home.

Davis and Morris get a call from upstairs. "He's pulling out!" The lead man starts the car and falls in a block behind Jake.

Smith took note of their car when they separated, and is driving with his eyes glued to his review mirror. A mile up Interstate 5 he spots them. "Those guys aren't that tricky." He laughs aloud and cycles through his scanner looking for their frequency.

Further, up the interstate, Smith pulls off on the Main Street exit and drives into lower Chula Vista. Jake spends the next two hours weaving through neighborhoods heading north. No other tail appears by the time he hits National City and he drives through to downtown San Diego and his loft.

That was too easy Jake tells himself.

CHAPTER FORTY-ONE
Jillian Ross

Jillian Ross walks into the offices of Hamilton-Adams Investigations Wednesday morning. Alex is behind her desk in the front office.

"Ms. Ross," Alex greets the ADA with a disgusted look. "What can I help you with?"

"Good morning, Alex. It's good to see you again. Is Jake around?"

"Have a seat. I'll see if he's free."

A minute later, Jake enters the room with Alex on his heels.

"Hi Jill, what's up?"

"Hi Jake, can we talk?" She glares at Alex. "Alone!"

"Alex is my partner now. Anything to do with HAI concerns her too!"

Alex slyly pinches his butt in thanks. Jake only reacts with a small grin. He knows he did well.

"Why don't we all sit in my office?" Jake holds his door open and motions Jill and Alexis to enter.

Jill starts by asking Jake how he is feeling and what happened in Mexico.

Jake only states that he is all right and asks if she would like a cup of coffee. The lawyer immediately accepts, knowing it will give her a few moments alone with her former boyfriend. Alex leaves the room to fetch coffees all around.

As soon as they are alone, Jill launches into how much misses Jake and would like to see him socially again.

"What about Jimmy?" Jake inquires.

"Jonathon. That was over before it started," she responds.

"Seems to me it started with a bang!" Jake remembers New Year's Day in nineteen-seventy when he walked in on them.

"Jake that was a miscalculation. I was only trying to force your hand into making a commitment."

Always a lawyer Jake thinks to himself. Before he can comment one way or the other Alex comes back carrying a small tray and three hot mugs. She hands one to Jill, sets a second in front of her man and sits holding the final one.

"Would you happen to have a little cream?" asks the attorney.

"Sorry, we're out." Alex grins.

"Black will be fine." A sickly sweet smile crosses her perfectly colored scarlet lips.

"So what have we been talking about?" questions the coffee girl.

"We were waiting for you," lies Jill. "I want to discuss Virginia Small."

"We're not involved in that case," states Smith.

"You're not?" Jill, acting surprised. "I hear you are investigating the Ortiz matter?"

"We're doing a little business research for his widow. The cops are investigating the murder," Alex pipes up.

"The cops, FBI, and just about every other federal agency. But, a private investigator doesn't get kidnapped and tortured in Mexico over *a little research*!"

"That was mistaken identity. They thought I was someone else." Jake has told that lie so often, he almost believes it.

"Someone else who had the *Federales* and FBI rescue him… and they get shot up in the process?"

"I respect our boys and their help. They apparently they return favors." Smith winks at his fiancé. He knows the district attorney's office is in the loop, however, two steps below the feds in his hierarchy.

"I realize you and Virginia have been friends for many years, Jake, and I thought you would like to help her. We are positive she is the killer, and I am prepared to offer her a deal and I would like you to talk to her first. You know, pave the way so she and Madison can make the right decision."

"What kind of deal?" Smith questions.

"Second Degree Manslaughter with a maximum ten years."

"That's not a deal for an innocent person!"

"I don't know how much you're privy to, but Ortiz was shot with a twenty-two and we have the gun!" Jill frankly states.

"Shot!" Putting on an act. "I thought he had been stabbed?"

"Shot first, stabbed second… a real crime of passion." Jill's turn to grin at Alexis.

"What do you think you have, Jill?" Jake is not sure how the crime actually went down but convinced Trujillo was behind it.

"Motive, opportunity, the murder weapon and a whole lot more," she responds.

"There are many people with motive and opportunity." Alex defends her partner's position but wonders if Jill's extra activities included Diego Ortiz.

"I have to get going. If you talk to Small, do it before Monday!" Ross stands. "And Jake, call me and let me know what you decide?"

When their alone, Alex asks, "What that was all about?"

Jake says he is not sure.

"Would you like some eggs?" she asks.

"Sounds good, dear."

As they share breakfast, Alex explains everything that she found in the last three ledgers. "*Immigration Cases* outline a complex human smuggling operation all across the border states and the money accounts. It's a huge operation managed by Jorge Hermie, living here, in San Diego. He is responsible for transportation and safe houses.

"Coupled with that, the *Import Record* shows that the illegal aliens brought in drugs at the same time. Once in the States, Lazarus Veliz took possession of the drugs and managed distribution. He also set up meth labs all over San Diego County.

"Both these men are under the direct supervision of Larry Hirsh. And, the *Money Channels* ledger refers to Hayden and

Reena Landry. It records investment partnerships with both Landrys and financial records of legitimate and illegitimate businesses and investments to launder the huge amounts of cash Ortiz was accumulating."

They spend the rest of the morning and most of the afternoon studying the books and making lists and flow charts. By three o'clock Jake tells Alex that he must take the files to the FBI and he will be back in a couple of hours. She tells him that she will keep working on the organizational layout.

Smith escorted directly to Davis's office. Morris sits at an opposing desk, in his upper-body cast, one-handed shuffling through stacks of papers. Bobby Blazer is on the phone, a desk over.

"Hey, guys," Smith interrupts, as he enters the room holding his wounded chest. A young suited FBI agent struggles with the three boxes of files, behind him. "I brought your stuff."

Looking up, Davis comments, "I started to think you weren't coming, Jake." Everyone refrains from mentioning the previous days tailing fiasco, except the PI.

"It's good to see you *all* you guys made it back from the border OK."

They ignore the comment. Everyone in the room knows Jake's border insinuation.

Looking at Morris. Smith asks, "How's the shoulder, Nat?"

"Fine, Jake. How are you feeling?"

The boxes are set on the floor adjacent to Davis' desk. Smith asks for a cup of coffee, Blazer sent to retrieve the beverage.

Jake starts in by saying, "I have been thinking, and came to the rather late conclusion that I don't want anything to do with Diego Ortiz. Alexis and I are planning our wedding and want to live a quiet peaceful life together. That said, here are your files and I'm out of it!"

"That's a wise decision, Jake. It's better for all of us."

One last thing… let me call it, a piece of advice; you should pick up Jose Contreras and get him up here."

"We're aware of Contreras, but Prieto hasn't been able to break him. If he ever comes to our side of the border, we'll will!" Morris adds, and questions, "What do you know about him?"

"I don't know any Pierto," Jake smirks. "So back to Contreras, he's culpable in both organizations and is in deep enough to know everything. He's a family man and if you offer him immunity and into the witness protection program he will probably be the easiest to turn."

They all thank each other and Smith leaves.

Davis looks at his two subordinates. "You know he's right!"

"About Contreras or getting out?"

The three agents belly laugh; all know Smith is never getting out!

CHAPTER FORTY-TWO
Mexico Calls

The following morning Jake Smith goes back to Mexico to see Jose Contreras and Siena Herrera.

He follows his same general procedure, parking and walking across into Tijuana. Jake grabs a taxi and goes downtown to Contreras' office.

He confronts the attorney head on, demanding to know about Ortiz's smuggling operations, both the alien and drug endeavors. When Jose declines knowing anything, Jake names Larry Hirsh, the San Diego manager, Lazarus Veliz, the drug supervisor, and Jorge Hermie, the coyote boss.

Contreras is astounded at Smith's understanding of the operation but continues his no knowledge of any illegal activity pertaining to his good friend and business partner, position.

After an hour of drilling Contreras, without learning anything he does not already know, Jake leaves and taxis south, to Siena's estate. Jake tells the driver to wait, that he will be an hour and agrees to pay for the time handing the man a US Benjamin.

The same approach follows with the familiar man picking Smith up at the gate and driving him to the main house where Siena is standing on the porch.

After getting comfortable, sitting in her living room and receiving a cup of coffee, Jakes asks her about Contreras and the illegal activities. Before she can answer, her intercom starts buzzing. Siena excuses herself and presses the receiver button. "Yes?"

"Señora, the police are ramming the gate!" frantic yelling coming from the voice box.

"Slow down, Manuel. I don't understand."

"There are five police cars and a pickup truck. They are ramming the gate to get in!"

"They didn't say want they want?"

"No, Señora, Men are everywhere carrying guns!"

"Thank you, Manuel." Siena turns to Jake. "I don't know what is happening!"

"I do. Contreras called his buddies, they want me!"

"What did you do?" she questions.

"It's a long story. I have to get out of here! Is there another way?"

"Yes, but you can't go north, they'll catch you. Come with me!" Diego's widow starts walking quickly down the hall with Smith close behind her.

"Where are we going?" he asks.

"We have an airfield east of Ensenada. I'll give you a car and directions. I'll call the pilot and get him ready."

Siena leads Jake to a new four-wheel-drive Ford Bronco and given him directions to the field. Siena tells him he will have to use four-wheel drive to get over the road leading in.

"Be sure to turn left right after the Tecate Beer billboard or else you'll have gone too far and won't be able to get back if they're after you! Watch your mileage closely. It's exactly forty-two point seven miles to the turn-off."

"Thank you, Siena. We'll talk soon."

Smith jumps into the vehicle and punches the gas. A few hundred yards down the road and he flies off the concrete onto a dirt road. Hitting the soft dirt, the Bronco slides wildly. Smith is panic-stricken trying to bring the vehicle under control. It ends up spinning and stalling in the deep sand beside the small road.

Smith springs from the truck and locks the hubs into four-wheel drive. Back in the driver's seat, he drops the shifter into low and lightly steps on the gas. The Bronco inches forward and he speeds up turning back towards the road, where he again hastily stomps on it. The vehicle fishtails wildly. Smith jerks the wheel into the slide and straightens it out before speeding down the road in a cloud of dust.

In the meantime, the cops have destroyed the gate and racing to the mansion. Siena is standing, under the car-canopy in the front yard waiting.

The cavalcade screeches to a stop on the concrete. One vehicle slides inches away from her legs before stopping completely. The army of men takes off running under the structure, towards the front door, while the charge man walks toward the woman yelling, *"Donde,* Jake Smith! *Donde,* Jake Smith!"

"I'm sorry, Sir, I don't know where Mr. Smith is," Siena lies.

He grabs her arm and squeezes as tight as he can, *"Donde,* Jake Smith, *Señora?"*

She screams in pain, "I don't know!"

"Teniente, there is a back road and a cloud of fast-moving dust!" A running officer hollers.

Men appear from everywhere, race to their vehicles, and speed off towards the destroyed front gate.

Siena says a silent prayer for Jake.

Hitting the old road south, the caravan pumps up the speed, lights flashing, sirens blazing.

Further south, Jake turns onto the main road and cranks it up to eighty. The sign he just passed reads EIGHTY KPM. All he saw is larger eight-zero. He glances at the speedometer and thinks *I'm doing eighty.* He missed the *kph* designation. The road is twisty and the old cracked asphalt rot with potholes. He bounces along crashing his head on and off the ceiling. The Bronco slams through eroded cavities and he yells aloud, "What the hell, nobody can do eighty on this stretch of crap!" He forced to slow down. Even sixty-five is too fast!

Jake takes frequent hurried looks in the rear-view mirror. At the end of a long straight away, the followers magically materialize. It scares the bejesus out of him and he tromps the gas again. For the next ten miles, Smith takes the curves too hard and the straights as fast as he can get his speed up. The vehicle bouncing and swerving like a Disneyland roller coaster.

The pursuers keep gaining. *How the crap, can they be going that fast* he stresses.

Smith glimpses at the odometer again, six miles to go, and the troopers are closer than two hundred yards behind. He has to push the Bronco harder.

By the time, he figures he is a mile from his turn-off the lead car is on his bumper. The front-seat passenger leans out the window and starts firing. Within a second, a man leans out the driver's side back seat joining the shooter in a barrage of gunfire.

Careening along through the ruts, only a few bullets hit their mark. The back window shatters as Smith's head missed by inches. Even his quick ducks would have been too slow if the air-splitting shots were true.

More and more bullets start whizzing by him through the cab. The windshield obliterates. He believes this is the end of old Jake Smith. Suddenly he rounds a corner and the Tecate billboard looms a quarter mile down the road.

How am I going to do this he thinks? Slowing down makes him a sure target, but without reducing speed, he will never make the turn! He has no choice and at the last minute, he slams on the brakes. The car behind him rams the Bronco. He is jolted into the seat. Whiplash instantly permeates his neck. Stitches rip from his excruciating chest wounds. Blood fills his shirt. Jake screams in pain as he jerks the four-wheel drive hard left into the sand. It is soft and he is glad the hubs already locked in four-wheel drive. The Bronco starts to slide. Jerking the wheel as hard as he can against the piling sand around the tires, he manages to get onto the almost impassable trail.

The ramming car slides sideways past the turn, tires locked and screeching. The second vehicle forces itself into the turn and ends up missing the road and into the sand. The driver presses the gas pedal to the floor. His tires spin, rooster-tailing sand, and digging in.

Jake takes a quick look in his mirror. "Two down!" he screams, as he shoots towards the first hill.

The next three are struggling to keep their vehicles moving.

212

Suddenly he spots the pickup jerking onto the sand and passing the slower cars. *Crap! That must be set up for off road too!*

The bronco and truck scale the hill in unison. Smith leads by a good fifty yards. The pickup cannot gain but is not losing ground either.

The two stay as one over the rough terrain and next two hills. Taking air as he crests the last summit, Smith spies the airstrip. It is within reach. The Bronco bounces to earth. Jake jerks the steering wheel back and forth trying to regain control. With the Bronco almost straight, he guns it.

Sitting on the hard oiled runway is a Cessna Citation 500, twin turboprop airplane. Both propellers are spinning as the aircraft warm's up. The gangway is down waiting for him.

The following pickup loses control after cresting the hill and hitting the ground. Off-kilter, midway down it veers off track. Unfortunately, for Smith, it does not roll and stays upright. The sand spewing the vehicle continues the pursuit. Fortunately, it gives Smith an extra minute to achieve freedom.

The Bronco slides sideways on the oil-covered tarmac and stalls forty feet from the plane. Smith jumps from the vehicle, grabs his oozing chest and starts running. He cannot turn his neck and has no idea how close they are.

Bullets start whizzing past him again.

"Prisa, Señor! Corre más rápido!" a man, standing in the doorway, yells.

Jake understands only that, he has to pick up his pace. The pain is unbearable, but life supersedes pain, and he tries to move his legs faster.

He makes the gangway and starts up the stairs. The truck slams to a stop with shooting men piling out of the back. Bullets are splattering the fuselage.

As soon as Jake dives into the cabin, the man starts raising the gangway and the plane moves forward. Within minutes, the plane lifts off. After a steep climb, they reach an altitude of eighteen thousand feet and a cruising speed of four hundred miles-per-hour.

Smith helped into a seat. There are only three people aboard, the pilot, the steward and Smith on the nine-passenger airplane. The steward runs for towels and water and helps Smith remove his shirt. Blood wiped and his chest cleaned. The man gets a first aid kit and the two try re-bandaging the wounds as best they can. Eventually, the steward lays a blanket over the oozing body and asks, "Would you like a drink of water or a sandwich, *Señor?*" Smith refuses food but asks for a bottle of aspirin and glass of water. He quickly swallows a small handful and reclines the seat.

Jake feels the plane make a hard left-hand turn, before passing out.

When he opens his eyes, he is mystified that they are over the Pacific. Jake strains to look out the window. He cannot see land and wonders where they're flying. Without much more thought, he falls back to sleep.

An hour later, the steward gently shakes Smith's shoulder. "*Señor*, we are preparing to land. You should sit up and fasten your seat belt."

"Thanks." He looks out the window. "Sir, where are we?" They seem to be flying very low over the ocean.

"We'll climb momentarily. We are landing in Ramona."

"Ramona? Why aren't we landing at Lindberg?"

"We always land in Ramona, Sir."

"Is that big enough?" the concerned passenger questions.

"Oh yes, Sir. They have a fifteen-meter runway and we only need nine hundred meters to set down."

Smith feels the plane raising and a few minutes later, they are over land and shortly on the ground.

The steward opens the door. "I'll call you an ambulance, *Señor.*"

"No need. I'll be fine. Thanks for the lift."

"Let me get you a new shirt." He goes to the closet and returns with a brand new Mexican style-wedding shirt. "Sorry, I don't have any clean pants."

"You've already done more than enough. Thanks."

"Take care, *Señor.*"

"Aren't you guys getting off?"

"No, we're heading back immediately."

Before Jake can walk to the small terminal, the Cessna is already taxiing to the runway.

Smith goes into the small lounge and phones Alex for a ride. As he is waiting the hour for her arrival, Jake spends most of the time in the one-stall restroom, attending to his wounds, and trying to figure out *why* Ramona?

In the waiting area again, Jake sees his fiancé running over and stands.

"What on earth are you doing here? Where's your car?" Alex loudly inquires.

"It's still at the border. How did you get here?"

As they walk to the parking area, Jake explains that Ortiz has a private runway hidden in the hills outside of Ensenada and flies into Ramona frequently.

"Why Ramona?"

"The only thing I can figure is because it has an uncontrolled tower and long runway, and no customs. Ortiz must have been flying illegals and drugs here!"

Before Alex can retort, Jake spots Jill. She sits behind the wheel of her car. He looks at Alex. "You had Ross drive you?"

"She's the only one I thought I could ask." Alex giggles.

"I'll tell you the rest of the story when we get home." He certainly is not about to let his former lover know anything that transpired.

CHAPTER FORTY-THREE
IRS Audits

Internal Revenue Service Auditor, Bryer Stobble, phones Hayden Landry Financial the same day Smith went back to Tijuana. When the receptionist answers the call, he identifies himself and asks to speak to Hayden.

Landry picks up the call and the auditor tells him that he is coming in the following morning to audit Hayden Landry Financial, Inc. and to have the books available. As he is on the phone to Hayden, another IRS agent calls his wife to give her the same message for RLD, Inc.

Before Hayden can hang up, Reena is already running across the breezeway to her husband's office. She barges in without acknowledging the receptionist and crashes through Hayden's office door. "Get off the phone now?" Reena screams.

Her man holds his finger to his lips, to quiet her down and continues, "So Agent Stobble, what time can we expect you to arrive."… "That will be fine."… We'll see you then."

Before the receiver reaches its base, Reena starts back in, "Was that the IRS?"

Hayden, with furled brow, answers, "Yes, it was. I assume you got the same call."

"Get Elon on the phone!" she shrieks.

Elon Mensah assures his client that he has the required documents ready for Gentry. At least the initial ones. He will be at their offices by eight in the morning, bringing the papers for the current auditor to start on. Reena closes the door and takes a seat.

Hayden relays what their attorney told him. They spend the next two hours discussing their dilemma.

Friday morning, August 24, Hayden, and Reena arrive before eight AM and wait for their lawyer. Mensah walks in at eight-thirty, with an overstuffed box of papers.

Looking into the couples distressed faces, he states, "Don't worry guys. This won't be that bad. I reworked your books and if I might say, they should pass with flying colors," he lies, only to calm the pair down. Elon is not going to jeopardize his business for these crooks. He is certain their records will not pass muster.

They talk and have coffee while they wait. Nine o'clock, Bryer Stobble enters. Introductions made and Stobble refuses offered coffee wanting to get straight to work.

The four of them go into a large conference room. Mensah carries his box. As the auditor explains the process to the Landrys, their attorney is removing papers from his carton and laying out supporting documents and a set of books for each business. When Bryer finishes, he excuses the other three saying that he will start with Hayden Landry Financial and if he has any questions, he will call them.

Three hours later, Bryer sticks his head into Reena's office. "I'm going to lunch. See you in an hour."

As soon as the agent is off the property, Mensah excuses himself and goes into the conference room. He looks over the jumble of papers spread across the table. Not seeing anything of interest, he glances around and picks up Stobble's briefcase, laying it on the high polished Oak conference table.

"*Oy vey,* it's locked," he mutters to himself.

Another glance around to be sure no one can see him, Elon starts trying a few three-number combinations, hoping the clasp will flip open. He keeps track of the time. Thirty-eight minutes later the hasp springs up. He twirls the dials of the second lock. Nothing! *Who would use separate combinations on the same case* he thinks.

After another time check, Elon re-locks the open hasp, and returns the case to the floor and walks outside for a breath of fresh air.

Just as he is about to enter Reena's office, Stobble comes up the walk. "Elon, I'm glad I caught you. Can you come with me? I have a few questions."

They sit opposite each other at the conference table. Bryer grabs his briefcase and sets it on the table in front of him. He quickly opens the first lock. Moving to the second, he stops short and stares at it. Then looks long and hard at the attorney. Neither says a word, but Elon knows the agent has trapped him.

He must leave a certain sequence of numbers when he locks the case runs through Elon's mind. *Who would do that and not just spin the tumblers?* He asks Stobble, "Is there a problem?"

"Well, yes, who was in this room while I was out?"

"I have no idea. I went to lunch myself," the lawyer lies.

The conference room door is still open, and Stobble yells for Reena and Hayden.

When they come in, he questions them about being in the room and both deny, but look at their attorney, as does the auditor.

Nobody utters a word until Stobble tells the Landrys to have a seat. He knows, beyond any doubt, that it was Mensah looking for his notes. *They must be hiding something.* Bryer is glad he called in re-enforcements while at lunch.

Before they start talking, an additional two women and a man enters. Stobble introduces his subordinates. One woman takes a seat. The other two keep standing.

"Do you have another room we can use?" Stobble asks.

"There's plenty of table space in here," Reena responds.

"We're going to be talking and going over a few items. These agents will need a quiet place to work." Bryer hands each a stack of papers and tears two yellow pages, full of notes, off his pad and hands one to each agent. Reena shows the pair to an adjacent office.

"Let's see… " Stobble looks over a couple pages of his pad. "… ahh, here we go. I've been going over RLD's books and have questions about the Diego Ortiz account."

"He was a good client until he started doing questionable things. I explained it all to Agent Gentry," Reena quickly puts in.

Elon glares at her trying to convey a *do not say anything until a question asked* message. She understands and mouths *sorry* back.

"What kind of questionable things?" Elon asks. His glare at Reena did not go unnoticed to Stobble.

"Tell me about Diego Ortiz and your LLCs," Stobble demands.

Reena looks at her attorney for approval. He nods. She states, "Well, he wanted to... I believe the word is skim money." She defers all blame on her dead partner.

"Skim money? What was his plan?"

"Oh, we never got that far. He just told me it would be easy to take a little extra money and make smaller entries in the books."

"That leads me to my next question. You have an entry for Disposable Waste Service for..." he checks his notes, before shuffling in a stack of papers. "for four thousand forty-four, but the invoice I found looks like it's been altered from one thousand forty-four." He slides the original invoice across the table and stands, leaning over pointing to the total. "See, the *four* looks like it's been altered from a one... " his finger traces the top triangle of the leading digit, "... and the total's entry for one thousand dollars is scratched out, with four thousand written below it. Obviously, this invoice was altered after the fact!"

Reena studies the document. She looks Stobble in the eye. "The entries were changed by Disposable before they sent out the invoice. I asked them to clean up a small oil spill at the City Center development project. We were working on it at the time, and I asked them to just, add it to the open bill. My accounts payable girl receives all invoices, and I just assumed they had generated a new one."

"That makes sense. And, it's certainly easy enough to check." Bryer hands the invoice to his new assistant. "Can you give them a call?"

Mrs. Landry has no retort and sits quietly; hoping Disposable Waste cannot locate the invoice.

"We'll just continue on and get back to that one. Maybe we should get your bookkeeping service in here. Who do you use?"

"Filson Accounting." Mensah states.

Stobble starts flipping pages of his notes and reading lines. "Filson, you say?"

"That's correct."

He stops at a notation. "Filson Accounting is linked to Diego Ortiz! It appears he is a partner in the business."

"His office is in the same building, that's all I know." Reena is now more nervous than she appears.

"Yes it is, and right next door to Ortiz's law firm." He looks at the woman under the gun, for an explanation.

With no response, he asks, "How do you explain that?"

"I don't. I didn't know."

"You didn't know? That's funny I have… " He starts looking through a different stack before pulling out a few papers clipped together. "Your husband set up that business and did the partnership between Filson and Ortiz." He turns his head towards Hayden for an explanation.

Hayden finally talks. "I recall now. That was years ago. I can't remember everything I did for Diego. There were many transactions and a lot of paper filing. He wrote up documents and I just filled them with the right offices. Attorneys are too busy to do their own legwork." He breathes a sigh of relief, after fending off that misunderstanding.

"Doesn't he have a secretary to do things, like filing?"

As Hayden him-haws around, the auditor finds what he is looking for. "I believe her name is Donna King."

"I know Donna. Diego was always overwhelmed with clients and Donna couldn't leave the office."

"I've glanced through Ortiz's books, not a full audit yet, but wouldn't it have been less expensive for him to hire another downtown firm or even a gopher rather than bringing you all his documents?"

"He probably did, but like I told you, I did a lot of work for him and he was here often. It must have been more convenient for him just to bring some of the work here," Hayden fumbles.

The four of them go back and forth for three hours. The Landrys only dig themselves a deeper hole with more lies. When there is a lull in the action, Stobble's helper leans over and whispers in his ear while pushing a note in front of him. He looks up and gives Reena a broad smile.

The IRS man glances at his watch. He reaches for his briefcase and sets it on the table. "It's getting late, we'll continue Monday morning." Stobble wants the Landrys to stew over the weekend to see what stories change at their next meeting. He stands. "Elon, I want the rest of the files and everything else you have Monday morning. Here's a list!" He hands two sheets of paper, retrieved from his briefcase to Mensah.

The four IRS agents leave. They need to get back to their office and compare notes.

"Elon stands. "I think that went well! I'll see you Monday."

He needs to get to his office; it is going to be a long weekend. The attorney figures, as soon as he drops everything off after the weekend, he will terminate the Landrys as clients.

Elon Mensah has to divorce himself as fast as possible to save his own skin.

CHAPTER FORTY-FOUR
Ramona to San Diego

Dench and Smith approach Ross' car. Smith opens the passenger door for Alex. Jill pops up, "Jake, you sit in the front. We have some things to discuss."

Jake looks that his girlfriend and shrugs. He opens the back door for Alex and slides into the front seat.

Before they are out of the gravel parking area, ADA Ross starts in on the PI. "So Alex tells me you went back to Mexico. What are you thinking?" Jill really wants to know what he is up to.

"Just a social call on an old friend," Jake answers. He tries to defray the Inquisition. "So tell me how the Small's case is going?"

The ADA gives Jake s disgusting look. "We're not here to talk about her! You can hardly move and you're still trying to get yourself killed!"

"Just doing what I'm getting paid for. I like to eat and need the money." Smart-ass Jake responds honestly.

"You won't be around to eat if you keep up this stupidity!"

"I'm glad you're concerned with my health, Jill."

The banter back and forth continues until they are heading up the mountain.

Jake tells Jill, "Can we continue this later? I'm not feeling too well and would like to close my eyes for a few minutes."

Ross takes her eyes off the winding two-lane backcountry road and gives a sympathetic look at her passenger. Alex, from the back seat, does not overlook it.

"LOOKOUT!" Alexis screams.

Absent-minded Jill has drifted into the oncoming lane. A huge box truck is barreling down on them. The truck's horn blaring

231

nonstop, exuberating thunderous honking. With brakes squealing, the locked up back tires leave the over-sized vehicle heading into the boulder encrusted embankment. The driver, using both hands, forces the truck back onto the roadway. It slides to a stop sideways across his lane.

Jill cranks the wheel hard right and her car starts spinning towards the opposite side cliff. Just past the guardrail is a two hundred foot drop off to certain death.

Alex's is screaming! Jake is gripping the dashboard. His knuckles turning pale. His eyes larger than a Harvest moon. Jill uselessly rocks the steering wheel trying to gain control. After an eternity on the Mad Tea Party ride, the fantasy cup crashes into the road guard and jumps wildly into the air with all three holding their breath. Seconds later, the car crashes back to earth with the left front and passenger-side rear wheels, hanging on the wrong side of the rail. Jill jolts forward and cracks her head hard enough to warp the steering wheel. Blood starts gushing from her forehead.

Jake pushes his door open and looks straight down the cliff. "I think I will get out on your side." He grins turning to Jill. It is the first time he sees her slumped over, out cold and bleeding.

Alexis is gasping for breath in the back. Jill's door flies open. A burly, dirty white t-shirted, man loudly questions, "Everyone alright?" Seeing the comatose woman, he blurts, "Is she dead?"

"She needs an ambulance," shouts Jake.

Two cars quickly pull over and three people appear outside Jill's car. "Someone call 911!" barks the truck driver at the newcomers.

"I'll go!" A young driver screams and sprints toward his older model compact Datsun pickup.

Twenty-eight minutes later, a California Highway Patrol, followed by a Ramona Fire Department truck, scream up the highway in a blur. The officer drives just past the accident and turns his squad car sideways across the road blocking traffic. He jumps from his car leaving the lights flashing. After retrieving a handful of flares, he sprints to the other end of the incident, to cordon off the road in front of the sideways truck. The highway now completely at a standstill.

Paramedics leap from the fire truck and run to the disabled car. "Please step back, Sir!" One attends to Jill where she sits. The other questions Alex, and then turns to Jake and sees blood filling his Mexican shirt. "Lay down here, Sir!" he commands, pointing to the asphalt.

"I'm fine. It's an old wound."

"Lay down! I need to analyze your condition," unrelenting.

Smith begrudgingly follows orders.

Cutting off Jake's new shirt, "You're going in an ambulance, Sir!" the paramedic orders.

A red over white brand new Cadillac Miller-Meteor *Lifeliner* comes screaming down the hillside road from the San Diego side. Alex exits the vehicle and refuses medical treatment. Jill has not come around yet and her blood pressure is dropping, and breathing labored.

The paramedics and ambulance personal load the injured woman on a gurney and shove her into the back of the *Lifeliner*. They shoot for Grossmont hospital in La Mesa, at least forty minutes away.

Two tow trucks arrive. The box truck has not sustained damage, other than a scraped and dented passenger side-panel. The driver pulls off the road and onto the shoulder. One tow truck dismissed and the other's operator radios for a crane to remove Jill's vehicle from the guardrail.

A second highway patrol officer loads Jake and Alex into the backseat of his unit and follows the *Lifeliner's* path over the summit and down the mountain.

In the meantime, a cleanup crew arrives and personnel start sweeping debris from the roadway. An hour after the accident, the Highway Patrol opens the eastbound lane. Flagmen alternately let, lines of cars past from each direction.

The boom truck removes the disabled car and loads it onto the tow truck hook. A half-hour later, the highway personnel disperse and not a remnant left that an accident ever occurred.

At Grossmont, emergency nurses and doctors attend to Jill and Jake. Dench sits in the waiting room for an eternity before Smith's wheeled in. Jake has been rebadged and given strict orders of recovery and is free to go.

After hours more of waiting, they're told that Ms. Ross is stable, though in a coma and she will be transferred to the critical care ward later that day. In addition, they should go home and check back the following morning.

Using Yellow Cab, Alex and Jake arrive back at their loft late in the night.

"Would you like me to fix you something to eat?" Alex inquires.

"I'm fine, thanks. I better call the DA and tell him about Jill." Jake thinks for a minute. "I could use a cup of coffee."

On the phone, Jake tells the answering service it is an emergency and to have Jonathan Jerrod phone him immediately.

When Jerrod finally calls close to one AM, Jake explains what had happened and where Jill is. "I thought you should know. Nobody can visit her until tomorrow," he concludes.

"Thanks, Jake, I appreciate the call. I'll let my boss know." After a long silence, he adds, "Jake, you know Jill and I never made it. We only had that one date three years ago. She is and always has been in love with you!"

CHAPTER FORTY-FIVE
Takeover

Derrik Filson has been working on expanding his control of the Ortiz organization for months before the murder. Late one afternoon, earlier in February, Diego took Derrik for dinner and drinks at the Butcher Shop Restaurant in Mission Valley.

They had a long dinner and stayed late drinking. Drunk Ortiz confided in his partner that he was having trouble with Pablo Melendez. The drug czar had been pressuring him to merge their organizations through a thug named Franco Trujillo. The more Ortiz resisted the stronger pressures Pablo exerted. Diego was afraid the Enforcer was going to kill him.

After that meeting, Filson started thinking and soon began planning. He came to the decision that he could set up his own consortium, rationalizing, it was only a matter of time before they got to Ortiz.

Filson made a day trip to Tijuana and met with Jose Contreras to see what the attorney knew. Contreras was cagey at first, never admitting anything, but hinted that he knew Melendez was pissed with Ortiz.

The accountant took a chance and suggested they take matters into their own hands.

Contreras was receptive to the idea, though non-committal. He stated that he would put some thought into the matter.

Filson came away with the distinct feeling that Contreras was not being completely honest with him and he feared he had made a mistake opening up to him. Filson figured that he better meet with Melendez before Contreras did.

A meeting was set between Derrik and Pablo. Filson is smart, but no match for Melendez or Ortiz.

Their meeting strained and left Filson feeling as though they played him. The consensus was the two organizations were destined to merge one way or the other.

The accountant went back to his normal routine and never uttered a word to his partner, though he was afraid Contreras would rat him out.

Over the next several months, everything continued as normal. Diego never made mention of Filson's visit to Mexico and Derrik became convinced his secret was just that, his secret.

The accountant was dismayed when Trujillo showed up at his home, late one evening, a week before Ortiz's murder and took him to see his boss in Mexico.

They met in a warehouse, on the East Mesa, on the outskirts of TJ. Pablo was overly friendly and charismatic. He quizzed Derrik for hours playing mind games and testing the accountant's abilities while pouring shots of high-end Cazadores tequila.

Finally, just before midnight, Pablo got down to brass tacks. "We want to partner with you." Filson floored.

Pablo laid out his plan. He expected the accountant to set up a network of dealers and cook houses to flood the San Diego market. Melendez omitted to tell the accountant that he was already a major drug exporter to the States, and only looked to have a more extensive operation in place by the time he puts Ortiz out of the drug business. He wanted nothing to do with smuggling aliens and Diego could continue his lucrative immigration practice unheeded.

Filson assured the czar that he could handle the north of the border operation. They shook on their deal and Trujillo drove Derrik home. Filson dreamed of unmitigated wealth and authority.

Over the next few days, the accountant started to worry about Ortiz's need for retaliation and his own future on earth. He called his new drug partner in hopes of relieving assurances of protection. His call went unanswered and unreturned.

Paranoia sunk in fast, *what have I done* constantly ran through his mind. The Friday morning of Diego's murder, Filson stepped into his accounting business partner's office. He was ready to confess everything.

Donna King told the man that her boss had gone to a meeting with Hayden Landry and not expected back that day.

Derrik was sitting at his desk, late that evening, contemplating whether to go into hiding or even commit suicide, when he heard Ortiz's office door slam shut.

CHAPTER FORTY-SIX
Smith Makes Rounds

Dench opens HAI at nine o'clock Friday morning. She sits at her desk going over everything for the umpteenth time. Smith's body wracked after the car accident, and his wounds throbbing and oozing. After a long night of tossing and turning, he sleeps late.

Jake finally wakes and stumbles to the washroom to take a shower, and clean and re-bandage his chest. Feeling slightly better after the hot water pulsates over his body, Jake heads for the coffee pot.

He sets down a fresh cup in front of his fiancé and painfully leans over and pecks her cheek. "Good morning, honey."

"Hi Jake, you had a restless night," Alex comments.

"My momma told me there would be nights like that... she just never said how many!" Jake tries a weak smile and sits across the table from Alex.

"So you better explain what happened yesterday?"

Jake tells her the story, underplaying the real perils of Mexican corruption and overstating the danger of Jill's car crash. "So how was your day?" He shows all his teeth.

"Rather mundane."

"What did you and Jill find to talk about?" Jake curious if he was the topic of conversation.

"Oh, you know, just girl talk." Alex's turn to grin.

"Nothing interesting then." Jake refuses to be outdone.

"If you weren't in such pain, I'd put you in some!" Alexis banters back.

Changing the subject. Jake asks, "What are you working on?"

"Just going through the Ortiz stuff again."

"And?"

"And, I not so sure Small is innocent. Jill surely thinks she did it!"

"Well, Small certainly didn't kidnap me or have the TJ police try to kill me!"

"Yeah, that's rather bothersome, isn't it? With Ortiz gone, what is Melendez thinking?" Alex ponders.

"He's thinking one down and me to go!"

"But what does he have against you, Jake?"

"He has me… us snooping around Ortiz's business and it conflicts with his. We're a threat just because he doesn't know *what* we know."

"*We*? Do you think I'm in danger?" Alex had never considered her safety.

"I'm afraid so. Hold on a minute." Jake walks to the bureau and retrieves two boxes. Jake sets both down in front of Alexis.

"What's this?" she questions.

"Open it," Jake retorts.

After examining the box of thirty-eight specials, it does not surprise her to see a shiny new stainless-steel revolver inside the larger container. "Do you really think I need this?"

"I do! It's a Smith & Wesson Model 60. They call it a LadySmith because of its compact size. The weapon has a two and a half inch barrel and the cylinder holds five shells. This will stop anyone coming at you. Have you ever shot a pistol before?"

"No, never had a reason. Of course growing up in Arkansas, Dad had a shotgun and a hunting rifle. We would go out and plunk cans once in a while," Alex tells Jake.

"A handgun is a little different. I'll give you a quick lesson."

Behind the closed door, Jake shows her how to load and hold the pistol in a two-handed shooting stance. He demonstrates the safety's on and off positions. The critical instruction, "Always aim for body mass! The gun recoils upward and you'll hit higher than where you're aiming!"

"Good to know, but I'll never shoot it… at least not at someone!"

"Certainly hope not. Anyway, keep it in your purse. We'll need to get you a carry permit." After thinking about it. "And, at the same time, we should apply for your PI license."

"Me, a real PI," Alex beams at the prospect.

"Honey, you already are. We'll just make it legal."

"Are you going to teach me how to pick locks too?"

They both laugh together. "Anything you want, dear."

Grimacing, Jake grabs his wounds. The belly laughs debilitating him.

Under control again, Jake tells his partner that he is going to the hospital to check on Jill and will probably stop by the jail to see Virginia. He does not mention he is going to Emily's first for a light breakfast and the DA's office second, to see who is taking over Ross' caseload and if there is still a deal on the table for Small.

Alex asks him to bring some things back from the store for dinner and writes out a quick list.

In Emily's Cafe, Smith sits at the counter and orders the morning special, eggs, sausage, and toast. The eating-place is packed and too busy for Emily to stop by his perch. Jake spots Montes in the pass-through window, handing up plates of food. Jake waves. Though they only met once, Montes recognizes him and waves back, shouting, *"Bueno, Señor!"*

Smith calls back, "Good morning, Montes!"

They do not make eye contact again in the forty minutes Jake sits there. He checks the time, decides he better get going, and heads over to the District Attorney's office.

Smith asks the receptionist who is taking over Jill's cases. The woman makes a call. In the middle of it, she puts her hand over the receiver, and asks his name, and what he needs? She relays the information into the handset and hangs up. "District Attorney, Grange Lövenberg is overseeing that case personally and says you can go up to his office. It is on the fifth floor, Mr. Smith."

H. David Whalen

On the elevator, Jake is racking his brain *I know I met him.* He remembers they held a joint press conference with the police department three years ago, *Jones and I were on stage with Chief Baker and introduced to Lövenberg.* He stews over why the district attorney would be involved in the Small case. It dawns on him that this is an election year and he is facing strong opposition from a woman in the race. *I guess he needs all the face time he can get, and Small-Ortiz is front-page news these days. That's not good for Virginia or himself.*

Jake asked to take a seat in the outer office and told that Lövenberg would be with him shortly. He sits twiddling his thumbs for ten minutes before Johnathon Jerrod steps into the room. "Jake, it's good to see you." Jon holds out his hand. "Have you heard how Jill is doing?"

"I'm stopping by the hospital after I leave here," he states in fact, without standing or accepting the shake.

"Good. Give me a jingle and let me know, would you?" the ADA asks.

"Sure thing, Jon." Jake smiles.

"Are you here on the Small thing?"

"It's a *big* thing, not too Small." Smith giggles at his little joke.

"I'll see what Grange wants. Talk to you in a few." Jon goes straight into the inner office without knocking.

Another twenty minutes of boredom and Jerrod sticks his head out the door. "Jake, are you ready to come in now?"

"I'm a little busy at the monument." Jake smiles at the stupid question.

Jerrod took back, before breaking into a tiny laugh. "That's rich, Jake."

Smith follows the attorney into the inner sanctum.

Grange Lövenberg jumps to his feet. "Jake Smith, it's wonderful to see you again. How are you doing?"

Always the consummate politician. He's got my vote! Smith laughs softly to himself. "Fine, Grange, it has been a few years."

"I heard you were back and investigating the Ortiz mess."

"Jill talks too much." Jake chuckles.

"That is tragic, we're all praying for her. I understand you were in the car too?"

"Car? I thought it was a bobsled. You must never have ridden with her?"

"Jill always said you had a sense of humor, Jake. So what can we do for you?"

"Jill was planning to offer Small a deal on a lesser sentence and I'm just trying to see who'll be handling her case now and if the deal is still on the table." Cutting to the chase.

"Are you working on her case too?" Grange inquires, eyebrows raised.

"Well, yes, Cooper Madison asked me to look into a few things."

"Cooper hired you?" Jerrod cannot help himself at the revelation.

Lövenberg stares at Jerrod. He thought it understood that he was only observing and not speaking.

"A *Small* pittance," Jake laughs at his pun.

"So, have you discovered any treasures the police overlooked... if I may ask?" Back to Lövenberg.

"Small is innocent for one!" Smith challenges the attorney.

"She is?" Faking surprise. "What do you know that the police don't?"

Smith looks longingly at his watch. "You better bring in a sack lunch."

Grange offers a loud strained laugh, and then continues, "If you're so sure of Small's innocence, you must know who really murdered Ortiz?" The District Attorney is well versed in the police investigation and knows full-well Jake Smith is on the suspect list.

"Let me ask you a question, why would the District Attorney be personally involved in a low life lawyer's murder?"

"This case is, as I am sure you know, Jake, a lot more than just Ortiz's death. The public is demanding a quick resolution. Again, if you have information on someone else's involvement, it's your duty, and the law that you divulge it."

"I don't have the sure answer, but the list of probable perpetrators is growing and Small isn't one of them. If Lieutenant Holden had the guts to put a competent detective team on it..."

"Jake," interrupts the DA, "Lyle and Terrance are seasoned detectives with decades of experience between them. Besides, Chief Baker, and I have all the confidence in those two fine officers, and it is my understanding they are not working on this case by themselves."

"That's reassuring." Jake's sarcastic response.

"Besides, they have the murder weapon and it belongs to Small?"

I'd better check on that Smith thinks and voices, "Is a deal on or off the table?" The reason Smith is there.

"OFF!" Jerrod voices.

"Jonathon, are you on or off this case?" Smith frankly asks, looking the lawyer in the eye.

"Jonathon is the lead prosecutor!" states Lövenberg and continues, "I'm just overseeing the case."

"Fine, is a deal for Small on or off the table?" Smith forcefully asks Lövenberg.

"Jonathon is making all the decisions as he sees fit."

Smith knows that an untruth, Jerrod barely allowed speaking privileges. He is not getting anything and it is time to hit the road. He thanks them for their time and leaves.

Instead of going to the jail, Jake drives to the county morgue.

"Hey, Doc." Jake enters the autopsy chamber.

"Jake, it's good to see you. I hear you live on the edge these days?" Edward Martin greets his friend.

"Yeah, a real roller coaster. To put it bluntly, Ed. I need a favor."

"I'm not surprised," replies Martin, with a small laugh.

"I assume you dug a slug out of Ortiz, and am wondering if you can call ballistics and see if it's a match for Small's gun?" Smith adds, "I'm not welcome in the lab."

"I think I can do that. Grab a cup of coffee. I like a shot of milk in mine."

Jake gets two mugs, one light, one dark, while Martin grabs the phone and makes the call.

After hanging up, the pair sits at the desk. The doctor asks, "Why are you interested in the slug?"

"I don't believe Virginia had anything to do with Ortiz's murder and don't believe her gun is the murder weapon."

"Why do you think that, Jake?"

"It's just not in her. We've known Virginia for years; do you think she could kill someone?"

"No." Shaking his head. "The slug didn't come from her gun!"

Jake almost jumps from his chair with glee. "So why are they still holding her?"

"I guess that's the million dollar question," Martin mumbles in contemplation. Finally, asking, "Do you think they found another gun linked to her?"

"No, those morons have nothing and are trying to save face." Smith thinks hard for many minutes, before voicing, "Lövenberg is running for re-election. He must know it's not Small's gun, but they don't have anyone else... so they hold Virginia while Lövenberg milks the press coverage for as long as he can get away with it."

"Doesn't sound like a solid campaign strategy to me?"

Smith goes on, "Then, they miraculously find new evidence after the November election, Small gets released, on page ten, but her life is ruined. Those bastards!"

"I would hope our elected officials are more honorable than that."

"Don't count on it, Doc!" Jake jumps to his feet. "Thanks for the coffee, I gotta run!"

"Jake, you cannot tell anyone, you heard it from me. They'll figure it soon enough!" Martin almost pleads, "Jake, it's my career here too."

"You never have to worry about me, Doc. Now that I know, I'll find someone to admit it to me!"

Smith enters the woman's section of the county jail and requests to visit Virginia Small. He told she is in conference with her attorney. Jake asks to tell them that he is waiting.

Minutes later, a guard pats Smith down and escorts him to the room.

"Jake, it's so good to see you," Virginia says, between tears.

"Likewise." Jake pulls up a chair and joins the discussion, "So what's going on?"

"We're talking strategy. It looks like we're going to trial. Have you found anything?" Cooper asks.

"As a matter of fact, I have, and it's great news."

Jake tells them everything he discovered. The police knew they had the wrong gun, and the DA's motives for going along. He highlights what he knows about the Melendez Cartel. Jake ends stating that Franco Trujillo is undoubtedly the murderer.

"Wonderful, Jake. When can I get out of here?" Virginia questions.

"There's a slight problem. I can't really prove any of this. First, I have to get concrete evidence that your gun is cleared." Jake keeps his promise to coroner Martin.

"You just told us it was!" Cooper worries that Jake does not know what he is talking about.

"Oh, I'm certain, but the police won't divulge their findings. We have to figure out how to abscond their files."

"I'll subpoena the gun for independent testing. We have the right to do that, but it'll take time." He pats Virginia's hand to console her. "You'll have to hang in there for a while."

"How long is a while?" Virginia asks as the tears start flowing again.

"It'll take a couple of months." Her attorney is not encouraging.

"By that time the DA will offer a deal... or even clear her!" Smith thinks aloud.

"Yes, but, if we can prove they knew all along, we'll have a major lawsuit." Cooper's pupils change to dollar signs.

"Or, you can tell the DA what we know and threaten to go public immediately. With the election in the balance, he'll fold faster than a losing hand at the World Poker Championship."

"Good thinking, Jake. I will set a meeting immediately, but you will have to get proof. If he thinks for a minute we're bluffing…"

Smith interrupts, "He'll know we're not bluffing because he already *knows* it's not Virginia's gun!"

A plan of action set into motion before Smith takes off for Grossmont Hospital.

Ross is still in a coma and the doctor tells Jake, "There's no way of knowing how long she'll be unresponsive, or if she'll ever wake up."

CHAPTER FORTY-SEVEN
Night Call

The private investigator goes through another rough sleepless night. By two AM, his chest wounds throb and he tosses constantly trying to get comfortable. Their car accident aggravated the pain and caused him a minor whiplash on top of his already whiplashed neck, and aching lower back. He slips as quietly as he can out bed, not to disturb Alex.

Jake fumbles in the dark early morning to find the aspirin bottle. He downs four and stands at the window waiting for them to kick in.

When he does not feel needed relief, Jake decides to go to the emergency room for some assistance. He slides quietly into the bathroom and brushes his teeth and dresses. Under the bright bathroom light, he writes Alex a note, lays it on the counter next to the coffee pot, and slips out of the loft.

Mercy Hospital in Hillcrest is busy and Jakes sits for over an hour before they take his vitals and lead him to a curtained cubicle and a bed. It is almost another hour before a doctor comes to see him.

In the meantime, Smith's chest is leaking blood with five stitches needing replacement, three on his right breast and two on the left. The nurse hooks him to an IV and Darvon drips slowly into his system. Twenty minutes later, a ward orderly wheels him to x-ray. They take Jake back to the room and he falls asleep.

After he is finally visited by a doctor, the nurse returns and requests an orderly to wheel his bed to a procedure room for suture replacement.

The doctor returns and after examining the radiographic images on the wall mounted light box, he tells Jake there is no internal damage other than muscle strains and removes the old and sews in new stitches. He tells Smith to take it easy and return in a week to have the sutures removed. He left alone in the cubical to get some sleep.

A couple hours pass, the sleep-inducing Darvon is wearing down and Smith wakes at the noise of a housekeeper scurrying around the room.

After dosing for a while longer, Jake wakes and pushes the call button. His nurse comes and asks how he feels. "I'm fine," he lies, anxious for release. She leaves him alone, telling him she will find the doctor and get the papers together so he can go home.

Smith finally leaves Mercy with a prescription for Darvon, a narcotic analgesic medication. Under the drug's influence, Jake barely feels any better than when he got up four and a half hours earlier.

Back at the loft, Alex is concerned and demands to know why he had not woken her for help. She chastises him for not, at least writing in the note which hospital he went to. After, a much needed, coffee, they relax in their easy chairs and talk for a period.

The sun is in the sky when Jake decides to call and check on Jill's status. No change. As soon as he hangs up, the phone rings, it is his ex-wife Cheryl.

"How are you doing, Jake? Roy read about you in the newspaper. Are you alright?"

"Fine Cheryl. You know me. You cannot keep a good man down. I haven't seen the paper, what did they write?"

"About the accident, you and Jill had."

"And Alex! There wasn't anything else?" Jake questions.

"What more would there be?"

"I don't know. I'm on meds, and not thinking clearly." He is relieved the FBI had kept his kidnapping confidential as they said they would. At least until the investigation is over.

After a little talk about their son, Adam. They get off the line.

Jake stands. "I'm going over Diego's ledgers again to make sure we haven't missed anything on Melendez."

"Jake, you need a day off. You need to heal!"

"I'm fine, dear. I need to do this!"

Thinking, Alexis comes up with an idea, "Why don't we go for a drive? We can go to the desert and have a Mexican dinner. It'll be good for you to get out of here for a while and get your mind off everyone else's problems."

"People are counting on me, Virginia's in jail, Jill's still unresponsive, and I need to see…"

"NOT TODAY! We're going to the desert!" Unyielding.

Alex is driving her new bright orange Ford Pinto subcompact. She pulls off the freeway just past Jacumba, into a gas station. Jake wakes from his slumber. "Where are we? Why are we stopping?"

"I need some gas. Hey, I saw a sign for the Desert View Tower and thought we'd have a look. Have you ever been there?"

"No. How far is it?"

"Just down In-Ko-Pah road a mile or so. The picture on the billboard shows a quaint rock tower where we can go up and view the scenery. It'll be fun," Alex voices.

"Do they have coffee?"

Laughing at his addiction. "I'm sure they must. They have a gift shop."

"Let's go."

"Oh, we're going!"

The place is closed. A woman is bustling around making coffee and setting up the register for the day. Jake bangs on the glass door. She yells through it that they do not open for a half hour. Jake pleads for a coffee and quick tour of the tower, conveying they are just passing through and would really appreciate it. He holds up two twenties as a persuader.

After handing the bills over, paying four times the amount for two tickets, they're allowed to climb the tower. Jake, carrying a large black coffee, follows Alex up the winding staircase. Alex is slipping an ice-cold Coke.

Diego Killer

They stand to marvel at the wide Soranan Desert from the un-glassed observation deck. The warm westerly wind is blowing up from the valley floor. Even at eight-thirty in Jacumba, the temperature is already hitting close to ninety-three degrees. The lower sand and cacti desert is already hovering at a hundred degrees and expected to rise to one-ten or higher by noon.

"Are you sure you want to continue down there?" Jake suggests, "Maybe we should turn around and hit the Cuyamaca Cafe. It sits right on the lakeshore up in the mountains. Nice, cool and relaxing." Trying hard to sell her on the alternative. "And, they have Mexican food."

Alex ignores the suggestion and points. "What's that big lake over there?"

"That's the Salton Sea and behind is the Chocolate Mountains. Mexico runs along the canal by Signal Mountain." Pointing to the southeast. "And Arizona is a hundred miles that way, beyond El Centro, where we *were* going to eat." Again pointing, Jake's a regular tour guide. He turns around. "The Cuyamacas are that way!"

"Do you think we can stop in the desert, and you can teach me to shoot my gun?" asks Alex, in thought.

"Good idea. You brought it, uh?" Now Jake is getting excited.

"It's in my purse! You told me to put it there!"

Surprised, she did. "I'm glad you listen to me."

He overlooks her disgusted look and starts down the stairs.

At the bottom, Alex voices, "I need to go to the washroom and freshen up. It wouldn't hurt for you to splash a little water on your face, too." She strides off.

After stopping at the bottom of the mountain in Ocotillo for a Frosty chocolate-shelled ice cream cone, they continue north on S2 for a few miles before pulling into a sand wash below the Carrizo Badlands to plink cactus.

Jake takes charge, loading the LadySmith, and firing off the first five shots. After a couple of quick lessons, Alex follows suit, emptying a few cylinders at various cacti. She is pleased that she managed to hit a couple.

Smith picks up the brass and they get into the car. Alex pushes the gas pedal and the drive wheel just spins in the soft sand. Distressed, Alex looks at Jake and states, "I think we're stuck, dear."

Jake puffs his chest out in pain. "I'll take care of it!"

She watches as he drops to his knees and starts hand-scooping sand away from the rear passenger tire. Looking up at her, he asks, "Can you find me some larger rocks."

After the cavity packed, he instructs her, "Get in and start real slow. I'll have to push and as soon as you get traction, keep the car moving until you get to the road. Don't stop! I'll have to walk out."

He sits on the bumper and pushes his back into the trunk as hard as he can. His wounds stress and he reels in pain. Unyielding, Jake, keeps pushing. The car moves a few inches on the rocks and breaks free. As soon as the Pinto is out of sight, he reaches into his pocket and retrieves his aspirin bottle. Jake chews up half a dozen dry, bitter pills, before slowly trudging through the sand.

Jake joins her on the road. "Let's keep going up to Borrego," he suggests.

They spend the day driving around the desert and past the south end of the Salton Sea before arriving in El Centro for dinner.

It's late evening by the time they are back home.

"I sure had a good time today, Jake."

"So did I." Bearing the pain while hugging Alexis lightly. "We need to do things like this more often!"

"I'll mark my calendar!" Alex giggles.

"Honey, I'm going to take a couple pills and lay down. I really need to sleep tonight."

"Are you alright, Jake?"

"Good as new, just a little tired."

They go to bed and snuggle to sleep. Alex is more in love with her man than ever.

It is just after three in the morning when Alex wakes. She stealthily sneaks into the bathroom and grabs her purse on the way.

She is out of Tampons in the washroom but carries two in her purse for emergencies.

Alex hears the steel front door squeak loudly, and thinks *where the hell is Jake going at this time of night?* She sticks her head out the door. Jake is breathing hard, still fast asleep in their bed. She stands deathly still listening. The floor squeaks softy from her office. Alex grabs her LadySmith and turns off the light. She leaves the door cracked and peeks through the slot.

After a good five minutes, she realizes she is just hearing things and ready to go back to bed when the floor makes another distinguishable noise. Alex scared but quickly turns mad over the fact that someone would intrude his and her space. She cocks the gun.

A small orb of light enters the room. She instinctively pulls back. The beam passes through the door crack and quickly moves on.

She peeks out watching the light beam sweep the room and stop on her sleeping boyfriend. A huge shadowy figure moves methodically across the floor. The black mass appears to be holding something in the left hand.

The shadow stops in front of Jake. After a few seconds, the hand rises. From streetlight dimly seeping through the open window, Alex recognizes a gun's reflection pointing at her man. Without a second thought, she flings open the door, and yells, "Freeze! Drop your gun!"

The figure spins. A reaction shot shatters the doorframe beside Alexis' face. The room fills with the earsplitting explosion. She returns fire. A single shot. She aims at the middle of the mass. The LadySmith pistol recoils high and to the right. The bullet penetrates the intruder's front left shoulder. Two more quick shots miss.

His gun drops and clatters on the hardwood floor. A slug spits out the barrel and lodges in Alex's foot. She screams in pain.

Jake, jolts wide-awake and instinctively rolls off the bed to the floor. The bathroom light comes alive and he recognizes the body standing next to him. It is Frank Trujillo. Frantically looking

243

around, Jake sees the gun lying at his feet and grabs it. Trujillo takes a step toward the pistol woman, as she is going down.

"One more step!" yells Jake, holding the silenced weapon pointed at the Franco's back.

Trujillo freezes at the all too familiar cocking sound.

CHAPTER FORTY-EIGHT
Madison Meets DA

Cooper Madison calls the District Attorney's telephone number Saturday morning. He leaves a message with the answering service. Not knowing who he is handling Small's case now, the message is an urgent call to ADA Jillian Ross.

A half-hour later his phone rings. "This is ADA Jonathon Jerrod. What is your emergency, Mr. Madison?"

"You need to call Lövenberg. I'll be in his office in an hour and he better be there or I'm going to the press!" Cooper slams down the phone.

He shows up precisely on time. Jerrod is waiting in the lobby. "What's your emergency, Madison?"

"Is Lövenberg here?"

"Not yet. I'm handling the Small case and you can talk to me."

Madison turns and steps towards the door. Jonathan runs over and grabs his shoulder, spinning him around. "What the hell is going on?"

"This is between your boss and Small. If he's not here in five, I am ruining his life!"

"Don't get excited! I'm sure he's on his way. Let me call and double check."

"FIVE MINUTES!" Cooper stomps down the hallway and into the restroom.

When he returns, Madison looks around, Jerrod is still alone and he heads for the door.

"Hold up, Cooper, he'll be here. He had a plumbing emergency and is just leaving his house," the ADA lies.

"How long?"

"Twenty minutes, maximum. He said he is sorry and asked me to have you wait." Another lie, the arrogant Lövenberg never expresses regret to anyone.

"Get me a cup of coffee!" Madison commands and takes a seat.

"Why don't we go up to my office?" Jonathan suggests.

Madison ignores him and looks at his watch.

"Don't leave. How would you like the coffee?"

"Cream and sugar… a splash of cream and two sugars!"

Precisely twenty minutes later Cooper walks out the door. Jerrod is on his heels begging him to stay. At his car, Cooper gets into the driver's seat. Jerrod scours the lot and spots his boss coming down the street. "There he is, please come back inside?"

After a pseudo-political apology, the three make their way to the District Attorney's upstairs office.

"This better be important, young man!" Patronizing the thirty-seven-year-old sitting across from him.

"Small's gun isn't the murder weapon and you covered it up! When the press finds out your finished!"

"Hold on, Mr. Madison, I don't know what you're talking about?" Grange asks his employee, "Jon, can you excuse us?"

Jerrod stands mesmerized by the gun revelation.

Jonathon, please," Grange begs.

As soon as their alone and the door is closed, the DA demands, "Now, you'd better explain yourself!"

Cooper lays out the story, accusing the man of burying the truth for the sake of publicity.

"First, that is ridiculous. I only go on what the police relay to me. If there is a problem with evidence, I certainly haven't been told!" Passing the blame directly to Lyle and Terrance.

"We're not playing here, Lövenberg. I have proof you knew all along and conspired with the police for your benefit!" Cooper stands to leave.

"Please, sit down Mr. Madison. If I had any knowledge of your claims or if there is any truth to them, I certainly would have had

Mrs. Small released and gone public with their screw up immediately!"

Madison plays his bluff to the end, staring at the DA before he opens the door and walks out.

Chasing him down the hall, Lövenberg, "Just tell me what you think you know. If there is any doubt in Small's involvement I'll have her released this morning!"

Jerrod had been waiting in the outer office and now is following them.

Madison continues out the front door. Lövenberg left alone with Jerrod, screams, "Get that F****** Lyle on the phone!"

Jerrod runs to the closest phone and calls PD headquarters.

Returning to the DA's office, Jerrod explains, "He's off today, but they are getting a hold of him. I told them to have him come here immediately!"

"Wait for him in the lobby!" the superior demands.

Jerrod leaves and Grange sits behind his desk with his head in his hands. Five minutes later, he is on the phone to Channel 8 telling Tina Tredberry how Detectives Lyle and Terrance messed up and not yet disclosed new evidence on the Small case. He is dropping all charges at this time and ordered her immediate release. Tredberry's report will broadcast immediately on a special news bulletin.

As he sits waiting for the detective, he calls Tredberry back twice more with new revelations to add to her story. Actually, it is just more of the same trying to his cover his own ass and shifting the blame to San Diego PD.

Lövenberg's phone rings, it is Detective Lyle. "What's so important, Sir?"

"You guys have a leak! Small's gun is not the weapon used to kill Ortiz." Acting as if he had not known. "I'm having her released and the story is breaking as we speak!"

After a long thoughtful pause. "I hope you didn't say too much! I think I know where this came from. Let me get back to you… before this goes public." The DA hears a click and the line buzzes in his ear.

Lyle radios his partner. "Meet me at Emily's Cafe now! We got a problem!"

Click!

Detectives Lyle and Terrance meet up and walk to Smith's office.

They stand in the hallway beating on his door and yelling for him to open up, before Terrance states, "I don't think they're here, Stephen."

"Let's go, we need to a BOLO out on him!"

CHAPTER FORTY-NINE
Damage Control

After getting off the phone with District Attorney Grange Lövenberg, San Diego Police Chief, William Baker, speeds to his office. Detectives Stephen Lyle and Donald Terrance, along with Lieutenant Holden called in and already waiting.

In the closed-door session, their boss demands to know what the DA is talking about, suppression of evidence, particularly concealing the fact that Small's gun is not Ortiz's murder weapon and why she's still in jail.

Holden speaks first, "She's all but confessed and we have lots of circumstantial evidence of her involvement other than the gun."

"The gun is your problem! Whose gun do you have?" Baker uncharacteristically yells.

"We don't know at this time, Sir. Small knows a lot of people and she could have easily obtained an unregistered weapon and ditched it," Lyle pipes up.

"What a load of poppycock!" screams the Chief. I want to know exactly what evidence you have on that woman!"

Lyle lists the feeble accusations of the longtime love affair and restaurant argument, ending with calling off the engagement, and Small's unverifiable alibi.

"That's it!" Baker still loud, "That's not evidence!"

"It's a little weak, but we're following other leads," Terrance tries to convince Baker.

"What other leads?"

"Uh, we're retracing her movements of the evening in question, constructing a timeline of her actions and interviewing people, who knew of the affair and Small's state of mind that night," Lyle flat out lies.

"You two are off the case and put on immediate paid leave. Give me your guns and badges!" barks Baker.

"But, Sir, we…"

There are no buts. When this hits the airwaves, everyone's heads are going to roll. Now get out of my office." Uncontrollably, "Holden, stay!"

After the detectives sulk out of the office. "Lieutenant, who do you have to replace them?"

"Max Marsh and Maurio Romero, Sir. They have been assisting Lyle… the other two are already up to speed, Sir." Contrite and now concerned for his job. Little does he know that Lyle and Terrance did not divulge much information to their new puppets.

"Good, get them on this *now*!" Baker asks, "Did you know?"

"No, Sir. I had no knowledge that it wasn't Small's gun." However, he had. It is time to throw Lyle under the bus.

"We have to be in damage control mode. Lövenberg states that he was in the dark too. I'm not sure about that, but he is clearly going to put the whole fiasco on our shoulders. It's going to be a media shit storm!"

"We need to get ahead of this, Sir!" Contemplating a move. "I think we should hold an immediate press conference, say that you just discovered the rogue detectives and apologize publicly to Virginia Small and state that she has been released." Holden's, on the spot, plan.

Baker considers the advice in silence for a prolonged period, before responding, "That's a good first move. You gather the reporters. I want every available officer standing on the steps with us. We must show solidarity! I'll call the jail and have her released."

Lyle and Terrance walk to the closest deli and phone Detective Marsh. He tells him to get Romero and meet them there immediately. It's an emergency!

Both the other detectives were together hanging out in front of Smith's business, waiting for movement. They had no idea that Dench and Smith were already halfway to El Centro. Romero flips on the siren and lights while Marsh fires up the company car, and screeches down the street.

They park in the closest lane to the deli, blocking traffic, and dash to their workmate's rescue with their guns drawn.

Lyle and Terrance burst into laughter at the Keystone Cop routine. "Not that kind of emergency!"

Lyle briefs them on everything crashing down on the Small investigation. Lyle stresses Smith's involvement. It is time to arrest Smith and his partner. "We've already put a bolo out on him!"

After hearing the condensed version, the new arrivals are stunned at their suspension and vow to vindicate the fellow officers and nail Small, once and for all. The four chat for a good hour before parting ways.

Marsh and Romero drive to the office. As they cruise past the front of the build, before turning into the back lot, they observe the press conference in full swing.

"What's going on?" questions Maurio.

"I guess the party started without us," quips Max.

After parking, the pair walks around the building to check out the commotion. They stand incognito at the back of the crowd listening to the offered BS from their boss.

When it is over, Romero turns to Marsh. "What was that all about?"

"Damage control. It's very possible we'll get a new boss!" Max suggests they get to work. The new case detectives have a lot of catching up to do before finding Smith and nailing Small.

Marsh and Romero spend hours looking through file after file. By late afternoon, they are exhausted and ready to go out for a sandwich and a cold drink before starting the night shift. Before they leave, Marsh decides to call Davis, over at the FBI and see what they have.

"Special Agent Davis!" He answers the incoming call.

"Good afternoon, this is Detective Max Marsh of the San Diego PD."

"You must be the new man on the Ortiz case?"

"So you heard?"

"I saw the news conference. What exactly did Lyle do? I thought they had wrapped it up and that reporter woman was beyond innocent?"

"Well, yeah... I guess everyone was under that impression. Anyway, my partner and I are involved now. Actually, we have been assisting Lyle and Terrance for a while. I was wondering if we could get together and share a little info." Acting friendly.

"Our case on Ortiz really doesn't overlap your investigation. We are looking into predisposed federal crimes and not specifically his murder." Davis rebuffs the detective.

"We're looking for Smith now, and making an arrest for obstruction. Just thought you might have something to add?"

"You know we searched his offices and living area and found nothing?" He omits telling him that Smith did have files and turned them over the day before.

"I didn't know that." After going quietly into thought for a moment. "If we find anything of value I'll give you a jingle," responds Marsh.

Davis thanks him and promises to return the favor if he discovers anything on the murder. Getting off the phone, Davis tells Morris and Blazer, "Looks like SDPD is going after Jake Smith and wants our cooperation.

CHAPTER FIFTY
Trujillo's Confession

"Get my handcuffs out of the drawer!" Smith barks at Alex.

She wraps a towel around her bleeding foot and hobbles slowly to retrieve the steel bracelets. "What would you like me to do?" Holding up the cuffs.

Smith looks at her and keeps the gun trained between Trujillo's eyes. He commands his prisoner to pull a kitchen chair to the center of the room and sit.

"Come over here and hold the gun?" Jake directs Alex.

"My pleasure. If he breathes, I'm blowing that asshole away!"

Trujillo watches her struggle back across the room. He believes her.

Jake hands the weapon to Alex and attends to the prisoner. He locks Trujillo's one hand between his back and the chair. Then thread the cuffs through the slats and locks his other hand, making the assassin and the chair one component.

As soon as Jake is done, he walks to a counter drawer and removes a single chopstick. Without a word, he approaches Trujillo and jams the stick deep into the bullet hole in the man's shoulder. Frank reels in pain. Smith continues spiraling the chopstick in a wide coning motion, around the hole, inflicting as much pain and damage as he can. After a full two minutes, he pulls the stick out and stares at his victim, without, so much as uttering a word.

Frank gyrates his shoulder wild agony. Stopping his smiles at Smith. "Is that all you got?"

Jake crams the chopstick back in with all his strength. Trujillo reels in the torture, but keeps the forced grin on his face. Smith projects his own sly smile and pounds the stick with the butt end of the gun as far in as it will go in. "Better?"

"Tell you what, Jake, take off the cuffs and I'll teach you how it's done."

Jake actually laughs hard at the unexpected humor. "I'll get better. We got all day and I'm a slow learner."

Alex is sitting on the bed, horrified at her fiancé's behavior. "Jake we should call the police and let them handle this. I need to get to a hospital."

Ignoring Alex. "I got a better idea. I'll give Pablo a jingle. He'll know what to do."

Franks pupils dilate uncontrollably at the suggestion. He knows exactly how his boss handles incompetent employees. He glares at Jake in defiance, trying to figure out if he is serious.

Smith walks to the small bed stand to retrieve his wallet. He returns to stand in front of the non-showing, terrified man. Not looking at him, Jake pulls a small slip of paper from his wallet with Cooper Madison's phone number written on it. "Ah, here it is." He looks up at Trujillo. "Relax, I'll be right back."

Smith walks into Alex's office, leaving the door wide open behind him, and picks up the phone. He acts as if he is calling Pablo, referring to the paper and dialing a number or two, and repeating.

As soon as Jake's index finger positioned in the rotor dial's last digit-hole, wide-eyed Frank yells out, "Jake, you win! Hang up the phone and tell me what you want!"

Jake looks over at the sweating man. "Oh, I am doing what I want!" Moreover, he pulls out his finger, letting the dial spin back to home position.

"JAKE, PLEASE HANG UP. I AM BEGGING YOU!"

Smith looks at Trujillo and without contemplating, hangs up the phone. He strolls back in front of Trujillo, closing the door behind him. Jakes pulls a chair over and sits, with the gun in his lap. "Well, Frank, first, let me ask you why you're using a twenty-two caliber gun."

"Lightweight and quiet, no loud pop. It's as deadly as any if you can hit your mark."

"And you are a good shot?" Smith asks.

"The best!" Sporting a wide grin.

"Tell me why Pablo wanted Ortiz dead."

"Juan, err, Diego and Pablo go way back. When Diego was a teenager, he worked for Pablo in Tijuana."

"What about Contreras?"

"Juan and Jose were inseparable. They worked as a team. Actually, they are the reason Melendez expanded so fast. I guess they thought they weren't getting their share and went out on their own."

"In competition with Melendez?"

"Yes, but Pablo found out almost immediately and put out a contract on them. Juan split to San Diego and changed his name. Nobody knows where Jose went. When he came back years later he was a lawyer."

"And Pablo didn't take care of him?"

"No need, besides, he really liked those kids. So, Contreras worked for a while unheeded and then Pablo needed a new representative and Jose owed him. Contreras had no choice... if you know what I mean?"

"And what about Ortiz?"

"Once Contreras worked out, Pablo decided to bring Juan back in and have him run everything north of the border. Diego was already entrenched and didn't need his old boss, so he refused. This went on for over a year until Pablo sent me to offer him one last deal. Again, Juan refused and Pablo called me. He was eliminating his competition one way or the other. Juan chose the other." Trujillo smiles.

"And you were sent to kill him?"

"Yes! I stabbed him in the chest."

"What the hell are you talking about? Ortiz was killed with a twenty-two!" Smith rattles the gun in front of the murder's face. "And then stabbed with a knife. I assume that was to send a message?"

"That was the plan, but when I got there Ortiz was already dead." Quickly realizing why Ortiz had not responded when he stabbed him. "I just shoved the knife in and took pictures for my boss." He reiterates, "He *was* already dead!"

"Dead? When you got there?" Smith is confused.

"That's what I said!"

After thinking about who else had a motive, Small's name is clearly the front-runner in Smith's mind. "Would Melendez have you *and* others as a backup? Someone beat you to the punch, so to speak?"

"No way! I am the man! Me and only me!" Trujillo states proudly.

"Ok, let me get this straight, Pablo has a beef with Diego and sends you, only it's too late?

"That is correct!"

"And what's all this have to do with me?"

"That was more Contreras' doing. He was getting nervous that you are learning too much and going to spoil his little nest egg. You know, from whatever Siena or anyone else, you talked to up here, spilled. Pablo wanted to know how, uh, how involved you were getting, and if you put him on a watch list on this side of the border."

"So why the electric works?"

"Fun for me!" Trujillo smirks. "Just no other reason and nobody would miss you anyway!" Frank laughs heartily for a long time. Jake does not appreciate his humor.

Smith goes on questioning about the Melendez's organizational structure and what all he is in to and how far his reach. Trujillo tries to dodge as many questions as he can and lies about everything else, minimizing his involvement, saying, "Above my pay grade." or "I have no knowledge of that," repeatedly.

Smith believes he got straight answers as Trujillo bragged about his job, but nothing more.

There is a banging on the front door and people screaming, "Police open up!"

"Saved by the bell, Frank." Jake pushes his chair back under the table while Alexis painfully hobbles to let them in.

As soon as the front door opens a crack, it jerks from Alex's grip. Caught off balance, she puts too much pressure on her wounded foot, and she screams in pain. Marsh and Romero lead an army of officers through the door.

"Alexis Dench, you are under arrest!" Detective Marsh states.

Before he can continue. An officer shouts, "Max, get your ass in here, NOW!" Marsh runs to the commotion.

Romero stays and handcuffs Alex. He looks at her blood-soaked towel-wrapped foot, and questions her. He ends up calling an ambulance.

Max Marsh stands dumbfounded at the scene. An unknown man is handcuffed to a chair and bleeding from his shoulder with a… a chopstick sticking out? Smith is on the floor face down with an officer's knee in his back. A gun with a silencer is laying on the floor at another officer's foot, close to Smith. He glances around and a third officer is standing by the bathroom door pointing at a second pistol laying on the bloody floor.

"Officer's you saved my life! This maniac tortured me and was going to kill me."

Not yet, out of the daze, "Who are you?" Marsh inquires.

"I came up from Tijuana to hire Mr. Smith and he went berserk shooting and accusing *me*!"

"Accusing you of what?" Detective Marsh questions.

"I… I don't know. He talked nonsense. The man is *loco* in the head."

"What were you going to hire a PI for, Mister… what's your name?" Quizzically.

"Manuel Juarez. I wanted him to find my wife. She ran away and I think she is in San Diego." Franco is good on the fly.

"Take the cuffs off him and call a *bus*!" Commands the detective.

"He doesn't need an ambulance," Smith screams. "Don't take the cuffs off! He murdered Diego Ortiz!"

"See, he's crazy. I do not know anyone by that name. I only want my wife back!"

An officer is on the phone with nine-one-one getting Trujillo medical assistance and Marsh shouts, "Everyone just shut up!"

"Get this monkey off my back!" Smith yells.

The detective stares at him, "Jake Smith, you are under arrest! Handcuff him!"

"What are you doing? This guy broke in here to *kill* me and we had to shoot him in self-defense."

"Shot him with a chopstick?"

"Of course not, I…"

Not prepared to listen to Smith's lies, Marsh breaks in, "And when were you going to call us?"

"We just got him under control and Alex was going to the phone when you knocked!"

"I'd be dead if you didn't come." Trujillo, trying to divert the conversation from Smith.

The paramedics show up and attend to Alexis first, then Trujillo's wound before two officers lead into each into waiting ambulances, one with Dench and one with Trujillo and escort them to the hospital.

Smith put in the back of a squad car and taken downtown.

CHAPTER FIFTY-ONE
Smith Arrested

Detective Max Marsh calls an investigation team to HAI's loft. Smith already arrested and transported to San Diego Police headquarters, while Trujillo and Dench are under guard and on the way to the hospital.

"What happened here?" Maurio Romero, out loud, but more to himself. Mystified and shaking his head.

"No idea, but we got Smith!" His partner gleefully chirps.

Alone in the room, the two detectives start photographing and bagging items of interest. They have taken pictures of the two pistols, bag coffee cups from the counter and collected papers strewn across the kitchen table by the time the investigation team shows up. After a short debriefing, the examiners get to work.

Romero starts tearing apart Dench's office and Marsh does likewise to Smith's office.

Jesse from San Diego Locksmith called in to open the backroom safe.

Within the hour, Romero has Dench's room boxed up, and is back in the loft area, standing behind the locksmith watching and waiting.

Jesse gets it opened.

"Max, you better get in here!" Maurio shouts out.

"What did you find?" Questions Marsh as he approaches the kitchen table. His partner is looking through a ledger and five more are stacked in front of him.

"Smith has all Ortiz's ledgers! That bastard *was* suppressing evidence, just like Lyle told us."

"Never a doubt," grins Marsh. "Let's bag them and head back." He tells the evidence team to finish boxing up Smith's office and bring everything to headquarters.

The detectives sit at their desks drinking coffee and looking through Diego's records. Two hours later, they have Smith taken to an interrogation room.

Jake handcuffed to the table when they enter carrying the six books and Max sits across from him. Maurio drags a chair against the adjoining wall and sits, tipping it back in relaxation.

"Be careful Murry, you don't want that seat slipping out from under you," grins Jake, purposely addressing the man with the wrong name.

Marsh stares at Smith. "Shut up! You have a lot of explaining to do!"

"That is an oxymoron." Smith acts serious and he fakes zipping his mouth with the thumb and forefinger of his right hand.

"Let's start with what happened at your loft this morning."

Smith re-zips his mouth.

"You're not getting out of here, this time!" snarls Marsh.

Smith says one word, "Lawyer!"

"Why do you need an attorney?"

Once again, the zipping motion repeated across Jake's snarky lips.

"Jake, I want to help you. I believe you are justified in everything you've done," Romero tries the good cop routine in vain. "You don't need an attorney at this time. We just need to know what happened here."

After no response. "Jake, we've been friends a long time and can talk man to man."

Jake thinks *friends! What, the hell, is he talking about?*

"You can talk to us off the record," Marsh's eyebrows rise and hands palm up feigning a state of sympathy.

"Lawyer!" Smith repeats.

"You're not charged with any crime, why do you need a lawyer?"

Diego Killer

"Not charged? Undo the cuffs, I'm out of here!"

"Don, take his cuffs off," Detective Marsh tells his partner. Turning back to Jake. "Would you like a cup of coffee?"

"Sure, let's go to Emily's," Smith suggests.

"You're can't leave. We are holding you until we get some answers."

"Why did you arrest Alexis?" Jake questions.

"Obstruction of Justice, same as you. You failed to turn over evidence." Marsh pats the journals. "We are really on the same side here. We both want Ortiz's killer. All we're asking is for you to *help* us solve the case." Again turning on the friendship charade.

"I'm glad you finally realize you need help," quips Smith.

Romero tries hard to control himself, but cannot and barks, "Call your attorney!"

While they are waiting for Cooper Madison to show up, Marsh keeps pressing. "Smith, who was that man you shot this morning?"

"I never shot anyone… at least not today," snidely Jake remarks.

"So what is that guy's name?" Persisting.

"Franco Trujillo."

"How do you know Mr. Trujillo?"

"Old friends." Jake smiles.

"You shoot old friends?"

"I told you, I *did not* shoot him."

"Ok, so Dench is the shooter. How did he get a chopstick in the chest?"

"Unfortunate accident. It was dark and I think he slipped. Anyway, when the lights came on, there it was," Jake fibs.

"You turned the lights on?"

"Don't remember, maybe Frank did?"

"That doesn't make sense, Jake!" Romero speaks.

"None of this makes sense. If I could help, don't you think I would?" Jake challenges.

"I know you wouldn't!" retorts Marsh.

Smith stares at the man. "You don't have a good Christian attitude, Max. Maybe a few more church visits would help."

261

"Here's what I think, you tell me if I'm close." Marsh, starting to put it together. "Trujillo comes calling. Alex shoots him and you torture him with the chopstick. How's that?"

"Too much TV and not enough church," Smith remarks.

"So tell us, what were you trying to get out of Trujillo?" Ignoring the crass remark.

"Franco Trujillo is a hit man for Pablo Melendez. Pablo and I don't see eye to eye and Trujillo pays me a visit."

"Who is Melendez?" Quizzing the suspect, and pleased to have Jake talking.

"Mexican drug lord."

"Why is a Mexican drug lord after you?

"Ask the FBI." Time to end this.

"What has the FBI got to do with you and Melendez?"

"You'll have to ask them. I have nothing to do with either." Smith is only telling enough for the police to keep holding the assassin.

"You're telling me, Trujillo came to kill you and was shot in self-defense?"

"That sums it up! Am I free to go?"

Cooper Madison storms into the interview room. "What's going on here? You didn't say anything, Jake?"

"Nothing important." Smiling at Marsh.

Cooper turns to Marsh, asking, "What's he doing here? Is he under arrest?"

"Yes. We were just about to take him to booking." Romero steps forward and lifts Smith under the left arm. "Let's go."

Max stands and informs the lawyer, "We'll bring him back in a few minutes. You can wait here."

"What are you charging him with?" asks the lawyer.

"Obstruction of Justice, Concealing Evidence, Impeding an Investigation, Conspiracy! Do you want more?"

"Conspiracy to do what!" Smith demands.

"Conspiracy with Alexis Dench on obstruction for one. Torture for two. When we are at the bottom of this, I'm sure there will be plenty more charges! You're going to jail, Smith!"

Diego Killer

Almost an hour later, Smith, escorted back the interview room. After he and Cooper confer, the detectives lock up Smith in a holding cell.

CHAPTER FIFTY-TWO
Landry Arrest

Monday morning a platoon of FBI agents, raid both Landrys' offices, home, Sorrento Valley Storage, Filson Accounting and Elon Mensah, Attorney at Law, all at the same time.

Bryer Stobble and his IRS team spent eighteen hours a day over the weekend scouring the Landry's improprieties and Sunday evening he phoned his counterpart, Fraser Gentry. In turn, Gentry called FBI Special Agent Davis. "Hate to bother you at home on a Sunday evening, but we got the Landrys!"

"What did you find?" questions Davis.

"We tracked a scheme connecting both Reena and Hayden to Diego Ortiz. They were actually in the money laundering business together. We have enough proof to arrest them. I want a raid and their arrest, as soon as possible. I'm positive we can get more on them and possibly others. Hayden has accounts set up in the name, Howard Griffin. Griffin was a former client that passed away a few years ago."

"What kind of accounts?" Davis inquires.

"It's a long list, running money through legitimate businesses, offshore accounts, understated entries. When we get all the records, we expect to find postal fraud, forgery and more."

They discuss a plan of attack for the following morning. As soon as they are off the call, Davis draws out a rough flow chart on the logistics of the raids. As all the suspects arrive at work, the agents will be waiting.

Two minutes after Reena unlocks her office door, FBI and IRS men and woman barrage her business. Davis immediately approaches and arrests her for money laundering. Reena is screaming for her attorney as handcuffed and set in an office chair under guard. She remains in that position the whole time her rooms torn apart.

Hayden shows up for work forty-five minutes later. His office door is wide open, but he runs into his wife's office to see what all the commotion is about. Blazer immediately puts him under arrest. He is taken to a different office than his wife. It amazes Davis that they did not pick up Hayden at his home, and wonders where he has been.

The radio comes jumps to life. "We got Mensah and Filson. When we're finished here we'll meet you at the office."

By the end of the day, the FBI has vans full of Reena and Hayden's property. Their offices and home almost bare except for furnishing. Filson and Mensah's offices are almost as bad. They turned up a couple of Reena's hidden boxes at Sorrento Storage. The cartons mismarked and placed with another company's records.

The four arrested people transported to FBI Headquarters and placed in holding rooms well before the searches complete.

By four-thirty, the last of the vans are pulling into the parking lot.

It takes two hours to move the confiscated material into various inspection rooms and start the tedious process of thoroughly going over and cataloging every scrap of paper. Agent Morris tasked with overseeing the procedure. Even with the battalion of agents assigned, the process could take weeks.

Davis and Blazer take Mensah into an interrogation room. They decided he would most likely be the first to break with a deal offer.

"So Elon, we have you dead to rights." Davis starts in.

"I didn't do anything illegal. I'm not involved with the Landrys more than representation!" Mensah desperately cries.

"Why don't you tell us about the *false* entries you made in their books?" Davis asks.

"That wasn't me. You need to question Filson. He's the criminal!"

"We'll get to him. Your problem is the first person to cooperate is the only one making a deal. Have you ever been to prison?" The agent threatens.

"No... No, of course not! I'm not a criminal. Only legal representation! I only know what Reena and Hayden have told me, and nothing more." Mensah puts his head down into his hands in shame.

"Elon, you knew about Disposable Waste Service's doctored invoices and covered for Reena. That's a crime in itself and Obstruction of Justice mandates up to ten years in Federal prison."

Mensah starts shaking and does not respond.

"What else are we going to find in your files?" Blazer questions.

Sobbing uncontrollably. "I have a family! What kind of deal?"

"I can't make any promises, but I can probably keep you out of prison. It all depends on you!"

"I... I will tell you everything I know. I just can't go to prison!" The man looks frail and ten years older than an hour earlier.

"Write down everything you know!" Blazer hands the lawyer a yellow legal pad.

Mensah stares at the paper for a long time, before taking out his pen and writing. The two agents vacate the room, telling him that they will be back.

In the hallway, they run across Nathan Morris. "That was the easiest flip we ever did, partner." Davis slaps him on the back.

Morris lurches in pain from his wounded shoulder.

"Sorry, Nat," Davis apologizes. His partner, wearing an oversized sweater over his cast with only his arm sticking out. In his jubilee, Davis overlooked Morris' bullet wound.

"I'll live!" through crooked cringed lips.

"After Mensah finishes we'll take a whack at Filson. Want a cup of coffee?"

The three agents retire to their desks for a much-needed break from the already long day, which is going to stretch into an all-nighter.

Blazer and Davis return to Mensah almost an hour later. The lawyer is sitting quietly with pages full of notes.

As Davis reads over the statement, he questions the broken man on several points for clarification. Mensah is deeper involved than either of them had suspected. Davis has him sign his statement and Blazer leaves with it to make copies. Now they know what specifically to look for first.

Davis stands and calls a rookie agent into the room. "Can you transport Mr. Mensah to the county jail?" The FBI substation has a few holding cells, but not equipped for longer stays.

"What! I thought you were letting me go! You said if I confessed you would let me go!" shouts the attorney in fear.

"I said I would try, but no guarantees, Elon. The District Attorney will not be here until the morning. I'm afraid you'll have to spend the night. I'll get this straightened out and see about your release." He adds, "Elon, we appreciate what you're doing and I certainly don't anticipate any problems, it might take a couple of days." Well, any problems Davis is willing to share. Elon Mensah will surely lose his license to practice at the very least, and they will see if he has committed any crimes outside of the Landry investigation, with which to charge him. *He must have learned how to play the illegal game and very well might have tried his own little schemes* think Agent Davis.

After Mensah escorted out, Filson brought in. Davis and Blazer cannot get a word out of him. He refuses to talk and demands an attorney.

Filson replaced by Reena. Likewise, she refuses to speak and demands a criminal lawyer.

Hayden's turn. He is not as strong as his wife is. Reena is obviously the brains of the operation.

After Mirandizing. "Do you understand your rights?" Davis asks Hayden.

"Yes."

"Do you want an attorney present during questioning?"

"I want to make a deal!" Hayden has watched too many detective movies.

"What kind of deal?" Davis raises his eyebrows at his partner.

"The kind where I don't go to prison!"

"I can't make any promises. You and your wife broke many laws."

"It was all Reena's ideas. That bitch was having an affair with Ortiz. She thought he walked on water and would do anything he suggested!" The agents stare at Hayden in disbelieve.

After many minutes of silence, Hayden continues, "I did have an account under Griffin Howard's name and made a couple of... of questionable transactions, but nothing close to what Reena and Diego were up to! They're the real criminals. I don't even know everything they did, but want to help any way I can."

Davis excuses himself and tells Blazer to follow him into the hall. "What do you think, Bob?"

"I don't think we need him, and I don't trust him!"

"I agree. No deal, then?"

"No deal!"

Back in the interview room. "Hayden, we'll need to speak with the DA in the morning for you. In the meantime, why don't you tell us what you know?"

Hayden Landry refuses to speak, without a lawyer and the DA present. They take him back to his holding cell.

CHAPTER FIFTY-THREE
DA Visits FBI

District Attorney, Grange Lövenberg, and ADA Jonathon Jerrod show up at FBI headquarters Tuesday, August 28 and meet with Agent Davis. Lövenberg has had a rough three days since the *wrong gun* scandal started. The public outcry is resignation and an investigation into criminal charges against him.

The FBI agent meets them with niceties, but the DA overlooks the political correctness and goes straight to the point. "Agent Davis, we need to know everything you have in the Ortiz case, specifically what Detectives Lyle and Terrance told you about Virginia Small's involvement!"

"I see you guys have a problem there. Frankly, SDPD has been uncooperative with us. The only thing we know is what we see on the news."

"Sir, we need your help." Jerrod tries again. "Did you have any inclination that the police lied about Small's gun being the murder weapon?"

"We're not involved in the murder investigation. The news said it was. That's all we know," Davis reiterates. "How's your ADA? I think her name is Ross?"

"Not good, she's still in a coma. Thanks for asking. We better get back to work." Lövenberg abruptly ends the meeting.

After shaking hands, Lövenberg and Jerrod leave. Davis heads down the hall to the room filled with agents pouring over all the Landrys' files.

Walking into the first room, he spots California Bureau of Investigation Agent, Beverly Good, sitting next to an FBI woman and looking at papers.

He approaches the pair. "Good morning, Bev. See anything you like?" Motioning at the papers scattered in front of her.

"Hayden Landry was definitely committing forgery on documents relating to Howard Griffin accounts, but nothing yet on Ortiz's forger activities."

"Incidentally, IRS Agent Gentry is in the other room, if you need to speak with him. He would certainly know about the money end," Davis mentions.

"It goes way back!" She looks at Davis. "It started when Griffin was still alive and kicking. Landry was forging his documents and transactions and stealing hundreds of thousands of dollars."

Davis asks Good, "What exactly do you think Ortiz did?"

The CBI agent studies Davis's face, asking herself *is he kidding or trying to bait me?* Not visualizing an immediate answer she asks, "What have you discovered about his illegally smuggling business?"

"We're sure he was into it. You know, bringing people across and getting them naturalized."

"How?" Good asks.

"That I don't know. Its INS' territory!"

The two agency representatives play cat and mouse for ten more minutes before Good realizes that the FBI really has no idea about the depth of Ortiz's forgery operation.

"Let's get a drink and go to your office, Egan," Beverly suggests.

After visiting the vending machines, they sit in Davis's office.

"Well, what's on your mind, Bev?" he questions.

"Egan, I get the impression you guys haven't followed the documents?"

"We just got most of them, what are saying?"

"Let me be blunt here. I know you're preoccupied with the RICO violations, and INS is on the illegal crossings, but I have been on the paperwork. Hardly been out of the office in months." She laughs. After thinking hard for a few quiet minutes, she confesses, "I brought in a team of undercover agents a while back…" Another pause. "… with what they discovered, we have come to this conclusion, and pretty sure we're right."

Davis sits quietly waiting for Good to spill everything.

"We all know, Diego Ortiz's business was booming, but how did one man work the system so quickly in every case. Each case takes so long he wouldn't physically be able to handle that much volume alone."

"So, he has partners!" Davis is unimpressed.

"No! That is the point. He had to be paying people off!" Good, states.

"Common practice. What people are you suggesting?"

"INS people for sure and probably DMV personnel. That's what interests me."

"Border Patrol's problem, not ours," Davis flatly states, referring to INS.

"Nor mine. But, getting people across is not the problem, processing is!" Still on the naturalization issue.

Letting it sink in before answering, "You think someone was helping Ortiz file bogus forms within INS?"

"Exactly. Ortiz owns Public Portrait. Therefore, he takes his own photos and he owns Southend Printing, making his own documents. Then, he had them hand delivered them to certain INS personnel, which in turn, enters the phony documents into the system and our government unwittingly approves status. Ortiz never went to court and never left his office while handling cases!"

"That sounds pretty risky?"

"Money talks and Ortiz never had a problem sharing the wealth! He must have done his research and found a vulnerable employee."

"Or he had a long-term plan and took the time to get his own person hired and moved up to the right position." Davis ponders aloud.

"Either way, Diego Ortiz infiltrated the system," Good speculates.

"Sounds like you need to talk to them."

"I'm planning on seeing Adams this afternoon. I'm convinced that his files contain forged documents linked to legitimate DMV records."

CHAPTER FIFTY-FOUR
Conspiracy

Agent Davis goes to the jail to visit private investigator, Jake
Smith. He requests an interrogation room and sits quietly waiting
for Smith to be brought in.

Eventually Jake shuffles in. His leg irons not letting him walk
freely. The guard undoes one of his handcuffs and sits Smith down
at the table. The officer slides the open cuff through the large
protruding steel ring and re-locks his free hand, securing him to the
top.

"That's unnecessary, unlock him immediately!" barks Davis.

"Sorry, Sir, orders!"

As the guard leaves, Davis takes a handcuff key from his vest
pocket and frees Jake's hands. "What's going on here, Jake?"

"The price you pay for fame and glory!" Jake laughs.

"I though obstruction was the charge? That certainly doesn't
constitute this kind of treatment."

"Obstruction and obnoxiousness!" He continues to have fun.

"Jake, we've always been straight with each other, haven't
we?" Davis uses a salesman's close.

"One of us has!" Jake leaves it up to Davis to decide who the
honest one is. Both know neither qualifies.

"I'm here to help you, Jake. This is just wrong that you're in
here!"

Smith does not respond, waiting to see where this line of bull is
going.

"You're a great PI." Davis starts with a fake compliment. "I
want... rather, need you to tell me everything who have uncovered
about Ortiz."

"His ledgers spell it all out, Egan."

"What ledgers?"

"The six I gave to Marsh."

"Six?" Stunned. "When did you turn them over?" inquires the agent.

"A couple of days ago," nonchalantly responding, not mentioning that they were confiscated and seized in the search of his place or that Dench made Xerox's of everything pertinent and hid them in his neighbor's basement storage locker.

"Is it one set of books spread over six volumes?" Davis questions.

"Six sets, one volume each. Covers all his dealings."

Smith has nothing to lose; he is out of commission and tells Davis everything he can remember. Almost everything. They discuss Ortiz, Melendez, Trujillo and various channels of businesses Diego setup up. The discussion lasts for hours.

Late in the afternoon, there is a knock on the room door and an officer sticks his head in. "There's a Cooper Madison here and demands to sit in!"

"Show him in," Smith responds.

"Who's that?" questions the FBI man.

"My attorney! Maybe we should have waited to have this conversation!" Jake laughs.

"I'm glad we had this talk. Jake, you have nothing to fear from our side!" Davis states, unsure if it is true or not.

Madison enters and takes a seat. "Who are you?" he demands of the agent.

Davis stands and sticks out his hand. "Special Agent Egan Davis, Mr. Madison."

"You haven't said anything!" The lawyer's standard line to Smith, ignoring Davis' handshake.

"You know me, Coop, not a word," Jake snidely remarks.

Davis takes his seat. An instant disdain for the attorney, not unlike most attorneys he meets.

"Can I have a word with my client in private?" Madison addresses the agent.

Diego Killer

Davis back on his feet. "We're finished here. I was just leaving anyway. Jake, we'll talk soon."

"Egan, you might mention to Adams that Diego was flying in the illegals."

"Flying them in? How in the world…"

"He has an airstrip outside Ensenada and a Cessna Citation. Unloads them at Ramona," Jake offers.

"Jake, don't help them!" Madison commands.

"And another thing…" Smith pops out before Davis can get out the door. "… Filson has to be in over his head with Melendez and Contreras."

"How do you figure that, Jake?" The FBI agent turns back into the room.

"Well, the only people I talked to was Contreras and Filson, before my incident." And, he adds, "Oh, and Siena."

"We're onto Filson and Contreras, who's Siena?"

"This is the interesting part, Diego Ortiz was born Juan Herrera and took a false identity from a dead child in Phoenix, who was born the same year as he when he fled Mexico and came to this country. But, he is or was married to a Mexican lady, Siena Herrera, and has a family living on a beach estate south of Rosarito."

"How did you find all this out?"

"So Diego, err Juan was a philanderer, which also gives Siena a motive for murder and access to his assets!"

"I need to talk to her. But tell me about this false identity!" Davis responds.

"When he came to San Diego, he met an immigration attorney, named Clarence Brown. I believe, though haven't been able to prove it yet, that Brown is responsible for setting up the illegal alien scheme. When he passed, he bequeathed everything to Juan. Juan was groomed to keep the operation going, only he was the real entrepreneur and expanded it into what it is today."

"What else do you have?" Already shocked by Smith's revelations.

"That's about it. If I think of anything, I'll give you a call."
Jake tries to befriend.

"Thanks, Jake. We'll talk soon." Davis leaves to find Detective
Marsh, and get his hands on the ledgers.

As soon as they are alone. "Jake, I filed papers on what you
told me, that you didn't come into possession of the ledgers until
the night Trujillo came calling. I certainly didn't say he brought
them with him. That part of your story is ridiculous! Tell me when
you really got them and how?" Attorney Madison demands.

"You don't want to know!"

"I need to know everything if I going to get you and Alexis out
of here!"

"You don't need to know about the ledgers. It would put your
life in danger!" Smith lightly rubs the wounds on his chest.

"We'll wait on that for the time being!" Madison understands
and quickly comes to his senses. "Anyway, I have a judge signing
a Writ of Habeas Corpus for you and Alex.

"What's that?" Though he roughly knows, it is his freedom
ticket.

Madison explains that it is for unlawful detainment and that he
will be their custodian to guarantee they show up in court.

"Have you seen Alexis?" Jake is concerned.

"Yes, I just left her. Her foot's in a cast and she's on crutches,
but she'll be fine." Back to the subject at hand. "You know as soon
as they prove you had the ledgers prior to Saturday night, you guys
will be back in jail!"

"They'll never prove that!" Jake is confident.
Madison and Jake sit for hours until the writ comes through and
the release papers are completed. The San Diego Police
Department surely did not rush to release Smith and Dench.

CHAPTER FIFTY-FIVE
Another Body

A headless corpse found rotting in the Mexican desert south of Mexicali by a couple of teenagers, dirt biking in the cool morning.

They report their findings as soon as they are back in the city before the midday heat destroys their riding pleasure.

The temperature climbs rapidly and hits one hundred and seventeen degrees on the open sand by the time Mexicali officials take the boys back out and eventually locate the body. They transport it to the local morgue.

The coroner takes a quick look. "This part of the anatomy is stinking and well chewed. Looks like the coyotes found this guy before you!" he comments, and adds, "The genital area must be the tastiest part, I can't tell the gender!"

"When you finish, give us a call!" One of the officer's command.

Two days later, they receive the final autopsy report. The body was so badly decomposed there is no definitive cause of death, but it defiantly is male. The doctor stresses that they must find the cranial.

Three off-road vehicles full of officer's return to search for the missing head. Hours and gallons of water later they abandon the fruitless search, and the remains eventually buried as a John Doe.

Davis picks up his ringing phone. "Agent Davis, this is *Capitán* Prieto."

"Yes, Edward, it's good to talk to you again."

"*Si, Señor*. Jose Contreras is missing. His wife reported it a few days ago," the *Federales'* official reports.

"Did he go on the lamb?"

"On the lamb?"

"On the run from Melendez or you guys?" Davis reiterates.

"No. I don't know. However, a headless body turned up in the desert. It could be him."

"The head wasn't there?"

"No head. Probably never, find it. The body was so rotten and eaten that no positive identification could be made."

"Eaten?" Shocks Davis.

"By animals, most likely coyotes," Prieto flatly states.

"What about fingerprints or dental id?"

"No head, no teeth!"

"Sorry, I'm just not thinking straight."

"Fingers and toes are a delicacy and first to go. The body too damaged to examine for burns or bruising. They already buried it. It probably is nothing, just a person lost and dying from the heat. But just thought I let you know about Contreras' missing."

"Thanks, Capitan. How's the investigation on Melendez faring?"

"Faring? You mean coming progressing?"

"Yes, progressing."

"Good, we're almost ready for an arrest. We cannot find Franco Trujillo. He appears missing too. Maybe the body is him."

"That should be easier to identify. Trujillo is a large man and the average head is about nine and a half inches. I presume you have the length of the body and if you add the two together, you'll get an estimated length. If I remember correctly, Trujillo is around six-six." Davis doesn't mention that the man is sitting in a San Diego jail.

"Yes. Hold on a minute."

Davis hears paper rattling and keys of a calculator pounding.

"Looks like our body could between five-eight and five ten. Not big enough for Trujillo," Prieto states.

"Well, that leaves Contreras or an unknown," Davis comments while in thought. "Can we find out how tall Contreras is?"

"Shouldn't be a problem. I'll let you know." *Capitán* Prieto ends the call and hangs up.

Davis turns to Morris. "Looks like Melendez is cleaning house!" He relays the conversation he had with the *Federales* to his partner.

After discussing the events with Blazer, Davis decides to phone Smith.

Jake suggests they put pressure on Filson. "That weasel might know something and if he thinks he's going to prison for life on Conspiracy Murder charges he'll do anything to save his own skin."

Davis agrees, but they are close to nailing him and do not want to tip their hand and spook the accountant. He tells Jake that he was thinking the PI could call his client and see if she heard anything.

Smith states he has to check in with Siena anyway and will ask her. Davis tells Jake to phone and never go back to Mexico!

"Don't worry. I learned my lesson… twice." He laughs, gripping his chest.

Jake calls Siena, "Good morning, Jake Smith here."

"Hi Jake, I'm glad you made it back safely. I hadn't heard and was getting concerned."

"Didn't your pilot report to you?"

"No, Roberto never came home."

"Roberto's your pilot?"

"Yes. He and the plane are missing. I think he got scared and maybe, went back to Honduras."

Hesitantly. "You know the plane was shot up pretty badly. They were worried it would not make it as far as Ramona. It surprised me that they even took off again." He speculates. "Maybe the airplane broke up over the Pacific on their return flight."

"Maybe, but I like to think he's alive and safe." Siena projects a positive attitude.

'I hope so too," Jake agrees, but not so sure. "So, what's new with you?"

"Your tax people froze all my accounts. I received a letter from an Agent Gentry that he wants to see me in the States."

"Don't come here! Do you have enough to get by?"

Laughing. "Plenty. Diego had money everywhere."

"I glad he looked after you and the kids. Hey, what I'm calling about, have you heard from Jose?"

"Nothing. Martha called and told me he was missing. She fears Melendez is responsible."

"Martha? Is that his wife?"

"Yes, Martha Contreras. She told me he was doing work for Melendez, which I did not know and I am sure Juan did not either. They were always like brothers."

"Why does she think Melendez is responsible?"

"Jose was gone a lot of evenings. Last week, when he came home, he was very scared. He told Martha that Pablo is getting paranoid and making mistakes. He told her that they might have to move and be ready on a minute's notice."

"That does sound scary! Does she know why he was worried?"

"Just that Melendez is a cruel man and he should never have gotten involved."

Jake touches his chest as a reminder and agrees with Martha.

They end their call and Jake goes back to work.

CHAPTER FIFTY-SIX
Adam Comes Home

Adam Smith, Cheryl and Jake's son visits San Diego. He takes an early morning flight out of San Francisco and arrives by nine-thirty Thursday morning. After visiting the Hertz counter, he drives to the county jail and then to his father's office.

Adam finds HAI's location and climbs the stairs. The large steel track-door open and he walks right in. He stands to look around the small room when the back door slings open and Jake rushes in and hugs his son. They have talked over the phone, but not seen each other for almost four years.

Adam returns the hug too forcefully and Jake grimaces from the pain in his chest. Quickly separating. "Sorry, Dad. How are you doing?"

"I'm good, just getting older." Jake smiles.

"I'm talking about your wounds."

"Must have slipped in the shower."

"Mom told me about your *accident*. Can we get a cup of coffee and talk?" asks the young attorney.

"That woman never could keep a secret."

"She's my Mother, remember?" Adam grins back

"Your, Mother?" Acting shocked.

"I'm sorry I couldn't get here sooner, Dad, tied up in court and all. I tried calling a few times. Didn't you get my messages?"

"I have been busy too, actually a little indisposed."

"I know. I stopped by the jail and they told me you'd been released."

"Mother again?" Not waiting for the answer to his rhetorical question. "Those damn cops still have a thing against me!"

They retire to the kitchen table. Alex has been watching and listening to the reunion on the closed circuit system, while hopping around, without crutches, making breakfast. She never met Adam and was pleased he came to see his father.

After introductions, the two men sit at the table. Alex sets a cup of Joe in front of each and returns to the stove. A few minutes later, she sets a heaping plate of food in the center of the table and a plate in front of each man.

"I have work to do in the office." Wanting to give them space to talk alone.

"Nonsense! Join us, dear," Jake suggests.

The three share an enjoyable morning chatting away like chuckling chickens. Finally, Adam starts inquiring about what they are working on, and about his Dad's wounds. Alex and Jake take turns laying out everything about the Ortiz case, each, and every detail.

"Wow! Unbelievable!"

"It gets worse!" And, Jake launches into the Melendez problem and the Mexican police chase through Jill's driving accident and ends with his jail story.

"Looks like you're in deep. How's Madison as an attorney? I can hook you up with the best criminal defense lawyer in town, Dad."

"Cooper's good. We're out!"

"Yeah, but not free! He should have been able to secure a release on your own recognizance and... "

Jake interrupts, "I'm sure he would have if we had a hearing, but he got us out as soon as he could."

"All I'm saying is that it wouldn't hurt to get a second point of view."

"Where are we going for dinner this evening?" Dad changes the subject.

"That reminds me; I better call Mom and let her know I made it."

Minutes later. "We're all meeting at the Charter House." Adam returns smiling.

Diego Killer

"WE!"

"Yes, Mom, Roy and the three of us." Adam is pleased with his diplomacy at getting everyone together.

The dinner outing goes better than expected. Jake had never met Roy and only spoken to him that one time they talked briefly over the phone about insurance investigations. Cheryl's husband is personable, friendly, and an intelligent conservationist. Smith figures that's why he was such a successful executive. He is surprised that he actually likes the man.

Roy knows many local politicians and city officials. He promises to make a few calls to see if he can dig-up exactly what is going on with the police and DA's office and why Smith's targeted.

As they leave the establishment, Jake hugs Cheryl and whispers to her that she did well and he is truly happy for them. Adam tells everyone that he needs to check into his hotel and begs off drinks at the El Cortez rooftop lounge.

Cheryl insists that he comes home. She has a room already set up for him. Adam wants to stay downtown to work with his dad and refuses. Alex tells Roy that Jake needs to rest and says they will also take a rain check. They all leave in opposite directions.

As soon as Adam settles into the US Grant Hotel, he calls Thom Fiumara at home. Adam had phoned Fiumara the day before and discussed his father's legal problems, as he knew them. Fiumara had given Adam his home number and told him to call, anytime, after he gets to town and finds out what is going on.

Adam gives a brief description of his dad hiding evidence, from the police and assorted agencies. Thom reassures that Jake has nothing to worry about, with the police's own scandal over manufacturing evidence on Small's gun. Though suppressing evidence from the FBI is a different matter. He tells Adam that his father is in good-hands with Cooper Madison, but he would also do a little digging in the morning.

Adam thanks him for his help and sits at the room's desk making notes and jotting down ideas for most of the night.

CHAPTER FIFTY-SEVEN
FBI Brings In Filson

The same day Special Agents Davis and Blazer pickup Derrick Filson. He released days earlier for lack of evidence after the Reena and Hayden Landry arrests. Now they are more than ready for him.

The three men sit in a small off-hallway room. "I want a lawyer!" Filson demands before anything asked.

"Calm down, Derrick. We're not arresting you, but want to offer you a little advice." Davis tries to befriend the accountant.

"I don't need counseling! If you have nothing, I am leaving!" Filson tries to stand, but Morris forces his shoulder, preventing it, without comment.

"We're working a joint task force with the *Federales* in Tijuana," states the lead man and lets it sink in before continuing. "Melendez is going down! And you're involved!"

"I have nothing to do with those people!" Unwittingly admitting he knows them.

"We have photos of you meeting Pablo at his warehouse!"

Pondering for minutes, before answering, "That was at Ortiz's request. I don't even know their connection!"

"Ortiz was already dead! What could you possibly have had to discuss?"

Squirming uncomfortably. "Ortiz had... had done business with them and I needed to clear their accounts," Filson lies.

"What kind of business would Ortiz have with a drug cartel?"

"I... I... How would I know? There was just an unbalanced account. Only numbers, no notes. I didn't know it had anything to do with drugs until I got there."

"So, why would you contact them again, two days later?"

"During the first encounter is when I realized Melendez was a drug dealer and I never went back again," he confidently answers.

"But you did call him! We have your phone records!" Morris steps up. "Why's that?"

"I... I was still trying to balance the books."

"Tells us about Hirsh!" commands Davis.

"Who's that?"

"You're telling me, you're Ortiz's accountant and business partner, and you don't know his San Diego manager?"

"Oh, that Hirsh. I know Larry, but had very little contact with him. Actually, I only met him once, years ago. He just mailed in his weekly reports and I did entries, that's all."

"Ok Derrik, let's get real here! We have *all* Ortiz's ledgers and files. You're up to your eyeballs in this!"

"I want a lawyer *now!*"

The agents ignore Filson's request. "You don't need a lawyer, but you should get your affairs in order for your wife and kids' sake." Davis gets up.

"What are you talking about?" The accountant takes the bait.

"Just offering a little advice. You must know Melendez has people everywhere, watching everything. And, I would bet, they're curious why you're at the FBI office twice in as many days. You're free to go. Nat, can you take him back to his office?" The fun is just starting.

"Wait! Wait! What are you talking about?" screams the less confident man.

"We're just going to save the government a lot of time and expense. You're free to go!" Davis repeats.

"I'm not going anywhere until you explain what you mean!" demands Derrik.

"I *mean* we have no more interest in you, but when word hits the street that you've been seen talking to us, I'm sure you'll have Pablo's interest! Nat, get him out of here! He has a lot of loose ends to tie up!"

"You can't do that!" cries Filson.

"Can't? We have no choice but let you go! It's your wishes!" Agent Davis smiles.

"They… They'll kill me!" The realization as bright as a thunderbolt.

"Probably! Of course, that is just another added charge on which we will arrest Pablo. The stronger our case against him the happier I am!" Davis sports an ear-to-ear grin.

Derrick sits crying hard for many minutes before Davis stands. "I need a cold soda! How about you Nat?"

"Sounds good. You want one Derrik?"

The question goes unheard through the man's loud, uncontrollable sobbing.

Davie shrugs his shoulders at his partner and leaves the room.

Returning later, Davis hands Morris a cold cola, sets one down in front of their suspect, and takes a seat and a long slow drink while staring at Filson.

"What… do you… want?" Between sobs.

"You know what we want!" Agent Davis responds.

"I… I don't… don't know anything. It's like I've been trying to tell you," the crying man.

"I believe you, Derrick. I am truly sorry. There is nothing, we can do for you."

"I'll warm up the car and take him back to his office," Nat offers. "Can you bring him down?"

"WAIT!" After a long blank stare at the table. "I'll tell you!" Filson caves.

The three sit in silence for a long time. "Enough of this BS! Let's go!" Morris taps Filson's shoulder.

Derrik looks at Davis. "Can you get me and my family into the witness protection program?"

"I don't think so. You should have chosen your friends a little more carefully."

"I know everything and will tell you!"

"Then you don't need the program. We'll keep you and the family in a secure location and protected until Melendez is off the streets."

"But, he has sons. They'll come after me!"

"Tell us what you know and if there's enough I send a request to the Attorney General."

Filson spends the next nine hours relaying Diego Ortiz's operation and his connection to Melendez. He confesses to government payoffs, and illegal refugee and drug smuggling. He lays out how Ortiz flies them into different states from all over Mexico, and how Hirsh manages a man named Lazarus Veliz, who sets up Ortiz properties to house drugs and manufacture meth. Veliz is also in charge of distribution.

He goes on to describe Jorge Hermie's functions, under Hirsh, as their transportation manager and safe house director for the illegals, in San Diego and Imperial counties. He is not familiar with out of state operations and assumes Ortiz has the same setups in Arizona, New Mexico, and Texas.

Derrik tells of the passport photo and document printing businesses and the names of INS clerks on the payroll. In addition, he outlines how Diego puts all the smuggled people to work in order to exploit them. It construes to lifelong enslavement and cash flow.

Finally, Filson outlines how the money laundering system works, through commercial and residential properties bought outright and with partnerships with Reena Landry. Included is skimming from his many businesses and investments and offshore accounts in a variety of countries.

When he finishes, Davis asks about Diego's illegal identity and Clarence Brown. Filson is shocked that the FBI knows. He confirms the identity scheme Brown had manipulated for Juan, and upon his death left everything to Ortiz, money, property and the organization. Brown was small potatoes compared to what Ortiz built.

Filson confesses to all he knows. He never mentions his plan to take over the San Diego connection.

The agents realize that Filson is a dead man, and sure, they can get him into the Federal Protection Program.

"Derrik, we are going to hold you here tonight. We will need a full written statement. In the morning, we will move you and your family into safe houses." They won't' reunite the family until after the hearing.

CHAPTER FIFTY-EIGHT
Forgery

California Bureau of Investigation Agent, Beverly Good compiles enough forgery evidence. She puts together a team to raid Southend Printing, and Public Portrait simultaneously. Friday, August 21 at eight AM. She includes Immigration and Naturalization Service agents and Drug Enforcement Agency officers. The local police and FBI are not included.

Southend just unlocked their doors for business, when twelve men and woman descend screaming, "CBI, SEARCH WARRANT! EVERYONE FREEZE!" While running from room to room.

Five undocumented aliens jet out the back door and run straight into a half a dozen INS officers with their guns drawn and beaded on the group. The four men and a young woman line up, against a cement brick wall, along, the sidewalk.

The last young man sprints down the alley and around the corner of a vertical wall. Two uniformed men give chase, yelling, "INS STOP, *ALTO!*" Repeatedly.

The first officer, in the chase, rounds the corner and cold-cocked in the face by the hiding man. He crumbles; his nose broken and squirting blood.

The fugitive takes off again as the second officer comes around running at full speed and goes down, tripping over his partner. Pants tore, the man cusses and jumps to his feet to continue the pursuit.

The bleeding man gets on his radio calling for backup, "Suspect running east on Commercial! Repeat. Suspect on run! East on Commercial!"

A siren blaring Border Patrol vehicle screams up the street past their running agent searching for the runner. A block further, they slide the corner. The perp is nowhere in sight! They screech a U-turn and back to Commercial. The officer on the sidewalk made the corner and doubled over gasping for breath. The car slams to a stop. "Did you see which way he went?" shouts the driver through his open window.

"No, he just turned this corner!"

"Jump in! We'll get him!"

"I'm going back to check on my partner!" The officer straightens and starts jogging down the sidewalk from the direction he came.

The vehicle pulls another U-turn and starts searching for the runaway again.

After the first two officers are together again, they walk back to the print shop to clean up. The man with the broken nose transported to the emergency room, while his partner finds his fellow officers interrogating the roundups.

In the meanwhile, the DEA agents, who have not discovered any drug activity, were packing up to leave.

After more than an hour scouring the adjacent streets for the escaped illegal, the car-team gives up.

Beverly Good and another CBI agent interview the manager and employees. The rest of her team pack boxes of records and crates them to waiting vehicles.

In the end, eleven suspected illegals detained and transported to an INS substation for further processing. Six prove they have proper papers, and taken with the others to CBI's temporary San Diego headquarters, along with twenty-seven cartons of paperwork.

In the office, Good goes in search of her other team leader to see what happened at Public Portrait. She finds the woman sitting at her desk and pulls over a chair.

They talk about the photo operation. Moreover, what the team discovered. Nothing of interest at this point, but seized documents that will have to be gone through. Pasqual Agosto and his wife are waiting in Room 2.

Beverly heads down the hall and enters the room. "Hello, I'm CBI Agent Good and will be asking you some questions regarding your business."

The man and wife are sitting holding hands and looking nervous. Neither respond to the agent.

Good takes a seat and turns on a recorder. "I'll be taping this interview. Please state your names for the record!"

She asks about their positions in the business and their relationship to Diego Ortiz. Pasqual only states that Ortiz brought them to this country and set them up to manage the photo business. After legalization, they only saw Ortiz twice in the three years they ran the studio and dealt primarily with the accountant, who they assumed owned the business.

Ortiz was a Godsend to them, but Filson treats them like underclass human beings. He is greedy and bossy, taking ninety percent of the business income. The couple lives in a cheap rundown apartment in Little Italy and barely survives.

They know of no illegal activity concerning Public Portrait. Beverly Good believes them and feels compassion towards them. After a long interview, the Agosto's released.

By Monday morning, Agent Good knows everything about the document forging operation and phones Immigration and Naturalization Service's, Agent Adams.

"Good morning, Beverly."

"Good morning, Silvester. Do you have a minute?" Under accentuating the amount of time, it will take.

"Sure, what do you have?"

"There is no question of Ortiz's document forgery. Actually, I am shocked at the extent of his operation."

Agent Adams sits silently waiting for the bombshell.

"Here's how it works, an attorney in Mexico, Jose Contreras finds candidates qualified to run or work in businesses in the States. He starts the ball rolling by contacting his partner, Ortiz.

Ortiz then smuggles them in. According to the FBI, who unbelievably, learned it from Jake Smith, Ortiz flew these people into Ramona. They were picked up in box trucks and taken to holding houses, which Ortiz owned." Stopping for a breath and a sip of water before continuing, "During the holding process, they are taken to Public Portrait for passport photos. The photos then sent to Southend Printing and applied to fake passports and work visas. Now, the people are put to work making Ortiz money in one of his many businesses."

"What other businesses did Ortiz own?" Adams questions.

"You name it, landscape, transportation, painting, and maintenance. Everything to self-contain his organization. In addition, he owed liquor stores, restaurants, and adult clubs… the list is huge. Anyway, after they're put to work, Ortiz files fake birth certificates, histories and other paperwork with you guys to obtain ligament documents."

"There is no way we wouldn't catch forgeries!"

"Well, that's what I thought, but he had some of your clerical staff on his payroll. They enter the fakes and approve issuing real visas and passports. Then, the illegals can obtain driver's licenses and social security cards and become completely legit."

"We have an extensive venting system with many checks and balances. It's impossible for a clerk to get anything approved on his own!"

"I only have two names for you, but there must be managers or supervisors involved?"

"Give me the names!"

Agent Good reads him the suspected clerk's names. Silvester thanks her and hangs up.

Now Adams has a problem, not knowing how far up the chain Ortiz's long arm reaches, he cannot just approach the INS station chief but has to conduct his own clandestine operation within his offices. He needs proof before alerting the Associate Director, in Dallas.

CHAPTER FIFTY-NINE
Adam Smith

Attorney Adam Smith walks into the District Attorney's offices early Friday afternoon. He steps to the reception counter, and identifies himself and asks to speak to DA Grange Lövenberg regarding his father's case. The woman calls her boss.

The receptionist gets off the phone. "Mr. Smith, you'll have to speak to ADA Jerrod, He's handling that case."

Adam, shown up to the ADA's floor to wait.

Finally, he led into Jerrod's office. Adam jumps right to the point, "Mr. Jerrod, my client has been falsely arrested and you your office is pressing charges. Frankly, it is another drummed up conspiracy by the San Diego Police Department and particularly Detectives Lyle and Terrance. I'm filing a class action suit against this office and DA Grange Lövenberg." Smith looks at Jerrod for a long period. "And *you!*"

"And, why are you here, then?" Jerrod asks.

"Professional courtesy, one attorney to another. I'm sure you and your boss can't fend off more publicity and I'm holding a press conference at four o'clock today!" Adam looks at his watch for dramatic effect.

"Why would those detectives be after Jake Smith?"

"My father worked as a detective for SDPD and has a history of problems stemming from Detective Lyle. It is a well-documented fact that he brought false charges against him three years ago and under pressure, Dad resigned and moved out of state. Now he's back and they started in again."

"That's not how I remember it! I was here at the time and... "

"It doesn't matter what *you* remember, I am going to have every case your office conducted in connection with Lyle *and* Terrance examined for improprieties and evidence tampering. And with everything going on in Small's *wrong murder weapon scandal*, it is going to be a slam dunk cleaning this department." Adam remains standing and waits while the ADA ponders the situation.

Before Jerrod can come up with a response, Adam Smith continues, "I hope, for your sake, you're not in bed with Lövenberg on this! Either way, your association will brand you! You'll certainly lose your job and maybe your license. Depending on how deep you are, you might even go to prison!"

"Mr. Smith, can you take a seat? I'll be right back."

Adam sits smugly while Jerrod runs to his boss' office.

The ADA does not wait and hurries past the secretary bursting through Lövenberg's door. Slamming it closed behind him. "Hang up the phone, we got more problems!"

The district attorney has his back to the door and looking out the window, talking. He jumps at the sudden intrusion and spins around.

"Hang up!"

Grange, looking at the drained, sweating face automatically replaces the handset on the desk unit, "Are you alright, Johnathon?"

"No, I'm not alright! And neither are you!"

Jerrod explodes with the new predicament and the forthcoming press conference. He embellishes his story reading apocalyptic disaster into every word Smith had voiced.

After the five-minute tirade, the ADA takes a breath and Lövenberg speaks. "Calm down Jonathon, this is the least of our problems."

DA Grange Lövenberg picks up the phone and calls Chief Baker. He sedately tells the police chief that after careful review, they do not have enough evidence to move forward with the Jake Smith case, and are dropping all charges. It ends with the DA reassuring that if more evidence found they will take another look.

Diego Killer

The DA hangs up and tells Jerrod, "Tell Attorney Smith that it's over and he can go back to wherever the hell he came from!"

Jerrod runs all the way back to his office hoping Smith is still there. Bursting through his door, he sees Adam sitting comfortably.

Trying to catch his breath, Jonathon gasps, "Would you like a drink?"

"I'm fine. Looks like you and your boss had a good meeting?"

Composed. "Yes, I told him that I reviewed your father's file this morning, which I had, and there wasn't enough evidence to pursue it. It's not your threat, I was planning on meeting him this afternoon already and dropping the case," Jerrod lies.

"I glad we had this little talk," patronizes Adam as he stands to leave.

"It's over then? You're canceling the press conference?"

"I'll take care of it immediately. Thank you for your understanding, Mr. Jerrod." Adam's bluff worked and he leaves. There is no press conference to cancel.

Adam goes straight to his father's office and tells him the good news. In addition, he states that if he ever has another problem with the police to call him before Cooper Madison.

Adam and Jake go out for a beer and spend an enjoyable father-son afternoon. Later, Adam excuses himself and calls the airport, arranging to fly home in the morning. While he is on the phone, his father calls Alex and Cheryl and makes reservations for a final family dinner engagement.

Jake is paying. He owes his son at least that much.

CHAPTER SIXTY
Witness Protection

Late Saturday afternoon, after two nights in a cell, Derrik Filson brought to Special Agent Egan Davis' office.

"Derrik we've got through your statement line by line and are satisfied with the evidence you supplied. At this time, the FBI is transferring you to the safe house here in San Diego. You'll be under guard until the arrests and trial where you will have to testify. Do you understand?"

"Yes, but what about my family?"

"We sent a car to pick them up, but couldn't locate them. I was hoping you know where they went?"

Acting scared for his wife and child, though smiling confidentially inside. "What do you mean you can't find them?"

"We went to your home and nobody was there. I've had officers staking out the place for two days and nobody has come or gone. At this point, we are looking for them." Davis' genuinely concerned for Filson's family.

"Gone! Melendez got them! You've got to go to Mexico and rescue them... or the deal is off!" threatens Filson.

"We're doing everything possible to find them. It doesn't appear they were kidnapped"

"What are you talking about? Of course, they were kidnapped! Where else would they be?" Almost screaming.

"That's what we're trying to find out. The *Federales* have been watching the Melendez Cartel and they don't have them. Would she go to her parents?"

"Her parents live in Wisconsin. I don't know how she'd get there?"

"Fly, drive, a number of ways. Give me the address and I'll have an agent check."

"I don't know the address off the top of my head, it's in Chippewa Falls."

"What's her parents' names?"

"Kathleen Burns. Her mother remarried, and her father's name is Carl Van Leeuwen. You've got to find my family!"

"We'll get them. In the meantime, we're moving you."

"And what about the Witness Protection Program you promised? I can't live in a safe house until a trial. It could take years!"

"Sorry, I misspoke; it'll only be until the arraignment. We'll make the arrests within days. After that, you and your family will be relocated until the trial starts, and then put into witness protection permanently."

"Just find my family!"

"Perhaps she went to a friend's or sibling's place?"

Filson lists his wife's two siblings and the cities they reside in. No friends come to mind.

"Robert, can you and Morris transport Derrik to the house?" Davis addresses his partner.

The two agents, with Filson in the back seat, pull up to a nondescript tract home in the heart of Clairemont. The garage door is open and Morris pulls in. Blazer jumps out of the vehicle. Filson opens the back passenger door.

"Not yet Derrik!" Morris blurts out. "Please close the door."

Confused, Filson shuts the door.

Agent Blazer pushes a wall button, and the garage door shakes and automatically grinds closed.

"Ok, Derrik, let's go inside," Morris states.

The three-step into the living room, where two more agents, suddenly stand up. Introductions made all around.

One of the guards gives Derrick a tour of the place, ending in his new bedroom before they return to the group.

Back in the living room, Morris explains the rules and the guard schedule to Filson, before saying goodbye and leaving with Blazer.

Derrik listens as the garage door rumbles open and re-closes.

"Would you like a drink or sandwich?" an agent asks.

"No, I am just going to lay down for a while." Derrick decides.

"Fine, just make yourself at home. You can help yourself to anything in the house. Just remember you have to stay inside. Stay away from the windows and do not open any curtains!"

Laying on top of the blanket on his assigned bed, Derrik thinks *what idiots these guys are. They're never going to find Jean and little Tina.* Derrik Filson knows precisely where his wife and child are!

CHAPTER SIXTY-ONE
The Kingdom Falls

Jake and Alex spend the day re-examining all the file copies she had made and hidden in the neighbor's basement storage unit.

Jake is especially diligent going over the notes he took after speaking to Emily and Montes at their home. The papers mention the top of their agenda is having Montes join her in the café business.

After Montes is part of her team, remodeling and expanding the café a top priority. Emily also mentioned they want to expand the cafe into catering and add a food truck.

Jake thinks hard about their plans for a long time. He is aware that she now solely owns the business and the building, but where is she going to obtain the expansion financing.

"Possibly take out a first on the building, since it is currently paid for?" he rationalizes aloud.

"Did you say something?" Alex quizzes, and looks up from her work.

"Just thinking."

Jake makes a mental note to have a serious discussion with Emily and have Alex perform a background check on her finances.

The rest of the day spent together, mostly each in solitude, reviewing everything they discovered in the last three weeks.

Jake and his fiancé are eating a pancake and fried egg dinner when the phone goes off.

Alex jumps up to answer it. Pain twinges through her leg, from her foot cast to her thigh. She returns to the table and informs Jake that Agent Davis is on the line.

Smith picks up the receiver. "Good evening, Egan."

"Hi Jake, how are you feeling?"

"As good as new! What's up?"

"The kingdom is falling! We're hitting all Ortiz's locations at six o'clock tomorrow morning. The *Federales* are descending on Melendez and his crew at the same time."

"Sounds exciting. Hope you get them all." Jake is pleased.

"Well, if you're up to it, I'm inviting you along as an observer." Davis offers Smith involvement since he actually assisted the FBI far more than he could possibly realize.

"Great. Thanks. Where are we meeting and what time?"

"We have gathered fifteen teams from every agency engaged in the various areas of the Ortiz investigations. I would like you to be with my team. We're hitting Larry Hirsh's home since he was Ortiz's San Diego manager and oversaw human and drug smuggling, housing, transportation, and distribution." He adds, "We're meeting up at five AM, in the SDPD lot."

"Thanks, Egan, I'll see you there," confirms Smith.

"Thank you, Jake. You really came through for us. We'll see you in the morning." Davis and Smith both hang up.

Jake shares the good news with his partner.

"Oh Jake, are you sure you're well enough?" Alex questions.

"I'll be fine, dear. You know just standing around drinking coffee." He smirks.

Smith is up by four the next morning and stops by Emily's Café for a hot cup of mud. The building and parking area cordoned off with yellow crime scene tape. He spots Marsh and Romero standing with the coroner, Ed Martin. He pulls his sports car onto the sidewalk and yells at the trio, "Hey! What's going on?"

The coroner walks over to Jake's car, while the detectives head back inside the café. "You're up early, Jake."

"Couldn't sleep," he responds, not wanting the word going around about the major bust gearing up. "What went down here?"

"They had a shooting around midnight. Some young delinquent tried to rob the place and the owner shot him!"

"Emily?"

"She apparently wasn't here at the time, kids or something. The triggerman was her husband."

"Crap! Is the robber still alive? Was he ID'd?" Smith wonders if he knows the kid.

"Never made it. Nobody admits knowing him yet."

"So, Montes packs?"

"They keep a twenty-two under the register. It looks like the kid fired first and missed. Montes didn't! He shot the kid in the chest, and he dies instantly."

Smith eyes Emily sobbing into the shoulder of one of her waitresses. He continues to look over the scene and spots her husband, head down, in the back of a patrol car. Jake needs to talk to Emily and gets out of his car. Before bending under the crime scene tape, he glances at the time. Jake gets back in the 'Vette and takes off. He will have to see her later.

Smith pulls into the police lot and hooks up with Davis. He is happy Marsh and Romero are preoccupied and will not be joining them.

Jake ends up riding in the back seat with Agent Blazer, as Davis drives and Morris rides shotgun. Their vehicle followed, by two unmarked cars, and one SDPD patrol unit, carrying four officers. The caravan drives *dark* to the residential home of Larry Hirsh.

They pull up to the house and all the officers, in pairs and threes scatter. Davis and his team slink up the steps to the front door. A uniformed policeman carries a battering ram. He positions himself in front of the main entry.

Seconds later. "Unit two in position," comes whispering across the radio. As soon as the other three teams check in, Davis barks, "GO! GO!" into his communicator.

Blam! Blam! Blam! The front and back doors crash open simultaneously. "FBI! Search Warrant!" shouts Morris, and the home bombarded with gun-drawn officers.

Davis runs straight to the master bedroom in the back corner with his two compadres on his heels. Smith follows at the back of the group.

Davis slings the door wide and it cracks into the wall with a loud whack! A man jumps from the bed and grabs a pistol from the nightstand. A woman bolts upright and screams, staring into the mass of flashlight beams.

"FBI! DROP YOUR WEAPON!" yells Agent, Egan Davis.

The man looks shocked at the black shadows and lowers his arm, and lets the gun rattle on the floor.

"Hands up!" Davis again.

Slowly the man raises both arms straight into the air.

"Are you Lawrence Hirsh?" questions the lead figure.

"Yes," comes the only word.

"Find the lights!" barks Davis.

The room brightens. Hirsh is standing naked, hands still stretch towards the ceiling. The woman, presumably Ann Hirsh, is holding a flowered bed sheet tight around her neck.

"On the floor face down!" shouts Davis. Larry immediately complies.

"Put your hands where we can see them," Morris screams, training his gun on the woman.

"I… I can't. I'm not dressed," she stammers.

"Now!" Cocking his gun as a precaution.

Tears stream down her face as she drops the sheet and raises both hands. Mrs. Hirsh is also naked and her small milk-white bosom appears.

"Get on the floor face down!" he commands, and she does as told.

One at a time, each ordered to stand and dress. The cluster of weapons never leaves their sighted positions on the suspects, until both are clothed and handcuffed.

The men lead the husband and wife into the living room, read them their rights, and place under arrest.

The other teams report in. One team has two children and calls in the outside waiting social worker.

Both Mr. and Mrs. Hirsh transported to headquarters in separate vehicles, while the rest of the agents continue to search the house. The children taken to Social Services.

All teams eventually show up back at the police station, bringing in Lazarus Veliz, Jorge Hermie, and the rest of the Ortiz personnel from each of his businesses.

Immigration and Naturalization take carloads of suspected illegals from the safe houses to their building.

Drug Enforcement does likewise, seizing illegal inventory consisting of meth cooking flasks, glass tubing, and equipment and vast bundles of money. People arrested include cookers, packagers, dealers and many more. The DEA had the largest contingent of teams and agents covering the vast majority of the Ortiz Empire.

Late in the afternoon, Agent Davis receives a call from *Capitán* Prieto. The Mexican arm of the operation has been just as successful with the Melendez Cartel in Tijuana.

CHAPTER SIXTY-TWO
New Regime

"Pablo! Pablo! Wake up!" Come the cries over the front-gate speaker system.

Pablo, Jr. explodes from a deep sleep, rolls over in his bed and stares at the black and white monitor trying to see who is at his front gate.

"Bebé, what's going on?" asks his droopy-eyed wife. She looks at the clock. "Pablo, it's only six-thirty."

"Armando's here. Something's up!" Junior pushes the gate button to let the man in before hurriedly dressing and running downstairs to meet his brother.

Their father, Pablo Sr. and mother, Juanita, have been married for thirty-one years since she was nineteen and he was twenty-nine. The young woman was pregnant at the time and Pablo Junior was born six months later. The couple bore four more sons during the following eight years, Armando, Aesop, Gaetano and the youngest, at twenty-two years old, Bonifacio.

Pablo, Juanita, and their two youngest sons reside in a large gated house in the south hills of Tijuana. It is at the end of a five-house cul-de-sac. The streets leading to the small neighborhood are a mixture of lower and middle-class homes. The middle child, Aesop, lives next door to his folks, in a house his parents also own.

Playas de Tijuana, the beach borough, bordering the Pacific Ocean, is the home of Pablo, Jr., and brother, Armando has a home in the *Pedregalde Sta Julia* district about halfway to his parent's place in *Camino Verde*.

Pablo, Jr., is only part way down the stairs when the pounding starts. "Open up! Open up! Let me in!"

Diego Killer

As soon as the alarm turned off and the door open, his brother shouts, between gasps, "There's shooting at our house! Men are attacking!"

"Slow down, Brother. Who is attacking your house?"

"NO! Our parents. Their security is fighting back! We've got to go!"

"Run? Where?" The sibling confused.

"To help them!" screams Armando.

"Is it the Aguayo's?"

"I don't know who's behind it. They're all dressed like *Federales*!"

"How do you know this?"

"Enough questions. Let's go! They need our help!"

"Armando, please sit. Five minutes aren't going to change anything!"

Armando remains standing. "I'm going now! Are you coming?"

"How do you know this information, Brother?"

"Aesop called me!"

Pablo considers the consequences. "If we go there, we'll be arrested with them! I do not believe it is the Aguayos. You and I can be more help from the outside if they all go to prison," states the levelheaded older brother.

"Arrested! They'll kill them all!"

"Maybe, Brother." Pablo rests his hand on Armando's shoulder. "But do you want to die in vain with them? We all knew this would come eventually. We must stay strong, together!"

Armando just looks at his brother in disbelief. They hear the front gate crashing open!

"They're here!" Armando screams.

The lady of the house had been standing at the top of the stairs, listening and runs to her young daughter's room.

"Go to the tunnel, Brother! I'm grabbing my family and will meet you there!"

The four of them hook up at the basement tunnel door, as footsteps running helter-skelter and yelling heard above. Heavy boots clomp down the stairs. Pablo quickly pushes his group into the tunnel and follows, slamming the door behind him.

The fugitives run through the escape burrow leading to a guesthouse, at the back of the property.

Pablo is the final one on the freedom ladder. He reaches to the sidewall, beside the hatch, and tugs a short rope dangling there. There is a series of explosions as the tunnel starts collapsing and he scurries up the final rungs. He bolts through the building and finds Armando sitting in the driver's seat of his Jeep, warming up the engine. His crying wife and daughter are huddled together on the back seat. Pablo dives into the passenger seat as Armando steps on the gas.

Seconds later the vehicle is speeding south on the hard-packed sand along the beach. Waves lapping the oversized tires.

Almost ten miles later, the jeep veers onto a sand-buggy trail. It hits the berm along the old road and flies onto the asphalt. A chicken hauling pickup with plywood siding slams on the brakes and runs onto the soft shoulder, overturning. The birds escape chucking and running in all directions.

Minutes later the fugitives approach the toll road. This time Armando stops and checks traffic before proceeding across the busier roadway.

They head east for four hours, turning on trail after trail through the desert and mountain maze, and down onto the desert floor. Another hour later, and they approach the outskirts of Mexicali. Staying on the sand, they detour the large Mexican metropolis and come out on Highway 5 heading south along the western edge of the Gulf of California towards La Paz.

More than halfway down Baja California, the Jeep veers into the seaside village of Punta Chivato and makes way to a Melendez safe house.

Pablo Junior immediately picks up the phone and calls his Tijuana Police contact, to see what has happened. He learns that the *Federales* have arrested his mother, father, and brothers, Aesop and Gaetano. Brother, Bonifacio killed in the gun battle. Their warehouse and other locations were all hit at the same time and very few of the gang members escaped.

He takes Armando for a walk along the beach and explains what his contact told him.

"Dad can run things from jail until we break him out!" Armando firmly states.

"I think the organization, as we know it, is gone, Brother. Dad won't be able to hold the remaining few together," Pablo ponders aloud.

They walk on splashing barefoot through the gentle waves washing the beach while carrying their sandals, and letting their pant legs soak up the warm salt water. Neither speaks.

Eventually, Junior tells his brother, "The old regime is out! We're in charge now!"

"No! It's not over! Father, will know what to do!"

"Father won't last a week in jail! It is us now, Brother, and if we don't move fast, we'll lose everything to the Aguayo Cartel.

"What should we do?" the younger brother questions.

"First, we get everyone that's left together and find new recruits." Thinking again, before continuing, "Then we have to take out Frederico Aguayo and his leaders. In addition, we have to get that *pechi* Filson. It had to be him that ratted!"

A new regime is born!

CHAPTER SIXTY-THREE
Smith Visits Jill

Later that Sunday afternoon, Jake and Alexis drive to the hospital to visit Jillian Ross. When they enter her room in the Critical Care Unit, at Grossmont Hospital, Virginia Small is sitting at Jill's bedside, crying and holding her hand.

"Hello, Virginia," Smith acknowledges her.

"Oh, Jake!" Small runs to him and hugs him tight for the longest time.

Alex stands, quietly aside, giving them a moment.

Jake finally pulls back. "How are you doing, Virginia?" He overlooks the throbbing pain pulsating through his chest

"Not very well. They won't give me my job back." The first thing out of her mouth. "I tried to call you to thank you for all you did for me."

"You can thank Alex. She is the driving force of this team." Jake gives his partner all the credit to her delight.

"Thank you, Alexis." Virginia hugs her tighter than she squeezed Jake. They part and Virginia, with tears in her eyes, takes turns looking at each. "I can't thank you guys enough. You saved my life."

"Doing our job, Virginia," Smith modestly answers.

"Oh, you guys." Small puddles up again.

"How's Jill doing?" Alex asks, as her man walks over to look at the comatose friend, and touch her forearm.

"The doctor is hopeful she'll recover."

"You talked to the Doctor?" Jake surprised that he did not get the call.

"A little while ago. He says that there is a good prognosis for recovery… but, not optimistic about no permanent brain damage."

Jake leans and whispers in Jill's right ear, "Come back to us, Jellybean."

"Why don't we all go to the cafeteria and get a cup of coffee?" Alex suggests.

Weaving the maze of halls, Virginia questions Alex about her crutches. Alexis underplays and states that is was an accident, without elaborating. There is no way she is telling this woman that she got shot.

Alex and Jake have not seen Virginia since her release from jail. The three of them sit and discuss Virginia's problems, Jill's health, the car accident, and other subjects concerning Jake's adventures.

The ex-reporter is stunned at Smith's revelations about his torture and escape, and all the rest of the on-going escapades.

After the Reader's Digest version of Smith's current life, he asks, "So, Virginia, what are you planning to do now?"

"Cooper wants to file a lawsuit against the police, city, DA, and everyone he can come up with."

"I think that is a good idea." Alex grasps her hand.

"I think so. They need to be held accountable, but it doesn't solve my problems."

"It doesn't?" quizzes Jake.

"Well, maybe, years from now. Cooper says that they'll offer me a settlement, but only after long procrastination and legal finagling."

"Short-term plans?" he questions.

"I haven't had a second to think about it yet, but I have to do something quick. I need to make money to live." After a short breath. "Madison isn't cheap. I'll be paying him forever!"

"If he files the suits, won't it be on contingency?" Alex voices.

"Yes, the civil suits, but not his criminal defense."

"Cooper seems like a reasonable man. Wouldn't he make allowances for you to pay him after the suits settle?" Jake wonders aloud.

"Possibly. We really haven't talked money since I got out. But I still need an income to live on, now!"

"What about the other stations or newspapers?" Alex suggests.

Virginia scrunches up her face. "I'm toxic! Maybe down the line, a long way down the line."

"If you're not a reporter, what else can you do?"

"Not much." Considering options. "I'm a good typist. Maybe a secretarial job or researcher somewhere?"

"What about sales? You're personable and wouldn't need much training." Jake interrupts their discussion.

Another twisted expression. "Me, sell used cars?"

"It doesn't have to be cars. There are unlimited sales positions everywhere."

They talk for another ten minutes before Jake makes an excuse and they part ways.

Back in their sports car, Jake tells Alex he needs to find Emily and see what happened the previous night at the cafe. Alex bows out and he drops her at the loft.

Smith parks in front of the Vargas home and rings the bell. Emily answers. Her eyes are bloodshot from crying for hours.

"How are you holding up, Emily?" Jake inquires.

"Good," she lies in response. "Come in. Would you like a glass of tea?"

"No thank you. I just stopped by to see if you need anything?"

"Montes is in jail!" she blurts out.

"I know. What happened?"

She relates the story of the robbery and her husband shooting the perpetrator. Jakes listens intensely. "It is obviously self-defense. They will release him after his statement." He looks at his watch and wonders why he not released yet.

"Jake, there are other problems." Emily goes on, "Our gun is illegal."

A long silence. "An unregistered pistol in a public place could belong to anyone. Have you retained an attorney yet?"

"Not yet. Waiting to see if they let him go, I guess. The gun is definitely ours. We kept it under the cash register."

"That aside, a good lawyer should be able to cast enough doubt that anyone could have placed the gun there." He reflects on Adam's lawyer friend, Thom Fiumara.

Emily does not respond. She is quietly contemplating hiring attorney versus expanding the restaurant.

"Is there something else you're not telling me?" Smith pressures.

She looks him in the eye and starts crying. "I think there might be a problem with our papers!"

"What kind of problem? Diego handled everything for you, right?" Smith questions, even though he knows the answer.

"Ye… Yes, but… but, I'm not sure he did everything right. I've heard rumors."

"From who?"

"Some of his other employees come into the cafe. He always promotes his businesses within his circle, like all our signs and printing has to go through Southend. We were never allowed to find someone ourselves… even if it is cheaper. I have overheard people talking about… about not real papers coming from the printers."

"I'll see what I can find out for you," Jake reassures.

"Yes, thank you, Jake." Emily continues, "I think one of Diego's partners might have gone to see my husband. Only he's not a… a criminal lawyer, I think is the correct term?"

"So, Montes has seen a lawyer, though?"

"I'm not sure. A man called and said something about going to the police station. I was so upset I didn't really understand."

"I'll go by there and call you back, Emily." Jake asks a new question, "I assume the police have the gun?"

She looks at him with an unsure face. "I don't think so."

"What do you mean, you don't think so?"

"Uh, Maria, a friend, and an employee might… " Emily stops mid-sentence.

"Might what?"

"She took the gun and hid it."

"What are you saying?" Jake inquires.

"She was in the middle of the naturalization process when Diego was killed. Now she is illegal. She took off before the cops came… with the gun."

"Why would she take the gun?"

"Probably to protect me and Montes?" Shrugging her shoulders.

"Emily, you weren't there!" Exacerbated. "How do you know Maria took the gun?"

Sitting quietly, she refrains from comment.

Jake pushes her. "Emily, I can't help you if you don't tell me the truth. Were *you* there?"

Softly, she admits, "Yes"

"Go on, Emily." Wondering if she is the shooter.

"As soon as Montes defended himself, I told Maria to run and to hide the gun. You know, since it is illegal."

"You shouldn't have done that. That's a crime in itself. And, it makes you look guilty. What happened then?"

"There was no way my husband and I could both leave. Montes told me the children needed me more than him and told me to go home."

Jake finds out that Maria lives in a room at one of Ortiz's houses a few blocks from the cafe. They chat a while longer and Jake bids her farewell promising to look into her husband's legal problems.

He drives straight to Emily's Café. It is still cordoned off with crime scene tape and Jake parks in the street.

Smith walks the route described to him towards Maria's place. Along the way, he searches hiding places and trashcans, for the missing weapon.

After arriving at the home, Jake pounds on the door. No one answers and he heads back to his vehicle.

On the return trip, he stops at a corner red light. As he is standing and looking around, Jake spots a city storm drain under the edge of the sidewalk across the street. He stands in thought and misses the green light. Jake, jaywalks over to inspect the drain.

The bottom of the cavity is dark and he cannot see anything. Lying on his stomach, Smith reaches as far down as he can and feels around. His arm is too short to touch the bottom and he gives up and goes home, dirty.

CHAPTER SIXTY-FOUR
The Gun

Jake returns to his loft after not finding Montes' gun.

"Where have you been?" Alexis questions him. "And, why is your shirt dirty?"

Jake explains what Emily had told him and that he had been looking for Maria and the gun. Nobody would answer her door, but he stood on the porch listening before knocking and heard people inside. As soon as he rapped, the place went as quiet as a church. He speculates that Maria is not the only refugee hiding there.

"What's the interest? Leave it up to the police to find the gun!"

"I just wanted to help Emily. She has always been a friend. I'm sure I mentioned that she was responsible for getting me hooked up with Diego."

"Help her for what, nothing but troubles!"

"I needed Ortiz's business." Jake reminds her. "That was during the time I wasn't sure if I would even be in business another week."

"You're a smart man and a good investigator, Jake. You would have made it with or without him." Alex compliments her fiancé. "And, you'd still be healthy!"

"Thanks, dear." Though, he is not as confident as she is.

"I'm sure Emily and Montes will figure out their own problems. You can't save the world, only us, and with all this over, it is *time* for us." Alex tries a little sympathy. "You need some time off to rest and heal. I'm here to wait on you hand and foot, and to see that it happens."

"Foot?" Jakes giggles as he looks at her cast.

"Yes, foot… such as it is!" she laughs with him.

"I'm not so sure it is all over," Jake states softly, not wanting to rock the boat.

"What are you thinking?" More a statement than a question. "Ortiz and his organization are toast, Melendez is in jail and Small's redeemed. What more could there be?"

"Diego's murder!"

Alex frustrated. "Melendez murdered Ortiz. It's obvious!"

"Not according to Trujillo. I mean, that was the plan, but he got there late, remember?"

"And you believe a liar and killer?"

"You're right, as always." Jake walks over and kisses her forehead unconvinced. *After all, Trujillo was sure he was going to die and had nothing to hide. His only hope would be to admit killing Ortiz so I would turn him over to the cops* Smith rationalizes to himself.

"Let's watch a little TV tonight, and then I think I'm going to turn in early." Alex ends the losing battle.

"Now, that's a plan!"

Alexis gives him a sexy smile of anticipation.

The next day the couple relaxes and in the afternoon, they take a slow stroll along the Embarcadero. Alexis cannot move very fast on her crutches. Jake is quiet all day and in thought. Alex assumes it was a combination of his pain and the sweltering heat. The early September day is reaching close to one hundred degrees even with the slight ocean breeze along the coast.

The couple stops for a cold drink in an air-conditioned cafe. "Jake, are you hurting today? You seem so quiet," Alexis questions.

"I feel fine, just a lot on my mind," he retorts. "How's your foot?"

"Hurts!"

"I am sorry I got you mixed up in my life."

"It's not your life that's the problem. It's just an occupational hazard that no one could have predicted. Both of us will be as good as new in a few weeks. I love you, Jake."

Jake looks lovingly at Alexis and mouths, *I love you,* back.

A moment later, Alex suggests, "We're getting a check from Siena soon. Why don't we take a few days and drive up the coast, Maybe Santa Barbara or Big Sur?"

"That sounds good," not really hearing what she said.

Alex looks out the window over the bay wondering what is bothering her man.

Jake interrupts her thoughts. "Are you about ready? I want to stop by the drug store."

"Are you out of aspirin?"

"I want to buy one of those new suction-cup stick things."

"What's that?" Alex asks.

"You know, we saw it on TV last night. It's a shaft with two suction cups on the end and you squeeze the handles to grab something."

"Why do you need one of those?"

Not answering right away, he finally admits, "It hurts when I bend over and I thought it will be easier… you know if I drop my pen or something." He hopes she buys the lame excuse.

"Honey, you have me for that!"

"I know, but I don't like to bother you when you hurt so much."

"I'm never in too much pain to help you, dear."

He is not going to win this and changes the subject. "I do need some more painkillers, too. And, need to lay down for a few minutes, when we get home."

He thinks it worked until she stands, and suggests, "You wait here. I'll go back and get the car so you don't have to walk."

This woman is wonderful he thinks, but voices, "I not an invalid. Let's just go together?"

"Ok, but don't push it. We'll take lots of rests along the way."

A few blocks from their loft, Jake turns the corner; Alex is halfway across the street before realizing he is not beside her. She leans hard into the crutches and turns her head. "Jake, where are you going?"

Still contemplating, he had not noticed that Alex had not followed him either. "To the drug store. Still, need that aspirin." He smiles.

They make their way up Fifth Avenue to a Longs Drug Store. It is in the old Woolworth building and is three floors high. The pharmacy and medications are located on the ground floor. While Alexis looks for Jake's pills, he goes to the counter and asks the pharmacy girl if they carry the suction cup grabber. She confirms they just came in, and are not on the shelf yet, but she would be happy to go to receiving and get him one.

Alex walks up with the largest bottle of Tylenol she could find.

"Three hundred pills!" Jake laughs. "That'll last until I die!"

"Don't talk like that!" She gives him a disgusted sexy look.

The cashier comes strolling up to the counter. "I found them."

Now he receives a *real* disgusted look.

"Great! Can you ring up everything in this register?" Jake asks the woman.

After supper that evening, Alex clears the table and starts washing the dishes. Jake mentions he needs some air and is taking a short walk.

"You didn't get enough air earlier? I thought you were in pain?"

"Feel great, now. Thanks to the pills. You're a lifesaver," his smiling comment. "I'll be right back."

Alex turns to the sink, her back to Jake. He slips on a light jacket and sneaks the grabber under it, and walks out.

He makes a beeline to the sewer drain.

With the grabber in his one hand and a flashlight in the other, Smith, scopes out the area for any evening walkers or transients. All clear. He kneels down and pushes the suction-cup end into the drain.

He cannot feel anything and shines in a beam. Still nothing. Jake lays on his stomach and tries again. With, the inch or so longer reach, the suction cups hit bottom. After a couple of sweeps, he hits something.

After more than five minutes of struggling, he pulls out an old brown loafer. "Crap!" he mumbles and tries again. This time he hit paydirt and pulls out the gun.

Quickly he drops it into a plastic baggie and shoves it into his pocket. He stands and looks around. An older woman is a block away, walking towards him.

Jake walks rapidly in the opposite direction and around the block back to the safety of his loft.

"That felt good, I needed a little stretch," he comments to Alex, as he walks in.

"Did you find the gun?"

Jake smiles, thinking *she's too smart for me* and lays the pistol on the table.

CHAPTER SIXTY-FIVE
Foist Revenge

On a dark unlit street, Pablo Melendez sits behind the wheel of an indiscreet white '69 Chevrolet G20 cargo van. He has a MAC 10 in his waistband. The weapon's thirty-two round magazine fully loaded.

In the passenger seat is his brother, Armando. He is cradling a sawed-off 12-gauge Winchester pump shotgun. The magazine plug removed to hold an extra two shells. With the one in the chamber, it is now a six-shot weapon.

The windowless back compartment holds four additional men, armed with AK47s.

The house they are watching, Frederico Aguayo's, sits on a cliff above *Arroyo del Padre.*

After finishing his cigarette, Pablo flicks the butt into the street and turns in his seat. "Let's go!"

The six men assemble, hidden beside the van. One man positions himself by the driver's window, able to peer through at the house and acts as a lookout.

Pablo is unsure how to proceed. A few minutes earlier, he had noticed a guard, inside the walled property, walk past the wrought-iron gate and stop to look through. An automatic rifle in his hands and two German shepherds beside him. Each dog shoves its nose as far as it can through the bars.

"Here's what we're doing." Pablo looks over the gaggle of men. "Manolo, Guillermo, go to the south corner wall. Hilario, and Alvar, you take the north corner. Armando and I will go to the front gate. On my signal, we climb over. Once in the yard, take out

319

everything that moves. Then we storm the house and do the family. *En total, comprende?*"

Armando speaks up, "Pablo, that's suicide! He must have a dozen guards or more. We'll be gunned before we can get to the house!"

"*Venganza! Venganza*! Who is with me?" The leader pumps his fist in the air.

"Get down. Someone's there!" the lookout whispers, as loud as he dares while ducking to his knees.

One man opens the gate just enough to squeeze through. He stands on the sidewalk, looking up and down the street. His eyes stop on the unknown van and he stares.

A second guard asks, "What is it, *Amigo?*"

"A van. It looks empty. I'll check it out."

"He's coming." The watcher barely peeking above the window seal.

"Follow me! Stay low!" Pablo quietly directs.

The band of men moves bent over and silently to the edge of the cliff.

"Over here," Armando speaks softly. He found a trail heading down. They rush behind him over the edge and hunker low.

A breathless two minutes and a beam of light pass over their heads, through the darkness, and back again.

"*Todo claro!*" The searching *hombre* yells to his companion and starts walking back to the house.

The man, still in the yard, pushes the heavy gate fully open. A black sedan drives through and stops in the middle of the street, fifty feet down the block.

Pablo stretches his head over the top of the ledge and looks at the vehicle. "Four men," he whispers.

A black Cadillac pulls slowly out and stops behind the sedan. Its windows dark.

"Two men in the front seat. Aguayo must be in the back," Pablo, still watching, whispers again.

A third black car pulls through and stops. The gateman closes and locks the wrought-iron barrier before getting into the back seat. The man walking back joins him. The car moves in line and flashes his light. The three-car caravan proceeds slowly through the neighborhood.

"Come on!" Pablo scampers over the rim and runs for the van. His gang of five on his heels.

The van stops at the block's corner and inches forward. The lead cars are out of sight and Pablo punches the gas. After racing down the hill, they approach *Ejido Francisco Villa,* the road south.

There they are! Turn right!" Armando spots the caravan a half mile or so up the street.

Pablo cannot wipe the grin off his face as he turns and follows. When the lead cars stop at Boulevard *Cucapah,* the main street out of the *Buenos Aires Sur* area, Pablo pulls to the curb and shuts off the lights. As soon as the convoy is on the move again, so is the van.

Two and a half miles later the Aguayo team pulls into a freestanding restaurant. The van keeps driving past, while Armando looks at the group walking across the parking lot. "Ten men and Aguayo and a woman."

Pablo drives around the block and parks. The armed men jump from the vehicle, and Pablo gives each one their orders.

The brothers walk around the building to the sidewalk. Looking in the direction of their goal, they spot three men standing outside having a smoke. Pablo and Armando causally stroll towards them.

Approaching, Pablo asks, *"¿tienes humo?"* Do you have a smoke in Spanish?

"A warm night for such a coat?" A suspicious guard mentions, looking at Armando's trench coat.

Without a word, the twelve gauge appears and Armando blows a hole through the man's chest.

Pablo's Mac immediately takes out the unsuspecting other two.

Gunfire erupts at the back door. At the same moment, bullets shatter the parking lot windows. Within seconds, the five outside guards are dead!

H. David Whalen

The Melendez gang burst through the doors in a hail of bullets from both sides. Guillermo takes one to the head from the man standing next to Aguayo's booth. Quickly, a shotgun blast cuts him down. Pellets spray over innocent dining patrons. The MAC 10 is blazing. The AK 47's are all destroying everything in sight. Bodies piling up. People screaming. The lucky ones, huddling and shaking under tables.

In less than two minutes, the massacre is over and quiet enough to hear a pin drop. The five remaining Aguayo's guards lay in pools of blood. A waiter is dead. The owner critically wounded, lying on the floor next to the kitchen entrance. Six diners dead or wounded.

Pablo walks up to Frederico Aguayo. His dead wife face down in her Caesar salad next to him.

"Señor, Melendez, por favor ten piedad!"

"Like the mercy you gave my family!" Pablo glares at the frightened man. He slowly lifts his gun.

"NO! NO! POR FAVOR!"

A volley of bullets rips Aguayo's body to shreds.

While the massacre at *Monteil's Restaurante* is underway, a second Melendez team of four hit the Aguayo warehouse.

Three men use M72 LAW rocket launchers. The Vietnam surplus *Light Anti-Amour Weapons* previously purchased by Pablo Sr. from a black-market arms dealer. The fourth man packs an AK 47 machine gun.

After the three rockets pulverize large holes in the front wall, the building catches on fire. Men start running from the building, only to be, taken out by the machine gun.

The fires rapidly spread, engulfing the building. Gas explosions start going off. The men get in their vehicle and drive away unfazed.

In like style, a Melendez *Capitan* leads the third team against the Aguayo headquarters using hand grenades and automatic weapons. The building is all but, destroyed in the attack.

Diego Killer

Four other teams of three each hit Aguayo homes, throughout the region. The drug organization fell in less than twenty minutes of mass murder and devastation.

The Aguayo's were not involved in the Melendez raids and caught completely by surprise.

CHAPTER SIXTY-SIX
New Queen

Fifteen miles south, on the coast, Siena Herrera is in the middle of a meeting with five men when interrupted by a phone call.

"I told you not to disturb us!" she screams, at the old woman coming into the room.

"*Lo siento, Señora,* but it is Reynaldo Tapia, and he insists to talk to you!" she softly mentions, and quickly turns and leaves the room.

"Please excuse gentlemen. I must take this!"

Siena is gone an inordinately long time. She returns with a huge smile covering her face.

Before she regains her seat. "Good news?" Asks a middle-age arrogant Mexican fellow. Surprisingly, sitting next to him is Derrik Filson, who the FBI lost from their San Diego safe house.

He was under light guard with only one agent babysitting at the time. The FBI misjudged him as weak and scared of retribution.

During Filson's second night, in the single-story house, he slipped out his bedroom window to a waiting car and hustled across the border to Siena's seaside estate.

During the two days, spent with Siena, Derrik satisfies his new boss, that her instructions followed to a T and everything in place. She explained to him that he will not be able to return to San Diego and will be in charge of their Texas operation out of Brownsville.

"Couldn't be better!" Siena responds to her *teniente's* question. She continues around the table and stands next to her seat at the head. "Those crazy Melendez brothers just took out the Aguayo's!" She cannot wipe the smile off her face. "One less competition. Now, it's their turn!"

The elation around the table is uncontrollable. Everyone has a drink in his hand and making impromptu toasts as they clink glasses. Laughter fills the room.

Finally, Siena holds her glass of red wine high. "Gentlemen to *our* future!" She smiles at each individually before chugging the nearly full glass.

"¡Salud! ¡Salud!" Loudly, the men return the toast, almost in unison.

"Let's get back to work!" Siena sits.

For most of the night, they revise their strategy once again. Mrs. Herrera had been planning the demise of the Melendez's *and* her husband long before the deed was done. With all the recent surprises, this should be the last revision and the finale!

Three incarcerated holdovers from the Ortiz organization are in La Mesa Prison and have obtained shanks and paid off a guard. At the appropriate time, he will let them into the solitary confinement cellblock, and hand over the keys to Pablo, Aesop and Gaetano Melendez's cells.

"Junior and his brother won't be expecting us and will be easy targets at their homes, as will the rest of their people. Those fools think this is over and they're safe." Siena lets it sink in. "We do it tonight! Tío, let your prison guard know and give him the word that it's this evening after lights out!"

After another celebratory hour, Siena calls her mother to show the men to their rooms. Before the old woman arrives and the men retire, Siena re-enforces that they must contact their soldiers early to have time to congregate. "Each of you will meet your group… " she glances at her wristwatch, "no later than noon. Stay off the streets after that!" She again makes eye contact with each. "*Te veré aquí más tarde esta noche amigos.*" In addition, she repeats in English, "I'll see you here, after your victories, Friends."

As they are filing out, Siena grabs Filson's arm and holds him back. She walks to the bureau, and retrieves a fat legal size envelope and returns to the mystified man. "Derrik, your family is already at your new home. You fly to Dallas tonight. Rent a car and drive to Brownsville. Everything you need is in the envelope, ticket, money, your new identification, and directions. Nothing disrupted outside California, so no changes in are in effect in Texas. Your captain and lieutenant's information are in here. Contact them as soon as you arrive. I won't be seeing you again for quite some time." She hugs him and wishes him much success.

Siena is oblivious to the fact that all the alphabet agencies are looking into Diego's national operations. She should have spent more time learning her husband's business and not trusted Filson as she had.

Derrik Filson has no idea that he and his family scheduled to be the next mishaps.

Later that night, the men are arriving one at a time, between nine and eleven o'clock. All of their assignments had gone off without a hitch.

Siena Herrera crowned the new Queen of the Mexican Drug Industry.

CHAPTER SIXTY-SEVEN
The Inquiry

Assistant District Attorney Jonathon Jerrod is nervous about his future. He sits in his office, after coming back from lunch, in a daze. His career in the District Attorney's Office is over, and probably his professional life as a lawyer.

Jerrod had just opened his mail and received notification from the State Bar Association that they are conducting an inquiry into his handling of the Virginia Small case. The letter states that a complaint filed and if proves true, a hearing on his conduct will be held. He knows that any misconduct finding could result in suspension or termination of his license to practice the legal profession in the State of California.

Grange Lövenberg, in the middle of a hard-hitting campaign to save his position, chose to keep the pressure on the disgraced Small and both their faces on the front page for as long as possible. The District Attorney blames the SDPD for mishandling the case and continuously tells the press of his conviction to seek justice and that he is sure the newly assigned detectives will find the evidence they need for her conviction.

Jonathon knew it was wrong, but complacent to his boss' decision. He went as far as standing beside Lövenberg and supporting him in press conferences.

"What a mistake! I knew it was wrong. That a-hole should have let it go when he had the chance! I should never have put up with his shenanigans. Now, this!" Jerrod grumbles aloud at the travesty.

Who could have filed the complaint? Was it Cooper Madison or that creep, Adam Smith? Or, even his father! The questions run repeatedly through his mind.

After hours of deserved self-loathing, Jonathon cannot come up with a solution and decides to leave the office and get drunk. He walks down the street to the Grant Grill and starts downing shots of tequila.

Jerrod decides he will not go down without a fight and needs to hold his own press conference, denying all forehand knowledge and pushing total blame on Lövenberg conspiring with the defamed detectives, Lyle and Terrance!

The ADA scribbles illegible notes on a damp cocktail napkin and shoves it in his suit pocket. He calls the bartender over, pays his tab and stumbles to the restroom. After relieving himself, he is standing and staring into the over-sink mirror. Water pouring from the spigot and splashing all over his clothes. "I need Jillian," he mutters.

"A beg your pardon, Sir?" asks the washroom attendant.

Jonathon looks at the man through blood-orange eyes. Not saying a word, he weaves out of the establishment and towards his car. He has to drive to La Mesa ten miles away and confront the love of his life. Jon's aware Jill's still in Grossmont Hospital, but oblivious to the fact that she is still comatose.

He manages his way out of the city and onto Interstate 5 North. On the Highway 8 interchange ramp, Jerrod cannot handle the corner and scrapes the guardrail for the half-mile turn. The screeching siren of metal scraping metal alerts a California Highway Patrol Officer leaving the Padre Cafe in Old Town. The cop looks up at the freeway. He cannot believe the flying sparks lighting the warm dusk air. He runs to his unit and flicks on the alert system and races to the Taylor Street on-ramp.

By this time, Jerrod is traveling east on the freeway at a high rate of speed. He is hitting up to ninety miles per hour as he weaves in and out of rush hour traffic from the lane to the shoulder and back.

Diego Killer

The officer's wailing siren clears traffic as he speeds down the fast lane trying to catch the killing machine. He is screaming into his radio for backup!

Fours mile later, the patrol car and the ADA's are traveling as one with only feet separating them. The freeway is rapidly clearing in front of the pair.

A second unit screams onto the highway from the Seventieth Street on-ramp and positions to join the chase.

Jon approaches the Grossmont Center exit. Now, four highway patrol vehicles and two sheriff's units are trying to box in the feeing attorney. He takes the ramp and runs the stop sign at the bottom. Cars slam on their brakes and cause chain reaction rear-ends in both directions on the city street. Jerrod tries to weave through the disabled vehicles, before crashing headlong into a large delivery step-van.

Immediately guns are drawn, and shouting officers surrounds his vehicle. "PUT YOUR HANDS OUT THE WINDOW WHERE WE CAN SEE THEM!"

Jerrod does not move. His eyes filled with gushing blood from hitting the steering wheel.

The order shouting continues to no avail and a standoff remains in effect for forty minutes. Finally, the lawyer struggles from his vehicle, one hand supporting his weight on the door frame the other arm broken and dangling at his side.

He looks over the faction of men staring at him before reaching into his back pocket for his wallet.

A young rookie deputy filled with trepidation yells, "GUN!"

Eight bullets riddle the man's body before he hits the ground. Assistant District Attorney, Jonathon Jerrod dies in a hail of police gunfire at six-forty-two on the evening of September 5!

The following morning Grange Lövenberg holds a press conference. "Ladies and Gentlemen of the press it is with great sorrow that I must report the untimely death of one of ours."

He goes on and on about how ADA Jonathon Jerrod will be missed, and greatest condolences to his family and friends.

He ends the session. "Unfortunately, our rising star has recently been plagued with improprieties. My office just *recently* became aware of his suppressing evidence in the Virginia Small case and conspiring with the San Diego Police Department to railroad that poor woman for the murder of Diego Ortiz. My department tasked with the quick resolution of the case, but personally, the *truth* and only the truth are of utmost priority in every case. I was convinced of her innocence from the onset, and I am, personally conducting a departmental investigation into Mr. Jerrod's involvement. My investigation is extremely close to concluding. Last week I contacted the California Bar Association and alerted them to the known facts in the Small case. I recommended Jerrod's disbarment. It *was* an easy decision. I will not condone any illegal activities within my department. No matter who is involved! Thank you for your time this morning. Any questions?"

After a battery of questions with each answer re-enforcing his reputation while denigrating Jerrod's. The District Attorney concludes and returns to his office.

In the coming November election, Grange Lövenberg is re-elected to a third term as San Diego District Attorney.

CHAPTER SIXTY-EIGHT
Smith Unsure

Jake and Alex are drinking coffee and glued to the morning news watching the Lövenberg press conference.

When it concludes, they discuss Jerrod and his premature death, and the brazen DA's crap about being unaware of the gun evidence.

When they arrive at the gun topic, Alex's asks, "What about the gun you found? Are you turning it over to Marsh?"

"I haven't decided what to do with it yet," Jake responds.

"What do you mean? You don't need more trouble! You're clear now, and that gun doesn't prove Montes' innocence or guilt."

"I know, but I've been thinking about Emily's story. Why would an illegal alien, who is running from the scene to save her own skin, take the gun and dispose of it. It just doesn't make sense!"

Their conversation ceases at the sound of their counter bell dinging. Both turn to the monitor and observe the mailman leaving. Alex goes to her office and returns with a handful of solicitations and an envelope addressed to HAI. She sets the only piece of real mail in front of Jake and throws the rest in the trash.

He tears it open and gasps at the enclosed check before reading the included note.

"Well, what is it?" Alex inquires.

"We've been fired!" Jake smiles.

"I need to phone Lynette." Alex assumes the letter is from Hartford Insurance, who they had been putting off for the last month.

Jake does not correct her. They need to re-establish relations with *that woman*. He will tell Alex, who the letter is really from when she comes back.

"Everything is fine, Lynette is very understanding. The three of us are getting together for lunch today."

"Understanding or *hungry*?" Smith grins.

"Be nice! At least she's helping us!" His partner reprimands him. "So, who sent the letter?"

"It's from Siena. A nice note and a check for twenty-five thousand dollars!"

"That's a year's worth of work!"

"I'm sure she feels guilty for almost getting me killed… more than once."

"But still… " Alex does not finish her thought.

"Yeah, but still, what?" Before Alex responds, Jake adds, "She's grateful that I put Trujillo in jail. Siena just doesn't know it is not for her husband's murder."

"You didn't tell her he was arrested for breaking an entry and attempted murder… of us?"

"Not sure how I put it, just made sure she knew he had been arrested."

"Jake, Jake, Jake." Shaking her head. "If you were a little more forthright with people, your life would be much easier."

Jake pours more coffee and the pair sit in silence.

Finally, Alex retreats to her office to make a couple of phone calls, trying to drum up more accounts.

At eleven o'clock, she returns to the back loft. "We better get ready and go. You know Lynette likes promptness."

"Her stomach likes promptness." Jake will not ever give her a break.

Alex gives him one of *those* looks and heads to the shower.

On the way to the grill, they stop at their bank and deposit Mrs. Herrera's check.

Walking back home after an expensive lobster and steak lunch appeasing Lynette's appetite, "That was nice of you to suggest the lobster today!" Alex comments.

"Just the cost of doing business. Jake grins; it is easier to accept the fact, now that he is flush.

They wander in and out of small boutiques on their way home. Jake buys Alex three new outfits and they both go home happy.

Jake sits on their love seat as Alex models, each outfit, in succession. Afterward, he needs to talk.

Alex sits next to her man. She is hoping it is time to button down their wedding plans.

"Siena had her husband killed!" Jake blurts out.

"I think not. We talked very personally for a long time. She was upset with her husband's cheating but living with it. Siena is so nice I don't believe she could have done it."

Jake had forgotten the photograph he took from behind the Matisse and now retrieves it. He looks hard at the woman in the picture.

"What do you have, there?" Alex asks.

"Take a look." He hands her the photo. "That could be Siena!"

Alex studies the blurry picture. "I don't know. It's possible."

"She had the most to gain. Diego and she spent very little family time together. With him gone, she gets it all, the money, the estate, businesses and her lover…" Jake sports a derogatory grin, "… the murderer!"

"So, why did she hire us?"

"A front. Take suspicion off herself." Jake pauses. "Now, with everyone thinking Trujillo did it, she is out of the spotlight… home free!"

"Jake, I still don't buy it! An affair maybe, but certainly justified." However, she is starting to wonder.

More silence before she voices her thoughts. "Besides, Trujillo admitted he went there to kill him! Why wouldn't we believe that is exactly what he did? It is his job!"

"Because he would have *said* he killed him."

"You're taking too many painkillers and not thinking straight!"

They share a laugh.

"My thinking is fine. Look at it this way, Trujillo thought I was going to kill him for what he did to me… "

"I thought so too. You scared me!"

"I'm not a killer," Jake, defensively states, showing a look of hurt. "Anyway, if he admitted it, he had nothing to lose and more to gain." Letting that sink in, before continuing. "Say Trujillo admitted it, whether he did it or not, he could have been betting that I would do the right thing and turn him over to the cops. Then he has time, years maybe, to figure out an escape plan… you know with Melendez's help… or he might have even got off!" Smith voices his previous theory for Alex's benefit.

"Oh Jake, that's just not realistic."

"Sure it is! He's buying time versus getting killed!"

"We're never going to see eye to eye on this. Siena and I know the truth!"

The couple laughs together and Jake changes the subject to their wedding.

Long after Alexis falls asleep that night, Jake sits deep in thought.

CHAPTER SIXTY-NINE
Baker Resigns

It's a month after Diego Ortiz's body found with a knife sticking out of his chest. William Baker is at work early. Margret has not come in yet and he is just sitting in quiet contemplation. His eyes never leave a legal-size white envelope lying in the center of his desk.

Jake Smith walks right in. "Morning, Chief."

Baker's concentration jolts and he looks up at the private investigator. "Jake? It's nice to see you. Have a seat."

Just then, the secretary has arrived. She sticks her head in and greets the two men.

"Margret, can you get Mr. Smith a cup of coffee?"

"Black, thanks, Margret!"

"I hope I'm not distributing you?" Jake sits.

"Not at all. I'm pleased to see you, Jake."

Baker has never been overly friendly with the man he fired years earlier. Smith wonders what is going on, and asks.

William stares at the envelope again and finally looks up and speaks, "It's a rough time for me. I should be happy to retire, but I never dreamed I would go out like this."

"Retire!" Smith is shocked. William Baker has been through rough times on the job before. "What's going, Bill?" Jake has never called him by his first name.

"This Virginia Small thing, as you well know, should never have happened on my watch," he mutters, barely audible.

Margret brings in Jake's beverage and sets the mug on the desk in front of him. She also brought her boss a fresh cup. She turns and leaves the office without a word, closing the door behind her.

"Chief, you cannot take the blame for what Lyle and Terrance did. If anyone is responsible it is Lieutenant Holden!"

"No Jake, the buck stops at this desk!" Baker rests his large right hand on the desk and he looks down in disgrace.

Smith stares at the lone envelope. "Bill, what are you doing?"

After a long emotional pause, the dejected man looks at Smith, his eyes moist. "The mayor thinks it better I take early retirement," comes slowly out of his mouth.

"You can't do that, Bill. You're the best Chief this city has ever had… "

Baker holds up his hand, stopping Smith mid-sentence. "I wrote out my resignation a week ago." Looking back at the envelope. "Just need to sign and date it. It will make my wife happy, anyway. She thinks we should move… maybe Phoenix." He picks up the envelope on pulls out a single folded sheet of paper and reads the words silently to himself. Looking back across the desk. "She's right, Phoenix would be nice. It's time."

"If you do this thing, do it because *you* want to. Hold your head high, Bill. That ass, Lövenberg is going down! You don't have to!"

"No, Jake, we're all responsible. Virginia has filed suit against the city and me personally." After a long moment of thought. "I'm ruined anyway you look at it. It's not going away!"

"I'm truly sorry, Bill." Smith's turn to contemplate. "Do you have a lawyer?"

"Ah… the city is fighting my representation, but they have to. Only I'm not sure I'll get a fair shake."

Smith suggests, "Thom Fiumara. Do you know him? My son Adam was home last week and recommend I use him. He's supposed to be the best."

"I never met him, but heard good things." Slowly Baker adds, "He's expensive. Cost me my retirement."

Jake slowly sips his coffee. "Bill, the reason I'm here can help you. I don't mean with Small, but I solved the Ortiz murder. It'll take the public pressure off and redeem you."

Baker again takes a long break. He eventually reaches into the top drawer of his desk and pulls out a pen. William Baker signs and dates his resignation. "Thank you, Jake, but I don't have a choice here."

Smith pulls out the plastic bag containing the twenty-two pistol and lays it on the desk. "I found the murder weapon." He looks sadly at his former boss, waiting for a response.

"You always were a top-notch detective, Jake." Back to thinking, before saying, "No, I've made my decision."

Eventually, Baker questions, "I thought that the Melendez's were behind it?"

"That's what everyone thinks, but it's just not true!"

"You can give that to Holden, he'll handle it."

"Bill, you can be the hero here and then make the choice for what's best for you and Mrs. Baker!"

"I am making the right choice." Baker stares at the gun, "Tell me what you have, anyway. Just for my curiosity."

"You have a man in jail. He's being held on immigration irregularities."

Baker is confused, "Are you talking about Trujillo?"

"Montes Vargas."

"Vargas? Who's that?" It suddenly dawns on him. "The guy who shot the robber at Emily's Café... defending his own life?"

"One and the same! It's just a stroke of bad luck that he used the same gun Ortiz was murdered with. Only, I don't think he knew."

"How did you deduce that?"

"It happened like this... " Jake launches into the whole story. "Montes and his wife are partners in the café, well, Emily was Diego's partner until his death and she took full ownership. Montes worked as a handyman for him. Diego found them in Tijuana, or Contreras did. Anyway, Diego flew them across the border and faked their documents getting them naturalized by INS personnel. I assume he had connections there, besides... "

Chief Baker, not privy to all the sorted details, keeps quiet and lets Jake talk.

"Besides, Diego smuggles illegals across the border and employs them at one of his existing businesses or sets them up in a new business. He works them as slave labor and takes the profits for himself. Emily Vargas gets fed-up with their dismal future. No way out! See what I mean?"

No response. Baker, not thinking clearly about anything but his problems. Regardless, he would never be able to follow Jake's convoluted story.

Jake continues, "So Emily was one of the first and Diego had to obtain a loan to finance the cafe. Since Emily is his partner, on paper anyway, she has to sign the loan documents. The bank insists on term life insurance." Thanks to Lynette for the education. "And if either one dies, the insurance pays off the surviving partner, which is Emily. With the building and equipment loans gone, Emily owns everything free and clear. There's your motive!"

"So Jake, how do you know that it is the same gun. And why would this Emily stab Diego after shooting him?"

"Good questions, Bill. Melendez's enforcer, Franco Trujillo, admits going to kill Ortiz. When he got there, he found the body, so he stabs the corpse and takes a picture to give to his boss as proof of death." Jake states confidently. "Now, the way I figure it, with Trujillo removed from suspicion that leaves Siena Herrera and the Vargas'. Herrera took me off the case satisfied with Trujillo in custody. Only we know it wasn't him and that leaves Montes or Emily."

After a couple of breaths and a swig of coffee, he goes on, "Here's how I figure it… how I am sure, it happened, Emily *was* at the cafe during the robbery, which she told me, and when her husband shot the kid, Maria, her employee, who doesn't have all her papers in order, yet, needs to run. Emily is a sharp woman. She knows if the gun is found, it is only a matter of time before ballistics link it to the Ortiz murder." Another deep breath, "So, she tells Maria to get out before the cops arrive *and* dispose of the gun."

Baker contemplates for a long time re-running Smith's theory through his brain. Finally, he stands, "I'm going to see the mayor and turn in my resignation. Wait here and tell your idea to Holden." He pats Jake on the back. "It was nice to see you again,

Jake. If you're ever in Phoenix look me up." The soon to be ex-chief stops at Margret's desk and asks her to have Lieutenant Holden come to his office.

Smith heads to the lounge for a refill.

When he is back, Stephen Holden is standing in the room confused and looking around. He looks at Jake and demands to know where Chief Baker is and what is going on. Jake skips telling him Baker is finished and launches into his story again.

When finished, Holden spends a long time and many questions trying to straighten out the jumbled tale.

Finally understanding, but not believing, he calls Marsh and Romero upstairs. He hands them the gun and tells them to take it to the ballistics lab for testing. Moreover, to match the slug from Ortiz's body to the slug from the robbery. "This is a priority. I'll call ahead and make sure they do it now, while you guys wait."

Getting off the phone, Holden starts firing questions at Smith again, and when every answer, not only sounds feasible, but appears to be logical, he makes Smith retell the complete story, including everything he knows about Montes and Emily Vargas, Diego Ortiz, Pablo Melendez, Franco Trujillo, and Siena Herrera.

Three hours later, Margret calls out, "Lieutenant, there's a call for you on line seven. It's Detective Marsh."

Smith sits still listening, "Ok."… "Yes."… "I see."… "Ah huh."… "Good," and finally, "Are you sure?"… "Come to the Chief's office!"

Holden hangs up and looks Smith in the eyes. "The kid's slug and Ortiz slug were both fired from that pistol!"

Holden calls the front desk. "Sargent, send two units to arrest Emily Vargas on charges of First Degree Murder!"

I hope you enjoyed my book!
I would appreciate a review, (positive or negative) on
Amazon.

Connect with H David Whalen

Here are my social media coordinates:

More Books:	hdwhalen.com
Blog:	Burning Writer
Friend Me on Facebook:	Facebook
Connect on Linkedin:	Linkedin
Google+:	google+
Twitter:	twitter
Instagram:	instagram
Email:	hdavidwhalen

About the Author

David Whalen was born in Northern British Columbia, Canada. At the age of two, his family moved to Vancouver Island off the southern coast of the province. He spent his early spent his early childhood romping the forests surrounding the small logging and mill town.

At age eleven, his family again relocated, this time to Southern California. Mr. Whalen continued his schooling through college, where he earned a multiple-major degree in marketing/retailing, from Grossmont College in the East County area of San Diego.

During his college years, he married and started a family.

Upon graduation, he promoted into management for a major drug store chain in their southeastern California desert location. After an eleven-year career, he left his position, moved back to San Diego, and started a national Christmas Décor manufacturing company.

Mr. Whalen soon became a serial entrepreneur. Through thirty-four years of self-employment, he grew many companies and sold three. While on this journey, he invented and licensed numerous products.

After selling his last enterprise, Mr. Whalen retired and is now pursuing a writing career.

About the Author

David Whalen was born in Northern British Columbia, Canada. At the age of two, his family moved to Vancouver Island off the southern coast of the province. He spent his early spent his early childhood romping the forests surrounding the small logging and mill town.

At age eleven, his family again relocated, this time to Southern California. Mr. Whalen continued his schooling through college, where he earned a multiple-major degree in marketing/retailing, from Grossmont College in the East County area of San Diego.

During his college years, he married and started a family.

Upon graduation, he promoted into management for a major drug store chain in their southeastern California desert location. After an eleven-year career, he left his position, moved back to San Diego, and started a national Christmas Décor manufacturing company.

Mr. Whalen soon became a serial entrepreneur. Through thirty-four years of self-employment, he grew many companies and sold three. While on this journey, he invented and licensed numerous products.

After selling his last enterprise, Mr. Whalen retired and is now pursuing a writing career.

Made in the USA
Columbia, SC
03 May 2018